Fancy Pants

CATHY MARIE HAKE

Fancy
Pants

BETHANYHOUSE

MINNEAPOLIS, MINNESOTA

Fancy Pants
Copyright © 2007
Cathy Marie Hake

Cover photography: Linda's Photography, Linda Motzko
Cover design by Jennifer Parker

Scripture quotations are from the King James Version of the Bible.

Published by Bethany House Publishers
11400 Hampshire Avenue South
Bloomington, Minnesota 55438

Bethany House Publishers is a division of
Baker Publishing Group, Grand Rapids, Michigan.

Printed in the United States of America

ISBN-13: 978-0-7642-0317-6
ISBN-10: 0-7642-0317-7

Library of Congress Cataloging-in-Publication Data

Hake, Cathy Marie.
    Fancy Pants / Cathy Marie Hake.
        p. cm.
    ISBN-13: 978-0-7642-0317-6 (pbk.)
    ISBN-10: 0-7642-0317-7 (pbk.)
    1. British—Texas—Fiction. 2. Ranchers—Texas—Fiction. I. Title.

    PS3608.A5454F26   2007
    813'.6—dc22   2007023564

To Deb Boone,

a cherished friend whose love, encouragement,
and insights make all the difference.
The Bible tells us to seek wise counsel—
and more times than I can count,
your words have been filled with God's truth.
Of the innumerable blessings our Heavenly Father
has bestowed upon me, I count you among the dearest.

CATHY MARIE HAKE is a nurse who specializes in teaching Lamaze, breastfeeding, and baby care. She loves reading, scrap-booking, and writing, and is the author or coauthor of more than twenty books. Cathy makes her home in Anaheim, California, with her husband, daughter, and son.

Fancy
Pants

Chapter One

New York, 1890

Rexall Hume planted his hands on the desk and leaned forward, his scowl rivaling a gargoyle's. "You've tested my patience far too long, Lady Hathwell. A year and a day—that's how long I've waited."

Sydney Hathwell met his gaze unflinchingly. "Surely you're not intimating my father was unworthy of a proper period of mourning."

"Which ended ten days ago." Hume paced across the intricate carpeting to the far side of the study and wheeled back around. Eyes narrowed, he studied her as if encountering her for the first time.

Sydney stood in silence and returned his gaze with equal frankness. In the week since she'd arrived, they'd shared only three stilted meals. He'd left orders for the staff to assist Sydney and her aunt whenever they required, then spent the balance of his time away from the residence. No small wonder he now stared at her as if she were a stranger.

What did they know of each other? Nothing. Over the past year, he'd not bothered to correspond with her. Oh, he'd sent condolences in the form of a telegram. She'd responded, as was proper, with a small card of acknowledgment. Silence then yawned across the Atlantic. She couldn't break it; a woman didn't pursue a man. It simply was not done.

A full year of no contact—then he'd telegraphed for her to come. She'd been more than a little surprised, but she understood she was obliged to allow him to court her. Sydney struggled to find anything more to write than the particulars regarding her arrival. She'd never seen his picture, heard his voice, or even read a single word written by his hand—yet she'd come to fulfill her obligation. Now that she'd traversed a wide ocean and been beneath his roof, he'd made no attempt to woo her. None whatsoever. How could he possibly think they'd pledge their hearts and lives to each other tomorrow?

Hume stalked toward her, a stiff smile plastered across his face. His hands were every bit as cold as hers when he grasped them. "You don't need to be upset, Cindy dear."

Cindy! He expects me to marry him, and he doesn't even know my name!

"There, there. I can see you're . . . distraught." He squeezed her hands. "Things come up at inconvenient times. It's an unfortunate fact in business. I had hoped you'd come along and consider this a wedding trip."

Maybe I've been wrong. Father respected and appreciated Mama's opinion. "Are you requesting that I assist in negotiations?"

"You?" A crack of laughter erupted from him. "Of course not. We can stop by the church on the way to the train station tomorrow. Since you don't know anyone here and you are just coming out of mourning, a quiet wedding will do. Then, while I tend to business in Boston and Philadelphia, you can visit museums and the like. Wouldn't you enjoy that?"

She pulled free from his grasp. "Mr. Hume, as I said earlier, I fear we do not suit."

He heaved a longsuffering sigh. "Perhaps this business trip is best done away with."

Is he putting me above his business?

"Once I return, we'll marry. That will allow you sufficient time to settle in and see to whatever little matters you women consider to be so vital." He looked inordinately pleased with himself.

Sydney couldn't help thinking Hume still resembled a gargoyle—cold and stonehearted. "Mr. Hume, I'm so very sorry—"

"No, no." He held up his hand. "No need to thank me, Cindy dear."

The butler appeared in the open doorway. He cleared his throat. "Excuse me, sir. Mr. Borland is here."

"Ah, yes." Hume sketched a perfunctory bow in her direction. "You'll excuse me. I must see to this."

Dismissed as though she were a cranky child in wont of a nap, Sydney managed a chilly nod and headed upstairs. She'd tried twice now to tell Mr. Hume that she couldn't marry him. He'd ignored her concerns on both occasions and brushed her aside so he could conduct further business. She'd tried to be honorable; now she'd do what she must.

⚬⚬⚬⚬⚬⚬

Five nights later a light, pattering knock barely gave warning before Serena Hathwell let herself in. Sydney whirled around. "Aunt Serena! What are you doing up at this hour?"

Serena stared at the hatboxes, trunk, and portmanteau scattered across the bedchamber. "That telegram you got yesterday! Just as your father swept your mother off her feet, Hume's coming to claim you! How very romantic! I never imagined he'd be the type to ask you to elope—but you know what they say. Still waters run deep."

"Romantic and Hume scarcely belong in the same breath. I cannot marry him." Sydney took what should have been her wedding gown from the ornately carved wardrobe and shoved it into her steamer trunk.

"You're acting in haste." Aunt Serena pulled the yards of satin and lace from the trunk.

"I tried. Marriage between us simply will not work."

Censure puckered Serena's features. "Even if you feel no obligation to Mr. Hume, you made a promise. A deathbed promise. Your father—God rest his soul—must be spinning in his grave."

"I promised Father I'd come to America and meet Mr. Hume. I didn't vow I'd marry him. Reflect for a moment, and you'll know I'm right."

Aunt Serena's eyes widened. "Oh my. That's right."

A small measure of hope sparked in Sydney's heart. Her aunt might help her. "Father loved Mama. He wouldn't want me to marry someone for whom I hold no affection."

"These things work out. Hume has every right to believe you'll wed him after honoring your mourning period."

"It makes no sense that I'd cross an ocean to wind up with the same aloof, unfeeling marriage others proposed back in England. I came seeking what Mama and Father had, and I won't settle for anything less."

Sliding a hanger back into the gown, Serena tutted. "Their marriage was unique. The time's come for you to put away childish dreams and settle down."

"Since we've been in America, Hume's never once shown the slightest interest in me. I didn't expect him to quote sonnets or attend to my every whim, but you must admit his neglect has been legendary."

"He's a busy man. You wouldn't want to marry a sluggard."

"So busy he couldn't be bothered to meet our ship? He ignored me most of the first week, then went off and left me alone the second. If this is his concept of courtship, marriage will be desolate!" *And I'm already so lonely. . . .*

"Mr. Hume leaves a little to be desired, but what man doesn't?" Serena hung the gown back inside the wardrobe and patted Sydney's cheek. "Bridal jitters. That's all this is."

"No!" Sydney grabbed her hand. "Monday evening I went downstairs to make one last attempt to explain matters. I didn't realize Mr. Borlan was still here. I inadvertently heard—"

"You stooped to eavesdropping! Sydney." The censure in Serena's tone then transformed into conspiracy. "What did you hear?"

Heat filled her cheeks. "Hume told his friend I'd serve his purposes well enough. Access to the peerage and a legitimate heir are all he wants."

"Of course he wants sons. All men do." Serena turned the same shade as her frilly, shell pink dressing gown. "Oh, dear. Is that what's worrying you? Your wifely duty?"

Still sickened and shocked by what she'd overheard him say, Sydney whispered, "Mr. Hume has a paramour and plans to keep her."

"He's a man, dear. They all stray. It won't matter. You'll have his name, his children, and generous funds to fritter away however you please. Do what other wives do: Turn a blind eye to his indiscretions."

Sydney shook her head so adamantly, her hair escaped the pins and tumbled to her waist. "I refuse to marry a man who won't honor his wedding vows. I can't."

"Madame du Marnier warned me that this trip was ill-fated. How many times did I tell you she warned me no good would come of it?" Rubbing her temples, Aunt Serena sighed. "I've chaperoned several young ladies and seen them wed by the end of their Season. You"—Serena shot her a meaningful look—"are the thirteenth."

"Well, this trip has been an unmitigated disaster."

"I know you don't put any store in such things, but Madame du Marnier gave me dire warnings about bringing you here upon hearing you were to be my thirteenth charge. 'Bad things come in threes and thirteens,' she said. Now that I think of it, someone stole your diamond earbobs, the ship practically sank, and . . ." Serena frowned.

Desperately grasping for anything to add, Sydney blurted, "The heel broke off my boot. My *left* boot. Do you know the Latin word for left? Sinister."

Serena shuddered.

"I knew you'd understand. Once given the facts, you've always proven to be sensible." Sydney grabbed a whole armful of dresses and tossed them on the bed. "We'll have to hurry. I have everything planned."

"The prudent thing would be to wait and discuss the matter with Mr. Hume."

Sydney fingered the lacy bodice of the wedding gown. "He's unsuitable, Serena. Completely unsuitable." Though Sydney could cite far more important and troublesome issues, she chose the one that would matter most to her aunt—trivial as it was. "The last evening Mr. Hume spoke to me, he had the gall to suggest we stop by the church on the way to the train station and marry. His business trip would be our honeymoon."

"The rotter!" Ever-so-proper Aunt Serena spewed a line of words worthy of a guttersnipe. "That horrid man would deny you a proper wedding? Every last one of my charges has boasted the grandest wedding of the year! What kind of man would cheat his wife out of the most important day of her life? You poor child! No wonder you put that exquisite wedding gown in the trunk first. I'm getting you out of here!" A mere second later, she'd relegated the elegant creation to the depths of the trunk.

Relief washed over Sydney.

"Whatever were you thinking, keeping something so vile all to yourself these past days?"

"I didn't say anything until I could make arrangements and keep us both safe." The sweet fragrance of freesia swirled in the air as Sydney pulled a dress of heliotrope foulard from the bed and shoved it into the trunk. "You'll recall Mama had a much older brother. I've contacted him. Uncle Fuller is expecting me."

Aunt Serena snatched the gown from the trunk, tucked it back in after fussing with the skirts, and grabbed the next garment. "Americans. You can't trust them."

"Mama was American."

"And she's the exception that proves the rule." Serena set aside the gown, took out the wedding gown, and positioned it between the other two.

Sydney chafed at how methodically her aunt disciplined the yards of satin to fold and lie in such perfect order. *I have to get us out of here, and she's fussing over a gown I'll never wear.*

"Distressed as you are over that cad destroying your wedding, something vital escaped your notice." Aunt Serena handed her a lilac gown and attacked the mauve one with enough force to scare it into obedience.

Under other circumstances, it would be comical to see a stout spinster in a dressing gown do midnight battle with an entire trousseau. Yet Sydney couldn't afford to be amused.

Serena didn't know the full extent of her plans—hopefully, she never would.

"Your uncle is an American, too." Serena scooped up a stack of small clothes, modestly stuffed them into a pillowslip, then wedged it into the trunk. "He's not to be trusted. You'll simply come back to England."

"I can't." Sydney added her glove box, a stack of dainty handkerchiefs, and a slender, lacquered case that held her fans. "Home isn't ... home any longer." Her second cousin twice removed had inherited the title and property. He and his wife had changed everything. Ultimately, Sydney had become an intruder in her own home.

"Harold and Beatrice have their peculiarities, I grant you that. But you needn't fret. Now that you're out of deepest mourning, we can arrange a match with another young gentleman."

Sydney rested her hand on her aunt's. "I know you mean well, but all my life, I heard Mama tell stories of her childhood. This is my opportunity to—"

"Run wild? Absolutely not." Serena disappeared behind a froth of petticoats she flicked into the air, only to reappear and have them completely bundled into an astonishingly small block.

"You're to prepare the Ashton twins for their Season. You gave your word, and their grandfather is counting on you. I can depend on Uncle Fuller until I find a suitable situation."

Serena sighed. "You never did cooperate. I'm firm, though: You're coming home. It's the proper thing to do."

"Doing all of the proper things put me into this predicament. It seems logical that something improper is the only solution."

"You and your logic." Serena managed to tuck a smaller hat into a larger one and pop them into a single hatbox. "Why your mother insisted upon your being educated like a boy is beyond me. It would have been far better if you'd taken voice and music lessons."

"I'm tone deaf. That would have been a waste of time and money." As fast as Sydney took something out, her aunt found a spot for it.

"Learning logic, Latin, and the like was just as much a waste." Aunt Serena took three pairs of gloves and burrowed into the trunk. Her head half buried in the clothes, she kept on nattering. "What man wants a wife who is smarter than he is? Men marry for money, property, and title. It helps if the girl is pretty, of course."

"Hume has the money. As for property—Harold and Beatrice inherited it."

"But you'll always be a lady. A fine lady. And a beautiful one. While I'm arranging prospective suitors, you simply must remember to let the men feel they're intellectually superior."

"Women have brains and shouldn't be ashamed to use them."

Aunt Serena half emerged and gave her a baleful glare. "Those brains are to help you employ your wiles." Her glare darkened. "No, Sydney. Keep out that traveling dress. You'll wear it on the ship."

"I'll keep it out, but I won't be on the ship." Sydney glanced at the prune-colored cheviot dress and didn't regret for a moment that she'd leave the ugly creation behind. "Uncle Fuller is expecting me."

"Expecting you? He ought to come claim you."

"That will take too long. I'm going to join my uncle."

Serena stopped everything and squinted. "I know that look. It matches your mother's whenever she concocted one of her hair-raising schemes. Just what do you think you're going to do?"

Her aunt missed her calling. She could have been an interrogator during the Spanish Inquisition! Sydney realized she'd have to divulge what she'd hoped to keep secret. "There was just a little misunderstanding, is all."

"What kind of misunderstanding?"

Sydney gave a dainty shrug. "Uncle Fuller presumed I'm a boy. No doubt it's because of my name."

"But you disabused him of—" Serena gasped. "Sydney!"

"Wait just a moment. Hear me out." Sydney barely took a second to inhale. "Traveling alone as a woman would be difficult. When my uncle's error dawned on me, I knew at once that he'd solved the problem."

Horror contorted Serena's features. "You couldn't ... you *wouldn't*! A woman of good breeding does *not* wear men's attire. If the news gets back home, you'll forever be ruined in the eyes of polite society!"

"Aunt Serena, no one would ever credit such a wild tale! I'll only need to manage the ruse for a short time. You have to admit, traveling in such a costume would keep me safe."

"Darling, how will you manage? You have no understanding of men or of a man's world."

Sydney turned away to hide her smile. Aunt Serena was starting to crumble. A little reassurance, and she'd come around. "It cannot be all that difficult. No one will expect a man from the British aristocracy to carry his luggage or do any other labor, for that matter."

"Even if you succeed in this scandalous charade, what will you do then?"

"I have it all planned out. While you see to launching the Ashton twins, I'll fulfill my dreams of experiencing all Mama told me about America. Uncle Fuller promised to see to my welfare. You must admit, Uncle Fuller is a closer relative than Harold and ought to be first in line for assuming responsibility for me. I'll reach my majority by January and receive my inheritance. By then, I'll know whether I truly belong in England or America. Either way, I'll be comfortable enough to be financially independent."

"January is months and months away. I scarcely can bear the thought of your being here alone that long."

Sydney let out a long, slow breath. "I am alone, even in England. Harold and Beatrice—it's their home now. And you're in high demand. Since creating a family with Mr. Hume is not my lot in life, the path is clear—I'm to go to Uncle Fuller in Texas."

"There's nothing at all proper or decent about your traveling plan." Serena looked as appalled as she sounded. "You're anticipating the visit you'll pay your uncle without giving sufficient gravity to the days you'd be in transit. What if someone discovers your deception?"

Sydney eyed her would-be accomplice and measured the doubt on her features. "I know I can make it. Uncle Fuller wired a generous sum of money. If you won't assist me, Aunt Serena, at least be kind enough not to give me away."

The older woman shook her head so adamantly, her jowls wobbled. "Even if I were fool enough to agree to your reckless plan, no one in his right mind would give you britches to wear."

For the first time in days, a smile lit Sydney's face. "No one has to give me any." She opened the bottom drawer of the ornately carved oak dresser and pulled out three pairs of trousers and several more shirts. "These strange Americans thought nothing of my purchasing men's attire."

Sydney folded a pair of britches and stuffed them in the

valise she'd pulled from beneath the bed. *Men's clothing is so much easier to manage.* "How difficult can it be? Men aren't slaves to fashion and etiquette. They do as they will and go where they want. Certainly I can play the role as nephew to a landed gentleman."

Serena stared at the shirts. "What about your ... ah, um ..."

Sydney looked at her for a second, waiting for her to explain the silence. Serena quickly patted her own chest. Sydney ignored the heat filling her cheeks. "Binding," she said succinctly. "It can't be any more uncomfortable than wearing a corset."

Her aunt spluttered, collapsed into the nearest chair, and used her hand to fan herself. "Bad enough you'll wear men's outer clothes—but you won't wear proper ladies' smallclothes? Oh, Sydney!"

"I'll be fine. You already have your return ticket, so I'm sure you'll get home safely. We'll go pack your things now." Sydney handed her an envelope of money. "This is for you."

Aunt Serena glanced at the envelope and pushed it back. "No, no."

"I insist. This way, I won't worry about you."

"Child, you never need fret about me. On the other hand ..."

Sydney hastily gave back the envelope. "We'll agree not to worry about one another."

"What about all of the women's things you're packing?"

"You'll take them with you to England. From there, you'll ship them back to America—New Orleans, to be precise. The rail line from there to Texas is quite reliable."

"You have sufficient funds to purchase appropriate clothing in the meantime?"

"Gracious plenty. As I said, Uncle Fuller was exceptionally generous."

A lifetime of watching Mama taught Sydney how to get her own way. Instead of throwing tantrums, Mama thought creatively. Her unique solutions took others off guard long enough to allow her to obtain whatever she desired and slip off before realization of the folly sank in. Sydney decided the time had come for her to do the same.

"Oh! Look at this coat. It'll be perfect!" Sydney pulled a bright green one from the depths of the wardrobe. "It's just like the one Billy Daniels wore to the Christmas party last year. Everyone raved over it, so I'll look like landed gentry. Americans will expect me to have a fine jacket like this."

"Child, you're wading into a sea of trouble."

"No more doubts. We have to hurry. I've booked passage for you. The ship doesn't actually weigh anchor until tomorrow, but no one here needs to know that—not now. We'll have the coachman take you to the docks just after lunch."

"I'm staying with you until the last minute."

Sydney folded the coat and tucked it in atop the other garments in her valise. "I appreciate your stalwart spirit, Aunt Serena. But you'll assist me far more by helping me fool them. Just imagine—when they discover I'm missing, they'll realize the ship departed a day later than they thought. It'll trick them into thinking I've joined you on the voyage!"

Serena rubbed her temples. "Something must be wrong with me. I'm thinking your scheme isn't crazy—it's brilliant."

"Nothing's wrong. And you know I won't be acting in the least when I allow the staff here to see how much I miss you. I'll retire to my room and sneak away to the train at dawn. Hume won't be back until the next day, so we'll both be long gone."

Sydney tugged on the trunk, but it refused to budge. "This has to be with your things. If anyone comes in here, they'll realize I'm gone."

Serena traipsed over, turned her back on the trunk, and proceeded to give it a hefty bump with her derriere. The trunk slid several inches on the carpeting. In a matter of minutes, the two of them shoved the trunk into Serena's room.

Aunt Serena's remarkable packing skills came in handy. It took little time for her to fill her own luggage. She even managed to call and order the maid to bring up a breakfast tray for two.

Sydney looked at the collection of luggage and dared to hope everything would go off without a hitch. "Thank you for all of your help."

"Don't try praising a woman who is fool enough to let you gallop off to certain disaster."

"Horsefeathers! This is nothing compared to what Mama did." As soon as the words left her mouth, Sydney regretted them. Aunt Serena always pounced on the least little opportunity to sermonize on the topic.

"And just look at the end result of your mother's folly! She met my brother and married him the next day, and when she died, she left him desolate. He wouldn't have died of a broken heart if Crystal had shown the good taste to live. Well, she didn't, and that's why you're here. You wouldn't have needed to cross the ocean and marry if your mother bothered to stay alive and nab the right man for you."

"Mama didn't die on purpose."

"It was a tragedy. So is this . . . this horrid excuse for marmalade." Serena placed the tray on the edge of the bed and tutted over the offering. "I specifically ordered things that would travel well. Hume's staff is as pathetic as the man they serve."

Sydney didn't have to feign sadness as she bade her aunt farewell. Fearing a maid would enter the bedchamber and see the empty wardrobe, Sydney couldn't accompany her aunt to the docks. She barely ate from the luncheon and supper trays the cook sent up. At midnight, the maid gave Sydney an odd look upon her request, but she woke the cook and soon thereafter delivered a breakfast tray. Sydney ate the fruit compote and eggs, then laid the rashers of bacon between the slices of bread. Wrapped in the napkin and stuffed in her pocket, the sandwich would be her first meal aboard the train.

Just before dawn, Sydney reread Uncle Fuller's telegram.

Funds wired. Pleased to have nephew. No use for females here. Bring boots, britches, shirts. I'll provide all other essentials. Regards, Fuller Johnson.

Serena assumed the masquerade would end once Sydney reached Forsaken Ranch. Sydney knew different.

One last detail needed to be addressed. Sydney brushed through her hair. Mama's had been the same shade of chestnut, and Father never ceased to wax poetic on its beauty. Though blond hair was the rage back home, Sydney didn't mind being different. She stared at her reflection. "Well, I can be different by having short hair, too."

She picked up the shears. Vanity warred with logic. Gentlemen wore their hair cropped quite close to the head and used pomade, but she couldn't bear to chop off that much. Compromising by cutting just below the level of her shoulders would be long for a man but short for a woman. Yes, that's what she'd do. After all, George Washington and Napoleon and Custard— no, Custer—all had hair they could tie back. Sydney steeled herself with a deep breath and snipped.

Nothing.

She hadn't cut a single strand. Or so she thought until she started to part her fingers. As the scissor blades opened, tresses tumbled down her arm and onto the floor. She stared at them, then looked back at her reflection in the mirror. "No turning back now." She lifted her chin, pulled another segment of hair forward, and measured it to the shorter length. Halfway though, she studied the woman in the mirror. Long, rich curls cascaded on her left while bluntly clipped strands hung starkly on the right. *That's who I was—and this is who I'll become. I'm cutting myself free.*

The fire sparked as Sydney burned the tresses she'd cut off. After tying the remainder of her hair back with a small strip of twine, she tugged on britches and promptly jerked them back down. The lace at the hem of her unmentionables made a distinct, lumpy line. Hasty whacks with the shears solved that problem. With the flounces gone, her britches pulled up without impediment and hung correctly.

Critically eyeing herself in the mirror, she grimaced. "I'm still shaped like a girl." Since the shirt was longer than she'd thought, she folded the hem up and bunched it just below the trousers' waistband. That bulk disguised her feminine shape well enough. Socks and boots finished the ensemble.

Thick, gaudy carpeting muffled the clomping of her slightly too-big boots as she tiptoed down the hall. The heavy valise slid along the banister quite nicely.

Pleased with how well her plan was working, Sydney reached for the doorknob. The massive brass fixture felt cold, and the door was unyielding. Never before had she needed to open more than her bedchamber door. Surprised at the weight of the massive door, she yanked with all her might. It opened quite suddenly. *Shuffle, clomp, thud.* Her boots robbed her of any ability to balance, and she fell in a graceless heap over her valise.

Afraid someone might have heard the commotion, she scrambled to her feet, snatched the valise off the floor, and hastened outside. *The one time a bustle might have come in handy, I don't have it on.*

By the time she made it down the brick-lined drive, Sydney wasn't alone. Oscar, Hume's whippet, ghosted along at her side. "Go home," she commanded.

Oscar didn't obey. He continued to trot as if she held him on a leash. Sydney decided having him might not be such a bad thing. After all, it was still dark outside. "I'm running away, boy. I can't blame you for wanting to do the same. He ignores you as much as he ignored me."

Soon a terrier joined them. "Shoo. Off with you!" He ignored her and gave a happy yip. Then a third dog accompanied her. Sydney rounded the corner, took a few more steps, and stopped. Where the fourth mutt came from, she didn't know. Exasperated, Sydney told them, "I'm trying to be inconspicuous."

Four furry tails wagged in the air as if to wave off her concerns. The terrier sat on her foot.

"Oh, honestly." Sydney bent to remove him and ended up scratching between his scruffy, adorable ears. "There, boy. Now you simply must let me go."

He didn't budge.

Oscar nosed Sydney's pocket.

"So that's the way of it! You're nothing more than a ragtag band of beggars." She heard herself and winced. *I sound like a girl.* Trying out a lower pitch, she said, "This had best be quick."

No more had she pulled the napkin from her pocket than the dogs crowded in for a bite. One growled at another. "Mind your manners." To Sydney's delight, the lower pitch and a distinct edge to her voice worked. The mutt sat and hung his head.

They snaffled up every morsel, and all but Oscar trotted away. "Go home, boy." He gave her a sad look.

The sound of hooves and the rattle of a carriage sounded on the street. As it rolled past, a man shouted to the driver, "Halt!"

Sydney's blood went cold.

Chapter Two

It's him! Yet it can't be—he's a day early! Sydney tamped down the urge to flee. She couldn't outrun Hume—especially not in these boots.

Her erstwhile fiancé opened the door of the carriage and charged toward her. "That's my dog."

Sydney hitched a shoulder. She didn't trust her voice.

Hume drew closer. The scents of cigars and brandy wafted from him—along with a whiff of a distinctly floral perfume. "Oscar. Go home!"

Oscar slinked away with his tail between his legs.

"Do I know you?" Hume squinted at her.

"Sir," the driver called to him. "Are you—"

"I'm fifty yards from home," Hume roared. "I can walk!"

"You owe me a dollar."

While Hume patted his pockets, Sydney sidled past him. She took pains to sound gruff. "I'm in need of a ride."

"Jameson Winthrop! I knew I recognized you. You're Preston's nephew! Going home again already?" Hume clapped a hand on her shoulder. "Take the boy to the train. This'll more than cover my fare and his."

She tugged on the brim of her hat and rumbled, "Thanks."

For a heartbeat, she waited for him to open the door and assist her inside. Sydney immediately realized her mistake, saw to the door, and scrambled in with a complete lack of grace. For the next six months, no one would see to the niceties she'd always taken for granted. The realization only added to her sense of adventure.

Leaning back against the seat so she'd be in shadow, Sydney took one last long look at what she'd be leaving behind. Hume shoved money into the driver's hand, turned, and swaggered off toward his mansion. Marriage would have been a lifetime sentence of misery, and no amount of money could ever buy love or change that beautiful prison into her home. Relief flooded her. She'd escaped.

Three days later Sydney strode up to the window at the Chicago train station, hoping her gait was a fair imitation of the men she'd been studying. "First class to Austin. Then on to Gooding, Texas."

"Did you want a sleeping berth?"

She nodded.

"One hundred eighteen dollars and twenty-nine cents."

Sydney shoved her hand into the pocket of her trousers. Men had no concept of how free they were to stuff things into pockets instead of having to tote around a reticule. She pulled out seven bank notes.

The teller took each bill separately and inspected it. "Planchette paper. They're all fine. You wouldn't believe how often people try to pass off counterfeit." He looked her straight in the eyes. "No one can fool me, though. I can spot a fake."

Sydney held her breath. *Does he know. . . ?*

"Here's your change, young man. It'll be just over an hour before your train departs."

"Thank you." She looked up and down the station and didn't see any chewing gum vending machines. Though she secretly thought the men chewing tobacco or gum resembled cattle chomping cud, she decided she ought to chew on something—and it certainly wouldn't be tobacco. Chewing a wad of gum might make her look masculine. She cleared her throat. "Pardon me. Where are the gum machines?"

The ticketing agent shook his head. "Don't have any of those new-fangled contraptions. Mercantile across the street carries gum."

Sydney crossed a busy thoroughfare and hastened ahead in order to sweep open the mercantile door for a woman. "Allow me, ma'am."

"Thank you, sir." The lady sashayed inside. While the clerk assisted the woman, Sydney ambled about. In London, she'd been in millinery shops and to a dressmaker's, but she'd never been allowed to do any practical marketing. This place was a veritable wonderland of items and scents. Such freedom! Sydney took a moment to relish her newfound liberty.

"Your valise will be safe over here by my register." The shopkeeper held up a basket. "You can fill this with your purchases."

"Wonderful!" Sydney realized she'd not disguised her voice and immediately coughed. "Pardon me."

"I have Dr Pepper just behind you. A bottle will cure that."

Sydney grabbed a bottle and traded her valise for the basket. Jerked beef and Semple's chewing gum seemed like manly choices. Sydney tried to choose foods that would travel well. Though a pint basket of fresh strawberries looked utterly scrumptious, she bypassed them. Fig Newton cookies sounded delicious. Five more days aboard the train would mean trips to the dining car, but Sydney figured she'd forego a few of those meals. The fare didn't taste very good, and she might as well save whatever money she could.

Until now, she'd said very little. What women could and would say depended on who was present. Since the first day she'd been dressed like a man, Sydney discovered a startling truth: Men changed how they spoke when a woman was present. Uncle Fuller's telegram let her know she'd be in the midst of a male bastion. Mimicking the clipped, direct style of communication would be pivotal to the success of her charade.

Listening to what men discussed startled her. And how they'd speak! Somehow, she'd thought they'd discuss family, work, and politics. Rarely did they say much about their families. Men identified themselves by trade or profession. As for politics—Sydney resolved to read newspapers to grasp what they were saying. So far, when men asked her opinion, she'd shrugged. "I'm British."

She headed toward the counter. "Have you any newspapers?"

"Kid on the corner sells 'em." The storekeeper pointed to the side. "I have a fine selection of books."

Poems by Emily Dickinson appealed to her, but Sydney refrained. "I say, are those penny dreadfuls?"

"Dime novels. They fly right off the shelf. You being English, you'd like Western heroes. Buffalo Bill's a man's man. Those two on the right"—he pointed—"are far better than the ones featuring Deadwood Dick."

"Very well." Sydney added the two thin orange-paper-covered books to her items. In the past, merchants presented her bills to Father. She cleared her throat. "What do I owe you?"

"Good deal on tobacco today." A crooked brow turned the statement into a question.

"The gum will suffice." Her valise loaded with her booty, Sydney boarded the train for Texas. Mile after mile chugged away. Page after page in her dime novels told of a brash man named Buffalo Bill and his hair-raising adventures.

She pluckily endured the gritty dust that choked her fellow travelers. As a matter of fact, it astonished her how easily she managed to take on the role of a young man. It had become almost a game. By studying and copying the men about her, she blended in as best she could, though she drew the line at spitting and wiping her mouth on her sleeve.

The farther the train traveled, the further the layers of civilization eroded. She'd originally considered Americans undisciplined, but as the miles and hours passed, she grew fascinated by their bizarre behavior and expressions. No matter where she was, they simply chalked up any gaffes she made to her English ways instead of looking past the britches and realizing her gender.

Sydney scarcely knew what to think about the wild territory through which they traveled. It was ruggedly beautiful, open and unpredictable. As the days passed and she spotted small outposts of "civilization," she came to understand that Texas was a world apart from all she'd ever known. Her deception might not be quite as easy to pull off as she'd planned.

***

Gooding, Texas

Spotting the boy from the vantage point of his saddle, Timothy Creighton shook his head. He stretched, pulled off his hat,

and ruffled his short hair in order to cool off a mite. The boy
ambled along so slowly, he hadn't made any appreciable progress
down the road. Tim leaned forward and squinted, trying to take
in more details. After a better look, he started praying what he
thought he saw was a result of too many hours in the saddle on
a hot day. A swig of water from his canteen didn't change the
view.

Fuller's nephew was every bit as bad as Tim feared he'd be.
Worse, if that were possible. The kid didn't have a muscle on
his twiggy body and could barely tote a stinking valise. Dragged
his feet along the dusty road like a schoolboy, too. Mr. Fancy
Pants Hathwell wouldn't make it to the ranch yard for another
hour at the rate he dawdled.

Unwilling to make the way even the slightest bit easier for
the boy, Tim tugged gently on the reins of his palomino gelding
and headed off in the opposite direction. He had time to go
check on the water level of the pond before heading back home.

"Lord, if you're of a mind," Tim said as he tipped his chin
upward, "I'd take it as a favor if you'd send Fuller back here
early. I've got a bad feeling about that kid."

"Will you get a gander at that?" Bert moaned as he saw the
new man walking up the road.

Tim stayed in the shadow of the stable and watched. He'd
come to the conclusion that his snap judgment wasn't fair. The
kid deserved a chance to prove himself. Watching how he got
along with the hands would give Tim a good notion as to how
he'd behave.

The men all followed Bert's gaze. They did double takes,
then openly stared for a long count. Disbelief painted their fea-

tures, and disgust followed close behind. Fuller had warned them his nephew had been reared in London's high society and probably knew nothing about hard living, but that scarcely prepared them for the fop who minced toward them.

"I seen an organ grinder once." Pancake spat a wad of tobacco off a few respectable yards. "His monkey wore a jacket just like that."

Everyone chortled at that pronouncement. It said more than anything else might. After all, no man worth his boots would be caught dead in a Christmas tree green jacket with glittering gold braid and gold buttons. Tim would shoot any idiot who dared make such a garment, then burn the offensive piece of trash . . . after salvaging those gold buttons, of course.

"Seems to me that monkey danced real purdy. Held a cup in his hand and begged. Wasn't good for anything else." Pancake scratched his ample belly and went on with his musing, "Coulda passed as this one's twin brother."

"The monkey—he had to be much more useful." Juan squinted at the strange sight.

"Fuller didn't really saddle us with that, did he?"

Gulp wiped his hand across two-day-old whiskers. His large Adam's apple bobbed as he took one of the deep gulps that had earned him his nickname. "Couldn't have known it'd be this bad. Drunk as a skunk, no one could ever imagine this."

Merle broke in, "I saw something almost as bad once when I got clunked in the head. Came to with Widder O'Toole kneeling by me."

Hoots of bawdy laughter met that assertion. Few things could be worse than being subjected to the Widow O'Toole. The woman had a tongue sharper than a razor and spared no words in giving her opinion about the evils of alcohol.

"I'm a-tellin' you, the woman's just addlepated. What man

calls hisself a man if he refuses the offer of a few mugs of beer to quench his thirst?" More laughter egged Merle on. He strutted back and forth like a scrappy bantam, his bowed legs adding swagger to his gait. "I'll tell the truth, though. Any man who overindulges and finds himself in Widder O'Toole's clutches learns to pray for deliverance!"

The kid drew closer. "Ho!"

"Ho!" the men repeated in a shout of disbelief.

Mistaking their volume for enthusiasm, Fuller's nephew beamed. "What a jolly greeting! I'm Lord Sydney Hathwell. My uncle is expecting me."

"Lord help him, yes," someone muttered in the sudden silence.

"It isn't necessary to use my formal title. Americans don't often do so, you know." The kid smiled. "But yes, I do hope to be a great help to my uncle. As I mentioned, he's expecting me."

There was a momentary silence as everyone digested the fact that the stupid kid hadn't absorbed the insult. "I'll bet he ain't expectin' you," someone else grated. "Some things aren't ever quite what's expected."

Jutting out his chin, the kid asked, "Is my uncle out riding, or will I find him in the house?"

"He needed to go to Abilene. Be gone a week or so." Pancake absently scratched his belly again.

"Then perhaps my aunt—"

"Sonny, Fuller ain't never been hitched."

"I see." Dropping the valise to the ground and setting off a small cloud of dust, the kid swept the men with a haughty gaze. "Might you think to exercise the civility to at least introduce yourselves?"

The men had the grace to look a bit ashamed. They shuffled around, and Merle jabbed his thumb at each individual and identified gruffly, "Bert. Pancake. Juan. Boaz. Gulp. I'm Merle."

Instead of shaking hands, the kid nodded curtly to each of the men. "Pleased to meet my uncle's staff."

Staff?! Tim bit back a moan. The kid's shortcomings could fill a catalogue, and he hadn't been here for two minutes yet.

The men stared at Hathwell. Merle finally broke the silence. "Velma went to help Etta Sanders with her baby. Took a day and a half, so she probably didn't get your room ready yet. Just go on in the place. Creighton's due back any minute."

"Creighton?"

Pancake nodded. "Tim Creighton. He and Fuller go back a ways. Practically runs the place. Owns a full quarter of the head and land, too."

"I see."

Taking that as a cue, Tim stepped out of the shadows. "This isn't a tea party. You men get back to work."

Sydney Hathwell wheeled around and gaped at him.

To keep from grinning, Tim ordered his crew, "Get busy! You're not paid to jaw with Mr. Hathwell."

The men disappeared without a trace.

Tim slowly stripped off his leather gloves, smacked them against his thigh, then wiped the sweat from his forehead with his sleeve. Even after doing that, the sight before him didn't change. If anything, the kid looked sillier with every passing minute. Before he said anything he'd regret, Tim ordered, "You heard the men. Go on up to the house. Velma's home."

The kid's back stiffened and his chin rose a notch.

Accustomed to men following his orders, Tim stared back in silence.

The boy looked away. He stooped, lifted the valise, and nodded. "Very well."

Though he decided to obey, the kid had to have the last

word. His lack of size, strength, and knowledge were huge liabilities; but the attitude—Tim shook his head. A kink like that could get someone killed. The first order of business was going to be setting Fancy Pants in his place.

Tim Creighton watched the boy lollygag toward the house. Pancake shuffled over. "*What* was that?"

"That," Tim said in a funereal tone, "is Fuller's kin."

"How in the devil did Fuller happen to get saddled with a nephew like that?" The bunkhouse cook wagged his head from side to side in disbelief. "He's prissier than any of the Richardsons' six daughters!"

Tim grimaced.

"His chin is still smooth as a baby's tail."

"I noticed."

Pancake yammered on. "Get a stiff wind going, and he'll be teacup over toenails. I got a look at his hands. Smooth as silk, not a callus on 'em. I'll bet he ain't never done a lick of work."

Figuring he ought to put an end to the honest assessment, Tim said, "He's young."

"Yup. Voice still cracks. 'Bout all the good he'll come to in life is maybe bein' a preacher. Knows fancy words and fine manners that'd make him a natural for that callin'."

Tim shot Pancake a wry look and didn't verbalize his thoughts. Much as he wanted to, it wasn't right. After all, that puny pup was his partner's nephew. This called for loyalty and discretion. "I can't let Fuller come home to that pitiful excuse. We're going to start whipping him into shape."

"Miracles take more time than that."

"I don't know about miracles, but I do know about men."

"Boss, you're gonna have to look long and hard to find enough material in that kid to scrape together anything manly. I've seen women who looked more like a man than he does!"

Pancake chortled softly. "Startin' with Widder O'Toole."

Tim broke into a fleeting smile, then glanced back at the house and grimaced.

"When Fuller gets back and catches sight of that pathetic excuse for a nephew, whatever cure he got in Abilene's gonna fly right outta the window."

"That's not going to happen." Tim's face tightened. "I'll do something."

"What's your plan?"

Tim's voice took on deadly resolve. "Whatever needs to be done will get done. It's going to be mighty unpleasant, though."

"That's plain enough to see, and I have eyes in my head." Pancake tacked on, "I've seen two-bit chippies with more taste in their clothes."

"Clothes can be changed."

Spitting a small stream of tobacco at a dandelion four feet away, Pancake demonstrated admirable targeting skill. "Doubt he's half as useful as one of them chippies."

Tim compressed his lips for a grim moment. There were times when life just handed you nothing better than a boil on the backside when you had to ride all day, and this was one such time. It galled him, but Tim Creighton wasn't a man to shirk his responsibilities or abandon his friends. He muffled a groan at the thought of what the next days would bring and resolved, "We're going to start whipping him into shape."

"Awww, Boss!"

"The Bible tells us to bear one another's burdens."

The cook's face darkened. "That's just one more reason I don't warm a pew. Besides, if you're quotin' the Good Book, you might as well pay close attention to what it says. There's a world of difference between bearing a burden and weathering a catastrophe." Pancake flapped his hand toward the house. "That kid's a catastrophe."

Eyes narrowed, Tim gave Pancake a piercing glare. "No job ever got done without being started, and we don't leave things undone at Forsaken."

"Someone's likely to get hurt."

"I'm painfully aware of that possibility." Tim's voice didn't betray the acid churning in his belly over that very fact. "It'll fall to me to work with the kid until Fuller shows up."

Pancake let out a bark of a laugh. "Should I take wagers on which of you gets buried fastest?"

"Try, and I'll see to it that you're in a casket first."

"Fuller's too old to handle this one. Betcha he ropes you into finishin' the job."

"There's where you're wrong, Pancake. Some things a man doesn't ask. This is one of them. Fuller is too honorable to saddle me with his dirty work." Fuller Johnson had ministered to Tim when his life was in ruins, but Tim knew the man wouldn't ever call in the favor. He added, "I'd do just about anything for Fuller. He knows it, too, but he'd lay down and die before he'd consider asking me to reform that boy—even if he is a relation. He wouldn't ask, but I'm stepping up to the task."

"Oh, I've known Fuller more'n long 'nuff to be shore he'd never ask. Fact of the matter is, we both know he's too long in the tooth to handle the duty. That rheumatiz in his back and hands makes him too slow to do what needs doing anyplace but at that desk."

"He owns most of the ranch," Creighton clipped as he scanned the landscape with a mixture of awe and admiration.

"No one challenges that. He's a great man. Fact still stands that you own a fair part and you do the bossin'. Just look—it's the middle of calving season, and he up and went to Abilene. That says it all."

Giving him an unyielding gaze, Tim said, "You've got work to do."

Pancake walked off and teased over his shoulder, "So do you. Oh, boy, so do you, and I don't envy you one lick of it!"

Sydney headed toward the two-story white clapboard ranch house. Wisdom dictated she leave those rough men and establish her place in the household, but pride demanded she do so with decorum. She refused to let the bossy one's cold disapproval bother her. Nothing was going to ruin her adventure.

And what an adventure this was turning into! She looked about and smiled. The ranch seemed to possess miles of verdant land with fresh spring grass for numerous grazing cows. A fair number of wobbly legged calves stuck close by their mamas and bawled if they were hungry. Birdsong filled the air, and clumps of colorful wildflowers dotted the landscape. Living in such surroundings shouldn't prove to be a hardship at all.

The weight of the valise pulled on her shoulder and arm. The servants here needed to be taught manners. They didn't introduce themselves and not a one saw to her luggage. That last man needed to be set straight on a few issues.

Mama always said even the best staff slacked off when the master is gone. From the topnotch condition of the grounds, the place must normally be run admirably. Uncle Fuller's not here now. Likely, that's the cause of their apathetic ways. Well—all but that surly one.

Sydney fought the temptation to glance back to make sure she hadn't imagined the black-haired man. She'd almost gotten a crick in her neck from looking up at him. The dust on his rugged blue denim pants proved he was a man who worked hard for his living. He smelled as if he'd been working hard, too. An acrid mixture of sweat and leather clung to him. At least he'd not offered her his hand to shake—though Sydney couldn't be sure whether he knew not to be so forward with his betters or if he'd been ashamed of how filthy he was.

Realization streaked through her. It wouldn't occur to that man to be ashamed of looking and smelling as he did; he was proud of it. It had earned him the others' respect and obedience. A smile tugged at her lips. Being male was . . . unique. Fun, even.

Sydney angled toward the house and managed to peek at him one last time. Even from this distance, he looked capable of doing everything Buffalo Bill did in the dime novels.

Her boots clomped up each of the wooden steps of the porch. Off to the side, a four-foot-long swing hung from chains. Sydney imagined sitting there reading and enjoying a glass of lemonade. After her travels, she'd finally arrived and could divest herself of these miserable boots, order Velma to bring her something to quench her thirst, and—

"C'mon in!" an unseen woman hollered before Sydney reached the screen door.

A short, heavy woman in a blue calico apron lumbered up. She bumped the door open with her hip and wiped her hands on a dish towel. A thin stripe of gray by her left temple was scraped back with the rest of her inky hair into a lopsided bun at the top of her head. Intelligence sparkled in her coffee-colored eyes, and laugh lines proved she had a sense of humor. "You must be Sydney. Been expecting you. Got two extra bedrooms upstairs. Go on 'head and pick one. I don't much care which. I'll have to put sheets on the bed. No use in letting sheets go stale on a bed that lies empty."

"Yes, I'm Hathwell. One of the hands mentioned your

name. I believe it was Velma, was it not?"

"Was and still is." She grinned. "Now get out of my hair. I've got plenty to do. Supper's in an hour. I'll holler once and only once. You show up or you go hungry. I'm not about to start toting water up and down the stairs for anybody, so you'll have to pump your own from the kitchen if you want to use the washbowl in your chamber."

She won't start, so that means she normally doesn't perform that task even for my uncle. Well, with only one house servant, allowances need to be made. "I'll see to filling my pitcher. Bert mentioned Uncle Fuller is in Abilene."

"Yep. Be back in 'bout ten days, give or take a few. Depends on how the cure is going. Your uncle ain't the kind to stick around and do any tom cattin'."

The housekeeper's frank acknowledgment of a man's baser needs astonished Sydney. Her eyes widened, though she did manage to keep her jaw from dropping.

Slapping her on the shoulder and nearly knocking her down, the housekeeper cackled. "Boy, ain't nothing old Velma don't know ten times over by now. My mama ran a bordello down in N'Awlins. Nothing surprises me."

"Out of respect for your sensibilities—"

Velma cackled even louder. "I don't pull any punches. The hands out there know not to pussyfoot around me. I take no sass, and I don't take any passes. Long as you remember those two things, you and me—we'll get along just fine."

"Fine," Sydney echoed in an unsteady tone. She looked at the stairs with dismay. She knew full well that no young man would stand there and complain about the heat and dust and his aching feet, though she was sorely tempted to do all three.

"Kid, you'd best move on. Big Tim's gonna be bustling

through soon, and he'll mow over the likes of you faster than a toad gulps flies."

It was not a reassuring metaphor. Sydney shuffled forward. "I'll locate a chamber and meet you for supper."

"You do that. Tim's going to give you a hard once-over. You ought to put on something a whole lot plainer if you don't want to have him squirm all through the meal. He's not a man to abide fussy manners and clothes."

Sydney noticed the cowboys were all in shirtsleeves, but surely landowners would wear respectable attire and dress for dinner. "I'm wearing a simple cravat!"

Velma threw back her head and roared in the most unlady-like display of sound Sydney had ever witnessed. "That was a good one. Now scamper on up and let me get back to work."

Lugging the valise up the stairs tested Sydney's mettle. Her shoulders felt as if they couldn't bear such a burden for a second longer. Once she reached the head of the stairs, she walked straight into the first chamber and dropped the valise. Nothing short of a pistol aimed at her head would convince her to pick up that load again.

The bedchamber held a modest bedstead and a nice three-drawer chest with a carved mirror above it. Heavy green damask curtains swagged back from the window, and faded cabbage rose wallpaper finished the decor.

Sydney smiled at the room. She could spruce it up with a little attention and care. In truth, it was far prettier than what she'd planned to find in the midst of this wild place. The glimpse she'd gotten of the downstairs let her know the other rooms, though well worn, were tastefully appointed, too. Perhaps Texas didn't entirely lack civilized touches. The mixture of refinement and commonplace struck her as oddly charming.

Sorting out when to apply rules and when to cast them aside would be a delightful challenge.

But that challenge could wait. She dropped down onto the edge of the bed. Her feet ached every bit as much as they did after a long evening of dancing with several suitors. Heel, toe, sole, and instep all burned and ached. Struggling out of the boots, she rubbed her toes and decided to fetch a pitcher of water so she could wash up and soak her feet. After that, she'd unpack and find her most unprepossessing shirt.

As she reviewed Velma's words and considered all of the men she'd seen, Sydney had an alarming thought. Big Tim would mow her over? Big Tim, as in Tim Creighton? That couldn't possibly be the rude giant whom she'd seen already. Shaking her head to dislodge the troublesome thought, Sydney convinced herself the man outside was too ... *something* to be the second-in-command. Terse and rough-edged and gruff and, well, *dirty*. Those very attributes convinced her whoever it was couldn't possibly be in a position of authority. Cheered by that thought, she went in search of water.

Under an hour later, the clock downstairs struck. Sydney heard Velma's call for supper and hastily smoothed her hair as she glanced in the mirror over the chest of drawers to ascertain if she'd done a sufficient job of binding herself. Twisting sideways, she craned her neck and examined the effect. A small smile tilted her lips as she gleefully judged, "Perfect!"

She left her room and started down the stairs. Halfway down, she practically got run over by an express train of a man who gallumped down the very same flight. His boots made a muffled thunder that carried an oddly rhythmic quality, and his large body didn't seem to move at all from the hips up as those log-thick legs churned with surprising agility and grace. Once he hit the foot of the stairs, the stranger stopped and gave her a cool, assessing look. Without a word, he wheeled to the right and strode off.

She remained rooted to the stairs.

He can't be Uncle Fuller's partner. He can't—even if he did clean up into a respectable-looking man. Truth be told, he cut a fine figure. For all of the refined gentlemen she'd seen in high society, none had ever looked half as imposing or innately capable of facing anything life might bring.

Following the scent of food, Sydney went in the same direction he had. With every step she promised herself Uncle Fuller's partner probably invited the rude giant to be a dinner guest. Yes, of course. That was it. Heartened by that realization, Sydney continued on.

She stopped cold in the doorway. *That* man sat at the huge trestle table. Alone. He'd already started serving himself. He'd spruced up on the outside, but that was it. The man still failed to exhibit even a hint of manners.

Velma thumped a bowl of mashed potatoes onto the table. "Sydney Hathwell, have you met Tim Creighton yet?"

"Mr. Creighton?" Her voice cracked like an adolescent's.

Grabbing for his coffee, Creighton nodded. "Hathwell."

Velma shooed her toward the table with a few brisk sweeps of her hands. "Don't just stand there. Your food's getting cold."

Sydney pulled out the chair and sat down. Unaccustomed to seating herself, she took several minuscule scoots to draw close enough to the table.

"We say grace at meals here." Creighton didn't pause for a response. He bowed his head. "Almighty Lord, we praise and thank you for this bounty. Bless Fuller and grant him your healing touch. In all things, let us be your servants. Amen."

Though they usually didn't pray at home unless company

joined them, Sydney considered Creighton's prayer lacking. She added a few extra lines of thanks for her safe arrival and begged the Creator for guidance and help. It looked as if she was going to need it. Mr. Tim Creighton was going to be difficult. . . .

I started out thinking this would be easy, but I was wrong. Well, the challenge will make my time here go by quickly.

As she slipped her napkin across her thighs, Sydney tried to approach conversation as she'd done back home. Civility might tame the beast a bit. "So, Mr. Creighton, where are your people from?"

"My people?"

"Yes. Your people. Your family."

"I don't have a family."

The curt clip of his voice let her know to cease pursuing that line of talk, so she segued, "Pity. You've certainly done well for yourself. Forsaken appears to be a fine spread."

"How would you know enough to make that judgment?"

"I walked the length of the road. The fence is well kept, and the house is quite stunning. Then, too, there are all sorts of cows everywhere."

"Cattle—not 'cows'—and they're not everywhere. We've moved them to pasture off at the southeastern sector for the moment. Other sections are empty at present to let the grasses grow."

"Oh."

"Do you ride? Most gentlemen are trained at horsemanship, aren't they?"

She fought the telling blush that heated her cheeks. Last night it had dawned on her that she'd have to ride astride. Such a skill must, of necessity, be altogether different from perching on a sidesaddle. Though she was quite proficient at riding in a lady's saddle, straddling anything would be a shock. "I . . . er . . .

excelled at studies. My time has been spent in academic pursuits."

"Hence the smooth, narrow hands and a complete lack of any muscle on those spindles you call arms."

The man shoveled food in like an animal! Nearly mesmerized by the precision with which he sliced off huge chunks of meat and devoured them, Sydney hardly felt the sting of his implied insult.

"Did you study anything of particular interest?"

"Oh yes. Greek history, Roman mythology, Latin, and poetry. I also appreciate fine art."

"So much for the frills." Tim took a big swig of coffee. "No one round here speaks Latin or walks around spouting poetry. Best painting in these parts is a sign in the feed store. Did you study anything useful?"

"I scarcely believe you'd find dancing or British history to be of practical application here in the West."

"You got that right." Waving a fork in the air and disregarding the fact that mashed potatoes plopped back onto the plate, Tim announced, "No one sits on their tail around this spread. You're going to have to carry your weight."

"I plan to do just that."

"Yes, you will. You'd best be ready—because come sunup, you're going to start earning your keep."

"Mr. Creighton, I'm not afraid of hard work. I'll also remind you that I'm not exactly a hired hand to be ordered about like some kind of liveried lackey." She wiggled in her chair slightly, squared her shoulders, and dabbed at her lips with the napkin. "There is my position to be considered."

Creighton leaned back in his chair, shook his head, and scowled. "Fancy Pants, you've got it wrong. That stinkin' title of yours isn't worth a hill of beans around here. I don't care if you've got a crown permanently affixed to your head—you'd better slap a hat over it because you'll still have to work."

The man wasn't just blunt; he was rude. He completely lacked couth. Sydney gave him a disbelieving stare.

He glowered straight back. "Fuller's a hardworking man. He expects every man on Forsaken to earn his keep. You're no exception."

Sydney reared back at the force of his words. "I say, there's no call to be uncivilized."

"We aren't civilized around here. Best get that through your head. Life is rough. Rugged. Hard," he hammered at her in a harsh tone. "You don't toughen up, you won't survive. Pure and simple, the useful survive. The weak don't."

"Are you threatening me?"

"Take it however you want, but you're due up at daybreak. I respect your uncle too much to let him come home to an English dandy of a nephew. By the time he gets here, you'll have learned enough to make yourself useful."

"That's only a week away!"

"Don't remind me. I already have indigestion from watching you eat. You chew meat longer than a cow chews a wad of cud."

Sydney's fork and knife clattered to the plate. "That was less than appropriate table conversation!"

"Spoil your appetite?"

"It's apparent nothing spoils your appetite. You've torn into a perfectly delightful meal with no more manners than a rabid wolf."

"Wolves tear apart baby animals that are wet behind the ears. Don't forget that, sonny." Creighton took a huge bite, gnashed on it only half a dozen times, and swallowed while staring at her.

Sydney caught herself swallowing along with him.

Tim gave her a smile that showed every last one of his teeth. After that, there wasn't any more supper conversation.

Sydney went to bed and lay in the dark, horrified. To be sure, the soft bed felt great, but her mind reeled with Tim Creighton's actions. How could Uncle Fuller have left her to the vagaries of such a boor? A big one, too. She'd tried to convince herself he wouldn't be worthy of a second-in-command position, and seeing him at the table came as a terribly rude shock.

The way he acted as if *she* were the problem galled her; yet, that was precisely his perspective on things—and he made no bones about it. *But if every man here works, he's right. I'm useless.*

Sydney had to admit she presented a unique challenge to the man. He obviously liked Uncle Fuller and wanted him to be spared the pain of seeing a relative who was pitifully inept. Just what would this deception demand of her?

The idea of misleading others went against her deep sense of honor, but it paled in comparison to the appalling alternative of becoming Rex Hume's wife.

Sydney determined she would have to be a man's man and quickly realized she'd have to develop mettle to make it through. *I always did love a challenge.*

Chapter Three

The door rattled on its hinges from a sound smack, but Tim got no response. Velma yelled from downstairs, "Sun's almost up! Get movin'."

Tim wrenched the doorknob, crossed the small bedchamber, and grabbed the mattress. One quick flick of his wrists, and Hathwell tumbled through the air and hit the floor with a resounding thud. The kid let out a shrill yelp.

"Velma gave you a wake-up call fifteen minutes ago." Tim dumped the mattress back down on the bed frame. Disgust twisted his features as he watched the kid clutch the rumpled bedsheets to his nightshirted chest. "Stop squawking. Get on your feet and get moving. If you don't show up to eat in five minutes, Velma'll use the flapjacks to slop the hogs."

"Five minutes!"

Tim shot him a heated look. "Don't ever expect me to tilt you outta your bed again."

"I won't!"

Tim didn't stick around to listen to the kid whine. No use in both of them eating Velma's flapjacks cold. He sat down to breakfast, said grace, and implored God to intervene with Fuller's nephew. If ever a situation existed that required divine intervention, surely this was it.

Eight minutes later Tim watched in utter disbelief as the youngster carefully cut a single, tiny bite of a flapjack and daintily slipped it between his lips. The kid even crooked his pinkie like a fussy old woman. Tim propped his elbows on the table and fought the urge to bury his head in his hands.

"Eat up, kid."

"I have gracious plenty, thank you."

One flapjack and two rashers of bacon. How could that possibly be enough? No wonder the kid is skin and bones.

Hathwell scanned the table and frowned.

"What's wrong?"

"I don't see the sugar or cream."

"Black and strong enough to float a horseshoe—that's how men drink their coffee. Finish eating. Work's piling up."

Piling up. Tim smothered a grin. After the words slipped out of his mouth, he realized he'd made an unintended pun. The stable reeked in the morning from the horses' piles. Fancy Pants Hathwell might not possess a single skill, but that wouldn't matter. Anyone could grab a shovel and muck out stalls—and that was precisely what Tim planned to assign the kid. Last night the conversation ruined Hathwell's appetite. If he knew precisely what awaited him, he wouldn't eat another bite.

Hathwell took a sip of coffee and cut another miniscule bite from his flapjack. "Organization is key to success. I presume you and my uncle have routines that keep matters well in hand."

"There's a general routine, but animals have a habit of putting a kink in whatever plans we make. There's not a man on this spread who lacks the full array of necessary skills." Tim gave Sydney a telling look. "I'll see to it you learn the ropes."

"Ropes!" The kid perked up. "That would be capital! I'd

love to learn how to throw the lariat!"

Tim inwardly winced at how the kid pronounced it "larry-ette." A Mexican *vaquero*, Juan called his a *riata*. Tim immediately discarded that possible term. The kid would mangle it, too. "It takes time, practice, and diligence to handle a lasso."

"Well, then, I suppose once I become proficient with the larry-ette, I'll move on to the lasso."

"Lasso is another term for lariat." Tim pronounced it *larry-ut* and hoped the kid would get the hint. "When someone learns the ropes, it means they gain proficiency in the essentials. You'll tend other basics before you throw a lasso."

The kid's brows puckered. Tim couldn't be sure whether it was from displeasure at that news, or from the sip of black coffee he drank. It didn't matter. Either way, Fancy Pants Hathwell was going to endure plenty of things he didn't relish.

"This is a cattle ranch, not a cotillion." Tim rose. "Finish up and be quick about it."

Sydney bolted to his feet. "I rarely eat breakfast. Shall we go?"

Tim gave no response. He pivoted and headed across the floor and out the door.

The kid scrambled to keep up with him as they went toward the stable. "I see the staff is hard at work. That's commendable."

"It's expected." Tim stopped and locked eyes with him. "Get this straight: they're not staff. They're hands or cowboys or the men—or punchers or pokes."

"Very well."

Tim scanned the kid and shook his head. "Whatever passed for men's duds in London won't cut it here. Baggy shirts and pants will get caught or chafe. Next time you go to town, get a few pair of britches and shirts that are boys' size."

Sydney's jaw hardened. "Mr. Creighton, I happen to feel

more comfortable in loose-fitting attire." Then the kid added in a quieter grumble, "Besides, these *are* boys'."

Tim nodded curtly and said nothing more. It doubtlessly galled Hathwell to have to buy boys' clothing at his age. Hopefully, he'd soon have enough muscles and height to take up the slack in what he now wore.

There were men who never did get bigger than this. Wizened old Mr. Farber at the land survey office was a prime example. Then, too, that horse trainer over at the Franklin ranch wasn't bigger than this. Tim knew some of it was a family trait, but he also suspected people were like crops. The ones that were tended and fed right grew best. Proper activity, training, and plenty of food might boost the kid into a sprouting season.

"I beg your pardon, but I didn't understand what you just said."

From Sydney's comment and quizzical look, Tim realized he must have mumbled something under his breath. He shifted his weight. "Good food and hard work are what you need."

"Velma's cuisine is quite tasty."

"Which leaves hard work." Tim strode to the stable. "Bert!"

"In here!"

Sydney trotted alongside Tim like a spaniel pup. "My, look at the size of the stable! How many horses do we have?"

Tim couldn't be sure whether the kid was claiming ownership or speaking in general terms. He decided to give him the benefit of the doubt. "The ranch owns two dozen. A couple of the hands own their own mounts, so the total tally is thirty-one."

Syd's eyes widened. "Thirty-one! I didn't realize there were that many men here."

"There aren't. We keep three mounts for each man." He shot Bert a look.

A slow grin creased Bert's weathered face. "Back before the railroad was close, we kept five mounts per cowpoke."

Craning his neck, Hathwell peered down the stable. "There aren't that many stalls."

Tim smacked him on the back. "Nope. Not that many at all. Shouldn't take you long."

"What shouldn't take me long?"

Tim accepted the shovel from Bert and thrust it at the kid. "Muck."

An eternity later, as she began to muck out yet another stall, Sydney shoved back a snarled tress. She shouldn't have bothered to brush her hair that morning. The stable stank worse than an untended chamber pot. Just about the time she had a stall cleaned, the unmistakable noise of one of the horses relieving himself resounded in a nearby stall. For the first time in her life, she wondered if people who used crass language might not be cursing, but merely speaking a raw truth.

"Well, well, if it ain't good ol' Syd Hathwell."

Sydney glanced over her shoulder. "Boaz." She recognized the rangy black man from the brief introduction in the barnyard yesterday.

"Easy for you to recognize me, but I hardly knew it was you."

Bert came over and elbowed him. "Don't distract the kid. He's got to concentrate hard to get the job done right."

"Bet the kid wouldn't recognize himself—not with a shovel in his hands."

After Tim Creighton's supper comments last night, Sydney anticipated the teasing and pranks that were bound to come her way. A woman would whine and chafe. A man would take it or even joke back. She flashed a cocky smile at him. "It beats scooping this muck up with my hands."

Bert chuckled and leaned into a railing. "You're gonna have blisters."

"Future tense is unnecessary."

"And you're still shovelin'?" He grabbed a handful of her shirt and yanked. "Dumb greenhorn, wash 'em and put on gloves before you get something festering!"

"I didn't bring gloves."

"What man worth his salt don't have gloves? Aww, forget it. We shoulda known you wouldn't have something that sensible." He turned loose of her shirt and strode to the far side of the stable. Yanking a pair of gloves from a dusty shelf, he looked at them and scowled. "These are gonna be too big. Blast, I ain't never seen a man have such small hands."

"It's a Hathwell trait."

"Ain't nothin' to boast about. It's gonna make life harder for you."

"I'll simply purchase boys' gloves when next I go to town."

Tim Creighton stepped into view. Sydney didn't know where he'd been, but a smudge of dirt on his rugged jaw testified to the fact that he'd been busy. Suddenly, earning his approval mattered. Her shovel scraped the floor. "I'll be done in a few more minutes."

"Fine. Bert, Velma said we've got a fox digging at the bottom of the henhouse again. Go fill it in and bury a few spikes for good measure."

"Add a healthy dash of cayenne pepper to the last spadeful of dirt," Sydney suggested.

"Huh?" Boaz looked puzzled.

"Cayenne pepper. Certainly Velma has some. It irritates the nose and eyes of a predator. The fox won't likely come back very soon after getting a sample of it."

Bert planted his hands on his hips. "'Zat so?"

"Indeed."

"Boss?"

A crooked grin quirked the corner of Creighton's mouth. "Try spikes in one half and pepper in the other. We'll see if playing cook in the mud pie makes a whit's worth of difference."

Sydney smiled. "Care to place a friendly wager on the results?"

Bert perked up. "Sure!"

"No." Tim scowled.

Boaz huffed. "Just 'cuz you don't bet, Boss, doesn't mean the kid can't."

"You men can bet among yourselves, but leave the kid out of it. He's underage."

Sure of her solution, Sydney shot Creighton an oh-so-innocent look. "Then why don't you and I have a gentlemen's agreement? Instead of money, perhaps we could settle on the loser having to do a chore." *Like muck the stable . . .*

Tim crooked a brow.

Hooking the heel of his boot on a wooden slat, Bert drawled, "Boss, isn't that henhouse due to be cleaned out?"

"It is."

"So do we have an agreement?" Sydney strove to sound blasé. "If the fox goes through the cayenne, I clean the henhouse. If he goes through the other section, you do the honors."

"Fine. It's a deal."

Sydney felt so smug, she hardly even noticed the weight or odor of those last few scoops of muck. "What next?"

"We're going for a ride."

"I'll be ready immediately after I've seen to ... matters. Where is the necessary?"

Creighton rolled his eyes. "There's a tree out yonder."

Heat shot through her. Sydney stared at him. She hadn't even given a thought to the problem of how she might obtain privacy for her most basic needs. At the moment, she couldn't imagine she'd been so ignorant. She murmured, "A moment with you please, Mr. Creighton."

"What now?"

Heavens, the man sounded even more impatient, if that were possible. She leaned closer and stammered, "I ... er, happen to have ... um, digestive difficulties."

"Why doesn't that come as a surprise? All right. The outhouse is back over that way. Hurry up. I don't have all day."

Sydney hastened to the outhouse and strained to think about anything else she might have overlooked. Carrying on this masquerade wasn't as easy as she'd hoped. While she had a few moments in that cobwebby, dank privy, she made sure the knot on her chest binding would stay secure. She wished she'd brought along powder. It used to keep her corset from chafing, and the binding rubbed dreadfully.

Chewing on a long shaft of grass, Tim watched her come back toward him. He didn't bother to move the grass when he muttered something to Bert.

Sydney pasted on a cocky smile and approached them. "Well? Did you decide on a suitable mount?"

"Diablo?" Bert suggested.

"Hmmm. Maybe ... if you want to kill me off before I reach my majority." Sydney grinned back. "Every horse given a name dealing with the occult seems to be wicked tempered. I could give it my best effort, but I do value my life."

"Fuller might take exception to us trying that stunt,"

Creighton agreed. "Coming home to a fresh grave would rile him. Let's make it Kippy."

"I'll saddle him up," Bert offered.

"Please, no. I need to learn to do it myself." Moments later, Sydney regretted her impulsive denial. The beast was huge, and the saddle weighed a ton. Everything in her arms and back screamed as she rose up on her tiptoes to fling the saddle onto the horse's back. She managed to get the halter and bit on correctly, even though she held her breath in fear that the horse would nip her with those huge yellow teeth.

After Sydney led Kippy into the yard, the men seemed to find cause to draw closer to watch the show. She tried her best to ignore their presence. It wasn't easy, since they gave a running commentary on how poor they anticipated her performance would be. They planned on having a grand time watching her fail, and it tickled her. They were in for quite a surprise.

She steeled herself with a deep breath, reached up, and barely clasped the pommel. Big Tim didn't clasp her waist to gently settle her into the saddle. Sydney didn't expect him to. But he also didn't lace his fingers together and let her put the sole of her boot in his hands as a makeshift stepstool. Instead, he grabbed her ankle and half tossed her upward.

Sydney flew clear over to the other side of the beast. Her near bootheel snagged and stuck on the saddle.

Never in her life had Sydney's legs spread this wide. Kippy shuffled forward a step. Bloody images of falling and being trampled spurred her to flex her arms and pull herself upward.

Just as her shoulders and head popped above Kippy's withers, Tim grabbed a fistful of her pant leg and tossed her leg over the horse.

She dipped for an instant, then found the stirrup and valiantly gained her seat. Sitting stiffly in the saddle, Sydney stared straight ahead. Her cheeks flamed with embarrassment. *Did Tim Creighton do all of that just to humiliate me?*

"You don't weigh as much as a barrel of flour," he said gruffly.

That would have been a compliment for a woman. For a man, it didn't happen to be very positive. Sydney gave him a stern glare. She wasn't sure if she wanted to forgive him for holding her ankle, either. No man had ever been that familiar— even if she was parading about as a boy and wearing britches.

"I have to adjust these stirrups, too." He tugged at a buckle near her shin. "You're short."

"Contrary to your belief, that particular flaw isn't my doing. If you wish to lodge a complaint, take it to the Almighty."

"Son, I already have a fair amount I'm asking the Lord for reckoning about. Plenty of things regarding you just got added onto the list." Tim fixed both stirrups and heaved a great sigh.

"At least he knows how to hold the reins. Must've ridden a little," Gulp proclaimed to the cowboys.

"Pointing those toes down, though. He's a greenhorn."

"Heels down, toes flat or up a bit," Tim stated under his breath. "Keep your back straight like that, but loosen up a bit. You're way too stiff, and the horse senses it. Relax and use your knees to direct him. A little thigh pressure, and he'll respond."

Tim slapped Kippy, but he may as well have slapped Sydney. No man had ever used such intimate anatomical terms as *knee* and *thigh* around her. She tensed, and the gelding started off at a brisk walk. The sudden move made her thighs tighten, and her heels instinctively dug inward to gain better balance. Kippy began to canter. It only got worse. She increased the pressure, and the gelding broke into a run.

"Sweet saints!" She leaned forward and hung on for dear life. Sydney then realized the pace wasn't any different than when she was on a foxhunt. If anything, sitting astride gave her far better balance and control. She relaxed her legs, and Kippy slowed naturally. Giving herself permission to use the opportunity to play around with this new freedom, Sydney kicked the gelding and got him to a full-out run. They circled around a tree and returned to the ranch yard.

"Dog me, the kid can actually ride!" Gulp declared.

"Who woulda ever thunk it?" Merle marveled.

Tim grabbed the halter. "I thought you didn't know how to ride."

"I've never ridden like this—in this kind of saddle." As soon as she made that proclamation, Sydney felt a sense of utter horror. How could she have been so stupid? She'd just given away her secret!

"Those bitty little English saddles are what you used? I've seen them. No wonder you questioned your ability."

"Yes," she breathed in sheer relief.

"I'll mount up and we can take a gander at the grounds." Tim turned and left her amidst the circle of ranch hands.

Surveying them, Sydney grinned impishly. "I do hope one of you was wise enough to put a few dollars down on my riding ability. In view of the general consensus that I'd be an abysmal failure before I got started, the financial return was probably quite satisfying."

Jack chortled as he gave her an open-handed smack of goodwill on her thigh. "Sonny, you just earned me three bucks. Next time we're in town, your first beer is on me."

Beer? She'd never had beer in her whole life. Still, Sydney knew she'd have to play along. Nodding, she lowered her voice as best she could. "Thanks. I'll look forward to that." What she truly wanted to do was turn around and smack him back and rub her leg. He'd probably left a huge wheal, and her thigh stung.

Tim Creighton reappeared. He fluidly swung up into the saddle of a handsome palomino. "Let's get going. You men, if you thought to keep jawing, just remember that Fuller wanted the north fence reinforced before he got back."

He jerked his head slightly to the side, as if to say, "follow me," and took off at a slow canter. Sydney experimentally nudged her heels into the gelding and felt a surge of pleasure that he moved faster. She watched Big Tim. The man could ride; he and his horse moved in perfect rhythm. She'd grown up watching gentlemen ride, but none of them ever commanded a horse as Big Tim did.

They rode a fair bit away from the others before their horses found a comfortable side-by-side gait. Tim pointed out a few salient landmarks, then halted his mount at the peak of a gentle hillock. Sydney had to not only stop Kippy, but struggled to get him to backstep. Her success felt good, though, and Tim's slight smirk of a smile was ample reward. They sat there as Tim gazed off at the horizon.

Sydney took the opportunity to study him more closely. His eyes were definitely gray. His hair needed a decent trim as the edges looked uneven and ragged. His shirt was frayed at the collar and cuffs, too. His body and the horse's seemed to blend as one, since his trousers and the horse's coat were the same shade.

"What are you smirking at?"

His words jolted her out of her perusal, but with her usual candor, Sydney informed him, "You look like Pan."

"Pan?"

"In Greek mythology—he was the god of herds. He's half man, half—well, not goat. Horse, in your case."

His brow crooked.

I'm babbling, she realized and cleared her throat. For a fleeting moment, she tried to be silent, but Tim's steely look set her off into an explanation. "There are creatures in other cultures' myths, legends, and tales. Satyrs have the top half of a man, and the waist joins where the neck of a beast meets the body. With your trousers and the horse's coat so similar in hue, the likeness is remarkable."

"And so you remarked upon it."

"Obviously."

He gave her a cold look. "Kid, I'm going to lay things on the line with you."

"Please feel free to do so."

"You need an education in just about everything except useless book learning. That kind of knowledge is likely to get you into real trouble. A satyr, for your enlightenment, happens to be insatiable. He lusts after anything in a skirt and exercises no restraint. I could take real exception to your characterization of me."

Heat scorched a path from her bodice to her brow. Even her ears burned. *Revelry. Pan was known for his revelry—but lasciviousness? Dear mercy, they sanitized—*

"Growing up privileged made a freak of you. Unless you do a lot of learning fast, the boys in the bunkhouse are gonna eat you alive."

"I've proved I can ride."

"Stick to riding. The way your hips sway when you walk, you look like a girl."

Cold terror washed over her. "A girl?"

"Knew that'd gall you. I'm of a mind to strap a holster around you to weight you down a mite. Between that and you using your butt instead of your thighs to move those nubs you call legs, that ought to solve the problem."

"Really!" The man had absolutely no class.

"Really," he drawled. "The difficulty is, you'll be fool enough to have a bullet in each chamber and blow off a few toes."

"Give me your pistol." She extended her hand.

"You aren't going to shoot me, are you?" Tim reached for his holster.

"Believe me, if ever I were tempted, most surely 'tis now. Nonetheless, I'll refrain from that and give you a demonstration." He still looked dubious, but Sydney decided to take the opportunity to prove she wasn't helpless. "Is the barrel true on this?"

"Absolutely."

"Capital. See that knob on the tree stump over in the clearing?"

"Yup."

She took aim and fired. Without even checking to confirm her results, she handed back the weapon. "Now you don't."

Amazement altered his tanned features.

"As Cervantes said, 'Thou hast seen nothing yet.'" She handed back the weapon. "Your pistol's nicely balanced."

"Kid, you're in Texas. Here you say, 'You ain't seen nuthin' yet.'"

Syd's mouth quirked. "You ain't seen nuthin' yet."

Creighton shoved the gun back into his holster and gave her an assessing look. "How old are you, anyway?"

"Seventeen."

He echoed in a disbelieving tone, "Seventeen?"

"I'll reach my majority in January." Sydney straightened her shoulders and sat tall in the saddle.

Squinting, Tim leaned closer. "I don't believe it. Kid, you're not even shaving yet. I thought you were somewhere around fourteen."

Offended, Sydney glowered at him. "Your estimation was obviously as faulty as your opinion of my marksmanship and equestrian abilities."

"Too bad your body doesn't keep up with your tongue, son."

"You, sir, are detestable."

"You're entitled to your opinion." He gave his reins a commanding yank. His palomino turned and cantered off.

Sydney stared at Tim's back. As soon as her birthday came, she'd make him pay for his arrogance.

Chapter Four

That evening the supper table remained devoid of conversation. The only sounds were of cutlery scraping the plates and glasses settling back on the wooden tabletop. Tim finished eating long before the kid did, so he sat nursing his cup of coffee. Finally, he breached the icy silence. "Listen, son, we're going to have to get along. I don't know what you're used to, but men out West don't mince words. Best get used to it quick."

Sydney gave him a truculent look.

Tim took another sip of the coffee, then set it down. "It's obvious you're just a late bloomer. It doesn't mean you won't fill out. Some good, hard labor will help with that. After a month or so, you'll have some muscles. Fresh air and plenty of meat will give you something to grow on, too."

The kid's jaw jutted forward. "Was that supposed to be some kind of olive branch?"

"You're as prickly as a porkypine." Heaving a longsuffering sigh, Tim rose. "Until Fuller gets back, I'm in charge around here. He asked me to take you under my wing. I'll hold up my part. I refuse to let him down."

The kid concentrated on buttering a slice of bread.

C'mon, Fancy Pants. Be a man. Say you'll do your part.

Sydney set down his knife with great precision, raised the slice, and took a bite.

I gave you a chance. You didn't take it. Tim shook his head in disgust. He strode from the dining room, out the door, and into the barn. Earlier in the day, he'd mudded a mare's foreleg. A cursory check showed the swelling and heat had gone down. *At least something's going right.*

"Boss?

He turned. "Bert."

"Wanted to tell you, I took care of the henhouse. Velma didn't want to give me some cayenne, but I talked her into it."

Tim folded his arms across his chest. "Just what did you have to promise her?"

"You know how finicky she is about her kitchen. . . ."

Tim nodded. The day was already a mess. Anything more wouldn't make it worse.

"She wants feed sacks traded. Seems she has her heart set on a particular yellow one for a dress, and she needs six or seven more sacks just like it."

"That shouldn't be too difficult."

A slow, sly smile tilted Bert's mouth. "Glad you feel thata-way. I'll fetch the one she wants matched so you can be sure to trade for the right one."

"Whoa! I said nothing about *me* getting them. You made the deal; you carry out your part of the bargain."

Bert wagged his head from side to side. "I was just following orders. Did what I had to, to get the job done. My part's finished."

Tim's eyes narrowed. He didn't put up with anyone questioning his orders.

"Before you get too het up"—Bert held up both hands as if to ward him off—"you might think on how that Hathwell kid was the one who wanted the cayenne. Maybe he ought to track down what Velma wants."

The plan had merit. Tim mulled it over.

"You gotta admit, it's probably all that scrawny little brat's able to do."

Scrawny? Yes. Little? Uh-huh. Brat? You bet. Tim resisted the temptation and glowered at Bert. "Chasing after feed sacks isn't part of the plan. We're going to whip that kid into shape."

"Pancake said you were set on that." Bert kicked a bale of hay. "No one's gonna blame you if you change your mind."

"What other people think doesn't matter to me. My aim's to do the right thing."

"Awww, Boss." Bert looked pained. "Some things can't be fixed."

"We won't know that until we give it a fair try." Tim thought for a moment. "I'll let Velma take tomorrow morning off to go visit Etta Sanders and the baby. She can drop in on the Richardsons and Widow O'Toole. That will give her a chance to trade and get the feed sacks. Tell Pancake the kid and I will join you men for lunch."

Smiling like a man who escaped the noose, Bert shuffled off.

The ranch never lacked chores that needed to be done. Tim looked about and mentally catalogued and prioritized what ought to be addressed. As Forsaken paid better than most spreads, the hands weren't blowing-in-the-wind tumbleweeds. Having experienced men who stayed long-term rated as important. At the moment, Tim realized just how much he depended on reliable, seasoned hands. Any man could do any job.

And then there was Fancy Pants Hathwell.

What could the kid do? Getting him to round up cattle and drive them to the next pasture would be a disaster. He'd likely start a stampede. Stretching barbed wire took a steady hand and quick reflexes. If the wire snapped and snarled, a man could get cut to ribbons. The kid probably couldn't figure out which end of a branding iron went where. No matter what task came to mind, Tim immediately eliminated it as a possibility for the kid. Frustrated, he strode back toward the house.

Lord, I'd take it kindly if you'd meet me halfway here. There's got to be something for Hathwell to do that won't run into danger. Can't be something brainy. Any dolt can see the kid's got enough schooling to last two men. He's got to develop his brawn. What, Father? What should I have him do?

Tim leaned against a split-rail fence and stared as the moon started to rise. A streak of silvery-yellow light sliced the yard. Suddenly, Tim grinned. He knew exactly what job to give the kid.

As soon as Velma banged on the bedchamber door the next morning, Sydney vaulted from the mattress. She'd gone so far as to set out the clothing she planned to wear. Last night she'd begun to braid her hair out of habit. The very lack of length kept her from making that terrible mistake. If Tim Creighton ever saw her hair in a plait, she'd be ... what was that saying she'd heard on the train? Fish bait. She'd be fish bait. Still, her hair had tangles the likes of which she'd never dealt with before. Her maid had always dressed her hair, so Sydney silently breathed a prayer of thanks that she'd chopped off at least part of the length.

Since she'd filled her pitcher the night before, Sydney quickly splashed herself clean, yanked the binding around her chest with vicious intent, and knotted it securely in place. She carefully tucked in the edges of the binding so she wouldn't have to worry they might flap around. The shirt was so big, she didn't need to unbutton more than the top fastener to slip it over her head. She made a mental note to repeat that time-saving trick. Fighting her way into the legs of some britches, Sydney decided men's clothing wasn't quite as simple as it once seemed.

Neither is being a man. Back home, the things men did seemed so simple. They rode and went on fox hunts. Courted women, played billiards, and went to gaming hells. Retired after supper to smoke and drink port. She shook her head. *It's so different here. It's far more involved and complicated than I imagined.*

She made it down the stairs before freight train Creighton rumbled down them. Still, he practically ran her over in the doorway to the dining table.

Velma poured coffee into three mugs and took a place at the table. Servants never sat at the table with their betters—but delight more than covered Sydney's surprise. She liked Velma, and with someone else at the table, maybe Tim wouldn't behave so impossibly boorish. "Good morning, Velma. Something smells—" She caught herself just before saying, "delicious." *A man wouldn't be that flowery.* "—smells good."

"Everything Velma makes is good." Tim shot the house-keeper a warm smile, then bowed his head. He was halfway through asking the blessing before Sydney got over the shock of realizing Tim could pay anyone a compliment.

They began to eat, and Sydney wondered what Velma had set before her. The taste wasn't objectionable, so she decided she'd inquire about the meal once Tim finished his and stalked off.

"Velma, Etta Sanders probably needs you to look in on her and the baby," Tim said between mouthfuls.

"Yeah."

"Why don't you take the morning and do that? You can trade your feed sacks so you have enough to make yourself a nice new dress."

Velma chuckled. "I wondered how Bert was going to get out of that."

Sydney gave her a puzzled look.

"Bert and I made a deal—he got the cayenne if I got my feed sacks. I shoulda known that man would weasel outta his end of the bargain."

"He's not weaseling." Tim gulped some coffee. "You don't want him out there trying to match fabric for you."

"Why not?" As soon as the question popped out of her mouth, Sydney wished she hadn't been so indiscreet. To her relief, Tim didn't seem to have heard her.

As soon as he finished inhaling his portion, Tim looked up at the housekeeper with a beatific smile. "Velma, honey, that's a meal to make a man's belly sing. Got any more?"

Sydney could scarcely fathom this side of him. *Maybe he's just had a few bad days and he's gotten over them.*

"I know it's your favorite. Of course there's more." Velma padded off to the kitchen and came back with a skillet clutched in a bright red dishcloth. "How about you? Do you want anymore, Syd?"

"Thank you, no. I've sufficient. It is quite tasty, Velma." She flickered a quick smile and took another bite.

Tim waited until her mouth was full. He patted his rock-hard belly and stated with notable enthusiasm, "Yep. Nothing beats a good plate of calf brains and eggs!"

Sydney completely forgot to chew, and she didn't really want to swallow, either. The very thought that she might have anything so horrendous in her mouth galled her. Tempted to bolt from the table and dash off to the outhouse so she could empty her stomach, Sydney sat perfectly still.

Then she saw the gleam in Tim's eyes. It took all of her fortitude, but she swallowed that bite. Giving him a mocking grin, she commented as she scooped up a bite of egg, "I disagree. Please don't mistake me, Velma. Your breakfast is lovely. It's just that I prefer kidney pie. Blood sausage is good, too. I even like liver."

"So you like unusual foods, eh?" Tim gave her an assessing look.

The back of her neck prickled. He was up to something, but she wasn't going to allow him to trap her. "I do enjoy a small selection of several things. I've never been one to make a glutton of myself over any particular dish."

"How ... proper."

She dabbed at her mouth with the napkin and echoed with a slightly exaggerated accent she dropped in register so it sounded more masculine, "Veddy."

Velma burst into raucous laughter and slapped her thigh. "The pair of you deserve each other in the morning!"

"Three. You're in here, too," Tim reminded her.

"So I am." She shot them an unashamed smile. "Lightning done set down in this house. There's going to be heat and fire. You're going to shake up the world, and I'm gonna sit back and watch the show!"

"You can't sit back and do anything. According to Mr. Creighton, no one sits around Forsaken. He'll give you perdition for being unproductive."

Tim glowered at her for her audacity.

Sydney merely grinned back.

Velma grinned at Tim. "Cheeky little rascal, ain't he?"

"Not for long."

Sydney should have taken that as a warning. Tim ordered

her to muck the stable again. The second she finished, he hauled her over to a barren patch of ground. "Velma wants a garden. Collect the rocks and lay them alongside the line I've scratched in the dirt."

The patch of land was at least thirty yards long and half again as wide. Everything from thumb-sized pebbles to huge pillow-sized stones dotted the area. Sydney gawked at the collection of rocks in disbelief. "I'm supposed to budge those huge boulders?"

"Those aren't boulders. I already moved them over there." He waved his arm negligently toward a collection of rocks that might as well have been the foundations for a fortress. "I left you the smaller ones. Get busy. I want you to till and hoe it tomorrow so Velma can plant it the next day." Tim gave her a walloping smack between the shoulder blades to set her into motion and strode off.

Her back ached and her hands were almost raw. Those lovely, long fingernails she'd clipped short now were chipped clear back to the quick. The strain of picking up the stones left her arms quivering.

A rock landed beside her. She reared back and looked around.

"Chow time," Tim said.

Sydney stared down at the stone. *Couldn't he have just called me or used a pebble? That thing's huge! He's testing me. That's what he's doing.* She nodded and dusted off her hands. "I'm hungry."

The men all lined up, and one by one received a pie tin full of food. Pancake thrust a tin at Sydney. "Here ya go, Hathwell. Puke on maggots."

Revulsion streaked through her.

Tim gave her shoulder a jostle and chuckled. "Pancake likes to give his food fancy-sounding names."

"He's quite ... descriptive." Sydney blinked at the tin and forced herself to smile. Just about the time she'd decided Tim Creighton had no redeeming qualities, he'd saved her from making a fool of herself.

"Did the kid just insult me?" Pancake scowled at her and Tim.

"He agreed. Your stew on rice looks like puke on maggots." Tim motioned to the cook. "Better give me extra."

"That's more like it. Blood or fire?"

"Both." Tim took his tin. "But I'll add them myself."

Tim shook a bottle over his plate. Red goo plopped out. The second bottle was smaller, and the reddish orange watery contents poured out.

"Stop hoggin' the Tabasco," Merle groused. "In fact, give some to the kid. It'll put hair on his chest."

"And singe it." Tim shoved the bottle at Merle.

Sydney ate almost half of what she'd been served. Tim ordered in a low tone, "Eat up, kid. You don't want to insult Pancake."

Sydney looked down at the food. She couldn't eat another bite. A hand slid over, swiped her tin, and replaced it with an empty one. Her eyes widened, and she looked over at Gulp.

He seemed to be staring off in the distance. A moment later, he ducked his head and shoveled in every last morsel. He didn't say a word—just pushed away from the table and sauntered off.

As she rose from the table, Tim murmured, "You owe him one. A man always pays his debts."

"I'll take that to heart." Reluctantly, she went back to the field of stones.

As suppertime drew nigh, Velma came out and perched her hands on her hips. "Boy, you done a good enough job for today.

Go on up to your room and wash up. I even toted up water for you. You're plumb tuckered out."

Nodding, Sydney trudged to the house, still carefully wiped her boots on the mat, and forced herself up each step to her bedchamber. She grimaced when she saw her reflection in the mirror. Her hair was lank and dusty, her face caked with grime. She'd never worn filthier clothes, and as she peeled off the shirt, she noted that the dirt went clear through the binding and actually made a small ooze of mud in the sweat that trickled down her front.

She almost cried when she started to unknot the strip of cloth. In her haste that morning, she'd left a raw edge up under her arm, and it seesawed with her motions enough to actually start abrading her delicate skin.

For a woman who had never in her life even had to sweat, let alone work, this was a terrible first. Still, she had no choice. Having chosen this path, she had to stay the course.

After all, she owed a debt to Gulp.

A single knock sounded on her door, and it opened before Sydney could react.

Chapter Five

Velma slipped in, shut the door behind herself, and whispered, "Don't you worry. Your secret's safe with me. These men are the world's biggest pack of fools God ever made. One look at you, and I knew straight off that you are a girl. Mercy sakes, you're a mess. Let me help you before you get poisoning of the blood from all that dirt in your hurts."

"I'm too tired to protest," Sydney admitted in a soft tone. "I'm afraid I'll have to put myself in your capable hands."

"Child, why you doing this, anyhow? It's got to be one of the craziest notions I ever did see."

Sydney winced as Velma started to help her.

"Didn't you bring talc along to keep from rubbing yourself raw?"

"Everything I had was scented with lilac. I didn't dare."

Velma scowled. "You're raw as can be. Best thing for that is burnt flour."

"Flour?"

"Yep." She nodded. "You dust it on just like those fancy talcs, and it'll help you heal right up. I'll burn you some. Look for it in your bottom drawer tomorrow morning. It'll be in a coffee cup, so don't go spilling it."

"You have my undying gratitude."

"Honey, that's about the onliest thing in this room that isn't dying. You look dead tired!"

Sydney groaned. "Don't remind me."

"You were going to tell me why you're going through all of this nonsense."

"I have to keep it a secret until January. Uncle Fuller made it clear he didn't want women here—I mean you no offense. If I want to stay here—and I do—then I have no choice."

"The truth doesn't bother me. I'm the only female he lets on the ranch. What you're saying makes perfect sense now. Fuller wants nothing to do with women."

"Why not?"

"I wasn't here. Years ago, he got sweet on the housekeeper. They even planned to marry up, but the week before the wedding, the gal ran off with his lead man. After a time, he took on another housekeeper. Several months went by, and it came apparent she had herself an embarrassing problem. Most folks blamed Fuller and demanded he salvage her honor. Things got pretty ugly, but she up and popped out a nine-pound baby after knowing Fuller only seven months. That put the rumors and questions about Fuller's morals to rest."

"Oh, my goodness."

"To his credit, Fuller paid for her to go back east to be with her family again. Other than me, he hasn't had another petticoat on the grounds since."

"I can't blame him. He's certainly been through enough to make him wary, but Big Tim Creighton is an absolute bear."

"He's got good reason, too." Velma took a washcloth and attacked Sydney's shoulders with gentle determination.

"Are you going to tell me why?"

"You sure that you want the gospel truth?"

"Of course I do."

"Well, you asked for it, child. Until he got that telegram, Fuller didn't have any notion that his sister ever even had a kid. His rheumatiz is acting up something awful, and he was talking mighty serious about selling out his share of the ranch to Tim. Heaven only knows Tim deserves it. They'd gotten so far as to start dickering over the price, but then when the letter came, Fuller felt honor bound to step back and think about leaving his land to his kin."

"Oh, dear goodness!"

"You got it. You stepped right into the middle of men's business. No worse place to be." Velma paused. "When they find out you're a girl, they'll be fit to be tied."

She finished washing Sydney's back and dabbed a bit of some smelly ointment on the chafed spots. She stood back, nodded, and decided, "That'll do. We're going to have to truss you up again till you're done with supper. Then you come on back up here and undo yourself."

"Thank you ever so much, Velma."

"It's a pure pleasure, child. It's high time someone set this rowdy bunch on their ears." Velma headed for the door. "Dinner will be on the table in ten minutes. The way you're moving, you'd be smart if you started down in five."

Velma joined them for supper. She even asked the blessing.

Accustomed to someone reciting something from the Common Book of Prayer, Sydney found the unstructured way Tim and Velma prayed to be intriguing. They said whatever popped into their minds. Keeping her head bowed a moment longer, Sydney decided to try their approach and silently prayed, *God, help me. This is much harder than I imagined. And God? Thank you for Velma.*

"You nodding off, Hathwell?"

Tim's wry tone made her head shoot up. *Oh, dear. He's gone back to being moody.* "I was thanking the Almighty for something. Someone, actually." She smiled at Velma. "You. I can say with all my heart, you are a godsend."

"Yeah, *she* is." Tim's agreement made Velma's already broad smile grow larger still.

Sydney pretended not to notice the emphasis. Logic dictated that by contrast, Sydney was a blight. *I worked my fingers to the bone today. A few more days like this, and Tim Creighton will revise his opinion.*

Sydney cut the fried chicken from the bone and ate it with her fork. Tim gnawed his off of the bone and even made a show of tearing off several large bites with his teeth. He was on his fifth piece as Sydney finished her only one.

"Kid, you're going to have to learn to be practical. You use tools when you shouldn't, and you don't when you should."

"Might you clarify that?"

He nodded sagely. "Use your hands to eat chicken. Plain and simple, it's a hands-on kind of food."

"It's evident you feel that way," she stated in a tone that clearly reflected she wasn't convinced to alter her dining habits in the least.

"You didn't use your head today. You lugged every last single rock."

"You told me to!"

"But you should have thought about what you were doing."

She stared across the table at him. "Since when did manual labor require intelligence?"

"Think, boy! Think! An ordinary wheelbarrow would have kept you from walking so much. You wouldn't have had to carry much at all."

Sydney gave him a stricken look and moaned.

"You should have rolled the larger rocks onto a board and had a horse pull them for you."

Her breath caught as shame and anger burned inside. She should have thought through those simple solutions. But she was new here. He'd purposefully let her half kill herself, all for the sake of showing her up.

"The only thing you got out of today was sore muscles. I hope you learned something important, though. Ranching is hard enough. Think through each chore before you do it, then carry it out safely and well. It's never good to hasten through only to have to redo it, but it's equally foolish to spend more time and effort than necessary. Believe you me, there's always plenty enough that needs to be done without wasting hours or energy."

Sydney gave him a cold stare.

Indifferent to her reaction, he pressed on, "Real men who have done the work of the world used their brains long ago. They concocted solutions and inventions that simplify the work and make it easier to accomplish. Since you've never gotten your hands dirty, maybe you thought those tools were strange looking or quaint—but wake up. Use them. Someone a whale of a lot more experienced than you came up with the idea, and a bunch of wise ones followed suit. They're the ones who succeeded."

Her face grew rigid. "Have you any other advice, or am I free to be excused?"

"Go on and get out of here. Go to bed. You have a full day tomorrow. You'd best be well rested. It'll be hard work."

"And you, Mr. Creighton?" Her anger got the better of her. "What will you be doing tomorrow?"

"That's none of your business."

"I disagree. My uncle owns seventy-five percent of this

ranch. Whatever is accomplished on the grounds ultimately concerns me."

"Don't be too sure of yourself."

Sydney stared at him. "Likewise."

His eyes went dark. "You might very well have been born with a silver spoon in your mouth, but I've earned every last cent in my pocket."

Heat crept into her face.

"No matter what percentage of the Forsaken partnership I hold, I'll always do my best. You got your first chance to do the same today. A man rolls up his sleeves and pitches in. He looks for where the need lies and meets it. Sure, his muscles burn and his back aches and the sun's hot. But he endures. That's what makes him different from a woman.

"Think about that, kid. The most important thing I did today was to force you to stop being an effeminate sissy and let you try out manhood for a change. Heaven only knows it's so unfamiliar to you, you don't know what to think about it."

A rueful laugh bubbled out of her before she could stop it. He was more right than he could possibly know.

Tim planted his elbows on the table, leaned forward, and glared at her. His eyes glowed like smoldering coals. "Kid, I'm right ... and I can outlast you. Just you wait. We've got almost a week left. I'm going to wear that fancy polish right off you and strip you down until you finally figure out you're a bull, not a steer."

Mortified by his sordid speech, Sydney very precisely put down her silverware, rose, and left the table without a backward glance.

Granted, she was tired when she went to bed. That was nothing compared to how she felt upon awakening. Everything ached. Even her eyelashes hurt. A loud groan rumbled out of Sydney as she threw off the sheets. She couldn't even jackknife into a sitting position. Instead, she rolled over and slid out of bed.

After dusting her binder with the scorched flour Velma had secreted in the drawer, Sydney struggled to wrap the long cloth around herself. Every move burned and throbbed. Lifting her feet to slide them into the pant legs made the muscles in her thighs quiver. Making it down the stairs seemed to be a task of Herculean proportions.

Afraid she couldn't manage to keep hold of her knife and fork, Sydney abandoned all civility. She slid the egg and three rashers of bacon between two slices of toast. Lifting the affair to her mouth, she saw Tim's astonishment.

"What in the world do you think you're doing?"

"I, Mr. Creighton, am borrowing a page out of your copybook."

He chuckled softly and left her alone.

Sydney strained to think of any reason that she could get out of work for the day. Certainly, the excuse of a headache would buy her no sympathy. She'd eat brains again before admitting her muscles were sore.

"Syd, I forgot I saw a speck of sumpin' in your coffee cup. Hold up a minute. I'll get you another." Velma exited the dining room and returned with another, much larger cup. She set it down. "You drink that. It'll put some hair on your chest."

At the mention of her chest, Sydney's gaze darted downward. Everything was still in order. She looked flat as a tabletop. She realized Tim happened to be staring at that part of her, too. She could feel his gaze, even if she didn't look up at him. She knew better. If she did, she'd feel the need to slap his face. Instead, she grabbed the mug and took a gulp.

Heat coursed through her veins. She set the cup down on

the table with a quick thump as she sucked in her breath.

"Too hot? Sorry." Velma winked at Sydney from behind Tim's line of sight.

On rare occasions back home, Father allowed her a few sips of watered-down wine. At parties, she invariably opted for punch. Whatever Velma added to the coffee could melt steel. Odd, though, that one mouthful made her feel warm all over and muted the streaks of pain she'd been suffering.

Creighton took Hathwell straight out to the garden plot after breakfast. He tried to ignore the kid's groan of disgust at the state of the ground. "We didn't want grass here. It'll choke out whatever Velma plants. You're looking at the best way to get rid of unwanted grass."

They stared at the garden plot, and Tim gave Syd a sideways glance. The look on the kid's face was thoroughly entertaining. A full two dozen cows stood within a roped enclosure. Indeed, they'd eaten off all of the grass. As if on cue, one nearest them answered nature's call. Tim chuckled. "Besides, now you won't have to haul over any fertilizer."

The kid gave him a dubious look. "I suppose I ought to be grateful for that labor-saving trick?"

"You're catching on."

"What am I supposed to do?"

"You're a plowboy today. I borrowed the Richardsons' plow. You can use it and return it tomorrow."

"Where do they live?"

"Seven miles or so thataway." He flipped his thumb to the right. "Gotta warn you, son, the man has daughters. Six of 'em. Not a single one of 'em even promised."

"You make that sound terrible!"

"It's worse than terrible. It's downright dangerous." Fancy Pants deserved fair warning. "Can't go over there without that whole gaggle of geese squawkin' and fluttering."

"There's nothing wrong with having daughters! The world wouldn't continue on without the female of the species."

"There's females, and then there are the Richardson girls," Tim intoned in a doomsday voice.

"Aren't they nice girls?"

"Boy, that's just the heart of it. They are nice. They're the nest-buildin', moon-eyed, ring-wantin' kind of gals who trap a man into marriage. Every time I go over there, I feel like a bone that every single pup in the whole starving litter wants just for herself."

Sydney laughed.

Slanting the kid a look, Tim brightened up a bit. "Hey! Did you want to do some courting?"

"Me? With a girl?" The kid's eyes bugged out. "Oh, my goodness, no!"

"Plenty of kids your age do more than their share of sparkin'." Memories made him smile. "By the time I was your age, I'd passed time with lots of pretty young things. Listen, son: The farmer has six daughters. All you have to do is check them out and find the one you like the best. It's simple enough."

"And what about you?"

Pain slashed through Tim. "I'm not about to get my neck in the noose. The last thing I'll ever do is to get married again."

"A—" Hathwell shut his mouth.

Tim had to give the kid some credit. He'd caught on and clammed up. Tim immediately redirected the conversation. "As I said, the Richardsons have six daughters."

"Six."

He nodded his head. "The youngest two are still playing with dolls. The older four are around your age—give or take a few years."

"The tone of your voice leads me to believe there's something you're not telling me." Hathwell met his gaze steadily.

So the kid's got some instinct. Good. If I expect him to act like a man, I have to treat him like a man. Tim cleared his throat. "Those girls are so man-hungry, their papa ought to send out warnings before he takes them to town. I respect a good woman, and I won't say a contrary thing about any gal who conducts herself with restraint even if it appears to be bordering on the teasing; but those Richardson girls . . ." He shook his head.

"I thought you said they were nice girls!"

"Oh, no doubt every last one of them is pure as the day she was born, but they all . . ." He winced. "I wouldn't be caught dead keeping company with any of them. Fact is, neither would most of the other men."

"Put that way, I'm more than reticent to consider socializing with them. You'll have to grant me the grace to bow out on that obligation."

Scratching his jaw, Tim admitted to himself that it was hypocritical to prod the kid into doing something when he wasn't willing to do it himself. "All right. I understand your stance."

As they spoke, Juan and Gulp quickly herded away the cattle. Boaz hitched the plow to a sturdy mare, and everyone gathered around for a few minutes to watch Tim give Sydney a lesson in plowing.

"Keep the plow tip in the ground. Don't jam it straight down. Keep it at an angle. The soil turns right over. Keep the furrows straight. Velma won't want a garden that looks like a drunkard plowed it."

Sydney muttered, "It would serve her right."

"What did you say?"

"Oh, nothing."

"Keep the reins over your shoulder and talk to the horse. Guide the plow, and there you go." Tim walked the length of a furrow.

Once he turned over the reins, Syd got into position and tried to copy him. Fancy Pants's nose wrinkled at the smell of fresh cow plops. Even worse, he intentionally stepped around them. After three feet, he'd already changed direction twice.

"Looks like a snake done plowed that row, boy," Boaz commented.

Tim coughed to cover his own laugh at the observation. He'd thought the same thing. "The kid's got to learn sometime."

"Yeah. Or somehow." Juan studied the winding furrow. "From the looks of it, it'll take a miracle."

Tim allowed the men their moment of humor, but they'd had enough. "You all have work to do. Get going."

The kid clicked his tongue and tried to slap the reins. He lost hold of the handles. When he bent over to pick up the plow, he jerked back his hand and made a sound.

"Keep going, Hathwell. You have all day." Tim wanted to bark an order to stop being persnickety. Reason dictated he refrain. Every few yards, the cows left evidence of having been penned in there. Sooner or later, the kid would realize he'd have to wash his hands and scrape off his boots at the end of the job. Once he did, the rows would be straight. He'd just better go back and redo the crooked ones.

As he saddled up a snappy pinto, Tim considered what to have Fancy Pants do next. Some things, like tilling the ground, he'd have to learn by doing. Other things, he'd have to be shown. Teaching took time—time Tim didn't have. Calving season was almost over. Two- and four-legged predators tended to pop up about now. He'd have to rotate the herd to another pasture farther away—and that necessitated scheduling a couple of cowboys to bedroll under the stars. Unwilling to order men to do something he wouldn't do himself, Tim made it a point to be among the first to do the duty.

"Lord, I don't know why you dumped this kid on me. I don't have the time or the patience for it. I'd take it kindly if you'd get Fuller back here so we could straighten out matters."

Fearing it would take her the better part of the day to finish a single row, Sydney clucked under her breath. The mare took that as an order to move forward. Sydney practically got pulled right over the plow. By the time they got to the end of that row, she knew she was in deep trouble. She didn't have the strength the job required. She also didn't have the arm span. The winged arms of the plow splayed so far apart, her hands barely reached them.

She stood in the middle of a huge, stinky, mushy cow patty and surveyed the zigzagging furrow she'd dug in the ground. Swallowing hard, she then looked at the plow. "Stupid men. Stupid tool. Stupid garden!"

A little sparrow landed on the ground and chirped at her. He happily hopped a bit, plucked up one of the worms she'd managed to reveal, and gobbled it up. He then cheeped a cheery little song.

"Oh, all right. I'll just have to keep at it. I've got to do something, though. . . ."

"What in thunder are you doin' here?" Bert asked as she entered the stable.

"Getting rope."

"Why?"

"Because I have need of it." Sydney had no idea ordinary rope weighed so much. She got the wheelbarrow, put two coils of rope in it, and went back to the garden plot. The first length she lay on the dirt to mark off a line. The second she used to make several circles from one plow handle to the other, much like coiling yarn around a partner's hands. She then hung a bucket from it and put in four fist-sized stones. Taking up the reins once again, she slid them over her shoulder and ignored the plow handles entirely. She crossed her arms and leaned her weight on the rope spanning them.

By the fourth row, she'd learned to lean her weight to counterbalance enough to keep the rows passably straight. She'd needed to add two more stones to the bucket to create enough drag for the plow to bite into the soil. Each row was an accomplishment. Each row was a victory. Each row took more out of her.

"Didn't you hear me calling you for dinner?"

"What? Oh! Velma!"

"Put down that plow and come on in and eat. You're getting a good job done, but I don't want you starving yourself."

Sydney beamed at that praise and hobbled off to lunch. Tim didn't arrive. Velma mentioned something about him doing work in a far pasture. The absence of tension at the table felt strange. Nice, but strange. Sydney ate more than she'd ever dared before.

"Honey, you're eating like a field hand." Velma ladled more stew into her bowl. "Then again, Tim's making you into one, ain't he?"

"It certainly appears so."

"Bet those uppity folks back in England would have a fit over this sight."

"Indeed." Sydney smiled wearily and finished every mouthful before dragging herself upright. "Thank you, Velma."

"You're welcome. I'll take a couple of pitchers of water upstairs so you can clean up pretty good tonight. We've got to work out something about baths. Mostly I just stick a tub in the kitchen and we've all taken turns, but that's not going to work."

"Why not?"

"Fuller and Tim think nothing about wandering through on each other."

"Oh, merciful saints!"

"Yeah, well, men don't possess a scrap of modesty among the whole herd of them. Let me think on it. I'll come up with something. You get out there and get busy. Tim won't take kindly to a half-done job at sunset."

It took every scrap of gumption Sydney could summon to go finish the job. She completed the final row by the last streaks of sunlight, then fought the urge to curl up right there in the dirt and sob. Or sleep. Most likely, sob herself to sleep. She'd never been so tired or sore. Or had such a sense of accomplishment.

"Take the plow into the barn. A man honors his tools with good care, and they take care of him right back," Tim quoted from his horse.

"For a man who doesn't much appreciate poetry, you sure do like to spout wisdoms and platitudes."

"Son, I never said I didn't cotton to poetry. It's just that I prioritize. Being able to keep food on the table ranks higher than talking in rhyming words."

"So you do like poetry?" As soon as she asked the question, Sydney grimaced. *That wasn't a question a man would have asked.*

"Haven't had much of an opportunity to read gobs of it. What little I've read spans from the nauseatingly flowery to the awe-inspiring religious."

Relieved he hadn't cornered her on that slip, she took advantage of his response and segued to a different topic. "So are you one of those churchgoing Christians?"

"I don't pray at mealtimes for show."

Sydney backpedaled. "I meant no offense."

"Look around you, son." He waved his arm in a broad, sweeping gesture. "How could any man see all of this nature and not think God made it?"

"I've read Darwin's *Origin of Species.*" Sydney shrugged. "When you prayed, I presumed you didn't accept his theory of evolution. But from what the hands say, you work on Sundays. I didn't know exactly where you stand."

"We attend worship on the Lord's Day. As for work—it's limited to the essentials on that day. I pledged my heart to God, and I do my best to honor His ways. What about you?"

"We always attended church back home. After all, it's a good example." The minute the words left her mouth, Sydney knew she'd said something wrong. She just didn't know what. "Of course, we attended all of the special functions, too—holidays, weddings, baptisms, and the like."

His eyes narrowed. "I see."

"Mr. Creighton, you aren't an easy man to figure out."

"Kid, believe me, I feel that way about you, too. Now get things put up. Velma kicks up a fuss if you don't get to the supper table on time."

As she turned away with the plow, Juan appeared. "Boss,

that kid's a real boot in the seat of the pants. Didja see what he did to that plow?"

"He's so skinny and short, he'd have never gotten the job done if he hadn't rigged that up."

Sydney didn't tarry. Hearing Big Tim complain about her stature instead of her accomplishment made her despair of ever pleasing him.

Moments later, Velma met Sydney at the door and pointed to the pump. "You're not stepping foot in here till you sluice some of that dirt off. Roll up the sleeves and get your hands and face. I put a cake of soap there, too. Duck your head and shampoo that greasy mess. Here's a towel."

Mortified, Sydney accepted the towel. No one had ever found her hygiene lacking. Indeed, it certainly was now. She smelled awful. She felt sticky, and her hair felt itchy. *What I wouldn't give for a nice, long bath,* she sighed to herself. Resolving not to complain, she headed for the water pump.

Though shockingly cold, the cascading water felt good against the scrapes in her palms and pain in her muscles. Her hands grew muddy before enough dirt was washed off to even let her see the flesh beneath. She knew her face couldn't be much cleaner, so she cupped one hand and thought about a kitten washing his face as she repeatedly splashed and rubbed at her cheeks and chin. Her hand even slipped back to get the nape of her neck. The cool water felt especially good there.

Sydney tipped her head so her hair fell forward. Soon she got the rhythm of pumping and rinsing it. The soap lathered quickly, and she was almost done rinsing out the last of the bubbles when a deep voice behind her urged, "Go on ahead and peel off that filthy shirt, too. You can wash to the waist."

Sydney jerked up so quickly, she hit her head on the spigot. "Never!"

"Suit yourself, kid. Velma's seen bare chests before."

"A gentleman wouldn't put her in such a compromising position." She grabbed the towel and began to rub at her hair.

"Kid, Velma's mama ran a cat house down in New Orleans. She's seen it all. Fuller decided the kid deserved something better than what her mama had in store for her on her comin'-out night, so he grabbed her by the hand and yanked her on outta there."

"Coming-out night?" Sydney echoed with a sense of dread.

"You got it. Her own mama set up a special auction to sell off her daughter's virginity. Those events draw good money."

"Her own mother!" Sydney couldn't keep her voice from rising at her disbelief.

"You got it. Fuller shared your outrage. He'd heard word on the street and went in to give the girl a chance to get away. To hear Velma's version, he used his pistol to convince everyone to stay put while he led her out of that place. He could have gotten into deep trouble for it, too. Kidnapping."

"Kidnapping?"

"It was her fourteenth birthday."

"Oh, dear goodness!"

"She's worked here ever since. Believe me, though—the woman's seen more than you'll ever think to imagine."

"It doesn't mean she appreciated the view," Sydney snapped.

"You're right. That's why Fuller brought her here."

"And that's why I'm not going to parade about unclad in her presence!" Sydney stalked off and waited until she made it up the stairs before letting out a shivering sigh of relief. Had she stayed there much longer, Tim might have noticed the bulkiness under her wet shirt.

True to her word, Velma left three pitchers of water. Sydney poured herself a glass to drink and used two pitchers for bathing. The last would take care of her morning needs; then she wouldn't have to carry water up the stairs tonight. Truthfully, there wasn't one chance in ten thousand that she'd make it up the stairs carrying anything heavier than a slice of bread.

When Velma hollered that the meal was on the table, Sydney opened her door and stepped out. Tim practically bowled her over. He scowled at the room behind her. "Son, why in tarnation did you choose that room?"

Turning around, Sydney glanced back inside, then gave him a bewildered look. "Why not? It's a perfectly lovely bedchamber."

He groaned. "You just put your finger on it, kid. It's *lovely*. Decorated for a woman. Flowers. Just looking at that paper makes me want to break out in a rash."

"I um . . . just took the first one I happened by."

"Then ask Velma to move your gear tomorrow while you work. Take the one next to mine. It has a single bed. The other one, next to Fuller's chamber, has a double bed, so you probably ought to leave that for when we have married folks spend the night."

"Very well."

"Fine. Not 'very well.' You've gotta stop sounding starchy." He headed down the stairs beside her and added, "And you walk funny, too."

Freezing on the spot, Sydney kept her gaze trained straight ahead and gritted, "Then get me the holster."

"I'll do that day after tomorrow. Until then, start using your legs instead of your rear. Here." He stood two steps below her and reached around to plant his large hand squarely on her backside. Ignoring her splutters, he gave her a few friendly pats and chuckled, "Yep. That's right. Pull tight and don't let it swish from side to side. Just use your thighs. Come on. I'm hungry."

This indignity was beyond all expectation. Sydney felt hotter than a July noon. She stayed completely still.

"Supper's getting cold, kid."

Velma came to the foot of the stairs. "Will the pair of you stop this nonsense? Skunks and possums, Tim! The kid's muscles are sore. If you want to do that kind of teaching, choose a night when he can move."

Pursing his lips as though it were a novel thought, Tim asked, "Are you sore?"

"Me? Sore?" Her tone dripped with sarcasm. "Whyever would I be sore? Just because I hauled enough stones to build a second Newgate prison and plowed enough land to sustain a tribe of wild savages, why would I be sore?"

"The two of you stop scrapping and get to the table. If you think I'll stand by and let a good pot roast go cold while you snarl and spit at one another, guess again."

Not long after supper was over, Sydney pulled on her nightshirt and decided that bed must be a foretaste of heaven. Getting into bed proved to be an exercise in pain, but she succeeded. A heavy knock sounded on her door. "Yes?"

"Syd," Tim said as he carelessly flung the door open, "I brought you some liniment. Stretch out on your belly, and I'll rub it into your shoulders."

"Liniment?"

Looking at the bottle, Tim shrugged. "It says it's good for folks, too. Can't say as I've ever tried it, personally."

"You want to put *horse* liniment on me?" She laughed in disbelief. "You're worse than the quacks and charlatans in London!"

"Son, from what I've seen, anything coming from England

is as bad as it gets." His eyes widened, then narrowed. They were trained on her chest. Stepping closer, he continued to stare.

Sydney cringed back even more.

"What are you doing with those?"

Cold dread surged through her.

Chapter Six

"What?" Sydney glanced downward and prayed that her breasts weren't poking out too far.

Tim's hand shot out and batted at the chain she wore. "A woman's locket? My sainted aunt, why would any man in his right mind wear a heart locket? And a ring?"

Her chin jutted forward. "The locket and the wedding ring belonged to my mother. I'm simply keeping them safe."

"Kid, put them in a drawer someplace. They'll be safe enough. We don't keep men I can't trust, so there isn't a thief or light-fingered hand anywhere around. You'll get your teeth knocked clean out of your head if anyone sees those dangling around your scrawny neck."

Sydney pulled the chain off over her head and dumped it onto the bedside table. "Fine."

Tim's mouth quirked, and he nodded. "You learn quick. Won't be long before you walk, talk, and work like a man." He studied the bottle in his hand and wrinkled his nose. "Stinks, doesn't it?"

She nodded.

"You're to return the plow tomorrow. Better not put this on you since you'll see the Richardson girls." Tim spun around and chuckled as he yanked the door shut.

"The Richardson girls," she moaned as she rolled over.

When she met the farmer's daughters, Sydney knew exactly what Tim meant. She'd been reared in London where girls were very aware of the marriage market. They knew the pedigree of every single male and could even closely approximate his wealth. Within a few minutes of dancing with a man, the debutantes were even able to guess, within a shilling, just what the man's cravat cost.

A few moments after Sydney stepped onto the Richardson farm, it became exceedingly clear the Richardson girls would have handled themselves admirably in London.

"So you must be Sydney Hathwell," Marcella cooed as she claimed "his" right arm.

"*Lord* Sydney Hathwell." Sulynn clung to Sydney's left side like a limpet.

Katherine stood so close, her toes bumped Sydney's boots. "I hear you ride divinely."

Apparently they'd planned upon this visit and wanted to extend it far beyond an introduction and a quick "Thank you for letting Forsaken borrow the plow, good-bye." Each girl wore her best dress. Ribbons perched atop hair that had been subjected to a curling iron. The eldest, Linette, sported suspiciously pink cheeks and lips. Sydney caught a whiff of cherry and knew the girl had resorted to boosting nature's lot.

Faced with enduring the simpering Richardson gaggle or returning to Forsaken and being put to hard work, Sydney chose the former. She turned on her upper-crust British accent, employed every flattering line she'd ever heard come from a man's mouth, and happily let herself be led into a parlor where she was fed any number of sticky, sweet items.

She silently wondered how she could diplomatically teach these creatures to brew a proper cup of tea. The brown liquid in her cup looked like the bilge water on the ship she'd voyaged upon to come to the States, and it probably tasted similar, too. Still, sipping it kept her from hauling rocks, so sip it she did. Slowly.

That night Tim sat on the porch and stretched out his legs. Crossing them at the ankle and studying the toes of his boots, he rasped to the housekeeper in a confidential tone, "Velma, I'm worried about that boy."

"Oh?"

"He's odd."

"In what way?"

"He squawks like a girl when he's surprised. His hips sway, and a peach has more fuzz than his chin."

"So?" She shrugged. "He's young."

"It's more than that. He chose a bedchamber with roses on the wall."

"Big deal."

"I caught him wearing his mama's locket."

Velma traced a spot on the skirt of her apron. "Don't be so hard on the kid, Tim. Both of his folks up and died in the past year and a half. If anyone in the world understands how painful that is, you should."

"I was three years younger and took care of myself."

"And you were the sorriest sight I ever did see when you eventually linked up with Fuller. Face it. You and me—we're strays he picked up. So's the kid."

Unwilling to think about that, Tim pressed on. "Well, get this, Velma: When I went to the Richardson farm to see what was holding him up, sonny boy was sitting in the middle of their parlor couch, surrounded by those girls."

"And that worried you? I'd think after everything you just said, that would thrill your gizzard!"

Wiping his hand down his face as if the act might erase the terrible memory, Tim shook his head and groaned. "Syd was talking about stitch work and poems. He actually rattled off one about a gal making a wedding gown, if you can stomach that!"

"How . . . interesting."

Tim didn't want to be spreading tales, but he desperately needed a second opinion. Velma wouldn't go gossiping, and she'd be forthright about her impressions. Tim decided to fill her in completely.

"That's not all. Fancy Pants actually suggested a combination of flowers to make a sachet. A sachet!" He shuddered at the memory. Walking in and seeing Syd with his legs crossed like an old maid and waxing poetic about female things almost had Tim gagging. He'd wanted to haul Sydney out of there, but Sydney proceeded to spout off a dissertation on the admirable qualities of lavender and lilac on a woman's delicate nervous system. Tim had wheeled around and stomped out onto the porch because Sydney's speech made him want to puke. "Velma, there's not another man alive who could tell the difference between lilac and lavender!"

"Now, Tim, Englishmen are educated differently. It isn't fair to compare, you know. Over there, rich men are trained in the fine art of conversation."

"Men, however rich or poor, don't get that involved. Not real men, anyway."

The housekeeper tilted her head to the side and gave him a searching look. "Tim Creighton, are you implying what I think you are?"

"Yup. I'm not going to stand for it. Fuller ought to be back in three to five days. Between now and then, I'm going to get that kid straightened out and toughened up."

Velma took one long look at him, burst out into hysterical laughter, and walked away.

"It isn't funny in the least," he groused.

The very next day, Tim pulled Sydney into the parlor and carefully shut the door. Sydney's eyes grew to enormous size. When Tim barked, "Sit!" Sydney did so at once.

Pacing back and forth, Tim thought of all of the possible things he'd mentally rehearsed saying and knew he wouldn't use them. His boots made a double sound of *heel-toe heel-toe* as he continued another round. Finally stopping in front of Sydney, he abruptly demanded, "Have you ever kissed a woman?"

"What!"

Tim glowered at him. "The question was excessively plain. Have you kissed a woman?"

"A gentleman doesn't kiss and tell."

"I didn't think so," he sighed.

The kid squirmed worse than a bucketful of bait. Tim sat down directly opposite him in the matching winged chair and leaned back into its depth as he hiked one booted ankle and rested it on the opposite knee. He completely filled the piece, in contrast to Sydney's skeletal frame creating a small slash of color in his. Without preamble, Tim rasped, "Are you one of those fops who prefers his own kind over a woman?"

The blood drained from the boy's face entirely. "A what?"

The shocked look on the kid's face made a wave of relief crash over Tim. Obviously he didn't have that particular preference if he didn't even know of its existence. So he was simply a late bloomer. Terribly late. Or maybe he was one of those men who earned a living with their intelligence by becoming professors or preachers.

Fuller's going to want his kin to stay on Forsaken and rear a passel of sons.

"Kid, it's high time you got off the settee and squired a few gals around. This Friday the town's putting on a Founders' Day shindig. You can mosey around and get to know folks. There's a barbecue and a square dance at night. By then, you'll have met some gals."

"I don't know any of your American square dances."

"There are just a couple of basic moves, and the caller hollers them out for you to follow along. The gals will be happy to teach you. It's a good excuse to get close to 'em."

"It's poor manners for me to approach a lady without an introduction. Will you—"

"Don't worry. I'll tell all the men to help out in that regard. We'll be sure you meet plenty of folks."

Hathwell's shoulders finally relaxed. "I appreciate your assistance. Shall I reserve Kippy as my mount, or do the men simply go pick whichever one they fancy each time?"

"Most of the men have a couple of horses in the remuda they prefer. No one says anything if you pick their favorite, but it irks them. Anything that goes wrong that day, they blame you."

"I'd appreciate your advice regarding one or two horses I could ride that wouldn't rile the men."

A small thread of respect spread though Tim. Asking for guidance on the matter showed the kid had some common sense. "Fuller doesn't ride much anymore. Kippy's gentle, so your uncle rode him."

"Could you recommend a different mount?"

Tim shook his head. "Fuller's been gone a week. Horses need to be ridden. Seeing as you and Kippy got on well, it's best if you use him for now. Enough talk. We need to get to work."

The rest of the week brought hard work with it. Tim took his charge seriously and didn't slack off for a single minute. From early morning to late night, he worked Sydney unmercifully. He ordered chores to be done and then made Syd redo them if he wasn't completely satisfied with the results. He pushed and growled and demanded more of the kid than any of the other hands. Velma and the others finally made a few offhanded comments, but the glare he shot silenced them at once. He had a mission, and their opinions weren't needed or welcome.

Fact of the matter was, the kid didn't do half bad. In many ways, he'd become like a pesky little brother—old enough to get into trouble, small enough to lack the necessary abilities to do a grown man's job. But little brothers eventually grew into valuable men. Fuller's nephew just might have enough of Fuller's blood in his veins to actually succeed at this life.

Chapter Seven

Rexall Hume paced back and forth in the study. Knowing snooty Brits preferred to do business within their own social circle made it essential to buy his way in—but that was too blatant and crass. Instead, he'd hired a lawyer to make discreet inquiries about English families with marriageable daughters. A list of their names soon landed on his desk—so Rex jumped at the opportunity to wed one. He'd expected a washed-out, horse-faced, stiff-rumped girl. Putting up with such a wife would be worth it for the money he'd gain. After all, he needed legitimate children, too.

He'd gone so far as to select Lady Hathwell, write her father, and seek his blessing. Things had gone all too well—too easily. Indeed, when Lord Hathwell unexpectedly died, Rex found himself trapped in a betrothal to a woman in mourning. The title fell to Sydney's second cousin; male lineage and all that nonsense. Nonetheless, once a lady, always a lady. Sydney Hathwell still afforded Hume the connections he coveted. He'd waited a full year for her.

Finally, she'd come. A high-strung beauty, she'd shown the strain of mourning and travel when he arrived home that first evening. He'd thoughtfully given her a few days to rest.

Beautiful, graceful . . . but stubborn. That was a drawback. It kept her from marrying him right away. For almost a week, she'd been standoffish. Twice, she'd had the unmitigated gall to tell him they "didn't suit." He'd already invested a year and a half of his life and business waiting for her. He wasn't about to start all over again.

In retrospect, he should have done a few things differently. He grimaced. Calling her by the wrong name had been an honest mistake. Leave it to a woman to get in a pique over such a trifling detail. He should have taken her out on the town. She could have paraded about in her expensive gowns and enjoyed the admiration and fawning of the local matrons. Aristocracy was undoubtedly accustomed to making appearances—and he'd not indulged her. It would have been wise—both for her pride's sake and for furthering his business. Being seen together socially would have cemented her obligation to wed him, too.

He'd even given her the choice of marrying immediately or having a whole additional week to stir up a grand wedding. What more could a bride want? The butler and maids all attested to how she'd brought an extensive trousseau and a beautiful wedding gown. Tossing a few flower arrangements about a church and whatever other minor details she felt necessary could have been seen to in no time at all. For the right amount of money, anything could be done.

He'd put all of his plans aside for her sake, and he'd hit the end of his patience. He'd been honorable enough to delay the marriage, but no longer. As soon as he found her, Rex was determined to wed Lady Hathwell.

Indeed, he'd built his life around getting what he wanted.

A restrained tap sounded on the door to the study. The door opened. "Sir," his butler intoned, "a Mr. Tyler is here to see you."

"Yes, yes. I'm expecting him. Show him in at once."

A man of middling height and weight in a dark blue suit entered. He'd blend in just about anywhere—unobtrusive, unremarkable. He swept the study with a keen gaze, then stared intently at Rex. Even then, he didn't speak because the butler was still present. Good. He understood discretion.

As soon as the butler shut the door, Rex proceeded. "Tyler, you came highly recommended, and I'm relying on your discretion."

"How can I help you?"

"It's my fiancée." Rex pulled the only picture he had of her from his desk drawer. "Lady Sydney Hathwell." Hume paused.

"I take it she's English?"

"Yes, yes." *He's sharp. Good.* "She's gone missing."

Tyler's brow crooked. "Do you suspect kidnapping, foul play, or has she run away?" He accepted the picture.

"I've read the paper to see if there's any mention of an unidentified young woman, and I've sent servants to the hospitals to ascertain whether she might have met with an accident and been unable to contact me. Nothing."

Tyler nodded a curt acknowledgment, but he didn't break eye contact.

Hume finished answering the question. "Not many people knew she was in New York. Her arrival was quiet." He forced himself to admit the humiliating truth. "She's undoubtedly indulged in a fit of bridal jitters."

Tyler's face remained impassive at that revelation. He studied the picture. "A beautiful woman. Do you have any notion where she might go?" Tyler pulled a small pad of paper from his pocket. "I assume she has friends in town."

Hume shook his head. "To my knowledge, she knew no one."

Tyler's brow arched. "How did you meet?"

Hume cleared his throat. "I was made aware of her and approached her father through an intermediary. Arrangements were made. Lord Hathwell died shortly thereafter. I permitted the lady to put off our marriage a full year in deference to her mourning."

"Such arranged marriages, though not commonplace, occur." Tyler tapped his pencil against the pad. "I'll need everything you can tell me about her. I assume you've saved the letters she sent during that year."

A beleaguered sigh exited Hume. "A distant male relative of hers who inherited the title sent a telegram, notifying me of the death. I received just two missives from her." He yanked open the desk drawer again.

The parchment envelope still felt crisp. Faultless script flowed across the front of it. The black bordered single sheet of stationery inside read as though a timid young woman had strained to say much. In the first, she thanked him for his condolences. The second told him when to expect her ship to arrive.

After scanning the note, Tyler commented, "She's a woman of few words. A rarity. Grief might account for the brevity of the first note, but the second is equally succinct. I've found such women are either secretive or painfully shy. Which would you say is more accurate in her case?"

"Neither." Hume paced across the carpet and turned. A strange sense of déjà vu struck him. He'd done the same thing before, only Lady Sydney Hathwell had been standing where the private investigator now stood. "Supposedly, she's well educated and capable of running a smooth household. Headstrong. I'd say she's headstrong. Within the first week of her arrival, she informed me she didn't feel we suited."

"Temperamental?"

"Undoubtedly. Stubborn too. She tried to cry off of marrying me. I chalked it up to her being nervous."

"Does she have any previous episodes of going missing?"

"Not that I know of." Hume parted his hands in an embarrassed gesture. "Lady Hathwell came over to be my wife. She seemed to be of the mistaken notion that the trip was merely to see if we would get along. She was here just a week." Looking down, he cleared his throat. "The last evening I saw her, I suspected I'd pressed her too hard and fast. She's young—seventeen. I realized she probably wanted the pomp and fuss of a society wedding—regardless of the fact that she knows no one here. I granted her additional time for that purpose."

"When and where was she last seen?"

Hume grimaced. "Six days ago." He anticipated the next question. "I arrived home at dawn from a week-long business trip, expecting that she'd had time to quell her doubts."

Tyler held up one hand. "You said she'd been here a week. Clarify for me, if you will—are you saying she refused to wed you twice on the day of her arrival, and it's been six days since then? Or are you saying you were present with her for a week, then took your leave and she bolted at once?"

"Neither." Hume shook his head. "I was home for a week, during which time she displayed her skittishness. The following week, she stayed as a house guest while I took an essential business trip. I came home last Thursday." He recalled coming home to find Oscar trotting down the street. Dumb dog had a habit of chasing after carriages and bolting after cats. He invariably returned; Lady Hathwell would return as well.

"How would you characterize Lady Hathwell's reception?"

Hume's hands slowly curled into fists as he confessed, "It being so early in the morning when I got home, I didn't disturb her. I'd scarcely been here an hour ere I got called away for an emergency."

Tyler scribbled on his note pad. "And that was six days ago."

Hume nodded grimly. "When I returned home last evening, my staff lined up in the expectation of greeting my bride. They presumed I'd arranged the emergency as a ruse in order to allow me to whisk the lady away in an elopement. It wasn't until I arrived home alone that we realized she'd gone missing."

"A transatlantic voyage runs five to six days. She's had sufficient time to be back in Britain. Have you telegraphed her family?"

"No! No. There's the possibility she'll sneak away and hide in a friend's country estate. If at all possible, I want this to be resolved without alarming her family."

"She isn't the first woman to get cold feet. I'll do my best to have her back to you as quickly as possible."

"You're reputed to exercise tact and cunning. Discretion and speed are essential. Find my bride, Tyler."

Chapter Eight

On Thursday, Tim pulled Sydney to the edge of the yard. She traipsed along beside him as fast as her too-big boots allowed. For all his bluster, Tim was an excellent teacher, and she'd started enjoying his way of explaining things.

He took up a lariat. "You have to learn how to rope. It's an essential. In a few more weeks, we'll do the branding, and you'll have to carry your weight with a rope. It'll take you that long to get good at it. Now watch how I knot this."

He made it look so simple. His big, rough hands moved with agile grace. It took her four tries before she produced anything vaguely similar to his demonstration.

He gave her a grim look. "Sit here and practice up. I'm gonna go see to that cow over yonder. I don't like the looks of her."

He strode over and came back. Grabbing Sydney by the arm, he yanked her up. "Take off your shirt."

"No!"

"Take it off, or I'll rip it off!"

"Just try." She swiped his gun straight out of his holster. His eyes narrowed.

A second later, Sydney lay flat on her back and Tim towered

over her as he shoved the pistol back into his holster. Exactly what he'd done eluded her. He'd moved so quickly, it was all a blur.

"Don't you ever draw a gun unless you aim to kill, son."

The magnitude of her action sank in, and she started to shake. Fortunately, the cow bawled and diverted their attention.

Sydney scrambled to her feet.

Tim produced a pocketknife and hacked at her sleeve in a few rough motions.

"Whatever are you doing?"

"See that? The calf is turned wrong. Only one foreleg's out." He yanked off her sleeve. "The sleeve's got dirt on it."

"What does my shirt have to do with anything?"

"Your arm is thinner, and it's long enough. Reach on up inside of the cow and fish out the calf's other foreleg."

"You're insane!"

"Son, that calf is gonna be winter chow for a whole family someday. His mama is one of the younger cows we've got, and she ought to be good for several more calves in the next few years. They'll both die unless you get down to business. Now do as you're told."

"Lord help me," she muttered as the cow's legs buckled and she collapsed on the grass.

"At least you're asking for the best on your team." Tim stared at her. "Now get busy."

Sydney took a deep breath, closed her eyes, and got started. Nothing had ever felt worse. Fighting the inclination to gag, she gritted, "This is worse than when Hensley Wentworth III pushed me into the Christmas pudding!"

"Trace the leg we already have. Go across the chest and find the other one."

"I'm doing ... the best ... I ... can." She stretched farther.

"If it's too slippery to hang on to, once you get the hoof, let me know. I'll feed you a rope, and we'll noose the leg and fish it out."

"That'll hurt!"

"Do you ever stop complaining?"

Her eyes flew open. "I didn't mean me. I meant it would hurt her or the baby."

He nodded curtly. "Sorry."

"Does ... this ... happen much?" She tried to take her mind off the sensations assailing her.

"More common with a first calf. She's one hundred percent Hereford; most of the herd is mixed. Anything with Longhorn in it calves easily. Have you found that other hoof?"

Her eyes widened. "I have it!"

"Hold tight. Finesse it. Sometimes it helps to tug in and up a bit."

Moments later, a sopping wet calf plopped out on the grass. The cow lowed and began to lick him. Covered in mess clear up to her armpit, Sydney gushed, "Have you ever seen anything so beautiful! It's a miracle! Oh, look! He's so cute! It is a he, isn't it?"

"He'll do. Back off and let her take care of him. If you get in the way, mothers reject their young. It's best you just walk away. Besides, you're a mess. Go clean up. We still have roping to work on."

Sydney resisted the urge to pet the calf one last time. Instead, she got up, visited the pump, then went to her new chamber. She hated this depressingly brown, dark room. The chest of drawers was scarred, and the mirror above it gave back a dim, distorted reflection. The chamber lacked much sunlight since a tree grew close by. When the wind blew, a branch scratched at the window.

She sponged off and put on a fresh shirt. Thankfully, Velma did the laundry and managed to do her drawers and get them dry when everyone was too busy or too far away to see them. Velma was an absolute godsend.

Sydney grabbed a pair of apples and tossed one to Tim when she went back out. His disappeared in four huge bites. She nibbled on hers and watched intently as he tied his rope once more for the purpose of demonstration.

Once she tied hers, he taught her how to spin a small circle. She did fairly well at it, and she made every effort to quell her sounds of excitement. His disapproving scowl after the calving made her aware she'd gone too emotional on him. A man never let his feelings show, and she'd broken that rule. She made a mental note to monitor her reactions more closely.

"Now try to change the attitude of the rope. Instead of horizontally by the ground, alter your wrist so it's perpendicular." He did so with his own rope and talked in a lazy tone. "You do it for a few revolutions, then feed more line so the hoop gets bigger. See?"

"By Jupiter! That's fabulous!"

He shot her a grin. "It's fun. Gals are impressed, too. Learn a few tricks, and then you can show off as a slick way of meeting some cute little filly."

A wry smile twisted her lips.

"Buck up, Syd. I'll teach you the ropes, so to speak, with gals." He flicked his wrist, and his rope spun away and rolled back.

"You're sly, Tim Creighton."

"Beginning tomorrow night at the dance, you'll be, too. Now give it a try."

Sydney started spinning the rope, then tried to tilt it onto the side. It hit the dirt and kicked up a cloud of dust.

"Keep trying." Tim stepped back.

"Very well." She tried three more times. Two of those three times, she flipped it too awkwardly. The lariat looped onto her and tangled in her hair. She set down the rope, retied the cloth at her nape, and tried again. It was a failure, too. She gave Tim a weak smile and set to work again. That one smacked her face.

Reeling from the impact, she stumbled backward. It took every shred of her self-control to keep from crying. Blinking rapidly, she said nothing.

"Kid, you're working against yourself. First things first. This has to go." Tim whipped out his bowie knife, grabbed the dangling length of her hair, and hacked off a good six inches.

Sydney's hands flew upward to feel the short tresses fall wildly around her chin and shoulders.

"At least it won't tangle in the rope now." Tim calmly flung the huge fistful of chestnut curls from his hand into the breeze.

Sydney disciplined herself not to let him see how horrified she was.

"Let's get back to roping. You're too jerky." He waited a moment while she picked up her rope. "Kid, I keep forgetting what a pup you are. Just how tall do folks grow in your family?"

"Papa was five foot nine," she croaked. After clearing her throat, she added, "Mama was five foot even."

"Fuller's her brother, right?"

"Yes."

"He used to be fair sized before the rheumatiz bent him. He was probably about your pa's height. Once you start to stretch out, you won't have cause to worry."

"Don't count on it. I'd wager that I take after my mama."

"Regardless, you're gonna help with the branding. Now see to the rope. Pay out a bit. About that much more. Good. Yes, a little more.... Now, see how I'm bringing your hand up and still keeping the wrist action? There!"

She got the feel of it as they did it together again so she would sense the rhythm. It was hard for Sydney to concentrate. His closeness seemed so . . . enveloping. She felt oddly smothered, but instead of wanting to inch away, she scooted a bit closer. Tim didn't seem to mind. Probably because he thought it let her move her arm more freely.

This stirring sensation in the pit of her stomach felt oddly warming. Sydney hadn't ever experienced it before, and she'd been in dozens of men's arms at formal dances. Then again, they kept the perfectly gentlemanly three inches of space as was proper and acceptable. If they hadn't, she quietly stepped on their toes and gave them a warning look that transmitted her opinion of their scandalous conduct. Even if his closeness tipped her into a dither, she was masquerading as a boy, so she didn't dare step on Tim Creighton's toes.

The thoughts were too confusing, too disturbing. She shook her head to dislodge them.

"What's wrong, Syd?"

"My . . . um, hair. It itches."

"Cut it real short. It'll keep you from getting buggy, too."

She almost dropped the rope. "I've never had a pest of any sort on my person!"

"That's bound to change. When we do a cattle drive, you'll have fleas and ticks. Sleeping on the ground and being around the animals—'specially the dogs—does it, regardless of how fastidious a man is."

She groaned.

Slapping her on the back, Tim shook his head. "Kid, you've got a long way to go. Forget all of those fancy drawing room ways and concentrate on things that really matter."

"For example?"

"The water level in the pond and well. The amount of rain-fall. The price of a barrel of flour and how to brew a decent cup of coffee over an open fire. How to talk sweet to a nice girl and let her down gentle if you decide she's not the one you want for your wife. Most important, setting aside time to tend your soul. If you're not right with God, nothing's right."

"You have a very interesting personal code."

"Works for me."

"Don't you want a son you can pass things down to?"

Growling, Tim let go of the rope. "That's a sore spot, Syd."

The words, alone, warned Sydney to drop the subject; but something about the sandpapery rasp to his voice and the look in Tim's eyes made it clear she'd best not bring it up ever again. She wanted to give him sympathy or compassion, but that was a womanly thing to do.

"I'd like to digress, if we might. You said that the Richardson girls are all nice girls. You also let me know that you avoid them like the plague. Word around here is that you just plain avoid women altogether. Why?"

Tim's jaw hardened. "Getting left behind once was more than enough."

Something in his tone let Sydney know he'd said all he wanted to. Men didn't pry, so she reluctantly changed topics. "I've never met my uncle. What can you tell me about him?"

"Kid, God doesn't make better. Fuller has equal parts integrity and grit. He started this place up and made it into a shining example of what a ranch can be. Hard work doesn't bother him. He makes others work just as hard because they're ashamed to give him a half-baked job. His word is better than anything written on paper. Folks consider his handshake a done deal, yet if something happens along the line, he's not one to hold another to something that turns unfair."

"Can you give me an example?"

"Me. I bought the land to the east. Some of the best pastureland around. Has a fork of the river passing right through it, sweet like. I was proud of that land. Fact was, I didn't have more than a few nickels to rub together after paying for the dirt. Times had been bad for me, and I figured on sitting tight and lickin' my wounds while I slowly built the place into something worthwhile.

"Fuller needed water. He and I settled on a fair price for him letting his herd water there. That was how I bought my starter stock. After a couple of good years, we had five of the worst drought years imaginable. The river turned into barely a trickle. Both of us had beef dying on the hoof for want of water, but he still showed up at my door and handed me payment for the river rights, just as we'd originally agreed.

"I'd never done a thing for the man. Fact was, I was so ornery, I barely spoke a word to anyone for the whole time I'd lived there. Still, I couldn't take Fuller's money. Then he told me he'd never be able to look himself in the eye if he'd back out on his word. He wasn't worth anything if he didn't keep his honor.

"I felt like a cow pie. I finally got him to agree that we'd take that money and drill somewhere on the border of our land and share whatever bubbled up. When we found the source of the spring, it was two feet on his side of the land, but the land slants. As soon as the well digging started, the ground crumbled, and the water all flowed to my side. Fuller refused to believe that the water was even half his. The only way he'd let his stock drink was if I took part of his place. We fought like crows over the last berry. In the end, he had me. He went to town and simply deeded over part of his stock and land without telling me."

"But droughts come to an end!"

"Yup. That one did the next year. By then, our stock had mingled so completely, it was impossible to credit the bulls for their studding, and the cows wouldn't keep to either land. He had me over a barrel."

"But you do more than your fair share now. Velma tells me my uncle's become badly crippled."

"Kid, I owe the man. Until he got so stubborn, I'd shut myself off from everyone. He forced me to start living again." Tim's face looked harder than granite. "Some things a man barely makes it through. Fuller has a knack for knowing when to step in and how far to push. I'll lay down and die before I let him see this place fall to rack and ruin."

"You're a good friend."

"Fuller taught me that. Let him teach you, too, kid. Not everything you learn in life has to do with money or things. Fuller's one of the few who knows that. If you turn out to be half the man he is, you can count yourself proud."

Tim pounded on Sydney's door. "Time to get movin', kid."

"I'll be right out!"

"Don't dally."

Sydney gazed at her reflection in that abysmal mirror and tried desperately to quell her smile. She turned sideways and looked at her profile. Did she look manly enough? The cravat she wore hid the bulk of her chest binding. The britches hung loosely. She frowned at her short, botched-beyond-hope hair. One of these days, she'd shave Tim Creighton bald for having hacked it off.

When she opened the door, Sydney stopped cold. Tim had

paced down the hall and was on the way back. He'd bathed and put on black trousers and a crisp white shirt. His boots shone with fresh polish, his chin had a small speck of blood that tattled on a fresh shave, and his hair looked sleek with a small dab of pomade.

Her mouth went dry. The man looked dashingly handsome. How had she managed to suppress her awareness of what a good-looking man he was? Beneath that rugged facade shone an impressive, stunningly masculine individual. He didn't just look cleaned up—he looked downright debonair. Had he the right set of clothes, he'd make every woman in London's high society swoon. As it was, he didn't have on tony clothes, but he was dressed as elegantly as any rustic man of these parts did. He even had on cuff links and a string tie. . . .

"Kid, what possessed you to wear that cravat thing? You look like you're wearing a silk scarf with ruffles. Honest to Pete, you look like a frilly sissy." He shook his head. "Maybe men back in England get away trying to look pretty, but out here, a man dresses like a man and leaves the fussy stuff for the gals. The last thing we need is for some drunken fool to mistake you for a pretty girl and start a fight. Ditch it, and we'll get moving."

His words thrilled her. He thought she was pretty! He thought men would be attracted to her. Even with her duded up in men's clothing, he still considered her feminine. Backhanded as it was, it was the first bit of male appreciation she'd had in days.

Tim gave her a dark look. "What're you standing there for? Take off that stupid cravat."

"You're wearing a tie," she rasped in a husky voice that couldn't truly be her own.

His big hand went up and fleetingly touched that bit of

masculine attire. "Yup. Plenty of the gals have a thing for them."

"Perhaps the ladies will take a fancy to my cravat."

Tim gave it a scowl. "Only because they might want to wear it themselves."

Sydney hastened to her room, stared in the mirror, and untied her cravat. With Tim in the background, she had to take pains to make sure he couldn't see the edge of her chest binding. In the mirror, she saw him lean against her doorframe. Her fingers fumbled with the top shirt buttons, then with the collar.

"That's good enough. Time to go."

"Very well—I mean, fine." The minute she passed through the door, Tim slapped her on the shoulder and practically sent her sprawling.

⚜

Tim thought about the holster he'd gotten for Syd. It'd weigh the kid down and stop that infernal sway to his hips. Then again, he'd seen Syd's temper. So far, when the kid got mad, he clammed up and stomped off—but men often felt obliged to take a stand when embarrassed in public. Those incidents gave ample room for foolishness.

"Velma already took the buckboard. She's mighty proud of her potato salad."

"I'll be sure to sample it and praise her."

"Good." Tim mounted up, then grimaced. The kid couldn't swing up into Kippy's saddle.

Fancy Pants casually led the horse to the porch steps, gained his saddle, and acted as if men always mounted in such manner. Unless aged or infirm, no other man in Texas would have stooped to requiring help to saddle up. The kid adjusted his hat and set Kippy at a comfortable trot.

Tim couldn't believe it, but stuffy English dignity worked in this situation. He nodded to himself. Whatever Syd did today that was off, Tim would cover for him by offhandedly commenting on how Brits had odd ways of going about things.

"Other than eating barbecue and dancing, what does a Founders' Day celebration entail?"

"The parson will say a prayer. The mayor will get long-winded, and old Mrs. Whitsley will poke him with her cane."

"Is that a Texas tall tale?"

"Nope. It's the unvarnished truth. She'll be sitting up on the platform because her grandfather founded the town. The woman's a pistol. She'll pound the platform with her cane and take the mayor to task for making everyone stand out in the sun when they ought to be sitting in the shade, eating."

"I take it that's what she did last year?"

"The last five years." Tim chuckled. "Some things never change."

Once they reached the outskirts of town, Sydney shot him a surprised look. "All of these people live hereabouts?"

"Sort of. Lots of the little whistle-stop towns surrounding us come for this and the Fourth of July. Not as many people show up for the Fourth, though."

"Whyever not?"

"Texas sided with the South in the War Between the States. Some folks still harbor hard feelings."

Beneath his hat's brim, Syd's face darkened. "I'd not thought about that. Thank you for bringing that to my attention. I'd not want to ruin someone's day by speaking out of turn."

"It's a subject best left alone." They dismounted, hitched their horses to a shade tree, and walked down the street toward the platform. Tim didn't want the kid lagging after him like a lost puppy. He had a few things he wanted to get done while in town.

Suddenly Syd halted and hunkered down.

Tim towered over him. "What are—"

"The Richardsons just arrived. My boot's—"

"Big Tim!" The girls all fluttered toward him.

Tim muffled a groan.

Sydney rose. "How did I know you ladies would all be coming to town? I just knew you would! And the town's all decorated. Did you help?"

Tim wanted to slink away, but Mrs. Richardson clamped hold of one arm while Linette grabbed the other.

Sydney listened to the girls for a brief moment, then heaved a sigh. "You ladies will have to excuse us."

"But why?" Katherine threaded her hand through the crook of Sydney's arm.

"Boots. Mine don't fit properly. I've admired Tim's . . ."

Tim seized the opportunity. "I promised Fuller I'd see to things. Since we're in town, it's smart to get Hathwell the proper equipment."

"We'll come along!" Marcella beamed.

"I simply couldn't bear the indignity of exposing such refined young women to my stockinged feet." Sydney made a shooing motion. "Off with you all."

"Good going, kid." Tim headed toward the saddlery. "C'mon."

"Isn't the mercantile—"

Tim shook his head. "Those gals will concoct a reason to go there. I'm taking you to Matteo. When it comes to boots, nobody makes 'em better."

Matteo was glad to get some business. While he measured

the kid's impossibly small feet, Tim looked around the shop. No use buying what the ranch didn't need. Then again, no use waiting till something broke before replacing it.

Odd, how Hathwell could be so nauseatingly priggish at one moment, then a stalwart man the next. He'd tried to help Tim evade the Richardsons, and when it didn't work, he concocted an honest excuse to part company.

Tim turned and watched the kid stand and stomp down to force his foot completely into a boot. He took a few experimental steps, then nodded. "Tim was right. He said nobody makes better boots."

Tim set a few articles on the table. "Put these on Forsaken's tab, Matteo."

The kid reached into his pocket. "How much—"

Tim shook his head. "Forsaken takes care of her men."

Being a man had some benefits. Sydney was free to roam around without a chaperone. She could eat as much as she wanted without anyone considering her a glutton. Instead of straining to make polite conversation, she could nod or be strong and silent. Well, silent at least.

A ragtag collection of people comprised a band on part of the boardwalk. They played with great zeal and very little talent.

Enterprising children ran a lemonade stand. Sydney bought a cup. It tasted dreadful. She couldn't resist buying a second one, though.

She'd meet folks at church on Sunday, but most didn't wait for an introduction. Men stuck out their hands and identified themselves by last name and trade or spread. If their wife happened to be with them, they'd simply introduce her as "the wife" or "the little woman." Daughters were a different story. Proud papas gave their names and boasted about their daughters' foremost accomplishment.

And oh, those accomplishments. Lacey could rope a steer faster than most men. Hedda took second place at the county fair with her fig preserves. Theodora inherited her uncle's knack for water dousing. Crawdads shivered in fear of Angelina. Odd as those boasts seemed, Sydney found them refreshing. Back home, fathers relegated their daughters to the care of a nanny or governess. Most didn't know their daughters well enough to dote on them.

For all the tony soirees, high-society fetes, and carefully orchestrated picnics she'd been to in England, none of them was half as fun. Once the dancing started, she stood on the edge of the planks and watched as folks whirled and stomped, promenaded and allemanded.

"Give it a go, kid." Tim slapped him on the back.

"After you." Sydney grinned at him.

Big Tim found crotchety old Mrs. Whitsley. She tossed aside her cane and joined him.

Sydney watched as Big Tim swept the old woman off her feet. Mrs. Whitsley pinched his cheek and said something. He threw back his head and belted out a laugh. Once the fiddle started, Tim carted the old woman to and fro, wheeled around, and slid her into another man's arms for one pass around the circle of dancers. He reclaimed her, wove around the opposite direction, and finally finished off the dance by carefully setting Mrs. Whitsley back down and making a courtly bow to her.

At that moment, any last scrap of resentment or anger Sydney had felt toward him evaporated. Big Tim, handsome and strong, hadn't chosen a pretty or rich young girl. He'd found a woman who needed a little lovingkindness and given her a taste of joy. Tim didn't stop there. He escorted Velma over to a group and helped form a square. Soon, they followed the lively fiddle music and the directions from the man Tim labeled the "caller."

Having taken dance lessons and learned all of the proper ballroom moves, Sydney possessed a sense of rhythm and movement. Far more verve and style went into square dancing, yet folks didn't adhere to strict postural carriage. She couldn't be sure whether someone stepped amiss or if they were just embellishing the moves.

Tim whirled Velma right by Sydney as their dance ended. He glanced from Velma to Sydney, and Sydney took the hint. She stepped up onto the planks and bowed. "Miss Velma, I'd be honored to partner you for the next dance, if you won't mind my inexperience."

"We'll have us a fine time!" She laced her arm through Sydney's and hastily introduced "Syd Hathwell" to the other couples. In ballroom dancing, men stepped forward and women moved backward. This dance didn't work that way. No one minded when she turned the wrong direction.

"You done good, Syd." Mr. Tomel pounded her on the back when the dance finished.

For the next hour, Sydney alternated between watching everyone and dancing. During one dance, Marcella Richardson was Sydney's "corner." That necessitated their dancing together for part of the set. When the piece ended, the man who'd been Marcella's partner vanished. Marcella sidled closer.

Sydney saw the hope in her eyes. *Do I ask her to dance, just to make her feel better? Or do I make my excuses so she'll have the opportunity to dance with a man? It's bad enough that I'm deceiving everyone. I can't rob these young ladies of the possibility of catching a young suitor.*

"In England, one dance—even a portion of that one

dance—is all that is permitted for a young lady with any gentleman. I'll not insult you by asking you to dance, Miss Richardson. You're so light on your feet, I'm positive the other men are all anticipating a chance to squire you about the floor."

Sydney bowed and made her escape. A few minutes later, someone grabbed her sleeve.

"Syd! I always pay up." Bert nodded. "It's high time we had that beer."

"Beer."

"Yeah. I told you soon as we were in town, I'd get you one. C'mon."

Gulp scrambled over. "Widder O'Toole just started in on Pancake. We gotta git while the gittin's good."

"The two of you go on ahead." Sydney squared her shoulders. "I'll be sure to engage the widow in conversation so you can make an escape."

"Toldja Syd's a good egg." Gulp gripped her arm and started striding off.

Bert took her other arm. "Us men stick together."

A moment later, Sydney found herself standing between the cowboys at the bar in the saloon. A lady ought never enter such a place, yet Sydney couldn't help enjoying the opportunity. The all-male bastion boasted a handful of tables. A smattering of bored-looking men played cards at those tables. Cigar and cigarette smoke mingled with the acrid smell of spirits.

The bartender smacked a meaty hand on the bar. "What'll it be?"

"Beers." Bert held up three fingers.

As the bartender shoved a sticky mug into Sydney's hand, she murmured, "I'm not all that thirsty."

"What does bein' thirsty have to do with drinkin' a beer?"

Caught by surprise by that comment, Sydney took a sip

before she remembered what was in the mug. Her eyes widened and her head came up. Then she saw the picture on the far wall and started coughing.

Bert poured the beer down her and gave her a friendly shove. "Best way to cure chokin' is to have a drink of something."

A few minutes later, Gulp elbowed Bert. A sly smile slanted across his face. Bert's face lit with the same scheming smile.

Sydney jerked on her cuffs to straighten her sleeves. "Well, Bert, you've certainly kept your word—"

"Oh, we just got started, kid." The cowboys each clenched a hand around her upper arms and headed up the stairs. "Tim said we're all supposed to make a man outta you. We aim to follow orders."

Chapter Nine

"Lord Hathwell, I presume." An elegantly dressed woman met them at the top of the stairs. She turned to Gulp, then Bert. "You men go on back to your beers. I'll make certain this young man returns downstairs in a while with a smile on his face."

One of the men roughly mussed Sydney's hair. She was too horrified to take note of which one. "This here's Helene. She'll match you up."

Rooted to the floor, Sydney realized the cowboys were tromping down the stairs, snickering.

Helene gave her a long look and a sly smile.

Sydney's blood ran cold. *This is wrong. And even if it weren't, they'll find out I'm—*

Stepping closer, Helene tried to draw Sydney's arm through hers. When Sydney balked, Helene murmured, "Nella and I were watching you. Your secret will be safe with us."

A young woman in a coppery-colored dress came around the corner. Her dress must have gotten caught in something, because the hem arced above her knees in the front. Sydney fought not to gape.

Helene cooed, "Nella, dear, this is Lord Hathwell."

Nella took Sydney's hand. "It's a pleasure to make your

acquaintance, Lord Hathwell." She tugged Sydney out of sight, into a small bedroom. Once the door shut, she leaned against it and muffled a giggle. "Oh, this is hilarious!"

Nervous as she'd ever been, Sydney rasped, "You won't tell anyone?"

Nella's curls bobbed wildly as she shook her head. Then her smile grew. "Folks are going to have to pay more, now that English royalty visited me!"

"I'm not royalty—just—"

"You"—Nella rested her hands on her hips—"are royalty. Close enough, anyhow. Nobody here'll ever care about the details. We'd better see to matters."

"Matters?" Sydney echoed.

"Rumple your clothes, Syd. It has to look like they've been dropped on the floor." Nella mussed her own hair a little. "And my perfume. Give a little squirt of it on your neck so's you smell like we was close."

"Why are you doing this?"

Nella's jaw hardened. "I'm doin' what I gotta. We all don't have rich uncles."

"Oh no." Sydney grabbed Nella's hand. "You mistook my question. I wondered why you're helping me."

The soiled dove let out a long, slow sigh. "Dunno. I heard about how Big Tim's been putting you through the wringer. Figurin' out that you're a gal—you've gotta be desperate to put up with it all." She shrugged. "Life is hard. Us girls—we gotta help one another out."

"What can I do to help you?" Never had Lady Sydney Hathwell imagined she'd speak to a woman of easy virtue, yet here she was . . . and finding Nella was an ordinary girl. Well, an ordinary girl who did something sordid to make a living.

"I got what I need." Nella wrinkled her nose. "Your hair. What did you do to it?"

"Tim sliced it off with his bowie knife."

"You ought to stab Tim for doing that to you. Sit down, and I'll even things up a bit." As Nella snipped at Sydney's ragged tresses, she whispered, "You're going to have to be sly to pull this off. What're you gonna say?"

Sydney thought a moment. "I'll stand on propriety. A gentleman shouldn't ever discuss his intimate encounters. It's in poor taste."

"Hey, I like that. You'd best have a bit more ammunition, though. That smirk you're wearin' is good as gold. Use it." Nella continued to use her shears. "Now as for what I'm gonna say . . . I'll waltz outta here and make like you was quite a surprise. A nice surprise. And it's the truth. You are a surprise."

Sydney twisted to look at her. "So are you. Nella, I don't know how to thank you!"

"Hey, it's a job, kid. You'll have to pay me for my time. I can't afford to give up time just to visit."

Sydney's breath caught. "I didn't bring any money with me. I promise—"

"It's a good excuse for you to come back." Nella nodded to herself. "I wouldn't trust nobody else, but you and me—we've got an understanding."

A thought raced through Sydney's mind. "Do you have a bathtub here somewhere?"

"'Course we do."

"Then I'll come and take a nice long bath. I'll pay you, and you can have the time all to yourself."

"Oh!" Nella closed her eyes for a moment. The tiniest, fleeting smile tugged at the corners of her rouged lips. "How about you bringin' some fancy bath salts for me? When you take your bath, I'll let you share 'em."

"Oh, that sounds blissful!"

A short while later, Nella squared her shoulders. "We need to go on back downstairs. Stand still. I have to get a little lip rouge on your shirt, back here just under your ear. You can act like you didn't know it was there, and the guys'll think we had us a grand old time."

Tim hauled Sydney off of Kippy and pushed him onto a mattress in the bunkhouse. The kid wasn't in any condition to complain. Tim yanked off Syd's boots and dropped them on the floor with a pair of loud thuds. The noise didn't even make Sydney stir.

Gulp tossed a spare blanket over him. "Gotta hand it to the kid. He managed to stay on his mount under his own steam the whole way home."

Keeping silent on the way home practically cost Tim his molars. He'd gritted his teeth to stay quiet, but now that his men were back on Forsaken, he let loose. "I won't put up with you corrupting the kid's morals. He's too young to drink. You knew better. As for you setting him up with a whore—"

"Aww, c'mon, Tim." Pancake plopped down onto another bunk and struggled with his own boots. "You want help turnin' him into a man. What better way ..."

"A real man is judged by the work he does and the character he develops."

Juan let out a bark of a laugh. "Well, the kid sure is a character."

Merle pulled off his shirt. "Give the kid some credit. He held his beer."

"Betcha he gets sicker than a dawg once he stands up," Gulp predicted.

"Didja see how much he drank? No foolin', he must have downed seven mugs."

"What!" Tim roared in disbelief.

Boaz nodded sagely. "Yep. Counted 'em, myself. Had a bet goin' with Johnson from Checkered Past. Won me a whole buck!"

Juan slapped Tim on the back. "That kid's gonna be one of us yet, if we work him hard 'nuff."

Tim widened his stance and stared at each man in turn. "As long as you've been able to pull your weight, you've been allowed to do whatever you please on your time off. A man has a right to live as he sees fit—but I won't tolerate you corrupting the kid."

"C'mon, Boss. You're startin' to sound like Widder O'Toole spoutin' on about the evils of alo—aklo—drinks."

"Sounds like her, but he don't look like her." Gulp squinted. "Well, maybe a little. But she's got hair growin' outta her ears. Big Tim don't."

Merle jabbed Gulp in the side. "Since when did you get that close to the widow?"

Tim tamped down his frustration. After the men had a couple of drinks under their belts, they squabbled and teased one another like a pack of orphans in a street gang. He cleared his throat and ordered, "You heard me. No more taking Syd to drink and carouse. Let him sleep it off in the morning. He's gonna have a roaring headache."

"But Nella," Pancake scratched his side, "Nella said it was more than worth it."

Sydney barely roused and zestfully slurred, "Zannnnnnnk yewwwww, Nella!"

The men roared.

Tim pushed the kid's shoulders back down on the bed. "Enough of that. Kill the lights and you men get to bed. Tomorrow's gonna be a demanding day."

Someone moaned. Sydney peeled her eyes open to see who had made such a pitiful sound. As she did so, she made the same sick sound and realized she'd been the one to be noisy. Her moan cut short when she blearily realized she wasn't in her bedchamber. There were men all around her. They were getting ready for the day—shaving, dressing, crawling out of their bunks with irritated oaths. The sight of them in various states of undress almost sent her screaming. Unable to sit up, she rolled over, dragged the blanket over her head, and groaned.

"Hey, Syd! Come on an' git up!"

She moaned.

"Leave the kid alone. He'll upchuck all over our boots if we don't clear outta here."

Sydney held her hands over her ears and pressed to keep her brains from exploding out of them. Bile rose up, and she swallowed it down. There was no way she could walk—or run—out of the bunkhouse at this particular moment. The men weren't even dressed!

A second later, an equally horrifying realization struck: The binding wasn't around her bosom anymore. It had slipped downward and looped loosely around her waist. If, by chance, one of the men snatched away her blanket, she'd be in terrible straits. She rolled onto her belly and huddled underneath the musty wool blanket and tried to remember some kind of prayer that might be suitable under such circumstances. Nothing came to mind. Nothing at all.

Finally, the bunkhouse fell silent. She timidly lowered the blanket and blinked. Dust motes danced on rays of sunlight. Even looking at them made her head ache. The sound of one of the hounds barking made her head ache. Breathing made her head ache.

Soft footsteps approached. She thought it had to be Velma. Turning around, she immediately clamped a hand over her mouth. The act was as much a reaction of shock as it was to keep nausea at bay. A terrified sound curled in her chest.

Tim held a battered old kettle in his huge hand. He shoved it at her, and she suffered the ignominy of being violently ill with him as a spectator. In truth, she nearly lost her shinbones into that kettle. Tim took away the kettle, grabbed a fistful of her hair, and tilted her head back. He briskly pushed a rough, wet cloth over her face and rasped quietly, "Kid, I hope you learned a real important lesson from this. Drinking doesn't make a man. Times when a man drinks to excess, he's liable to make some mighty big mistakes and live to regret them. Right about now, you're wishing you won't live; but if that's the biggest regret you got, you're lucky."

Sydney blearily blinked back her tears. Even in her hung-over state, she had enough presence of mind not to cry. She slowly nodded and bit back a moan as the bunkhouse whirled.

"I'll dump out this puke and leave the kettle here. You're responsible for any more cleanup. The guys'll have your hide if you leave a mess in here. The place is a sty, but that's where they draw the line. I'll tan your hide if I ever catch you drinking again until you're old enough to make that decision legally. I'm hoping you're smart enough to figure from this one episode that getting soused and womanizing aren't all they're cracked up to be."

Sydney moaned and nodded her head very faintly before letting it droop down to her chest.

"Why're you hanging on to that blanket?"

Her fingers clutched it even tighter as she rasped, "Cold."

"Syd, we're gonna have to put some meat on your bones. All the guys were jawin' 'bout how hot it is in here. I've been aiming to put in another window or two. You're acting like it's the dead of winter."

Slanting him a jaundiced look, Sydney whispered, "I feel half dead along with it."

"Yeah, I'll bet you do. Sleep it off. A bunch of the idiots'll tell you to have a nip of the hair of the dog that bit you, but that just makes it worse. Sleep. Drink loads of water, and eat as soon as your guts calm a bit."

"Fine."

Tim said nothing more. He simply walked away with the kettle and returned with it a few minutes later. He set it next to Sydney, pressed a hand on her shoulder, and walked out.

She was more than grateful to him for having been so understanding. It would have served her right if he'd thundered at her. A bellow might well have made her faint, though. That would have been disastrous. But he'd intentionally kept that booming voice of his very low and muffled, given her more kindness than any drunk ever deserved, and then held his peace. A few days ago, she wouldn't have pegged him as a man who possessed a scrap of compassion, but he'd proven her wrong. Maybe all that praying he did resulted in him showing a little mercy on rare occasions. She felt a wash of relief that he'd demonstrated it just now.

Praying that no one would walk in, Sydney hesitantly let go

of the blanket and lifted her shirt. She unwound the binding and rewrapped it. As she did so, she inhaled and smelled the scent of Nella's perfume. The sweetness of the fragrance made her want to retch, but at the same time, she relished that small bit of femininity. Having always been every inch a lady, the complete lack of woman's touches in her everyday life tried her sorely. Even if the scent came from a soiled dove's dresser, it was delicate. She didn't want to wash it off.

Miserably clutching the kettle to her chest, Sydney staggered to the house. She still needed to sleep several hours, but staying in the bunkhouse certainly invited any number of disasters. Stumbling up the stairs, she made it to her new bedchamber. During a fleeting moment of lucidity, she counted it a blessing that the place was so dark. The very lack of sunlight helped lessen the horrid throbbing in her head.

Velma came up and quietly put three pitchers of water in the room. "Drink the first, then wash up with the other two when you finally decide to join the living. Best you try to nibble on the bread crusts on the plate. Don't you dare eat another bite until I make you some broth at dinner."

"I never want to eat again!"

Velma chuckled softly. "At least not for today."

"Mama would be mortified," Sydney muttered as she curled up on the counterpane and buried her head in the pillow.

Petting her cropped hair, Velma whispered, "Child, I'd wager your mama never imagined you traipsin' about dressed in a getup like this and doing the work of a field hand, neither. Sure as shootin', she didn't picture you visiting a cathouse."

"I can do this." Each word rasped through her scratchy throat. Sydney tried to convince herself, "It's only until January."

Velma sighed and pulled a blanket up to Sydney's shoulders. "Girl, it's gonna be the death of us tryin' to keep this cat in the bag. You're just too tender to take all of this for long." She padded out of the room and shut the door.

By suppertime Sydney managed to splash herself into an alert, though not totally presentable, state. She wobbled down the stairs and made it to the table without her knees giving way, though they seemed to be mere lengths of soggy string rather than flesh and blood.

Sydney ate slowly and tried to ignore the odors of the food. It should have been a wonderful meal—well balanced, plentiful, and cooked to perfection—but her stomach still lurched at the least provocation.

Tim inhaled his food with the gusto for which he was famed. He looked over and scowled. "Remember how you feel. That'll keep you out of too much trouble the next time temptation arises."

She moaned. "I'll keep that in mind."

Propping his elbows on the table, Tim commented, "You did all right by yourself the first half of the night."

"How would you know?" she mumbled sickly.

"I saw you meeting neighbors and dancing. You picked up on the steps just fine."

"Of course he did. I danced his first square and taught him how." Velma nodded. "You did great, Syd. I'd dance with you anytime."

"I'll remember that."

"That reminds me." Velma hopped up. "Pancake was supposed to bring home my dishes from the picnic. If I don't go get my bowls, there's no telling what he'll do with them. The last time, he stuck them in the bunkhouse as spittoons!"

As Velma bustled away, Tim shoved a bowl of string beans across the table and ordered, "Eat more."

"I don't dare."

"You're just too plain skinny. Bet you don't have more than a pound of muscle on that body. Tomorrow, I'll have you chop firewood. Chop three cords a week, and you ought to get some bulk on those spindly arms."

Sydney put down her fork with a bang and winced at the sound. "Have you no couth?"

"I'm not saying a word that every man for miles around isn't thinking. You've got a long way to go before you amount to a hill of beans."

"Are you implying that I am worthless?"

He locked eyes and nodded. "Yup. That's about the size of it."

"Size? Is that all that matters? Brute strength?"

"Kid, stop right there. Size counts because if you aren't able to do the job, you can't have it. You gotta earn a living. Men won't work with you or for you if you can't keep up."

"I'm keeping up."

"Really," he drawled in disgust. "Fuller sweated blood to build this place into its current state. He'll demand that you be part of it, or you won't stay. Plain and simple."

"I suppose that would suit you just fine."

"Kid, that does it." Tim rose and came around to her side of the table. His eyes flashed with anger and his lips thinned to a line. "Get up."

Chapter Ten

There was no denying it. In her anger, she'd issued a challenge. Horrified at her carelessness and audacity, Sydney wondered how to extricate herself from this coil, but there was no plausible excuse or escape.

"Get up. Now." Tim's voice dropped below any register she'd ever heard. That rumbling bass carried such an implicit threat that Sydney slithered from the opposite side of the chair, gulped, then raised her fists as she'd seen in pictures depicting pugilistic exhibitions.

Contempt painted Creighton's features. "I'd flatten you in a single punch, you spoiled brat."

There wasn't a doubt in her mind he was right. Sydney's hands dropped. She nervously adjusted her clothing. "You're more than right. I'm obviously still shockingly in my cups. I spoke out of turn."

"You sure did. If you were a little kid, I'd wallop your backside. Don't think I'm not sorely tempted to do just that."

She stepped back a huge stride and croaked, "You wouldn't!"

Silence crackled in the room. The look on Big Tim's face clearly showed how he tamped down the urge to paddle her.

Sydney fought an urge herself: She wanted to slip her hands behind herself for protection. They eyed each other as tense moments passed.

"You're supposed to be a man." Each of Tim's gritty words came out so carefully enunciated, they sounded like individual gunshots. "Men measure their actions and words. In my book, you get one time of getting drunk and one time mouthing off. Try either again, and I'll level you."

"Skunks and possums, what's goin' on in here?" Velma asked as she stormed over. She planted herself between Tim and Sydney.

"The kid decided I'm trying to get rid of him. He thought maybe we ought to punch it out."

"Merciful saints!" Velma gave Sydney's shoulder a shove. "Kid, when you get soused, you really do take leave of your senses."

Thoroughly humiliated, Sydney met Tim's scornful gaze. "Sir, I owe you an apology. You've been honorable, and I spoke out of turn."

Tim looked less than mollified. "Don't you ever challenge my position here again. I won't have anyone question my motives or actions." He stomped out and disappeared through the door with a loud bang.

Velma whistled softly under her breath.

If being hung over wasn't misery enough, a delayed reaction to the narrow escape she'd had tilted Sydney into tears. She kept her hand clapped over her mouth to contain the noise, but huge, salty tears rolled down her cheeks and dripped onto her shirt.

"Honey child, this little masquerade of yours has gone on long enough." Velma gathered Sydney to her ample bosom and tenderly rocked her.

"I have no other choice."

"Yes, you do."

"No." Sydney pulled away. "If anything, this is a point of honor now!"

"Honor? Girl, honor was that big ol' cuss walking away when he had every right to deck you." Velma wiped her hand off on her apron with agitated swipes. "I just can't let this go on. You were a breath away from having Big Tim whale away on you!"

"I'm going to prove myself. Don't you dare tell!"

"I don't know. . . ."

Sydney gave the housekeeper a pleading look. "You have to keep your silence! I've already endured far too much to turn back. The first week has to be the worst. The men have begun to accept me."

"I'm not promising anything. I'll ponder over it and let you know what I think in the morning. Till then, you'd best get on upstairs and stay out of sight. Tim's hoppin' mad. Any other man would have stripped a length of hide off of you, but he didn't. Any man suggesting Big Tim's been less than generous and fair with Fuller is either a fool or a liar. You issued fighting words. He's man enough to know he don't have to prove anything to you, so he walked off. You got off easy, if all you got was a sound warning."

Sydney crept up the stairs, huddled pitifully under her sheets, and sobbed even as she vowed she wouldn't cry.

<hr />

Tim couldn't remember the last time he'd gotten that steamed. He stomped out to the barn, ignored the necessity for a saddle, and ripped out of the place on his gelding. He rode the palomino and finally cooled down enough to pull in on the reins. "Whoa, Hombre."

The horse stopped, then gladly obeyed Tim's lead and paced at a slow rate to cool off. He nickered softly, then blew. When Tim patted his neck, he tossed his head and sidestepped a bit. "Sorry, boy. I got pretty hot under the collar there. Too bad the kid isn't half as smart as you. He'd be far better off."

Tim looked around. The moonlit meadow all about him was beautiful. Cattle lowed and calves bawled here and there. Crickets and cicadas chirped and whirred. No matter how rotten a day went, he'd always managed to find a few seconds of peace in a place like this. It was why he'd bought the land. After having lost his wife and baby to cholera seven years ago, he'd needed seclusion and serenity. After riding for days, he'd camped overnight in this meadow and found a solitude to slightly ease the impossible ache in his chest. The very next day, he'd sought the owner and bought the place.

He didn't regret buying it. At least now, he didn't. A week after he'd spent his last dime on it, he certainly did. Tied to that parcel of land, Tim couldn't leave. The loneliness of building a home without anyone to share it settled into his heart and turned him into a virtual hermit.

Only Fuller managed to break through his seemingly impenetrable shell and talk to him. Oh, he'd been rude to Fuller. He'd been down right nasty. Fuller didn't even notice. He'd continued to be neighborly. He slowly chipped down the stone wall surrounding Tim's heart enough to make him speak to others and relate to the world again ... at least to the men. Tim knew he'd never love a woman again, though. It had been awful enough losing his folks when he was only fourteen. Losing Louisa and Tim, Jr. was more than he'd ever live through again.

The familiar ache of loss radiated in his chest. He forced

the air from his lungs in a long, steady flow. "That's it, isn't it, Lord? You're trying to show me the kid's acting angry at me like I acted toward the world after my loved ones passed on."

The gelding's head bobbled, as if to agree.

"That kid's got spunk to him. Nothing but a scrawny matchstick of a body and a big head that takes nothing to strike him into a fiery temper, though."

An owl hooted, and Hombre stirred.

"You know, Father, I'd take it kindly if you'd see fit to send Fuller home. Fuller'll take care of the kid. He's got a knack for handling the rough edges on folks. Sure as shootin', he did it with me and Velma." Tim sat and felt the dry wind ghost past. "I mean it, God. I know I'm supposed to listen and let you talk, but I'm desperate here. Your Word says you don't give us more than we can handle. I've hit my limit."

Sydney slid into her seat at the breakfast table and noted Velma hadn't set a place for Tim.

The housekeeper plunked a plate onto the table in front of her. "Tim got an early start. Always does on Sundays. Tim goes over and rings the bells to wake folks who don't have clocks, then sticks around to open windows and such. He's that kind of man—the solid, strong-and-silent kind. But he gets more done at church and around Forsaken than three other men put together."

"I see."

Velma slid into a chair and took a slurp of coffee immediately after praying. "D'you know how to drive a buckboard?"

"No."

"Then you're gonna learn today by driving me to church."

The housekeeper shook her head. "Doesn't seem right, me taking you to church and lying to everyone about you."

"I could stay home."

"Nope." Velma gave her the gimlet eye.

Desperation clawed at her. "But you've decided to let me continue on as I have, haven't you?"

Velma didn't give a prompt reply.

The bite Sydney had just swallowed threatened to come back up. Her eyes pled with the housekeeper.

"For now." Velma's voice sounded anything but reassuring.

Even so, Sydney took a long, deep breath to steady herself.

"This pretense of yours—I reckon it's your business. But I'm not going to lie."

"I won't ask you to. You can say . . ." Sydney strained for a moment to concoct something. "You can say I'm Fuller's kin. That's truthful."

"Hmpf." Velma salted her hash browns. A small smile tugged at the corner of her mouth. "You had to work to come up with what to say. Tells me you don't indulge in lies or deception."

"Of course I don't!" Just as soon as she spoke, Sydney bowed her head. "Truthfully, this whole masquerade bothers me. But I don't have a choice. You even agreed with me—Uncle Fuller would send me away." Her nose tingled and tears welled up. "I . . . I can't explain it. I've never even met him, but I have to be with whatever is left of my fam—" Her voice cracked.

"Family." Velma finished for her. "Fuller was pleased as punch to know he had kin. He's got a blind spot when it comes to dealing with women. I guess in this situation, your need is bigger than his whims."

Sydney tried to blink away her tears. Until now, she hadn't admitted to herself how desperately she longed to still have a family. Her lips moved, but almost no sound came out. "Thank you."

"But I'm putting you on notice here and now, missy." Velma shook her finger. "If Tim tries to tangle with you at all, I'm gonna spout off. I won't have you getting hurt. I owe Fuller that much. He'd be mad as a wet hornet if I let that big galoot clobber you."

Sydney nodded.

Velma taught her how to drive a buckboard on the way to church. "What're you going to do about singing?"

Sydney laughed. "I'm tone deaf. I simply read along and don't sing because the sounds coming out of my mouth would frighten small children."

Velma slanted her a sideways look. "Then maybe you could play the accompaniment."

Shaking her head, Sydney confessed, "My music tutor quit. He told mama in all his years, he'd never once failed to teach a pupil a passable skill—until me."

"You danced just fine the other night."

"Thank you, but I was moving to the music, not making it. Do you always take your Bible to church?"

"You don't?" Velma looked shocked.

Sydney shrugged. "At home the vicar reads the verses aloud. Our family Bible sits in the parlor. It's quite substantial, so carrying it seems pretentious."

During the service, Sydney wasn't sure what to think about these Americans and how they worshiped God. The hymns were the same, but thereafter things went differently. One of the older men went to the altar, turned, and spoke about parishioners! He mentioned ailments, concerns, and needs. At her church back home, such things were private. The preacher then prayed.

He specifically asked for the Lord to see to each and every person who'd been mentioned.

Instead of staying at the pulpit, the parson sat back down, and Big Tim stood there and read from the Bible.

Sydney could hardly imagine she was hearing the story correctly. This wasn't something she'd heard before. A man named Jacob pretended to be his older brother. By wearing Esau's clothing and using animal skin to seem hairy, he fooled his father and received his brother's birthright.

What a dreadful man. He had no honor. In the next instant, Sydney looked down at herself. *I'm wearing clothes that I shouldn't be in so I can trick someone, too.*

She fought the urge to squirm.

I'm not stealing anything. That's the difference.

Reverend Bradle preached in an animated voice. Instead of sounding somber and profound, he preached as if he were talking to a room of dear friends. There was no mistaking he spoke with authority. Instead of coasting off into a daydream as she used to back home, Sydney hung on every word.

As she left the church, Sydney looked around. She'd met most of the people at the Founder's Day celebration. A nod of recognition at a distance or a handshake worked well. Sydney enjoyed seeing the neighbors again. They all seemed like good, decent folks. She escorted Velma out to the wagon, then frowned. The horse wasn't standing right. Seeking out Tim was the last thing she wanted to do.

Gulp stood a ways off. He shuffled from one boot to the other and even the tips of his ears glowed bright red as a woman spoke to him. He glanced over at Sydney.

She made a beeline toward him. "Madam, please do accept my apologies for intruding. Gulp, it appears the horse to the buckboard is going lame."

"We can't have that!" Gulp wheeled around and practically ran away.

Sydney found herself the subject of squint-eyed scrutiny. "Gulp's very knowledgeable regarding horses. I'd best see what there is to learn."

The moment Sydney reached Gulp's side, he stooped over, pulled up the horse's right front hoof, and pretended to study it with great concentration. "Kid, you done that real smooth. Gotta hand it to you. You pulled me away before that old battleaxe started harping."

"Widow O'Toole," Sydney guessed aloud.

"Yep." Gulp muttered, "She's lookin' this way. Frown and act like something's awrong." Gulp pulled a knife from his belt.

Sydney could scarcely credit it—the man wore a weapon into a house of worship?

"I know you coulda dug this bitty little stone outta the hoof." Gulp pried it free. "But you saved me."

"Forsaken's men take care of each other."

He shot her a grin. "Kid, there's hope for you."

"Are the two of you going to stand there jawing all afternoon?" Velma tapped her foot impatiently. "I left a roast in the oven."

"We're done here." Gulp let go of the horse's leg and straightened up. "That could have bruised him, so go at a walk on the way home."

Sydney climbed onto the buckboard while Gulp helped Velma, then headed toward his own mount. They'd no more driven fifteen feet than Velma elbowed Sydney. "What did you think about the sermon?"

"The reverend seems very knowledgeable and lively."

"He is. But I didn't ask about him. I asked about what he

talked about. I figured you might latch on to something he said about Jacob."

"I did." Sydney nodded. "Jacob and I hold something in common."

"Pretending to be someone you're not?"

Sydney acted as if she hadn't heard Velma. "Jacob and I were each our mother's favorite. Then, too, our fathers doted on someone other than us."

"Your daddy didn't baby you?" Velma couldn't hide her astonishment.

Talking about Father wasn't easy, but Sydney couldn't bear the thought that someone might think ill of him. "He was so besotted with Mama, everyone else paled in comparison. Father came to America and met her here. They married the very next day."

"Impulsive rascal."

"They adored each other. I hoped I'd be as fortunate in finding a mate."

"Hmpf." Velma gave her a scathing look. "That's not likely with you tromping around in those duds."

"Just as well. I came to America to explore the possibility of marriage, but things went terribly wrong."

Velma grabbed the reins. "Whoa!" The buckboard jerked to a halt. "Are you running from somebody?"

"It's of no consequence."

"We're not budging until you tell me the truth."

Sydney didn't say anything.

"I'm waiting."

"Velma, your roast is going to burn."

The housekeeper gave her a disgruntled look, then a sly smile lifted her lips. "I'm not above blackmail. Either you tell me what's going on, or I'll tell Big Tim—"

"Very well." Sydney glowered at her. "All the gentleman cared about was making an advantageous marriage so he could gain access to lucrative dealings with the peerage. When I arrived, he couldn't be bothered to meet my ship or spend any time with me. After a single week of ignoring me, he addressed me by the wrong name and expected me to wed him the very next day. I was supposed to accept being left to wander museums alone on our wedding trip whilst he saw to business matters."

Velma didn't react.

Feeling completely adrift, Sydney let out a small sigh. "I also learned he has a paramour he planned to keep even after our marriage. I couldn't pledge my heart to such a man, so here I am."

Nodding sagely, Velma declared, "And here you'll stay. Doesn't matter to me whether you're in britches or a bustle. We'll make sure you don't have to worry about that scoundrel."

"Thank you, Velma. But until my birthday, I'm wearing britches."

***

Bam! Bam! Bam! "Wake up, kid."

Sydney rolled out of bed, noting the sun had barely broken over the horizon. The very thought of Tim Creighton thundering into her room and dumping her out of bed again served as ample motivation. She'd become adept at dressing quickly and racing downstairs.

Tim seemed preoccupied at breakfast. Sydney didn't mind. After shoveling in his food at record speed, Tim shoved away from the table. "We're rotating the stock to another pasture.

Hathwell, ride with Boaz. The fence on the west edge of the property is looking weak."

Sydney nodded to acknowledge the order.

"Don't be in too big of a hurry or careless. Barbed wire can cut you to ribbons." Tim scowled at her. "Talking of ribbons. That hair of yours looks girly. Next time you're in town, have the barber whack it."

"He will not!" Velma poked at Big Tim's shoulder. "That there is stylish. Little Lord Fauntleroy—"

"Is a fictional kid. Syd is—"

"Handsome just the way he is." Velma shook her finger at Tim. "Stop fretting and leave Sydney alone. He's pulling his weight around here."

"He doesn't weigh much." Tim shot a look at Sydney. "You've got to eat more. Maybe Doc ought to check you out."

"That's not necessary." Sydney grabbed her coffee.

"Completely ridiculous," Velma agreed. "Syd's appetite has improved since he first got here. He's eating loads more."

Tim's brows *vee*-ed. "But it's not making any difference. Maybe he's got worms."

Sydney choked on her coffee.

"Tapeworms. That's the problem." Tim nodded. "I'm sure of it. Copper's the cure for it. Nature's vermifuge." He strode from the room.

Velma slapped a hand over her mouth, her shoulders shaking with suppressed laughter.

Sydney gave Velma an it's-not-funny look. "If he brings in horse liniment again, he'll be the one who needs to see the doctor."

Tim returned and slapped something down on the table. A self-assured smile creased his face. "There. Swallow that. It'll cure what ails you."

She glanced down and jolted. "I'm not about to swallow a coin!"

"It's just a penny. Either you down it, or you go see Doc." Tim folded his arms across his chest. "Decide."

Velma burst out laughing and left the room.

Sydney stared at the penny. *I can't go see the doctor. He'll see straight through my ruse. But how will I ever manage to—*

"Drink it on down."

Grasping for any excuse, however slim, she rasped, "What if it gets stuck?"

"I'll smack you on the back."

Sydney realized Tim would stand there until she swallowed the coin. She picked it up and groused, "Cow brains, puke on maggots, and now a penny. And you wonder why my appetite is off."

Boaz was in a talkative mood. He jawed on about any number of things and seemed more than content to carry on the bulk of the conversation. He already had the horses saddled up, so they took off. Boaz showed Sydney how to determine if the fence needed to be reinforced.

"Now you ride next to the fence and call out when you see the next place that needs fixin'. I'll follow behind ya and catch things if you miss 'em."

"Very well." Sydney clicked her tongue, and Kippy stepped on. About fifteen yards later, she pulled back on the reins. "Whoa, Kippy. We have work to do."

"Good goin', kid. Here. This is what you do." With a couple of quick whacks, Boaz managed to hammer the loose nails. Sydney watched his technique. As they continued on, she observed him closely and managed to improve her aim in short order so she was able to do the job.

When she came in that evening, Velma yanked her off to the side. "Fuller sent a telegram. He's aiming to stay in Abilene another few weeks. Some doc there says he may have a treatment to help out that rheumatiz. You know he's got it real bad, so he sent word not to fret. Told Tim to keep control of things."

Sydney moaned.

"Don't go stirring trouble in the pot. Just keep your mouth shut, and Tim'll leave you be. He's not a man to carry a grudge. What you said to him the other night was unforgivable, but he showed Christian charity by walking away. He's back to being his regular self and treating you like nothing ever happened."

"He made me swallow a penny."

Velma snickered. "Just lie low. Do what you have to, and keep out of the way. It's the only way to handle this."

Sydney took the housekeeper's advice. It made sense . . . it was the only thing that did make sense. Any man she'd ever met would have set her in her place for impugning his integrity. Tim got riled, but he'd leashed his anger. He'd not let pride and temper dictate his response. Why? Why hadn't he just demanded satisfaction? And why had he put it behind him and acted like she'd not insulted him?

It can't be that he's a Christian. That's too simplistic. When I get to know him better, I'll be able to anticipate Big Tim's reactions to things. And I'll learn to respond the way he does. Respect and admiration are earned here, not conferred by social standing.

Feeling too restless to sit and read or go to bed that night, Sydney decided to pamper herself. In the past, whenever she felt this way, she indulged in a long, hot soak in a bubble bath, so she slipped off and rode to town. To her disappointment, the mercantile was closed. Vowing to find an excuse to come to town during the daytime in order to buy the bubble bath or some oils as she'd promised Nella, she turned toward the saloon.

Her heartbeat thundered in her ears as she pushed through the batwing doors and into the saloon. For an instant, every-thing went still. Then one of the poker players started to snicker.

"Syd!" Nella beckoned from the upstairs. "C'mon up."

Throwing her shoulders back, Sydney walked down the worn strip of red carpeting toward the stairs.

"Brazen little cuss," someone drawled.

"Syd's got plenty to be proud of. Y'all mind your own busi-ness." Nella let out a low chuckle. "Syd and me—we'll be mind-ing ours."

Heat filled Sydney's face. She hastened up the stairs and trained her gaze straight ahead so the men down below couldn't see her blush.

They had no bubble bath, but Nelly added a few drops of her perfume to the water for Sydney. The fragrant steam rising from the tub beckoned. Sydney sank into the depths of the water and soaked until the water went cold. After she dressed, Sydney slipped into Nella's room. "I need to pay you for tonight and the last time, too. If I give you more, would you go to the mercantile and buy bubble bath?"

"Sure."

By the time Sydney got back to the ranch, she felt loads better. Pancake and Bert were playing poker when she returned. They ignored her as she unsaddled Kippy, but as she walked past them to get to the doorway, Bert lifted his big nose and sniffed loudly. He peered over his cards and nodded sagely. "Yup. Told ya so. The kid even smells like a bunch of spring posies. Betcha Nella's gonna be tellin' tales again."

They're definitely tales. Sydney didn't bother to hide her smile, but she stayed silent. She had no more stepped from the small halo of light the men's lantern yielded and out into the shadows of the yard than a big hand clamped around her wrist and jerked.

Chapter Eleven

"No more tomcatting around." Tim bit off the words and glowered at the kid. "Bad enough the cowboys nudged you that direction. But you didn't have to go back. Whoring never did anything other than stain a man's soul and empty his pockets."

The kid looked offended.

Tim didn't care. "You don't know how many men that chippie's lain with. There's a good chance she's got a disease and will pass it on to any man who beds her."

Syd's eyes grew huge.

The smell of flowers hovered in the still night air—honeysuckle. The scent brought back a flood of tender memories of his wife. The reality that Louisa was gone savaged him all over again. And the scent came from the kid. He and that harlot abused the gift that belonged between a man and his wife. Tim snarled, "If I ever catch you with a two-bit whore or smelling of her perfume, I'll tan your hide till you can't sit. Get upstairs, strip naked, and scrub every last inch of you."

The next morning, Tim looked across the table. "Ride with Gulp today."

Sydney dipped his chin in assent.

Velma came in and gave Tim a heated look. "Creighton,

news is that you let a fox in my henhouse again!"

"I did?"

"Three of my layin' hens are history!"

"Now, Velma . . ."

She leaned into him and jabbed her finger into his chest with every word to punctuate her meaning. "Don't you, 'Now, Velma' me! The dirt with my cayenne pepper hasn't gotten dug up a-tall. Those spikes you buried are pushed apart farther than Orville Jantzen's teeth. The varmint got my hens, and you're to blame!"

"Cryin' in a bucket," Tim groused.

"You'll be crying if you don't get your eggs and custard, Tim Creighton! That's eight hens I've lost in three weeks. I can't lose another."

"We'll just buy eggs."

"We most certainly will not! You get your tail end out there and fix up the soil with more pepper, and you set a hound out there by the henhouse from now on."

He gave her a dirty look and shoved her hand away from his aching breastbone. The woman could certainly make an impression when she was of a mind to. Those stubby fingers of hers were downright vicious. He'd bet two bits that he'd have a mark on him from her nasty jabs, and he didn't bruise easily. "Eight? Why didn't you tell me?"

"I didn't want to vex you too bad. What with Fuller being gone, you were busy."

"How long will it take to hatch new hens?" Sydney asked.

Velma gave the kid a scornful look. "Chickens hatch mostly in the bright months. Not that it matters. I can't afford to let any hens sit. Every last egg I'm collecting still isn't enough."

Tim tapped his foot. "Jakob Stauffer's got the biggest henhouse in the county. I bet—"

"That man has better things to do than worry about replacing our hens. Leota loved her chickens. You can't ask a widower to go sell off his wife's hens."

"They're chickens, not pets." Even while he muttered the words, Tim knew he was wrong. After he'd lost Louisa, he couldn't bear the thought of parting with anything of hers, regardless of how trifling it was.

Sydney looked down and mumbled, "The Richardsons had plenty of hens."

Her words made Tim perk up. "Did they, now? Isn't that great! Tell you what, Syd. Forget all about riding with Gulp today. Those hens are more important. Maybe you ought to get yourself on over there to the Richardsons' farm and buy Velma some."

"Me?" The kid wore a stricken expression.

"Hold on just a second there, Tim Creighton. Don't you dare try to weasel out of this. It's your fault my hens are gone, and you're responsible for replacing them!"

"Syd can do it." Tim smacked his hand on the table. "After all, we agreed whoever was wrong would have to clean the coop. I'm going to be busy." *I never thought I'd see the day where I'd clean another coop—let alone be glad to do it!*

"Who do you think you're fooling here? I wasn't born yesterday! Fancy Pants doesn't know diddly squat about hens. He'll likely come back with a rooster and half a dozen scrawny-necked fryers." She shook her finger in front of Tim's nose. "You're responsible, and you'll see to it that I get fine hens. I'm missing eight, and I reckon you owe me a couple more than that for all of my vexation and trouble. Now shoo on out of here and get me my hens."

Tim swallowed his pride. "Awww, Velma, you can't send me over there! Those gals practically drag me to the parson's as soon as I set foot on their farm. I swear, the oldest, Linette, practically eats me alive!"

"Then take Syd along."

"What? Oh no! Not me!"

"Button your lip, Syd," Velma warned, then turned back to Tim. "He handles women just fine. He took to those Richardson gals just great last time. The men said he did fine with Nella, too."

Sydney's mouth dropped open.

Tim scowled. "Kid, by now, half the territory has probably heard about you in the brothel. It's not the kind of reputation you want to earn."

"Agreed." A sly smile slanted the kid's mouth. "And because there's a blot on my name, I shouldn't go keep polite company with nice girls."

"Don't keep company with them," Velma instructed.

Tim groaned inwardly.

Velma continued, "Just go along and drag Big Tim back after they make him stay to dinner."

"Dinner!" Tim roared.

Drying her hands on her apron, the housekeeper huffed, "Oh, don't get your socks in a knot. You know full well you can't tromp over there, buy hens, and skulk off. Mrs. Richardson's turned her daughters into man-hungry bits of fluff. They're our neighbors, and we can't afford to offend them. I fully expect you to have dinner there. In fact, I'm not even gonna bother cooking one here. You make some small talk and keep the girls from extracting any wedding-ring promises. I don't want a bit of lip from you, Tim. It's justice, you having to face those gals."

"But I didn't do anything," Sydney objected. "I already endured them when I took back the plow!"

The corners of Velma's eyes crinkled. "Then you're right in practice."

Sydney moaned. "I'd rather do something—anything else."

"You're not the only one," Tim grumbled. He then brightened up. "Tell you what, Velma. You know exactly what you want. I'll give you twice as much cash money as you need. You go on over and pick out just what suits your fancy, then you can keep the extra."

"Wipe that hopeful smile off of your face, you rascal. You're responsible for this problem, and you're going to fix it. I'm not bailing you out." Velma gave Sydney a jaundiced look and planted her hands on her hips. "Men on this spread watch one another's backs. You go and do your duty. Protect Tim from Linette. Marcella, too, for that matter. Tim, you do likewise. I'll bet Sulynn or Katherine are already doing inventories on their hope chests after seeing our Syd."

"I hate eggs," Tim muttered darkly as he stalked from the room.

<hr />

Tim and Syd rode in silence until the Richardson farm came into sight. "You've met the Richardson girls."

"I returned the plow."

Tim shot the kid a look. "You stayed and sat in the parlor with 'em. Founder's Day, you even danced with one."

"Only as good manners dictated—nothing more."

"Manners don't work with the Richardsons. 'Specially Linette. She's getting desperate."

Sydney crooked an eyebrow. "Are you concerned for yourself or for me?"

"Both. Just take a word of advice: If someone suggests a

ride or a walk, don't accept. One scrap of attention, and they hear wedding bells."

Squaring his shoulders, Sydney nodded. "This calls for teamwork."

Whew. "You got it."

"I'll make a deal with you. I'll control the women. You decide on the hens."

"Kid, you got a deal!" It went against Tim's personal code to make lopsided bargains. "I'll mind your back."

"I suppose I'll need it. As Cervantes said, 'Those who'll play with cats must expect to be scratched.'"

"Kid, with these girls, a scratch is the least of our worries. They could eat a man alive."

As they rode into the yard, a high-pitched shriek sounded off to their left. Tim turned in time to see Marcella's hands fly up toward her roughly plaited hair while Katherine hurriedly started to straighten her droopy, faded gown. Linette emerged from the chicken coop and promptly dropped the egg basket as she blanched. Eggs cracked and rolled willy-nilly around her bare feet.

"Good day, ladies," Sydney called out.

"Yeah. Howdy," Tim echoed.

Just then, Marcella emerged from the outhouse. She was singing off tune quite loudly, but as the wooden door banged shut, she caught sight of her callers. The song died out at once. Crimson filled her cheeks.

"Wipe that smirk off of your face and act like nothing's amiss," Sydney growled. "If you don't, they'll go get fancied up and we'll have to offer to take them on those walks for all of their trouble."

"Tim! Tim Creighton and Lord Hathwell!" Mr. Richardson strode forward and grinned. "What brings you here?"

Sydney dismounted and sketched a comical bow. "Ah, Mr. Richardson, I do hope we've timed our arrival appropriately. I didn't know which day your daughters conduct their at-homes."

"At-homes?" Mrs. Richardson echoed in a bewildered tone.

"Oh, but of course you Americans must have another name for the days upon which your daughters accept callers. I'm certain with such a bevy of eligible daughters, your farm is overrun with eager young swains on that day. But this is a business trip." He nodded his head quite adamantly. "Yes, business."

"Oh," Sulynn gasped softly.

"Business?" Richardson inquired, "What business?"

"Hens," Tim rasped. "I need laying hens."

Linette nearly squealed with delight. "I'm taking care of the chickens today! I'll be so happy to help you. If you'll accompany me, Big Tim, I'll help you select fine hens. Just come with me! The henhouse is full, so you can take plenty of time to select whatever your heart desires."

"Steady now, old man," Syd rumbled softly behind a gritted smile, then raised his voice. "Oh, so we get to select the fowl! I hadn't anticipated such an event!"

"Yes," Mrs. Richardson beamed. "Tim should help Linette choose them."

"Capital! I'll come along. We'll have a jolly time, won't we? I'm afraid I'm not countrified enough to know much about fowl, other than I adore eating a good squab or duck every now and then. However does one select a decent laying hen?"

"I owe you one, kid," Tim growled under his breath.

Marcella raced over. "I'll have to help you!"

"Jolly!" Sydney waved his arms. "Why don't all of you girls come? Mr. Creighton was telling me that he wanted to purchase ten hens. He's so very kind to Velma, you know. He's a dashing good man. A fine man."

"Yes, he is." The Richardson parents' unison forced Tim to twitch them an obligatory, albeit sick, smile.

Sydney kept matters well in hand. The kid shepherded the girls to the coop. "After you, after you. Ladies first."

Tim balked at being confined with the girls. He rumbled under his breath, "What happened to your voice?"

Sydney cocked a brow.

"You sound even more British."

Fastidiously plucking a speck from the sleeve of his shirt, Syd whispered, "I'm adhering to our agreement. I'll handle the lasses by providing them with something a bit foreign to intrigue them—namely, my voice and stories. You handle the rest—unless you wish to renegotiate."

Tim scowled.

Syd made a sweeping gesture toward the door. "After you."

With all the enthusiasm of a man digging his own grave, Tim ducked his head and went inside the coop.

All four of the girls grabbed for the nearest thing with wings. "I'm afraid I simply cannot be a decent judge of chicken flesh. Big Tim will have to determine which ones."

"Isn't this a lovely one, Tim?" Linette simpered as she backed him into a corner and produced a Rhode Island Red. "She's a terrific laying hen."

"No!" He pointed to the hen in the farthest corner on the coup. "I want that one."

Sydney stepped beside him. "I don't much care for her either. Those feathers are such an odd shade." He deftly pushed Linette away. "You'll simply have to find a better one."

"What about this one?" Linette produced the healthy-looking specimen Tim had indicated.

"Capital, I say! Now stand here and hold her. Oh! And hold this one that Miss Sulynn found, too. You can handle these cackling creatures. Busy hands and all, you know ... I don't truly remember that saying."

"Idle hands are the devil's playground," Katherine quoted.

"Ah! Then no deviltry here!"

After Tim approved all ten hens and they were safely put into a crate, Sydney clapped his hands. "Oh, now wasn't that a corker! I do believe it was every bit as fun as the day we went rowing on the pond back home at the Huberts' summer estate."

Linette stepped closer and tried to clamp hold of Tim's arm again.

The kid stepped in her way and continued to speak as if he hadn't executed that strategic maneuver. "The ladies weren't nearly as sweet tempered when the ducks flapped their wings at us." He sighed. "I confess, it probably had something to do with the fact that the ducks were swimming right beside our little boat, and the ladies did end up the slightest bit wet."

The girls burst out laughing.

"Okay. That's taken care of." Tim sensed freedom. "I need to get back to Forsaken. Now."

Mr. Richardson called over, "Not yet, Tim. We need to talk about studs. I'm interested in one of your bulls—"

Tim figured it was his turn to get the kid away from the girls. "C'mon, Syd." He strode toward the farmer. The girls followed along.

"Perhaps it would be best for me to accompany the young ladies inside whilst you speak with their papa about the bulls."

"Nope. Stick around. You've got to learn. Pay attention."

"Oh, I'll pay close attention," Linette declared.

"Now, you girls shouldn't let such an indelicate discussion singe your pristine ears. Shoo! Along to the house with you."

"We're farmer's daughters, Lord Hathwell," Linette stated as she scooted closer to Tim.

Sydney deftly reached over, grabbed hold of the hand Linette tried to thread through Tim's arm, and gave it a reasonably strong tug. "Miss Richardson, I'm more than impressed that you're so very diligent about helping your father tend to business, but we men certainly wouldn't want to offend your maidenly sensibilities. No woman of decency would be caught discussing such base subjects back home. I'm most positive that the same strictures for decent women hold true here, too."

"I guess I ought to go help Mama with dinner," she pouted. "You men are staying, aren't you?"

"Of course they are," her father broke in.

Tim opened his mouth to offer his regrets, but Linette leaned forward and blurted out, "I made apple tarts!"

"Apple tarts?" Tim echoed in a strangled tone. He held a decided weakness for apple tarts, but he couldn't decide whether the treat was worth enduring the present company.

"Yup. Apple tarts. Now you girls get." As soon as all of his daughters flocked off, Mr. Richardson scratched his side. "I'm aching just to hear a voice that ain't soprano. I love 'em, but I sometimes wonder what in thunder I did to offend the Almighty so much that I got six daughters and not a single son!"

Tim sucked in a deep breath and forced it out of his lungs very slowly. "I don't know, but if you ever recollect whatever it was, do me the great kindness of letting me know. That way I won't do it!"

"He meant no offense, of course, Mr. Richardson."

Tim looked down at Syd. "Kid, I don't need you to do my talking for me. I speak my own mind."

"Everyone knows I love my daughters, but God sure pulled a fast one on me, saddling me with a whole blessed gaggle of 'em," Richardson said. "Not a man in the county hasn't teased me about it."

Syd cleared his throat. "The teasing is simply because folks are aware of how difficult it must be without sons to assist you with the heavy labor on such a grand and sizable farm."

Richardson gave Sydney a good once-over. "I'm looking forward to having son-in-laws."

For the first time, Syd looked suitably horrified about the whole situation. "I wish you the best of luck finding them!"

"We all know you're too young to gallop to the altar, kid." Tim let out a throaty chuckle and slapped him on the back.

The men milled about and conversed about the weather and some of the civic matters. Sydney kept fairly quiet, since he didn't know the persons and situations under discussion. It wasn't long before the youngest daughter dashed out, her pigtails flying behind her. "Papa! Papa! Mama sent me to fetch you and our guests. Chow's on!"

"Such an enchanting young lady!" Sydney smiled at the girl. "What is your name, child?"

"Bethany!"

"Well, then, Bethany, thank you for summoning us. I confess, I'm quite famished. Back home in Londontown, we reward those who bring good tidings. I fear I haven't a treat in my pocket to give you. Whatever shall I do? I know." He leaned forward. "I'll sit beside you!"

Bethany's eyes shone brightly. "Would you, please? The girls are fighting about you. They said that I'm too little to count."

"I find youth extremely refreshing. I'd love to be your meal companion. That settles it. You must sit at my side."

"Can I really?"

"But of course. And you called Mr. Creighton, too. I do believe it is only just that he should have the privilege of sitting on your other side, too."

"Really?" Bethany squealed in delight.

Syd tweaked the little girl's braid. "Really and truly. Your sisters will be pea green with envy."

"Holy cats!"

"You go save our places. Mr. Creighton and I must go to the pump so we don't offend your mother by appearing at her fine table with soiled hands."

As they washed off at the pump, Tim chuckled. "That was brilliant. I have to hand it to you, Syd. You've got it down. I'm enduring this meal only because of the tarts for dessert!"

"Steady, old man." Sydney's voice was rich with amusement. "I can see the girl's mama over your shoulder. The woman could have led Napoleon to victory."

Tim let out a crack of a laugh. Syd thinking in military terms—that was manly. Witty too. "Just tell me one thing now, kid. We have little Bethany between us. How do I cover my other flank?"

"Elementary, my dear man. You insist upon honoring Mrs. Richardson with that place. Of course, sliding her chair out for her would make that possible. I'm snagging the other youngster, so don't get in my path."

"It's a sound plan. The other kid's name is Charlotte."

"Thanks. Come now. Dallying any longer would be unforgivably rude."

Later, as they rode home, Tim started to chortle. "Did you see the looks on the older girls' faces when you arranged those little squirts beside you?"

"I've spent more than my fair share of time with young girls of fine families who are in training for the marriage market. I could tell you tales that would raise your brows."

"When Mrs. Richardson wanted me to take Linette for a walk, I about died. What was that you said?"

"I declared—quite emphatically, mind you—that Miss Linette's delicate constitution and fair complexion precluded such exertion in the heat of the midsummer day."

"How did you cook that one up?"

"Simple logic. Linette would have to proclaim that she was hale as a draft horse and weathered as a fence post to get you to walk out, and no girl is desirable if she is of such constitution and complexion."

"Kid, you did good. Can I count on you tomorrow? Mr. Richardson said they're showing up at the Smiths'."

"I recall hearing something about that at church."

"Yeah. Smith's first wife died. He remarried and has a passel of kids. His mother-in-law from the first marriage showed up, destitute and with three of her grandchildren. A bunch of us are putting up a cottage so she doesn't upset his household any more than necessary."

Syd frowned. "How will they manage to feed and clothe that many more?"

"It'll be a strain. It's going to be a mighty bitter pill for Smith to swallow, accepting charity for them."

"So tomorrow you want me to concoct some method of keeping the Richardson maids from your doorstep, so to speak?"

"Absolutely!" He shot Syd a grim smile. "Gotta hand it to you, kid. We all have our strong points, and yours certainly goes toward coping with vexatious women."

The kid gave him a cocky grin and drawled, "You ain't seen nuthin' yet."

Chapter Twelve

Trip unfruitful.

Rex Hume stared at the telegram. He'd hypothesized a woman unfamiliar with anyone in the States would likely return to England. Ethan Tyler had agreed. The next day, Tyler had examined passenger lists for ships departing for England on the day Lady Hathwell disappeared. He'd located her name and jumped aboard the next voyage.

Hume's hand clenched. The telegram crackled into a ball. He stared down at it as his mind started tallying up the lost time. Six days before he knew she'd slipped off. Two days when he'd engaged Tyler and he'd researched passenger lists. Five days' voyage to England, and six more spent scouring Britain for the girl. Now, another five days lost on Tyler's return voyage. Twenty-four days.

Twenty-four days was an eternity.

Where was she?

And what had she been doing?

Not that he'd ever let on that where she'd been or whatever she'd done mattered in the least to him. He'd still marry her. He needed to. Had to. Couldn't afford another year of searching for a different prospective wife. Even more, he couldn't very well "lose" a fiancée. The aristocracy with whom he wished to deal would shun him if harm befell one of their own while in his care.

Never once had it occurred to him that his fiancée would behave in such an irresponsible way. Aristocracy understood the importance of image. They cut their teeth on propriety. Upholding the family name mattered above all. Honor. Duty. Even self-sacrifice.

Self-sacrifice. A rueful bark of a laugh left his lips. What could she possibly claim as a reason to object to being his wife? A quick glance in the diamond dust mirror confirmed he was a handsome man. Though not especially tall, he measured a good five inches taller than Lady Hathwell—and that was plenty. As would any conscientious man in his position, he engaged a decent tailor who saw to it his attire reflected the Hume family's success. That financial stability would surround a woman with capable servants and afford her whatever trinkets that struck her fancy. Indeed, many were the women who would gladly wed him—yet he'd held out for something more.

But as of yet, he'd gotten nothing.

It galled him. He'd reasoned that he would be able to mold a young, aristocratic bride into the kind of wife he desired— pretty, sociable, an asset who knew her place. Young and pretty—yes, Sydney Hathwell was both. But once he found her, things would go his way. He'd see to it.

Chapter Thirteen

A collection of over twenty men and as many women and children showed up at the Smiths' place. When Mrs. Richardson tried to buttonhole Tim and Sydney, Sydney gave her a brilliant smile. "Ma'am,. I'm new to one of these events, and Tim vowed to keep me apprised of all the necessary steps. Those handsome bucks over there seem more than besotted with your lovely daughters. Most assuredly you know by now that Mr. Toomel and Mr. Valmer have expressed interest in marriageable young ladies of distinction. Why don't you have them help you set up the quilting frame?"

"Why, yes," Mrs. Richardson murmured.

Sydney leaned closer. "Ma'am, if those dearlings of yours extended an invitation to those selfsame men to join them for the meal, I'd not take offense. I'd just bet men flock to them like bees to nectar. There is a strange appeal to some women, you know. Men seem to surround them, and that only makes them all the more beguiling."

A few seconds later, Tim clapped Sydney on the shoulder and handed her a hammer. "Kid, you may not have an ounce of brawn, but there's nothing wrong with that brain of yours. That woman's going to keep her girls circulating today if it kills her."

Male banter died out as the men gathered and reviewed plans. A solid foundation stood ready. Within three hours, all of the walls had been constructed. Sydney felt a surge of pride. She'd only hit her thumb with the hammer once. The time she'd spent repairing the fence had taught her how to handle a hammer effectively, and she didn't shame herself by fumbling once. An odd sense of satisfaction filled her.

All four walls were raised and braced together. Before she knew to object, Pancake lifted her high onto a beam. "Sit up there and crawl from beam to beam as we hand 'em up. You have to knock them in place and secure them. Over on the other side is William Bedford. Match his speed, and you'll do us proud."

"William?"

"Yep. The two of you are the lightest. Too much weight up there might well make the whole place collapse. Be careful."

Glancing at the distance from her beam to the floor, Sydney stated with great feeling, "Don't worry, Pancake. I'll be more than careful!"

Her arms ached and dozens of small splinters prickled in her hands. Her head swam to be at that height, but Sydney did her job. She kept up with William Bedford, too. Doing so earned her the approving nods of those present. When her feet hit the floor, Tim jostled her shoulder. "Kid, you did good. Real good."

When she got home that night, Sydney ached and gladly soaked her hands until the splinters swelled sufficiently for Velma to pluck them out. Velma glanced over her shoulder and whispered, "I gotta say, you're doing fine. Big Tim told me today you'd started to shape up. Said soon any man in the state would be proud to claim you as his son. Never thought I'd see the day when that man would admit it, but he actually decided he likes having you underfoot."

Though Tim didn't say a thing to Sydney, she sensed a subtle shift in the way he treated her. She no longer felt he was pushing her to change, but pushing her to be all a man ought to be.

She'd changed, too. Aunt Serena spoke the truth when she'd said Sydney knew nothing of a man's world. Basic observation helped with mimicking masculine behavior—but that was all. Tim was mentoring "Syd" and teaching her the responsibilities, concerns, and requirements. In doing so, he'd allowed her an unguarded view of what a woman never saw. She'd come to admire and appreciate him—and the impossible had happened. They'd become friends.

Two days after the Smiths' construction, she was mucking the stable when a rider came in and shot off his pistol. Men gathered around him at once. "Stauffer's little girl fell into the test hole the well digger started. We need Hathwell to go down and get her. No one else'll fit."

Sydney wasn't at all certain she wanted any part of this. By the time she was at the Stauffers' place, she was sure she'd gladly decline the rescuing opportunity. She took one look at the small, deep hole in the ground and swallowed hard.

Tim gave her a stern look. "Stauffer lost his wife and son two months ago. That little girl is all he has."

A wave of grief washed over her. Sydney knew what it was to have everyone she loved gone. Resolve replaced her fear. She'd do anything to spare someone else that anguish.

"Syd, they need you. For once, that scrawny body of yours is just what the job requires. Any other man strong enough for the task has shoulders far too wide to get down more than a few yards."

She nodded.

Tim shoved a rope in her hands. "You're going to do this. You have to. Tie that around your middle. Pull it tight. I'm knotting another length about your left leg. That way, if one snaps, we'll still have you."

"If that was supposed to reassure me, it didn't."

Tim locked eyes with her. "Duty makes a man. This is one of those times."

"Duty," she echoed in a voice filled with iron resolve.

"We're all counting on you, Syd. Look at Stauffer. He can't take another heartbreak." Tim paused a moment and tested the ropes. She barely felt the strong tug he gave to the one at her waist. He took the ends and twisted them into one more knot for good measure. "When you first got here, I wouldn't have bet a plugged nickel you'd last a day. You proved me wrong. I wouldn't send Fuller's only blood kin down that well if I didn't firmly believe he'd come back up in one piece. Fact is, you've got what it takes. We're all counting on you."

"I'll do my best."

Tim abruptly thrust one arm up into the air. Folks went silent. He clapped hold of Sydney's shoulder and bowed his head. "Lord, we come to you in this hour of need and plead with you for divine mercy. Grant Hathwell the necessary strength to do this task and reunite Stauffer with his little daughter. In your name we pray and claim victory, amen."

A chorus of amens sounded.

Sydney trained her eyes on the hole in the ground and felt bats fluttering wildly in her stomach. She knew that she had to do this, though. The time had come.

Sydney crept to the edge of the well's test hole. Dirt sifted in. She drew in a deep breath before sliding in, hands first. For a brief second, she fought the instinct to back out. She swallowed her fear, thought of the little girl, and scooted farther in.

"He fits," someone said.

It made perfect sense that they didn't dare send anyone larger down. Broader shoulders would have gotten wedged after the first two feet. As it was, very little sunlight filtered past Sydney's body. She couldn't see anything.

Then she heard a whimper.

"Lower me!" she shouted.

The rope bit into her waist as they lowered her. Dizziness assailed her as all of the blood rushed to her head. Dirt got in her mouth, and she spat it out. As the hole narrowed, she had to use her arms to turn herself at a different angle so she could continue.

Small, jerky sobs filled the well hole.

"What's your name?" Sydney asked.

"Emmy-Lou."

"Emmy-Lou, I'm Syd. I'm coming to get you."

"Please hurry!"

"Believe me, I have no desire to stay down here any longer than is absolutely necessary." She blindly reached ahead of her and thought she felt something. "Put both hands over your head, Emmy-Lou. I have to find you."

"You touched me. Come closer."

A voice from above called down, "That's the end of the rope!"

Sydney hoped Emmy-Lou hadn't heard those words and that God had heard Tim's prayer.

"My hand is hurt, Syd," little Emmy-Lou whimpered. "Will you still help me?"

"Yes, Poppet. Reach very, very high with your other hand." Emmy-Lou's fingers brushed hers. "Good. Now pretend I have a treat in my pocket. You can't have it unless you stretch farther.

You have to hold on to my wrist, and I'll hold your wrist back."

"Do you have a treat?"

Sydney fought back a hysterical laugh. "I'll get you one next time I'm in town."

"All right."

Once they connected, Sydney curled both hands around the thin, cold wrist, then kicked and whooped. Both ropes jerked at once. Her descent had been very controlled, but the ascent was wild. Dirt showered down around them, and Emmy-Lou screamed. In fact, the little girl let go. Sydney held fast, even though her arms felt as if they were being yanked out of their sockets. She felt Emmy-Lou's sleeve give and heard the ominous sound of fabric ripping. "Hurry!"

Suddenly the rope at her waist dug deeper as her left boot was jerked clean off by the rope. The waist rope now bore all their weight—and if the knots failed, she and Emmy-Lou wouldn't survive the downward plunge.

When Sydney's legs hit open air, seemingly dozens of hands grabbed at her trousers and yanked. She popped out, and someone snatched Emmy-Lou from her.

Sunlight never looked so sweet. Sydney managed a shaky grin, but tears slipped down her cheeks.

"Don't cry, Syd. We're safe now," Emmy-Lou piped up.

"Syd ain't crying," Pancake groused. "He's got so much dirt in his eyes, he's probably half blind."

"Let me take you to the washstand," a woman's voice offered.

"I'd be obliged, ma'am."

Mr. Stauffer clasped his daughter tightly to his chest. He couldn't even let go long enough to shake Sydney's hand. In a choked tone, he began to express his thanks, but the words got lodged.

Sydney gave him a cocky grin and shook the dirt from herself.

"Come along, then." Once in the house, the woman turned to her. "Mr. Hathwell . . ." Her voice fell away.

Sydney gave her a wobbly smile. "I'm afraid I'm going to have to insist that you be my accomplice, ma'am." She stopped holding her right shoulder, revealing how the binding had slipped.

"My dear Aunt Gussy! You're a woman!"

"Don't you dare let on! Promise!"

The woman bit her lip and nodded. "I owe you my niece's life. Silence is the least I can do. Let's put you in my bedroom. You can borrow one of Jakob's shirts."

"I'll be able to see to myself. Emmy-Lou said something was wrong with one of her arms. Please see to her."

Twenty minutes later, Sydney emerged from the Stauffer home, freshly bathed and shampooed, her chest carefully bound, and her secret still intact.

Tim stuck out his hand. Sydney put hers in it, and he gave it a strong shake. "I told you duty makes a man. You did well."

His words were the highest praise she'd ever received. Sydney's heart soared, but she knew she couldn't give too much of a reaction. Men didn't allow themselves shows of emotion. "Thanks. I'm glad the lass is fine."

Mr. Stauffer came over. Filthy as could be, little Emmy-Lou still had her legs and one arm wrapped tightly about him. "Hathwell—"

Afraid she'd become too emotional if he said much, Sydney interrupted. "How's her arm?"

"Sprained her wrist. That's all. Can you believe it?"

Sydney nodded curtly. "Creighton prayed." She turned to Tim. "We have work waiting back at Forsaken."

"Yup." When they got home, Tim pointed to the ax stuck in a stump. "Get to it, son. You've got enough time to chop half a cord by supper."

Sydney marched over to the wood and stared at the ax. How was one to accomplish this task? She hadn't the faintest idea. For the next two hours, she tried every conceivable way to hack the logs into manageable pieces of firewood. Nothing she produced was vaguely usable. What humiliation after she'd finally earned Tim's respect!

Boaz sauntered over. His features screwed with puzzlement. "Why is Tim bothering to have you make kindling?"

"I'm not producing kindling."

"Sure looks thataway to me!"

"Looks like that to me, too," Tim said from several yards away. He paced over, grabbed the ax, and managed to split several pieces all with single, well-placed, powerful swings.

"Watch, kid. You set the piece down." He took a good-sized log and positioned it on a stump. "Hold the ax like this. See?" He gripped the long handle with casual grace and ease, his large hands fitting with plenty of room to spare around the smooth wood. "Keep an eye at the center point, and swing with a fluid move."

He made it look so simple. He hefted the heavy tool up, and the arcing swing was fluid and loose. A single blow, and the wood seemingly fell apart, each half obediently dropping off to either side as if they'd been awaiting the ax's mastery. He grabbed a second piece, positioned it, and the ax bit once again. The area rang with a strange sound from each strike.

Sydney watched the muscles in his arms bulge and ripple with the action. There was a rugged beauty in the way he accomplished his labor. She didn't know a single man who could match this kind of masculinity. By the sweat of his brow and the power of his muscles, he earned everything he owned.

If only Papa had sent me to marry him! The thought stunned her. Back home, he'd have been a nobody. He was far beneath her in class. Papa wouldn't have let him in the front door. Here, things were different. Men were measured by their accomplishments instead of their pedigree. In the days she'd been here, Sydney had grown to respect Tim Creighton. Measured on his own merits, he was head and shoulders above any man she'd ever known.

Tim turned. "I'll get you started, Syd. Next time, if you don't know how to do something, just say so." He put another log on its end up on the chopping stump. He moved behind her. "Here." After placing the ax in Sydney's hand, he clasped his hands over hers and took her through the entire motion slowly. "Do it."

The act nearly shattered her molars. Force jolted all of the way up her arms, into her jaw and head. Though the wood split, so did her head. Tim didn't leave it at a single piece, either. He guided her through four more. "Get going now."

Weak from the pain in her arms, Sydney longed to confess her gender. She wanted nothing more than to go take a long soak in a tub full of sweet-smelling bath salts and put on a lacy dress. Still, she couldn't give up now. Not when Tim had finally accepted her and was mentoring her. She drew in a deep breath and adjusted her grip on the ax.

"Awww," Boaz groused. He held his palm up to the sky. "It's fixin' to rain."

Sydney swung the ax and connected with the wood. It split halfway, and she had to bang it down twice to finish splitting it, but she'd hit her target. By the time she set the next piece on the stump, the skies opened.

"You'd best put that ax away," Tim ordered. "I don't want

it flying out of your wet hands."

"Hey, Boss, what's with him?" Boaz frowned at her.

Tim's eyes narrowed.

Sydney looked down and felt horribly sick. Her soaked shirt stuck to her skin, and the binding around her chest showed through very plainly. She closed her eyes in horror.

Rough fingers clamped her jaw and squeezed. "Kid, why didn't you tell me you busted your ribs fishing Emmy-Lou out of the well?"

Shocked by his assumption, she remained utterly silent for a second. Her luck couldn't take any more twists and turns than this. Sent down a hole, fished out, almost exposed, gaining another accomplice, then almost being revealed again by the presence of her bindings. Just thinking about the day made her dizzy.

"Did Miriam wrap you up good enough?"

Sydney nodded vigorously.

"Go on in the house. That wet binding will chafe. I'll be up in a minute to rewrap you."

She stepped back. "I'll do it."

"Nope. Tell you what—it's muggy. Leave it undone and crawl into bed. Tomorrow, I'll strap you up."

"I'll manage, but thanks anyway." She hastened away before he became any more observant.

The next morning, Velma stationed herself in Sydney's doorframe. "Leave the kid alone, Tim. He's not complaining, but he's not in any shape to get out there today." She glared at the behemoth man.

"I'm checking on him, then."

"I'm standing over you to make certain you aren't too rabid."

Tim plowed into the bedroom and gave Sydney a long, hard look. "Kid, your skin doesn't have a drop of color to it."

"You near sent Syd to his death down that well hole," Velma accused.

"Close only counts in pitching horseshoes. Let me see your ribs, son." Tim grabbed for the blankets.

Velma slapped his hands away. "No need. I just inspected them. I wrapped them right and tight, too. Right shoulder matches his back for color, too. Left one isn't quite so bad, but it's gotta hurt like the dickens. He's got a huge rope burn ring around his waist and left ankle, too. Far as I can tell, little Syd ain't budging for three, maybe four days."

"Four days! If it's that bad, I'll have Bert fetch Doc."

"Doc is a brainless leech. I know my stuff. You know that for a fact, as often as I've patched you back together."

"Hey, I admit, Doc's no prize—"

"You got that right. He near killed Slim Garner by rubbing goose grease and ashes on that nasty burn he had. Then, there's what he did to the Tyson kid. That boy's gonna have one leg shorter than the other because Doc didn't set it straight!"

"Dear saints," Sydney moaned.

"Yeah, but we can't let Fuller's nephew weaken."

"Fuller went to Abilene to get squared away. He wouldn't even let Doc see him! Leave Syd to me. Now get outta here. You make me nervous, what with the way you pace about."

Tim threw them a disgruntled look and headed for the door.

Sydney barely choked back a surprised yelp as he came back in.

"How's he breathing? When a broken rib pokes the lung, men go white like this."

"But his lips would turn blue. He's breathing good enough. Did you ever get that laudanum I told you to pick up in town?"

"Nope. The men prefer a stiff belt of whiskey."

"I swear, you men nigh unto drive me out of my mind! Now get!"

After his footsteps died out, Sydney whispered gratefully, "Thank you, Velma."

"I don't know if you ought to be thanking me. I'm not doing you any favors by leaving you to Tim and his man-making ways. Long as Tim thinks you're a boy, he's going to find ways to work you, and you're not strong enough to withstand much. Tim's going to expect you to bounce right back."

Tim got restless on the second day, and by the third, he propped his elbows on the dining table and stared at Sydney. One curt nod, then he pronounced, "You've got your color back. That means your breathing's fine. After breakfast—"

"After he's done eating, Sydney is going to rest." Velma glowered at Tim. "You said you'd abide by my advice, and now you're about to go off half-cocked and put the kid to heavy work. He'll be bedbound for a week—maybe more—if you try that stupid stunt!"

"One more day," Tim groused.

***

Tim watched Syd come downstairs. His eyes narrowed. The kid held the banister like a woman afraid of tripping over the hem of her ball gown. A few days lolling around, and the kid was back to being Fancy Pants again.

Fancy Pants paused for a brief moment. Strain flickered across his features.

Maybe Velma's not completely wrong. At least the kid handles pain like a man. Babying him would be an insult. "You're good enough to go on into town and pick up some supplies. Velma's got a list."

Syd bobbed his head.

"I don't care what Velma said about Little Lord Fauntleroy. Your hair looks girly. While you're in town, mosey over to the barber."

Immediately after breakfast, Sydney left for town. Velma stayed at the table and gave Tim a scowl. "Creighton, you're gonna live to regret how you're treating Syd. Mark my words, one of these days, none too far off, you're going to be one shamefaced devil."

"Velma, the kid had to grow up sometime. Little Lord Fancy Pants has come a long way, and you have to admit it. He's downright passable now—like a brother who grew out of being a pest and turned into a friend. Given more time, we'll have him trained well enough to take over Forsaken when Fuller and I kick the bucket."

"Yeah, if he doesn't kick the bucket first! I swear, I've practically gone gray watching how you've whipped him into shape. He's mucking stables, clearing fields, plowing, building a house—and then he yanked a little girl out of a well hole. Just you remember that he's busted his ribs and been drunk as a skunk, too. To my way of thinking, he's getting a far sight too much living crammed into two short weeks."

"It's been almost three weeks."

"Yeah, and I'll bet the kid thinks it's been an eternity."

"Give it up, Velma. He's having the time of his life. Fact is, he's pulling his fair weight. What more do you want?"

Velma huffed and walked off.

An hour and a half later, Tim squinted at the road. The kid hadn't gotten home yet. "Probably talking to some woman about flowers and sachets," he muttered.

Almost an hour more, and Tim started getting antsy. Velma didn't fuss and squawk without reason. If she was right, Syd might have put on a manly front and still been hurt enough to run into trouble. Tim headed toward town.

Forsaken's buckboard was parked by the saloon.

Filled with wrath, Tim pushed through the batwing doors. A few men stood at the bar, but Syd wasn't among them.

The tacky, worn strip of reddish carpeting leading up to the stairs didn't muffle the angry stomp of Tim's boots. Taking the stairs two and three at a time, Tim reached the second story. The stairs ended at the far side of the room where just a tiny landing gave way to a hall. He stormed around it.

Four doors lay wide open, the rooms empty. Three soiled doves and the madam were using the fifth room as a parlor. A cursory glance let Tim know Sydney wasn't there. He ignored the giggles and gasps, turned, and spied one last door. It was closed.

He heard a splash of water. "Syd!" He banged on the door.

Sydney didn't answer.

Tim banged on the door again. When the kid didn't respond, Tim threw the door open.

Syd's clothes lay on the floor along with a woman's unmentionables. Bubbles cascaded from the deep tub and surrounded the shoulders of a shampoo-frothed woman. She stared at him with enormous blue eyes.

Tim spun around and stayed in the open doorway. He crossed his arms. "Soon as the kid runs short on air and surfaces, I'll pull him out of here."

The madam stormed toward him while the chippies stared at him from the parlor. "Mister, get out of here."

"Just as soon as Syd crawls out of the tub."

A woman rounded the corner with an armful of towels.

"Syd, I—" She caught sight of Tim. The towels tumbled from her arms.

Anger at Syd and discomfort at being in such a place left Tim off-balance for a second. But something more was wrong. *Sydney should have come up for a breath by now. But he hasn't.*

He glared over his shoulder. Yep. Those were Syd's duds. Tim didn't intend to look at the woman. He just wanted to be sure Syd wasn't sneaking another breath. Then the girl's wide blue eyes jolted Tim.

Four doors. Four whores. All accounted for.

The stricken look on the face of the woman in the tub was all too familiar, too. His mood went as black and cold as a bank of thunderclouds as he bellowed, *"Syd!"*

Chapter Fourteen

Tim paced downstairs like a caged tiger. A hungry, caged tiger. Sydney could hear the sound of his boots ringing on the floorboards as he made another circuit around the saloon. Each step sounded like a muffled explosion of dynamite.

The last thing she wanted to do was go down the stairs. After all, the grand finale and the biggest detonation of that dynamite would occur as soon as she made an appearance.

"You look lovely, Lady Hathwell," Helene praised softly.

"Please, call me Sydney."

The madam smiled and shook her head. "That wouldn't do. You deserve to be treated in accordance with your station."

"I don't want that. Right about now, I need a friend more than anything else!" *And I just lost my best friend. Tim won't ever forgive me.*

"I'll accompany you downstairs."

"I don't know how I'll even make it back home. The man's angry enough to shoot me on sight." Remembering the power of his hands, she shivered. "Forget the gun. He'll tear me apart with his bare hands!"

"Now, Lady Sydney, don't carry on so. You're letting your imagination run off with you. He's mad, but he won't raise a hand to you. Tim Creighton has a sterling reputation. He might bellow like a bull, but he won't hurt you in the least."

Sydney took a slow, deep breath to steady herself. In the past, it had always worked. This time, it didn't. The sound of those angry steps grated on her nerves.

"Just one more stitch." Nella threaded the needle through the fabric of the dress Sydney wore. "You're too short for this dress, but tacking up the hem will get you through."

Helene smiled as she finished uncoiling Sydney's hair from the curling iron. The softly curled tresses caressed her nape and cheeks. A small, pale blue ribbon kept the weight of the hair off of her face and echoed the color of the demure, flowered dimity dress that one of the other girls had donated to the cause. The effect was spoiled the moment Sydney took a step, because she still wore her boots.

She looked at her reflection in a gilt-edged peer glass and tried to recall how it looked and felt to be a woman. The shapely woman who gazed back at her didn't appear familiar in the least. Including her traveling time, she'd been in britches for almost a month. With short hair and a borrowed dress, her reflection was completely unfamiliar. She tentatively ran her hand down the skirt, as if to convince herself that this was real.

Nella bobbed her head in approval. "You know, Lady Syd, you're right pretty all fancified. You must be a sight for sore eyes in a fancy ball gown."

"That feels like a lifetime ago."

Helene patted her hand. "Not really. Now that you're back in skirts, you'll slip back into your role as a woman. It's more than skin-deep. Even as a make-believe man, you had gracious manners and speech. All of the decent folk are going to be thrilled—you're high society."

Sydney gave her a hesitant smile. "Honestly, after all I'd

ever heard about . . . er, soiled doves, I must say something: You women have been kinder than most of the girls I knew in Londontown. I do hope that you'll still do me the honor of a friendship."

Tim's steps grew more emphatic.

Helene grimaced. "That's very sweet of you, but this is hardly the time to fret over such things. We'd do better to get you through the next day or so. I fear Tim Creighton's a man who shouldn't be crossed. His pride is going to be aching the minute he catches sight of you in a dress. He won't fathom how he was fooled into accepting you as a boy."

"It wasn't just him. Everyone else did, too!"

"I fear, dear, that he won't care about that. He's a man who stands on his own. You've duped him, and done quite a spectacular job of it, too. Take my advice and be as feminine as possible."

"Won't that make it worse?"

"Undoubtedly, but it is also your protection. He won't hurt you, no matter how livid he may be."

A low, rabid growl filtered up through the floorboards.

Helene fingered a tress into place. "He'll behave himself. It may kill him, but he'll behave."

"Thank you all for your help. I do suppose I cannot delay my Waterloo."

The madam patted her cheek and grinned. "The British won Waterloo, dear."

They descended the stairs, and Tim stomped closer as soon as he saw them. He planted himself at the bottom and glowered at Sydney's every single step. His voice dripped with sarcasm. "Lady Hathwell, I presume?"

She inclined her head with a regal bow.

He strode up the last two steps toward her, unceremoniously

grabbed her wrist, and started toward the door with her in tow.

Sydney dug the heels of her boots into the carpet runner. "Turn loose of me this instant!"

His eyes shot fire, and he continued to drag her along, completely disregarding the fact that they gathered several feet of carpeting since she stubbornly refused to lift her feet.

"I'm getting you out of here. Fuller'll never forgive me for letting his niece spend five minutes in a saloon or a cathouse!"

Sydney yanked free. "I've already spent far more than five minutes here!"

"Don't remind me." Without warning, he simply bent, plowed into her middle, and tilted her over his shoulder.

Sydney couldn't catch her breath. The saloon's batwing doors clattered wildly as Tim stormed through them and outside. "Put me down this instant!"

Tim dumped her onto the buckboard seat. He scrambled up next to her and flicked the reins.

Sydney turned toward him and opened her mouth.

"Don't get started, *woman*."

✦

"Don't say a word." Tim's jaw jutted forward at an impossible angle, and he kept his eyes straight ahead. He'd had some powerful fits of anger in his life, but he'd never come close to being half this livid.

How dare she come down, looking for all the world like some sweet, innocent girl who belonged at a church picnic? She was in a dress, for Pete's sake! *A dress!* It looked all airy and those short, puffed sleeves gave him a view of creamy skin.

She looked like a girl from every blessed angle. He felt like an absolute idiot for having missed out on something so obvious. Oh, the clues had been there, all right. He'd even commented on them. Her walk, her overblown modesty and smooth cheeks. The lack of height and muscle bulk, the squawks and emotions that simmered far too close to the surface. How could he have been so oblivious? So stupid? How could she have dared make a buffoon of him? The flames of anger burned higher.

A breeze made the perky blue ribbon in her hair flutter. That jaunty little final touch set his teeth on edge.

A blue ribbon—an award that indicated first place. And he'd been a first-rate fool. Here was living proof why he and Fuller agreed not to have women on the ranch. Inevitably, women got under your skin or into your heart—and left. Whether by choice or death didn't matter. Once forsaken, a man learned to shield his heart.

Only Sydney Hathwell's deceit got past that barrier. He'd treated her like a protégé—and this was the thanks he got: betrayal.

The buckboard rounded the corner, and they were out of the town's sight. Tim pivoted and locked eyes with the woman who bristled beside him. Her haughty look got under his skin. He needed to bring her down a peg or two, and he knew exactly how to do it. "Don't take on any aristocratic airs with me, Sydney Hathwell. You're nothing more than a liar."

She twisted away from him. Fearing she might jump, he filled his fist with cloth from her skirts. "Stay put! You're not going anywhere."

She squared her shoulders and gave him a cold glare. "I wouldn't give you the satisfaction."

He let go of her dress and wiped his palm on the thigh of his britches, as if doing so would take away the feel of that garment in his hands.

No matter what he did, it was a mistake. Grabbing her wrist

on the stairs had been a mistake. Without the benefit of a shirt cuff between her flesh and his palm, he'd clamped his hand around her soft, slender wrist and known momentary panic. Talking to her rankled—the pitch of her voice had gone from a crackling tenor to a distinct contralto. Even sitting near her and breathing vexed him because her hair now smelled of flowers.

He closed his eyes and moaned. He'd cut her hair. Yep, he'd done it, all right—lopped it real short with a knife in a single whack. Memories of how those several inches had the inclination to curl at the ends taunted him.

He felt her shift beside him. When her hip barely grazed his, she hurriedly pulled away. He felt burned by that fleeting contact. It irritated him that she acted as if the momentary and accidental touch soiled her ... until he remembered resting his hand on her backside. *"You walk funny ... start using your legs instead of your rear. ... Pull tight and don't let it swish from side to side."*

A thought slipped into his mind and left him breathless. He'd dumped Sydney headfirst into a crumbling well hole!

Embarrassment and horror gave way to anger again. He'd discussed things with her and in front of her that no woman ought to hear. *"I'm going to wear that fancy polish right off of you and strip you down until you finally figure out you're a bull, not a steer."*

By the time they got back to Forsaken, Tim was stewing mad. They'd both been utterly silent for the rest of the trip, and hostility crackled between them. He pulled the buckboard right up to the front of the house and reached up to grab her waist so he could set her down on the porch. She glanced over to the other side of the bench, visually measuring the possibility of getting down on her own, and he knew full well what she was going to do. Lunging, he clutched her waist and gritted, "Don't go making matters any worse than they already are."

"They couldn't get any worse."

"Hey, Boss! Who's the gal?" Pancake's boots made a soft, plopping sound as he sauntered over.

"I'm wondering that myself," Tim growled.

"Pretty lil' thing," Pancake announced as he came closer.

From the other side, Gulp paced by with an armload of firewood. He almost ran into them. "Oh, 'scuse me, miss." He gave Sydney a big smile, then suddenly dropped the logs. "Syd? Is that you? It can't be! It is! It's Syd!"

"Now there's no reason to go insulting the young lady," Merle chided him.

"Doggone it! Take a look. A close look. It's Syd, all right!"

All the men started to talk at once. Sydney wrapped her hands around Tim's wrists and squeezed hard. "Put me down."

Caught up in his anger, Tim hadn't paid attention to how he'd kept his hands clamped around her slender waist and left her dangling a foot off the ground. He still kept hold of her. "Enough, men. It's Sydney, all right."

"Can't be," Boaz declared. "Syd got drunk and spent the night in the bunkhouse." Boaz sucked in a loud breath. "I took her to a whorehouse! Oh. Begging your pardon, miss."

Tim wasn't sure whether Boaz was apologizing for his language or the place he'd taken Sydney. *What does it matter? Everything that's happened was wrong. All wrong.*

Merle cleared his throat. "We sent that girl headfirst down the well hole, too."

"We're all very aware of those facts," Tim bit out. "Lady Hathwell has been several places and done many things that were far and away beyond the scope of a woman's realm. As soon as she gives me an explanation, I'll have her give you her apologies. For now, get back to work."

As the men mumbled and walked off, Sydney trembled. "Mr. Creighton, you're hurting me."

"Not a chance, *woman*."

Sydney closed her eyes, but a tear slipped down her cheek.

"Stop that right now." His fingers tightened a bit more. "I've had more than enough of your acting. You're not going to use your tears to twist me around your dainty little finger. Hear me?"

Her voice came out in a tight, high shiver. "The rope burned my waist."

A wordless sound of frustration tore through his throat. Instead of setting her down, Tim swung her higher and slipped her into the basket of his arms. He stepped closer to the door and noted that she was doing her best to keep from weeping. He'd been mad and held her far too tightly. Truth be told, he even felt a bit of a cramp in his left hand from it. Doubtlessly, he'd hurt her, and that bothered him. Regardless of how livid he might be, Big Tim never held with a man hurting a woman. He softened his tone. "Calm down. I'll get you inside and have Velma take a look."

"I'll be fine. Please just set me down."

She looked far from fine. She'd gone pale as a winter moon, and the shimmer in her eyes accused him of having hurt her.

"I guess the cat's outta the bag." Velma bustled out of the parlor. "Tim, why are you carrying her?"

He glowered at her. It was bad enough he felt led on by Sydney's ruse; knowing Velma participated only compounded his sense of betrayal. "You knew?"

"Wasn't my business to interfere."

Tim nearly bellowed, "That never stopped you from anything else!"

Velma crossed her arms over her chest and stared straight back at him. "Anybody who bothered to take a minute and get a good look would've known she was a girl. Don't you dare think about blaming me for your own blindness."

"Please put me down."

"Hush," he rapped back at Sydney. He then frowned at Velma. "She's too young and empty-headed to have thought this through, but you should have known better."

"I take umbrage at that remark, sir!"

"I told you to hush. Velma, take her things back to the room with roses. You're gonna have to move into that room she's been sleeping in till Fuller gets back."

"Do stop acting as if I were some terrible burden!"

"I'm not acting. You *are* a terrible burden!" he retorted.

"What a perfectly rotten thing to say!"

Giving her a dark look, Tim bit out, "Leave it to a female to get her feelings hurt. I don't care about your feelings. I'm hauling you upstairs so Velma can check you out. After that, you're going to get your b—er, yourself back down into the study, and we're going to have us a discussion."

"I'm able to mount the stairs on my own."

"Yeah, but I don't trust you to obey orders." For all of his anger, Tim didn't give in to the temptation to dump her on the bed. He carefully balanced her in his arms. Once he stepped foot in the bedroom, he even turned a bit to the side to keep her feet from hitting the doorjamb. He lowered her gently until the bed took her full weight, then slid his hands out.

The housekeeper nudged him in an attempt to get him to leave the bedchamber. He planted his boots. "Take a good look at all of her. Every inch. Don't let her sweet talk you into disobeying, either. Let me know if I need to send for Doc."

"Doc? You're overreacting, Tim. Now scoot off downstairs. Lady Sydney will be with you shortly."

"One more thing before I leave here." He sidestepped to the foot of the bed. "I'm not taking any sass on this, either. I'm pulling off your left boot and getting a look at the rope marks on your ankle. It'll be in better shape than your waist, so I'll at least have a gauge as to how honest you're being with me."

Sydney scrabbled toward the head of the bed. "You'll do nothing of the sort! It's indecent!"

"Tim Creighton, don't you talk to her like that!"

"Aww, hush." He grabbed Sydney's boot and wrenched it off. Though the young woman struggled, he flipped her hem up and clamped hold long enough to get an eyeful of the way a snowy stocking hugged her dainty ankle.

"The boot leather protected me." Sydney wriggled and squirmed. Her efforts were to no avail.

Heaving a loud sigh, Velma stepped up and pulled off Sydney's stocking.

Tim scowled at her bare ankle. Lady Sydney Hathwell had the prettiest ankle he'd ever seen. She probably had it just to torment him.

"I'm no happier about this than you are." She desperately tried to cover herself up.

Tim kept hold of her foot and tentatively touched the angry red line around her ankle. "You're still marked. You didn't have leather to absorb the chafing from the rope that sustained both you and Emmy-Lou on the upward haul. That means you're marked a lot worse around your . . . um, middle."

Once he let go of her, Sydney rolled onto her side and curled into a tight ball.

"Are you hurting that bad?" Guilt mounted. He'd been a fool to have missed the cues about her masquerade, and he'd pushed her far beyond her endurance. He'd been nasty tempered and rough ever since he'd discovered the truth. Tim fought the urge to pick her up. He wasn't quite sure whether he'd rock her or toss her right out the window if he did.

"Get on outta here." Velma pushed him to the door. "I'll have her downstairs in a few shakes."

A moment later, Tim grabbed a steaming mug from the kitchen counter and took a swig of . . . "Tea." He dumped it down the sink. Sydney was just like that cup. Masquerading as something worthwhile, she'd proved to be nothing but a disappointment. As he watched the fluid slide down the drain, Tim knew Sydney wouldn't be half as easy to dispose of.

Sydney took a dresser scarf and used it as a shawl of sorts. She needed to find out if the emporium had ladies' garments. As of yet, she hadn't been to the one in town.

"The mercantile has just a few ladies' corsets and stockings. The rest we're gonna have to rig up," Velma said, as if she'd read Sydney's mind. "Won't much matter. You'll be inside with me from now on, so you'll have plenty of time to make whatever else you need. You do sew, don't you?"

She nodded her head. "I'd best go downstairs. Mr. Creighton is not a man to be kept waiting."

Velma cocked her head to the side. "So he's Mr. Creighton now, is he?"

"Circumstances have changed. I cannot be familiar."

Velma shook her head. "This is going to be a mess."

"Indeed." Sydney gathered her resolve and approached the stairs. Since they were indoors and her ankle was so sore, she opted to wear stockings and forego the boots. Slippers were definitely in order, so she mentally added footwear to the steadily growing list of items she needed to purchase.

The housekeeper gave her arm a squeeze. "I'll come along with you in there if you want."

"I think I'd best beard this lion on my own."

Velma pursed her lips. "If that's what you want, I'll abide by your wishes; but I'm going into the study first, just to make sure Big Tim isn't spitting fire."

"If he is, 'tis nothing more than I deserve."

Velma gave her a reassuring pat on the arm. "Give me five minutes."

Velma had barely shut the study door before she started shouting. Sydney could hear every word clearly.

"That little miss has hit her limit, Tim. Don't you dare upset her any more. She's plumb wore out. You dragged her all over the township, trying to make a man of her when all it would have taken was one good look to get the truth."

"No decent woman would—"

"Oh, she's as decent as they come. Brave, too."

He bellowed, "Don't mistake stupidity for courage!"

"You shoved that little lady straight down a well hole! And she's got the marks to prove your folly."

Sydney winced. Eavesdropping was wrong—but with them shouting at the top of their lungs, she couldn't help overhearing the argument. *But it's my fault. They wouldn't be fighting if I hadn't lived a lie.*

"No, Doc isn't going to see her! That quack's likely to kill her off with one of his patented salves."

An unintelligible reply left a momentary silence.

"I'm sending her in to have a talk with you, and it had better be just that—a talk. Don't you dare raise your voice at her. All of the rules have changed." The door opened. Velma stepped out. "Lady Hathwell, Mr. Creighton would like to see you."

Tim filled the doorway. "That's not the truth. I wish I'd never laid eyes on you, but since you're here, you owe me an explanation."

Sydney entered the study and took a seat. Minutes later, she found herself getting dizzy watching him pace circles around her chair. Even if she hadn't heard him roaring at Velma, Tim's emphatic gait pounded out proof of his anger. Sydney mentally braced herself for whatever might come next. Waiting for him to speak stretched her nerves taut.

Finally Tim stopped in front of her. His hands fisted at his sides. "You had no right to deceive me—us. You had no right at all to lead us to believe you were a boy."

"I had no choice."

"Of course you had a choice. Deception," he grated, "is purposeful. You obtained boy's clothing. I'll bet you even took on that boy's name. What's your real name? Cindy?"

Hume called me Cindy. You're not like him. Don't be like him. She faced Tim. "Sydney is a girl's name when spelled with a *Y*."

"That still doesn't explain the fact that you wore britches."

It took a sheer act of will to keep from twisting her hands in her lap. They'd always been white and soft and beautifully manicured until she came here. Now they were suntanned, scraped, and bore jagged nails. Her palms were full of healing blisters and pinpoint holes from a few dozen splinters, too.

"Well?" he demanded in a steely tone. Upon discovering her deceit, Tim withdrew his friendship. His glower could very well set the chair on fire.

Her relief to be free of the lie warred with the keen loss she felt. *Perhaps if he understood* ... "I knew Uncle Fuller believed I was a boy, so I presented myself as one. My only defense is that had I not, he would have fobbed me off on someone like—" Her voice skidded to a halt.

Tim's eyes narrowed. "Like who?"

"That is none of your affair."

He towered over her. "Girls from fancy families aren't

allowed to travel unescorted. You may as well come clean. It'll be simple enough for me to see to whom Fuller sent the telegram."

Sydney stared at the arm of the chair. The very edge of the upholstery was frayed, and she fought the urge to play with the threads. Seconds ticked by as she decided whether to tell him the humiliating facts regarding her recent foray into the marriage market. *What will happen if Mr. Hume finds out where I am?*

After taking a deep breath, she decided she had no choice. "I arrived in the States to consider marriage with someone. My title and connections interested the man; I did not."

Air hissed between Tim's teeth. He tilted her face to his and assessed her with his piercing gaze. "Let me get this straight: Your father sent you here to marry a money-grubbing social climber?"

His evaluation stung. She momentarily compressed her lips, then pulled away. "Father loved me. He sent me to decide if I could be happy with the man in question."

Tim *harrumpfed.*

"It's the truth. F-Father would have gladly let me return home." She sucked in a breath to steady herself. "He's passed on. Since I couldn't get home, I contacted Uncle Fuller. In his telegram, he said how pleased he was to have a nephew and that females are useless." She extended the telegram as proof of her assertion. "Being forthright about my gender would have left me in dire straits."

Tim scowled. His boot scuffed the hardwood floor as he stepped back from her. "Fuller wouldn't do that to kin. He'd far rather have a niece than a liar." He paused. "As it turns out, you're both."

"I confess, it was a ruse—but I perpetrated it only out of necessity!"

"Convenience, not necessity." He snatched the paper from her, wheeled about, and slapped it down on the desk without bothering to even glance at the contents.

"Oh, bosh! Speak to me of convenience! Uncle Fuller would rather leave me to fend for myself than allow me to live in a home with relatives because he can't stand women." Bitterness tainted her voice. "I put myself through Hades to keep up with your demands, and I did it just so I could have a family and a safe place to stay until I turned eighteen!"

As soon as the words were out of her mouth, Sydney pressed her fingers to her lips, dipped her head, and whispered thickly, "Please excuse me. That was unforgivable." She slid to the edge of the seat.

"Don't go yet."

Sydney shook her head. "I shouldn't have said anything. I have no right to burden you with such a private matter."

"If Fuller knew how desperate you were to come here, he'd allow you to, even if you are a girl."

She blinked away her tears and tilted her face up to his. "Mr. Creighton, I'm afraid I may offend you by saying so, but it seems to me you're not being completely honest."

Tim schooled his features so she couldn't see his reaction, but his eyes still gave him away. He heaved a sigh. "This is getting far more complicated than it ought to. Soon as Fuller returns, he'll decide what's in your best interest. I'll ask him to speak with you first so you can tell him how you feel."

"That is most kind of you."

"I'm not making any promises."

She nodded. "I'm quite aware of that fact. Women are not welcome at Forsaken. It would be foolish for me to presume my wishes would weigh heavily in the decision, since my uncle's preference is both longstanding and strong."

Tim stared at her. How had she managed to fool him by

wearing baggy boys' clothing? He must've been blind to miss such an hourglass shape! Curves like that were blatantly feminine.

The sun danced on all the curls in her hair, glossing the chestnut color. The tips of those cropped tresses had been subjected to a curling iron, he knew. The style was beguiling, even if it was terribly short for a woman.

She ventured away from the chair, toward the door. Tim closed his eyes at the sight. Those hips swayed, and the hem of her skirt shifted slightly from side to side, revealing slim, stockinged feet. That made her look half woman, half child.

He didn't want to deal with either half.

"There are many devices in a man's heart; nevertheless the counsel of the Lord, that shall stand." The proverb that he'd read that very morning ran through his mind. *Lord, I'm more than tempted to come up with a bunch of plans right about now. I don't understand what your purpose is in all of this. I'd appreciate a heap of your counsel real quick.* No great inspiration hit. Tim opened his eyes and wished something other than her feet would come into view. They were so small and vulnerable and . . . womanly.

"Velma can take you to town tomorrow to get some of the necessities. I don't think the mercantile carries ready-made gowns for women."

"I'm handy with a needle. Besides, it will give me something useful to do and keep me from beneath your feet."

"Fine. Maybe you could borrow something from the Richardson girls. I'm sure they must have whatever you need."

Sydney finally turned to look at him. "The Richardson girls?"

"Don't be choosy, Syd . . . ney. Sydney." Anger streaked through him yet again. He'd mind his tongue—a slip like that might make her think he was feeling friendly. Nothing was further from the truth.

"I'll be as social and polite as necessary, but I do implore you to remember those girls grate on one's nerves."

"There's a shortage of decent young women. Get along with them."

The corners of her mouth tightened. "I'll take care of my needs without troubling you."

"Good." Relief surged through him. He didn't have the faintest idea what she needed—didn't want to find out, either. He cleared his throat. "Velma can take you to town. Forsaken has an account, so you won't need to take ready money."

"Thank you." She paused for a heartbeat. "I cannot blame you for being angry. I'll do my best to stay out of your way."

"Fine."

"I do apologize, Mr. Creighton. And you were right—I owe the men my apologies as well."

"You're not to go out there unless I'm with you. I have something to see to here first."

"Very well. Let me know when you're ready." Sydney left the study, closing the door very quietly behind her. The scent of flowers lingered after her.

Fuller's telegram lay on the desk. Tim didn't care what it said. Sydney took advantage of a simple mistake. She'd lived a lie and made a fool of him. Just because she was an English lady, she thought she had the right to use other people to her advantage. *She did it to me. Well, no more.*

Chapter Fifteen

Juan whipped off his sombrero, and the other hands immediately yanked off their hats as well. Sydney fought the urge to wring her hands as she stood on the porch and faced them. "Gentlemen, I owe you all an apology."

"I shoulda helped you clear the stones from the field." Merle nervously tried to buff the toe of his right boot on the left calf of his jeans. Bowlegged as he was, it made him resemble a cricket.

Gulp's Adam's apple bobbed as he swallowed. "And some of them words I said round you—they wasn't fittin' for your ears."

"Mine, neither," Merle added. "I ain't proud at all of my cussin'."

Ruddy as could be, Bert rasped, "I shouldn'ta took you to the saloon or upstairs to—well, you know."

"Miss Hathwell dressed and acted like a man." Big Tim stood beside her and grated, "She has no room to complain about anything that happened."

"She hasn't complained." Pancake waggled his finger at Tim. "You know good and well she hasn't. Not even about you whacking off her hair."

"Or," Boaz shouted, "you tying her up and dropping her down that well hole."

"Headfirst!" Juan tacked on for good measure.

Horrified that her apology was turning into a hailstorm of accusations, Sydney raised her hand. The men all fell silent. "Gentlemen, I take full responsibility for all that has happened. No one—and I mean no one—is to blame but me. I put myself in this situation for selfish reasons and regret deceiving you. Please forgive me. I sincerely hope we can put it behind us and start afresh."

A rumble of pledges sounded.

Tim let out a deep sigh that, though silent, Sydney sensed with every fiber of her being. "We've wasted enough time. Work's waiting. Get to it."

Once the men left, Sydney turned to face him.

His expression was remote and his eyes icy. He didn't say a word; he just turned on his heel and strode off.

⸻

One place setting. The next morning, the breakfast table held only one place setting. Sydney let out a silent sigh and slipped into the seat. Velma bustled in. Sliding a plate in front of Sydney, she made a face. "Eat up. Fast. We're about to have visitors."

Sydney glanced at the clock. "At seven-thirty?"

Velma swished her hand at the plate in a rushed gesture. "Yeah. They waited till after breakfast and morning chores."

It felt odd to start eating without a prayer. Sydney searched for a memory of something appropriate. *For the gifts we are about to receive, we give thanks. Amen.*

Velma was already dashing back toward the kitchen. In the

weeks Sydney had been in Texas, she'd never seen Velma in a dither. That, more than anything, made an impression.

"You use tools when you shouldn't. . . ." Tim's words flashed through her mind as she reached for her fork. Sydney tore open her biscuit, slid the ham inside, and ignored the egg. Getting up from the table with her plate, she headed toward the kitchen, eating as she went. Dumping the egg into the swill bucket, she took in how Velma had already put a pot or kettle on each of the stove's burners.

"Shoulda known word would get out." Flour puffed into a small cloud as Velma dumped it into a large red-striped earthenware bowl.

"How do you know anyone's coming?"

"Dust. A horse doesn't make much 'less he's at a full gallop. Look out the window. Dust moving slower than that. Means a wagon. Since none of Forsaken's wagons is gone, it means the wagons are coming to us."

Sydney's eyes widened. "Three?"

"Four. One's hidden by that stand of trees."

A rueful laugh bubbled out of Sydney. "I have an odd suspicion they're not going to drop off calling cards so we know to visit them in the next little while."

"Well, we're going to make the best of it. Finish that food and dash upstairs. The bottom drawer of my bureau has a dress-length in it. Yellowish. Go fetch it."

Beggars couldn't be choosers. Yellow wasn't an appropriate color for someone in second mourning—but it was more proper than britches. Sydney complied with Velma's order.

The kitchen door banged. "Velma!"

Sydney found the fabric and, clutching it to herself, she crept to the head of the stairs. Eavesdropping wasn't right; then again, Tim's booming voice didn't indicate that he wanted privacy.

"Folks are coming. Women are okay—but no men. Got that? Not a one."

"Men ride a horse when they're going on a visit." Velma sounded calm as could be.

"Not when they want to court!" Something banged, as if to punctuate his frustration. "I knew this was going to happen. What a mess. I don't have the time or patience for this."

"Look out the window. It's just women and a baby or two."

"For now." Tim's voice vibrated with irritation. "Keep it that way." The door slammed shut.

Sydney let out a deep sigh and looked down at the material in her arms. This was the beginning of the end. Now that Tim knew she was a woman, he was going to grouse and growl over everything until he got rid of her.

In a little while, four wagons pulled up to Forsaken's front porch. Miriam Stauffer was the first one to arrive. She had little Emmy-Lou with her. She'd sewn two petticoats for Sydney, knowing the day would come when the truth came to light.

Mrs. Smith and the older woman for whom the cabin had been erected arrived next. Three children accompanied them. Emmy-Lou joined them on the porch, and they started playing.

Waving a magazine, Lena Patterson cheerfully announced, "I have April's *Peterson's Magazine*. We'll have to make Lady Hathwell a gown!"

Until now, Sydney had to meet and remember men's names. Now it was women. She made a quick mental connection—Lena Patterson with *Peterson's Magazine*. "How thoughtful. But please, just call me Sydney. I do hope we'll all become friends."

Velma grinned. "Sydney, you'll love these gals. Women hereabouts all pitch in and help one another."

Sydney gave a reply. It must have been acceptable, because the women were all smiling. *I'm going back to a woman's world. I've already slipped back into the manners and know the rules. But the time I spent as a man—I'm going to miss it! The challenges and the excitement and my time with Tim. No friendship ever meant as much to me as Tim's.*

"Well, here's Etta!" Velma brightened.

Sydney turned toward the woman in the doorway. "I've heard your baby is beautiful."

"Thank you." Etta allowed Velma to swipe the tiny, blanketed bundle from her. "If it weren't for Velma, I don't know how I would have managed. I need to go back out. I brought a bowl of my carrot-raisin salad."

"Nobody makes carrot-raisin salad like you, Etta." Velma cradled the baby. "Sydney even commented on it the day we built the cabin over at the Smiths'."

In Etta's absence, Velma turned to Lena. "I'm glad you brought that magazine. I bought that material over on the table, and we were going to make Sydney a dress today."

"That hue will look lovely on you. Any shade of yellow is the height of fashion this year. The color of that piece reminds me of goldenrod." Lena went over and lifted the fabric. "It'll drape beautifully. Let's decide on a style."

The magazine featured a fold-out. "I've not yet seen an American magazine. So Parisian styles are all the rage here. In England the fashions are going more toward plain or gored fronts to the skirts with ample draping over the bustles. Oh, look at this print—someone hand-tinted it quite elegantly."

"The carriage and walking dress—we could make that gown for you." Lena indicated that model. "Aren't the sleeves on it marvelous?"

Sydney gently took possession of the magazine and turned the pages toward the front. "Here we are!"

"But those are everyday dresses." They all eyed the three sketches.

"Precisely!" Sydney tapped the second one. "I especially like this one."

"A wash dress?!" Mrs. Smith sounded scandalized. "Besides, you'd need striped cloth in addition to the solid."

"Velma has a wonderful selection of feed sacks. Do you mind if we use a few, Velma?"

"Not a bit."

Mrs. Smith let out a nervous giggle. "You'd use feed sacks? A lady wearing something made of feed sacks like us commoners?"

Sydney smiled at her. "Each and every one of you are ladies. Furthermore, I find your gowns quite pretty."

By midmorning, a skirt from the amber material was sewn together. Etta sat off to the side to nurse her baby while Lena and Linda White matched the stripes as they pieced the jacket bodice.

Sydney started hemming the skirt. "That postillion back is the height of fashion, yet so practical."

Linda commented on how a few gathers or pleats yielded so much more ease to a garment.

Pants, dear ladies, were far more liberating.

"Gramma!" A child ran in through the open door. "A wagon is coming. It gots lotta ladies in it."

A few minutes later, Mrs. Richardson and her three eldest daughters rushed into the house. "It's true!" Katherine shrieked. "You are a girl!"

Marcella gawked at her. "I heard Big Tim was mad at you. If I ever told a lie like you did, Daddy would take a switch to me."

Linette shook her head. "You made a laughingstock out of Tim. He'll never forgive you."

Sydney swallowed hard. "We cannot make fools of others, only of ourselves. Mr. Creighton has proven to be both wise and kind. I, on the other hand, fear I've succeeded in making an utter fool of myself."

Linda White cleared her throat. Her eyes reflected confusion, not condemnation. "We were all wondering why you did it."

I didn't just fool Tim and the hands. I did it to everyone. "I owe everyone an apology. It started out as a misunderstanding. I telegraphed Uncle Fuller, and he thought I was a boy."

Velma wrapped her arm around Sydney's waist and squeezed. "Fuller wrote her and said he had no use for a girl. So there our Sydney was, stranded and alone in New York."

"You poor dear." The old woman for whom the cabin had been built pulled a hanky from her sleeve and dabbed at her eyes. "I know how hard it is. You lose someone, and you can't think straight."

Mrs. Smith took the old woman's hand in hers and gave it a tender stroke. "But you're with us now, and everything is working out fine. I'm sure Sydney will settle in, too, given a little time."

"While you're all helping her settle in, I'm going to go stir the soup and take the bread out of the oven before it burns," Velma said.

"We brought over cobbler." Mrs. Richardson slid a pan into Marcella's hands. "Didn't want to come empty-handed."

Sydney realized Mrs. Richardson didn't intend to be mean, though the Smiths couldn't possibly afford to have brought anything. She simply didn't think about what she said any more than her daughters did. "I'm sure we'll all enjoy it. Each of you brought something sweet today—the offer of your friendship. I'm deeply touched."

"My baby's blanket," Etta said from the corner, "was a gift from Linda. Every time I swaddle my daughter in it, I know Linda made it with love. I hope you'll think kindly of us whenever you wear this dress we're making."

"I'll be robed in your thoughtfulness." Sydney ran her hand over a small scrap. "Velma chose the perfect color. Friendship is golden."

Tim descended all five church steps by stepping only on the center board, strode over across the churchyard, and elbowed no less than three men out of the way before reaching Forsaken's wagon. A gaggle of women had invited themselves over for a sewing bee yesterday, and he knew they'd stitched up a gown for Sydney—but until that moment, Tim hadn't known exactly what they'd accomplished. His jaw tightened as he reached to help her alight from the conveyance. Illuminated by the bright morning sun, the woman resembled a golden statue.

He'd quelled concerns about coming to church early to see to things, but he refused to compromise his commitments. He hadn't dropped his standards when Syd was a "boy," and he sure wasn't going to now that she'd revealed her duplicity. In one aspect, gender didn't matter: As a boy or a girl, Sydney had to change to fit in at Forsaken. But then things took a savage twist. As a woman, she posed a whole new, bigger set of problems now—and the proof surrounded him in the form of a pack of men gawking at her.

"Miss Sydney," Orville Clark proclaimed, "you're a sight to behold."

"It's Lady Hathwell. You have no right to be so familiar, Clark." Jim Whitsley poked out his elbow to offer Sydney his arm. "I'll be happy to escort you to worship."

Tim yanked Sydney away from them and rested his hands on her shoulders. The minute he did so, he knew he'd made a mistake. New fabric ought to be stiff and a tad bit scratchy. Well, her dress was, and it probably itched. The bubble-covered shoulders he'd seen in that bathtub were milky white and undoubtedly sensitive. With her habit of causing trouble, she'd probably end up rashy.

"What's wrong?" Nestor wondered aloud.

Tim's hold on Sydney tightened. "This young woman is young." *Great. I'm making a fool of myself.* "By that, I mean she's still a minor and Fuller's kin. By all rights, any matters pertaining to her go through him. Until he gets home, Forsaken—and Lady Hathwell—are off-limits to all the bachelors."

More than a few men moaned. Jim Whitsley looked outraged. "Nothing awrong with being sociable."

"There's nothing wrong with giving Fuller the courtesy and respect he's earned," Tim shot back. "That's the way it's going to be." He motioned to Velma, who bustled over and stood on Sydney's other side. They escorted her into the sanctuary, and Tim made sure they sandwiched Sydney between them.

Sydney folded her gloved hands in the lap of her new gown and looked straight ahead. At some point—Tim couldn't imagine when—she'd managed to locate a little straw hat. Flowers made from the same yellowish material from her dress and a cream-colored ribbon decorated the affair. She looked every inch the demure lady.

And he'd been fool enough to believe she was a boy.

Parson Bradle's eldest son slipped into the pew in front of them and turned. "Miss—I mean, Lady Hathwell, Ma—she said to invite you to Sunday supper. We'd all be glad to have you."

He looks at Sydney like she's what's for lunch. Tim glared at him.

Sydney gave her head a small, definitive shake. "Thank you for your kindness, but I cannot. As Mr. Creighton has said, it's only proper my uncle be consulted."

Well, at least she had the good sense to follow suit.

Mouth opening and shutting like a dying trout, Bradle went beet red. "Velma, you and Tim could come, too."

"No, thanks." Tim locked eyes with him. "Velma already has Sunday supper all planned."

Monday at lunch, Velma stuck one plate—albeit heaping—on the table in front of Tim. Sunday dinner was the only meal he and Sydney had shared since he'd discovered the truth. Velma's cooking tasted great, but the crackling silence at the Sunday table yesterday made it clear everything was out of kilter. Today wasn't going any more smoothly. In two short days, Sydney had turned Forsaken upside down.

He rubbed his knuckles along the edge of the snowy linen tablecloth. "What's this doing out?"

Velma cocked a brow and said nothing.

"You prize this. It only comes out for special occasions like Christmas."

"What good does it do, moldering away in a cabinet?" Velma smoothed out an invisible wrinkle. "Irish linen. You have to admit, it's mighty fine looking."

"Too good for everyday," he muttered.

"Since when did you care about how the house looked?" Velma moved an arrangement of flowers over a few inches, then scooted it straight back to where it had been in the center of the table. It wasn't just a fistful of blooms jammed into a jar. Three different kinds of green stuff wiggled and stuck out around a variety of flowers that were all varying shades of blue. Nothing other than blue. In a crystal vase. Tim hadn't ever seen the vase before.

Syd had gone all girly on him. Every last fussy frill festered—no matter where he looked, something reminded him of his foolishness and her betrayal. He refused to ask Velma where Sydney was.

"While we were at the mercantile, Sydney heard that the parson and his wife are both feeling puny. We paid a mercy call."

Tim raked his fingers through his hair. Sydney was about the same size as Louisa. This was exactly why he didn't want a woman around. They were too fragile. "Why take her somewhere she could get sick? What if it's the cholera or typhus or—"

"Nah. Parson's back has a kink in it again, and his missus got hornet-stung, so she's itching something awful. Sydney offered to stay and help out."

"She's more likely to set their house afire."

Velma shot him a murderous look.

"Fine," Tim huffed. "Maybe while Sydney's there, they can calm her down a notch or two. The woman is as touchy as a ready-to-foal mare."

"You're the antsy one."

Tim scowled at her. This whole thing was a mess. Friday, he'd gone back to town and sent Fuller a telegram. Wording it had been tricky. He didn't want the whole nation knowing he'd been duped, so he'd settled on an informative directive: *Your niece, Sydney, needs to meet with you.*

Saturday, no reply. The telegraph office was closed on Sunday. *Today. Today I'll hear from Fuller. He'll hightail it home now. He has to!*

But the day passed without any contact.

Velma's mood hadn't improved at all when he sat down to the supper table that night. She slid a plate in front of him and headed back toward the kitchen.

He felt utterly ridiculous, sitting at a flower-decked, linen-covered table all by himself. "Where's Sydney?"

"She's spending the night over at the parsonage. Ella Mae's broken out in the worst case of hives imaginable, and Parson Bradle can't help her. As for their sons—well," she sniffed, "they're as useless as horns on a hound."

A wave of anger swamped him. "You mean to tell me you left Sydney in that household, overnight, knowing they have three full-grown sons?"

"All three are mighty fine-looking bucks"—Velma nodded—"but Sydney didn't seem to take much notice. She was busy reading aloud to the parson and putting baking soda compresses on Ella Mae."

"Do you think I care if Sydney noticed those boys? No!" He shoved away from his untouched meal and rose. "I care if *they* noticed *her*, and I can tell you here and now, every last one did. Fuller'll skin me alive if any of them lays a finger on her."

"Land o' Goshen, Tim, she's in the parsonage! Only place safer would be the church!"

"I'm going to go get her."

Velma planted herself squarely in his path and stared him in the eye. "No, you're not. It takes a fair bit to rile me, but you've succeeded, Tim Creighton. You're a fine one to talk about how anyone else treats that gal. Those boys are treating her like she's every bit as special as she really, truly is. You tromp in there, breathing fire, and they'll wonder why you're so overprotective."

"I don't care what they think!"

"Perhaps you ought to. You've kept to yourself too much,

too long. You stopped caring about everything when your wife died. Folks cut you plenty of slack, but time's come for you to move on." She put up a hand to silence the protest that had him opening his mouth. "You may not want to admit it, but truth's the truth. The minute you go thundering around and kick up a fuss about little Sydney, it'll make folks sit up and take notice. They'll think you're claimin' her as your very own."

He froze. "Oh no! Now you just wait a minute!"

"No, you wait a minute. You stop and think, and you'll know I'm right. 'Sides, this buys you some time. I know you sent Fuller a telegram. I'll wait till afternoon tomorrow to go fetch her back, and by then maybe you'll have a reply."

***

"Of course I can do it." Sydney took the sheets from Mrs. Bradle. "Would you care for a cup of fresh-brewed chamomile tea? It promotes rest, you know."

A tired smile flitted across the parson's wife's face. "I doubt I need it. I'm so exhausted, I could sleep through the Second Coming."

"If you and the reverend need anything, don't hesitate to summon me."

"You're a dear. Good night."

Sydney opened the door to the other bedchamber. The Bradles' sons were sleeping elsewhere tonight so she'd have a bed. If she'd ever had brothers, Sydney knew they would have been just like the Bradle boys. The three of them were just over a year apart, stacked in size just like porch steps. They all washed up and combed their hair neatly before sitting down to the supper table. Sydney recognized the "best behavior" look on their faces—she'd worn it herself more times than she could count.

Sydney stripped the linen off the center bed and lifted a crisply folded sheet. For the first time ever she set about changing the sheets on a bed. She managed to bungle the job; the mattress kept slipping when she lifted it to tuck the sheet underneath. The sheets wanted to migrate anywhere other than where she intended them to stay, and she had no idea how to make the corners lie flat at the precise angles they did when her chambermaid back home saw to the matter.

A giggle welled up inside her. *I'll strip the bed at daybreak so no one will ever see what a terrible job I've done.* Sydney crawled into bed wearing a borrowed nightgown and lay there for all of a minute before she felt a wrinkle beneath her shoulders. She squirmed, and the wrinkle seemed to widen like the Thames until it ceased irritating her upper arm ... and started feeling like a bale of barbed wire beneath her hip. "Princess and the Pea, my foot." She crept from the bed and gave the sheet an impatient jerk. The wrinkle almost disappeared before her eyes. Delighted with that discovery, she gripped it more firmly and gave it another tug. The feather mattress came sliding off the rope straps and fell around her knees.

By the time she hauled the mattress back up, Sydney came to a firm decision. She'd been a fool when she thought cooking and cleaning and all of the other myriad domestic chores were far less physically demanding than ranch work! She swept the sheet toga-styled around herself and fell onto the mattress. *Tim thought I made for a pitiful man, and he was right. But I'm no better at being a woman.*

Tim was rubbing bag balm on a cow's udder when Velma

walked out to the fence. She waved a piece of paper and called out, "Fuller responded!"

"It's about time," he groused as he stood and wiped his fingers off on his pant leg as he strode over to meet her. "What did he say?"

Velma made no pretense at having left the contents private. "It's hard to tell what he thinks."

Her words didn't exactly encourage him. Tim had hoped it was a simple notice of, "I'm on my way." Obviously, it wasn't. His molars grated back and forth.

"Here." Velma handed him a bucket first.

Tim accepted it and drank from the dipper. "Is this your way of trying to cool my temper?"

"No call for you to be in a temper, but if you were, there's not enough water in all of Texas to do the job."

He drank more and said in a wry tone, "There's not much water, period. We'll have to drill." He set down the bucket, took the telegram, and unfolded the paper. *Take good care of Sydney for me. Treatment promising. Need to stay here longer.*

His hand fisted, crumpling the telegram into a small ball.

"Now, Tim. It's not half as bad as you're making it out to be."

His eyes shot fire at her. "It's worse!"

"Aw, stop whining. Sydney's a sweet gal. She doesn't have a mean bone in her body."

"Don't mention her body!" He took off his hat and smacked it against his thigh. "Likely every randy cowhand in the territory is already lusting after her, and Fuller expects me to chase 'em all off!"

Velma poked out her lower lip, then sucked it in, raked it between her teeth, and stared at him for a long, uncomfortable interval. "Seems to me you're mighty antsy about it. No reason to be. Just keep her here and don't allow any visitors till Fuller gets back to deal with her. That announcement you made in the churchyard put all the men on notice." She let out an irritating laugh. "If your words didn't scare them off, your scowl should have."

"There's a world of difference between what should happen and what does. All I have to do is turn my back for one minute, and some yahoo can try to sneak by. It's not neighborly for me to break an arm, but I'll do it if I have to."

"Now, Tim—"

"Don't you 'Now, Tim' me!" He kicked a small stone in frustration. "Orville Clark took a mind to suddenly come deliver supplies this morning. He's never left his mercantile and brought stuff out to Forsaken. Never. Not once. He thought I wouldn't know you'd just stocked up on flour and sugar."

Velma had the nerve to shrug. "Could always use more."

Tim stared at her. "I sent him back to town with his wagon fully loaded. Velma, I'm counting on you to back me up."

"I will, I will. Besides, all the hands here will help out. Forsaken's men think she's cuter'n a bug's ear, but they treat her like a cross between a fairy princess and a baby sister, so you don't have to worry about them."

Thoroughly disgruntled, he muttered, "The only thing worse than this would be the herd getting anthrax."

Velma pried the telegram from his hand and stuffed it deep into the pocket of her apron. "When do you plan to go get her?"

"I'm sorely tempted to leave her at the parsonage!"

"You're a man of duty and honor, Tim. We both know it."

He sighed and squinted off into the distance. "Nothing like being condemned with a word of praise."

Sydney made egg salad sandwiches for dinner and fretted over which seasonings to add. Ella Mae, mostly recovered from her hives, sat down and gave her suggestions. The meal went well, and Sydney was basking in the praises when Tim arrived to take her home. All three of the Bradle boys lined up by the front door alongside their mama to tell her good-bye. After Ella Mae's embrace, it became apparent the young men planned to follow suit. The first one barely got his arms about her. Tim dragged her back, interposed himself, and growled, "Sorry we can't spend time socializing. See you all at church."

The eldest son shoved his hand out, shook Tim's hand, and nodded. "Thanks for letting her come. Ma and Pa appreciated the help. Speaking of help ... you gonna need some help with roundup this year?"

Tim gave a noncommittal response, then had her in the buckboard before she could blink. As they pulled down the road, she turned and arched a brow. "I can't believe he thanked you for letting me help, as though I were your chattel or child!"

Tim didn't bother to look at her. He studied the horse's rump with great interest. "You'd best get used to it. Until Fuller gets home, I'm in charge of you."

Sydney started to laugh. Her laughter died out immediately. "You cannot be serious! I make my own decisions."

"Then decide to behave yourself. This doesn't thrill me any more than it does you. I got a telegram from Fuller."

She sucked in a quick breath. "When is he coming home?"

"Didn't say. His treatments for the rheumatiz are helping, so he's staying in Abilene for a while yet. In the meantime, he specifically put you in my care." Tim finally turned to face her.

His gaze held hers as he bit off each word. "And yes, he knows you're a girl."

Her chin lifted. "Being a girl is no crime."

A wry smile twisted his lips. "That's a matter of opinion. Still, you're staying put till he comes back, so you may as well resign yourself to it. I have."

"How very noble of you."

Unwilling to let her have the last word, Tim nodded. "Nobility isn't necessarily passed on in a family line. It's cultivated in the heart and mind by men who choose right when wrong would be much easier."

"That is character, not nobility."

"Sydney, from what I can see, most nobles don't have character, they *are* characters."

Try as she might, she couldn't help it. Sydney started to giggle. It made her wonder about herself. Three months ago, his words would have appalled and offended her; now they amused her to no end. "You Americans are an irreverent lot."

"I'll take honesty over pretensions any day."

His barbed words made her breath hitch. She'd earned his wrath. "Clearly, you aren't a man to pretend."

Tim's features shifted. His eyes narrowed.

"For whatever it's worth, you have my word that I won't deceive you or anyone else again. I deeply regret having done so. You've been nothing but honorable. More than any skill you tried to teach me, that is what I've learned most from you."

He didn't reply.

I can't expect him to smile and say all is forgotten. I'm going to have to prove myself all over again.

When they got home, he lifted her down from the buckboard. Velma stepped out on the porch. "Jeb Richardson stopped by while you were gone. Said he'd like to go ahead with that deal you discussed regarding the bull."

"Fine."

"He brought along an apple pie one of his girls made."

Sydney watched as Tim spun back around. The man virtually slobbered. "Pie?"

Velma nodded. "Apple. Your favorite."

"Why didn't you say so earlier?" He sped past them and headed for the kitchen.

The housekeeper grabbed Sydney's arm. "You'd best hurry on in here and claim a wedge, else that man'll eat the whole pie in five minutes flat. Never saw a man half as crazed about apple sweets as him. I swear, he goes weak in the knees whenever there's any to be had."

"But you rarely bake sweets."

"Fuller can't eat them. Says they make him feel crazier than a bronco." Velma patted her own belly. "I don't need to get any fatter, and I won't bother to spend hours baking something Big Tim wolfs down in nothing flat."

"Perhaps I should ask Linette to teach me how to make an apple pie."

Velma cast her a sideways glance. "You starting to go sweet on Big Tim?"

Sydney's face went hot, and she hid behind the multipurpose phrase Mama had taught her to use in such situations: "Oh, merciful heavens!"

"Just checking. He'd be an easy man for a young gal to love. You'd go a lifetime before you found a better man."

"Tim's made it abundantly clear he matches my uncle in not wanting to take a wife. I don't know what my future holds . . . but it won't be here."

Chapter Sixteen

"How can you be so sure she's not in England?" Hume glowered at Tyler. "Did you interview the crew and ascertain that her cabin remained empty for the entirety of the voyage?"

"It was occupied." Tyler held up a hand. "In point of fact, a Lady Hathwell occupied the quarters. What you failed to mention was that Lady *Serena* Hathwell accompanied her niece, Sydney, to America."

"That squatty old woman was a relative?"

Tyler gave no response.

Hume turned to stare out the window. Travel arrangements and accommodations were customarily made in the lady's name, not in the servant's or chaperone's. By seeing S. Hathwell on the passenger list and assuming it was Sydney, they'd lost invaluable time. He'd made several costly miscalculations in this entire affair. His mouth twisted wryly. *I failed to address her by her correct name—why would I have recognized her servant was actually her aunt?*

Even so, that was no excuse for Lady Sydney to flit off in a pique. Family honor and a well-deserved sense of obligation ought to have been more than sufficient motive for her to overcome whatever petty annoyances or misgivings she'd had. This whole affair had gone too far and lasted too long. His bride-to-be was proving to be more of a headache than all of the paper work spread across his desk. Logic. Numbers. Facts—those, he handled with finesse. How could one young woman create such disorder in his life?

"Since the aunt knew Lady Sydney best, I traced her steps. It appears she specializes in chaperoning young ladies of good families and marrying them off. Immediately after disembarking, she went to the Ashton home in London. At present, she's got her hands full with launching their twins. The old woman's thrown herself into the task with notable zeal. In my limited time there, she took the girls to any number of supper parties, soirees, and the like. A string of bachelors pay calls on the girls in the morning, and Lady Serena often accompanies the couples on carriage rides and picnics."

"With all that going on, how can you be certain you didn't miss something? My bride could well be there or somewhere close by."

Tyler inclined his head. "With the volume of notes, callers, visitations, fetes, and telegrams, that possibility occurred to me. On the chance that it might be so, I bribed one of the servants to alert me if Lady Serena sent or received any missives, telegrams, and the like."

"Rather unreliable, don't you think?"

"It seems the Ashtons are less than generous with their staff. A modest bribe with the promise of thrice as much for any information works wonders."

"Not," Hume said in a low tone, "in this case."

"At least, not yet. Your insistence that I not inform the lady's family of her disappearance significantly reduced my ability to gather information. Are you willing to reconsider?"

"No. Not yet." Hume strove to control his frustration.

"There's the possibility Sydney's in England and simply hiding away."

Tyler shook his head. "Not likely. I managed to get into the estate and found my way to her chamber. The lady's a woman of detail. She kept a book in which all of her friends' and relations' birthdays and anniversaries were listed. I tracked down each individual and ascertained—with great tact, I assure you—that Lady Sydney was not in their keeping."

Hume rubbed his temples. "What about other properties her family might own?"

"There are none. As you're undoubtedly aware, the family's finances have become . . . unstable. The country estate was sold several months ago. The family now in residence there boasts nine children, and every last room is in use."

Tyler's thoroughness, though noteworthy, proved also to be irritating. Hume had hoped that he would locate Lady Sydney and drag her back. For a seventeen-year-old girl to manage to carry on this escapade for a prolonged period of time was more than a mere inconvenience. Hume's business and reputation hung in the balance.

"As it appears she's not in England, we must concentrate on any other possible destination. During the time you spent together, did Lady Hathwell express interest in any place in particular?"

Rex had gone over it in his mind a dozen times a day. She'd arrived at an awkward time, and many business obligations couldn't be rescheduled. He didn't realize how scant their time together had been until he scoured his mind to pick up the faintest hint as to where she'd gone. How very odd, that she'd left the book containing her friends' and relations' personal information back in England. That certainly indicated she'd not taken her commitment to wedding him as seriously as she ought.

Then again, perhaps that was her way of making a break from her old life and a sign that she'd been willing to cut ties and start anew. Well, as soon as he got her back, he'd see to it that she got a pretty little book in which to keep track of all his associates' wives. As many as there were, she'd have plenty to keep her busy. Yes, and it would also be good for business. English aristocracy still held a certain cachet, and his standing in the community would go up with every little note she penned or call she paid. A dutiful wife and helpmeet would be more than willing to do such things on her husband's behalf.

"You're thinking." Tyler nodded approvingly. "So what did Lady Sydney like doing?"

Hume cleared his throat. "I'm given to understand she enjoyed shopping."

"For any specific item? Does she have a hobby or a passion for anything?"

"Not that she mentioned." One of the suppers they'd shared was after she'd spent a day shopping. He hadn't asked her what she'd bought. After all, it would have been indelicate. A bride-to-be's purchases just days before the wedding had to be of the more intimate nature. Hume cleared his throat. "I presumed she was attending to last-minute personal items. You can ask my housekeeper if Lady Sydney purchased anything that might give us a lead."

Tyler's features remained impassive, but his voice took on an almost lazy air. "The intermediary who assisted with the arrangements—was he a personal friend of yours, or someone with whom she might have plotted?"

Hume let out a mirthless laugh. "He's the friend of a friend. Mine was to be the third such marriage he'd coordinated. The other two were situations in which the lady's family required a large infusion of cash. I, on the other hand, stipulated I'd rather her family be solvent. It would indicate their connections would be more advantageous once the marriage took place and business deals could be brokered."

His jaw thrusting forward, Tyler demanded, "Just how much are we talking about? Enough for her to—"

"No." Hume's mouth twisted. "Things change. The cousin who inherited the title managed to squander just about everything. I assure you, after paying for that return voyage, Lady Hathwell didn't have enough to survive on her own for even a fraction of this time."

"You led me to believe Harold and Beatrice Hathwell were Lady Sydney's only relatives. You knew nothing of the aunt. Could there be others?"

"In your absence, I had the intermediary prepare a dossier. Before now, for the sake of privacy, I'd shunned committing anything to print. Discretion is relative, if you will forgive the pun. I've found that perfectly legitimate deals of the most sensitive nature, when put in print, can somehow be misread to take on an unsavory tone. Upon receiving your telegram, I admitted to myself that I had no choice but to gather all of this in order to expedite the continued search." He handed over the charcoal-colored folder. Why, though, he didn't know. He'd pored over it countless times and hadn't found a single clue.

Tyler tilted his head toward a table by the window.

Hume gestured toward it. As Tyler worked, Hume got back to his own business. It was already suffering from his bride's benighted escapade. It wasn't simply a matter of time and attention that had been compromised—certain connections could not be made, specific affiliations wouldn't be forged until Lady Sydney wore his wedding band. Time was money, and many of the deals could not wait indefinitely.

Fingers drumming on the tabletop all of ten minutes later, Tyler demanded, "What do you know of her mother's lineage?"

Hume froze. Title—and therefore the vital business links—followed the paternal line. He'd studied all of the financial records, detailed holdings, and countless other matters and neglected something appallingly simple. Facing an unpalatable fact head-on was better than pussyfooting around it. Especially in this situation. This might well be the key to finding Cindy—*Sydney,* he corrected himself. He turned to face Tyler. "Nothing. I know absolutely nothing of her mother than her name. Crystal."

Already on his feet, Tyler had one arm in the sleeve of his coat. *"Debrett's."* A smug smile slashed across his face. *"Debrett's Peerage* will list her father's name, title, and where he lives."

"Her father's?"

Tyler nodded. "Where's the nearest library?"

Hume leapt up. "Not far." Hope flared for the first time in days as he entered the library alongside Tyler. They located the book and Tyler flipped through several pages, then stabbed his blunt finger on an entry and read in a hushed tone, "Sir Herbert Eustache Hathwell. Duke of ... Eton ... Cambr—here! Married to Crystal Avery Johnson, daughter of Robert Johnson, Esq. *Chicago, Illinois ...*"

Tyler snapped the book shut. "American. She was American!"

Hume pulled out a stack of perfectly folded bills and shoved them into the investigator's hand as he yanked the book away. "Go. Find her."

Chapter Seventeen

Ever since her true identity had been revealed, Sydney's time had been filled, but the initial social whirl abated. She woke and wanted to be useful. *Needed* to be useful. Fuller and Tim didn't think there was a place for a woman on Forsaken. Well, if all she did was act like a wilting violet, she'd confirm that opinion. She wanted to stay here; she still had to prove herself. Donning her everyday gown, she headed out to the stable. Tim considered her a liability; she'd prove otherwise. She'd learned to pitch in, and it felt wrong to do nothing other than arrange flowers, sew, and pay mercy calls.

"What"—Tim's voice vibrated with anger—"do you think you are doing?"

Sydney didn't turn around. Fingers gripping the shovel tight, she continued to muck the first stall. "It's plain to see what I'm doing."

"You're not doing this." He yanked on the handle.

Sydney didn't turn loose. "I can still pull my weight around here."

Merle moseyed over. "Boss, tug o' war is done with a rope."

"So is a hanging," Tim snapped. He gave the shovel a jerk that nearly pulled her off her feet.

Merle let out a low whistle and made himself scarce.

Tim glowered at her. "You've already stirred up enough trouble around here. You apologized for what you did. Part of an apology is meaning that you won't cross the line again."

She still didn't let go. "Mr. Creighton, I apologized for misrepresenting myself, not for having done any work."

"You worked as a man. Don't come out here and think you can do whatever you please as long as you're in a skirt. Man's work is a man's. Now go back inside."

Slowly, Sydney uncurled her fingers and turned loose. "I meant no offense, Mr. Creighton. I simply wanted to help."

He heaved a sigh. "Velma can find something to keep you busy."

Sydney nodded and left. She'd made a bad miscalculation, thinking to meet him on his turf and continue on as if nothing had changed. All it did was vex him more. As desperately as she wanted to stay, she'd have to approach the problem a different way. Sydney stopped by the henhouse and gathered eggs before going back to the house. Even if Big Tim didn't want her working as she once had, she'd find ways of helping out.

They lived with a tentative peace for the next few days. Sydney busied herself with sewing. She'd always loved taking strolls, and the weather lent itself to her spending time outdoors. She'd taken a walk each afternoon, and Tim didn't object. Each time she went out, she found more about the land to admire. She'd go a different direction, find a new vista, and had determined to buy a sketchbook and pastels the next time she went to town. Though she couldn't paint well at all, she enjoyed drawing and could do a passable job when inspired. Forsaken lent itself to such emotions.

Friday, Sydney woke early. She dressed and decided to go out for a dawn constitutional. As she descended the stairs, she sighed. The cowboy boots Tim bought her were far more comfortable than the spool-heeled, kidskin ankle-high lady's boots she now wore.

Once out of the house, she aimlessly wandered down the road. The birds warbled praise for the sunrise. Sydney glanced about, knew no one could hear her, and tried to whistle. No lady would ever attempt anything quite so vulgar, but she couldn't help herself. There was something about the wilds of America that tempted a body to break free of strictures and restraints. Indeed, the energy she felt led her to break into a skipping pace that took her down the road until she had to slow to catch her breath. Other than her weeks posing as a boy, she'd never behaved in such a hoydenish manner.

The springtime green had fallen victim to summer heat. In a matter of one week, the Texas landscape had changed dramatically. Knowing the only place she might find flowers would be in the field by the pond, she headed that direction.

A bit farther down the road, she climbed over the fence and toward the pond. Busy enjoying the sights instead of watching where she stepped, her heel sank in a puddle of mud. She tried to tug free, but to no avail. After fumbling with the buttons, she got her foot out of her boot. Once liberated, she was able to twist the boot to pull it loose. Sydney stood in the middle of the road, studied her boot, and laughed. Since she didn't have a buttonhook with her, there was no way for her to fasten it back on!

One thing led to another. It made absolutely no sense to hobble about only half shod, so she divested herself of the other shoe and stockings. She'd never been barefoot outside. The grass felt like wet velvet, yet it tickled. Her toes curled at the icy feel, yet her shivers were of delight.

She bent down, wiped her boot on the grass to clean it, then had to smear her hands back and forth to tidy them, too.

"Oh, am I ever a sight!" she laughed. "Aunt Serena would have apoplexy if she saw me now!" The rigid rules of high society seemed so very far away. Glorying in the moment, Sydney started to pick wildflowers. She stuffed them into her boots until they were both filled with a profusion of Texas blooms.

Tim frowned at Velma. "Where is she?"

"I don't know. I just woke up. Sun's barely even broken the horizon."

"You check the outhouse and kitchen. I'll go look in the henhouse. So help me, if she went to the stable . . ." He paced off and yelled, "Sydney!" The young woman didn't respond, so he increased his volume. Still, she didn't materialize.

Velma and he met up again. "Tim, I checked her chamber. She didn't pack or take anything. The window is shut. Her blue dress is missing."

His heart thundered like a locomotive. "Where could she be?"

"Saints above, I don't know."

"Fuller trusted me with her!"

Velma rubbed the back of her neck. "Her boots are missing and her nightdress is up there, so she dressed herself."

Tim glowered at her and shook his finger. "So help me, if she ran off with one of Parson Bradle's sons, I'm going to do something rash!"

"Oh, stop worrying over that. Likely it's nothing of the sort. We'll find her. You saddle up and get going. I'll rouse the bunkhouse."

Tim wasn't sure what to think. Had someone kidnapped her? Had she run away? Worry ate at him. He didn't bother to saddle up. He simply slipped a halter on Hombre and mounted bareback. If Sydney was in trouble, she needed help now.

Men tumbled out of the bunkhouse. "Gulp, you and Juan go west. Merle and Pancake—go east. Burt and Boaz—north. I'm heading south. Keep an eye out, fire three shots if you need help. Two if you find her and she's fine."

He set out, scanning every nook and peering around trees. None of the grass was trodden, and no fresh hoof prints were visible, so no one had slipped in during the night.

He kneed Hombre to turn around a sharp curve in the road, then pulled him to an abrupt stop. For a moment, Tim stared at the sight before him.

Lady Sydney, always so very correct and proper, stood in the middle of a meadow. The early-morning sun shone like butter, setting an infinite number of dewdrops into prisms and glitter. A chaplet of woven wildflowers wreathed her hair. She clutched her skirts so high, her bare calves were visible. The skirts of her blue dress swayed as she danced to and fro.

Unaware of her audience, she puckered her lips, blew out, and made an airy sound. She shook her head, giggled, then tried again. This time, a slight whistle sounded. Engrossed in the attempt, she remained oblivious to his presence. The crazy, beautiful woman let go of her skirts, clapped her hands with glee, and let out a trill of a laugh before she tried once again.

She stuck her arms out like wings on a bird in flight and sprightly scampered in a shaft of sunlight. Before he could call to her, she bent and rose again. She clutched her dainty boots to her bosom. A huge bouquet of wildflowers spilled from them in a colorful profusion.

He'd never seen anything more beautiful. She moved with a dancer's grace and smiled with childlike simplicity. Her boots full of flowers bespoke moments of innocent self-indulgence.

He watched her pucker and whistle once again. It was a pathetic whistle—faint, short, and toneless; yet she seemed inordinately pleased with her accomplishment. Tim caught himself grinning.

"Sydney!"

She let out a shriek of surprise. Her arms tightened around the boots, and the flowers convulsed. The sudden tide of color in her cheeks matched some of the blossoms she carried. "Tim!"

Suddenly his appreciation of her appearance evaporated. He drew his pistol and fired into the air twice. She flinched with both reports and stared at him, wide-eyed.

"I hope you're happy. The whole ranch is out searching for you!"

She hastened toward him. "For me? Why?"

"I didn't know where you were! I'm responsible for you."

"But I just went for a little walk, and I'm on Forsaken property."

"And how was I supposed to know that?"

"I'm sorry you worried," she said softly, her head bowed. "I'll be more careful to let you know where I am."

Her regret didn't settle well with him. Part of him wanted to give her a good shake for the vexation and worry she'd caused. The other part of him felt strangely warm and tender that she'd felt so confident and safe on Forsaken land.

"Come on back out of there."

She nervously moistened her lips and drew closer to the fence that separated them. He watched as her features repeatedly went taut and her normally smooth gait lurched and swayed. He heaved a sigh. "Show some common sense, Woman! Dump out those flowers and yank your boots back on! You must be out of your mind to be barefoot out here!"

She continued her transit. "I fear I cannot."

"Why not?"

"I don't have a buttonhook with me."

Tim dismounted, climbed over the split-rail fence, and impatiently strode to her. He scooped her up, carried her back to the fence, and set her down on the top bar. He grabbed her boots, upended them, and ignored her small cry of upset as all of the flowers she collected littered the earth. "You had no business taking these off in the first place."

"I had no choice. My boot got caught in the mud. I had to remove it before I could free myself."

"So what? You could have put it back on."

"Out here? Where was I to sit, and how was I to refasten the buttons?"

"You could've plopped down in the dirt. Your dress is already a mess." He drew a stocking out of the toe of one of the boots. As it exited the shoe, it slid into a sensuous stream of sheer black silk. What business did she have wearing such a thing? The garter was dainty as could be—a soft, peachy rose thing that made him want to shake the teeth right out of her head. What business did an unmarried woman have wearing such lingerie?

Mortified, Sydney grabbed the stocking and balled it up in her lap. "Sir!"

"Hush and stuff your foot in this." He ringed his hand around her ankle and twisted her bare foot into the boot. It didn't want to go, but he forced it in place. He dumped the stocking out of the toe of her other boot, and it fell into her lap. He crammed her left foot into it. A small red slash still faintly marked her ankle—a reminder of how he'd sent her down the well hole. It fanned his temper. "You're lucky you didn't step on a snake or twist your ankle in a gopher hole."

She let out a strangled gasp.

"What now?"

Color washed her features. "My limbs are not to be discussed!"

"You're the one who had her skirts hiked up to Christmas morning when I came round the bend!"

"You could have been gentleman enough not to look!"

"I'm a man. I never pretended to be a gentleman."

"More honest a confession was never uttered!" She struggled to turn around and break free from him. Her skirt tangled on the splintered wood.

"Not much of a getaway, there, Miss Priss." Tim easily stepped over the fence, then stooped to gently tug the material free.

"Thank you." She hopped down. The wreath she'd so playfully woven drooped lower over one side of her brow.

Tim's mouth quirked in an amused grin. "Your, uh, crown is slipping, princess."

She snatched it off. "I'm not a princess."

His amusement evaporated. "There's nothing regal in the least about you prancing off. You set me back on this morning's work."

"I never asked you to search for me!"

He strode toward Hombre, effortlessly mounted, and tipped his hat. "Fine. Then you can wander on home now."

"But my shoes!"

"Get home and cool your heels in the house. If you try this stunt again, I'll personally tie a bell around you like I do a wayward cow."

"A cow!"

"I can't be bothered with your fits and pranks."

"I didn't ask for your opinion!"

"And I didn't ask for your presence," he shot back. He

kneed his mount. "I have important things to do. You get on home."

The whole day turned into one continuous headache. One of the new cowboys decided to settle an argument with his fists. Tim broke up the fight and sent that man packing. Richardson showed up a day early for the stud bull. Velma's clothesline inexplicably fell over and had to be repaired. She grumbled the whole while about having to rinse all those dusty clothes again.

Come suppertime, Tim headed up the porch steps. He halted and stared at Sydney's lap. "What are you doing with those?"

"Hmm? Oh. I helped Velma with the laundry today. I noticed your shirts required some mending. It seems the least I could do."

"You don't need to bother."

"It's no trouble at all, Mr. Creighton. I've been doing embroidery, so whenever a color that matched your shirt was on my needle, I whipped up a few stitches. I'm almost done."

Sydney handed him a stack of four neatly folded shirts. "They'll last you a short while. As soon as I have a few more garments completed, I'd be happy to make you a couple of shirts. I think something in a gray plaid would suit you nicely."

His wife Louisa had loved to sit in the sunshine and sew. He remembered the last thing she'd made for him: a gray shirt. He'd prized that shirt, worn it, and told himself it was like having her arms around him—but it wasn't. Pain slashed through him.

Tim scowled. His blue shirt lay on the swing next to Sydney's hip. Other than the ones he now held, the only other shirt he owned was on his back. He didn't need some highbrow English girl pointing out that his clothes were in tatters. The tip of her finger traced a penny-sized hole in the elbow of the last shirt. For just a moment, the corners of her mouth turned down disapprovingly, then they crooked back up into a smile.

She pities me. His temper soared. "So now that you're back in skirts, you think you can put on airs and find fault with us commoners? I work hard, and my clothes show it; but I'm not ashamed. I'd choose work over vanity any day."

Sydney's smile melted into a look of bewildered hurt. She blinked, then stabbed her needle into the embroidery hoop and set it aside. Without another word, she brushed past him and went into the house.

Tim stood on the porch and smacked his hand on his thigh in acute frustration. Dust swirled around from that action. The moment she got that wounded look, he realized he'd mistaken her motive. He was a coarse, big man, and she was a refined slip of a woman. How did she manage to get his goat? Just as bad, why was he being so rude to her?

His shirts needed mending. He'd noticed it from time to time, but he was as hopeless with a needle as the Richardson girls were at a dance. The fact of the matter was, men walked around with their clothes in fairly sad shape most of the time. Ranching ruined clothes. Men wore their garments until they plain fell apart. It was just the way of things.

Tim noted that she'd stitched small sprigs of forget-me-nots in the center of the embroidery hoop. It was charming. Like her. She'd been humming as he came up—atonal, berserk bee sounds that amounted to a poor excuse for music—but she hadn't cared. She'd been happy. It had been sweet, coming home to that bit of cheer after a long, hot, dirty day. In a few terse, harsh sentences, he'd silenced that perky little woman and made her leave her flowers behind. The embroidery hoop with its still needle accused him of cruelty.

Velma thumped a heaping plate in front of Tim that night

and snapped, "Go on ahead and eat up. Lady Sydney seems to have lost her appetite. No use in good food going to waste."

"Is she sick?"

"Sick of you. Doggone it, Tim! That little gal went and fixed all of your sorry old shirts without giving it a second thought. She mended my dishcloth, too. I had to haul her down from a chair because she climbed up on it so she could tack a ring on the parlor curtains that was pulling loose. You're spouting off words to make it look like she's put herself on some fancy pedestal and stands there jeerin' at us common folks."

"No one asked her to act like some kind of nest-building housewife!"

Planting her hands on her hips, Velma shot back, "You'd fault her if she sat around and twiddled her thumbs. The girl can't win no matter what she does."

"Can't a man eat in peace around here?"

"I don't see why not, but then again, I don't know why a woman can't sew in peace, either."

Tim glowered at her. She scowled right back. "Our gal's feet are sore. I don't know what possessed you to make her walk back all that way all on her own."

"She wandered out there. There's no reason she couldn't come back under her own steam."

Tapping her toe, Velma glowered at him. "She had stockings and buttoned-up boots on the way out. No stockings and loose boots are a recipe for a crop of blisters that'd make you wince, and she's got 'em."

"Soak 'em and use a little salve. They'll be fine in a day or so."

"We already did." Velma sniffed. "I've got me a bad feelin' 'bout her."

"She'll come down to eat when she's good and ready. You're

busy enough without having to fetch and carry for her."

"She wants to go to town tomorrow—checking into finding herself a place to go."

Tim nodded sagely. "Fine. That way, we'll have somewhere all lined up when Fuller finally gets home."

In the middle of the night, Tim woke up. He had a roaring case of indigestion. It had to be from Velma's lousy meal; for the first time Velma's pot roast had been tough and stringy, and the vegetables were undercooked. He wouldn't give any credence to his conscience suggesting that maybe he felt a bit guilty over the way he'd treated Lady Sydney. Men didn't let their guts knot up over a woman's tender feelings. He decided a glass of milk might help, so he padded downstairs.

An arc of light let him know someone was in the kitchen. Still wearing every last piece of proper day clothing, Sydney sat at the table, a fancy teacup in her hand.

Tim nodded his greeting and walked past her, hoping to smooth the tension between them. "Velma hardly ever bakes treats. I've got a powerful sweet tooth, so when she does, I gobble up every last crumb. Want a few cookies or some custard?"

"No, thank you. The tea is sufficient."

"Tea isn't gonna keep your slats apart." He tested the top of the stove and jerked back his finger. "The hens are laying well, and the stove's still hot. You could fry yourself a couple of eggs to hold you till morning."

"I'm not overly hungry." She finished her tea and went to the sink to rinse out the cup.

"Sit back down and talk a bit." He motioned toward the custard and cookies. "Eat too."

Folding her arms across her ribs, Sydney shook her head. "Mr. Creighton, we'd do best to avoid one another's company unless we have specific reason for conversation."

"Awww, c'mon! My mouth got the best of me earlier. I admit it. You got your feelings hurt, but that doesn't mean that you have to dash off and starve yourself."

"I'm scarcely in danger of starving."

"But you ran off like a kitten that some kid squeezed too tight."

Her eyes coasted across his broad shoulders and quickly scaled his height from floor to hairline. Staring directly into his eyes, she rasped, "Your analogy was exceptionally appropriate."

Raking his hand through his rumpled hair, Tim sighed. "Listen, Fuller's bound to be getting home soon. It'll be different with him here. He's good at handling people. He'll manage this situation far better than we are. I trust the man."

"Then at least one of us is looking forward to his appearance."

"Is that what this is all about? You're scared of him giving you the boot, so you're worrying yourself sick in the meantime?"

She shot him an icy look. "Mr. Creighton, I've been far from the wilting-and-hysterical type. The mere thought that I'd stoop to such an intentional manipulation is hardly flattering, and I assure you, it's not in the least bit accurate."

"I think you're only half right. That's precisely what's going on." He held up a hand as she made a sound of protest. "You're unaware you're doing it."

"There are so many flaws in that logic, it is impossible to address them all. Do you think I'd intentionally make myself ill when there's every likelihood that my uncle will send me away? I've already determined to find a suitable situation for myself. No one would engage me if I were sickly."

"You?" He let out a rough bark of a laugh. "Work?"

Sydney didn't laugh. The lantern illuminated the temper

sparking in her eyes. "Like it or not, Mr. Creighton, you cannot deny that I worked—and hard—for three weeks. I'm not about to suddenly languish."

She was right. He couldn't deny that she'd done whatever tasks he'd put before her. *But only because of her manipulating scheme.* He stared at her. "What would you do?"

"America is the land of opportunity. Education is valuable. A place at a school is a strong possibility. I'm skilled with a needle, and my mathematical abilities would allow me to work in any shop or bank." Her chin came up in defiance, but her voice faltered. "I'll do whatever I need to."

Tim pounded on the tabletop in frustration. "I didn't want to have to shepherd some greenhorn kid for a week, and I certainly didn't plan on having to guide the prancing fop who arrived. That was bad enough, but I never would have consented to playing nursemaid to a little English miss who wears her feelings on her sleeve!"

Sydney sat there for a long moment. Her tone went icy. "Now you tell me, Mr. Creighton, just who is venting emotions?"

His face went hot, but his stare scorched her.

Rising from her seat with all of the elegance of a queen from her throne, Sydney spoke in an irritatingly well-modulated tone, "Furthermore, I'm far beyond the age to require the services of a nursemaid. That being revealed, I bid you a good night."

"I agreed to watch Fuller's nephew for one stinking week."

"And you've had to endure my undesirable company for nearly a month." Sydney turned around by the door. "Don't feel too put out, Mr. Creighton. If your actions and attitude are any hint as to how my uncle will conduct himself, you can safely plan on being rid of me forthwith."

"Now, hang on a minute here—"

"Please, Mr. Creighton, spare me any platitudes or defensive commentaries. The simple fact of the matter is, I'm not wanted here. I do happen to possess enough pride to insist upon living where I'm accepted. That, obviously, is not the case here. In the morning, I'll go to town and send out inquiries regarding a suitable situation for myself." She slipped away and left him to sit in a pool of lantern light.

Tim shoved the cookies and custard away from himself. She'd ruined his appetite for good food.

⁎

The next day, Sydney went to town. Velma accompanied her, and they returned with two newspapers and a short list of boarding schools for young ladies. Sydney sat down at Fuller's desk. Miss Stern's Boarding School clear out in California and Trenwith's Anglican Home for Orphaned Young Ladies in Chicago . . . just the names gave her the shivers. Carefully sorting through the possibilities, she ruled some out immediately, then set herself to writing.

As Velma made dinner, Sydney wrote a letter of inquiry to a ranch in Kansas. As the last few lines of ink dried, she began another inquiry to a place in the Dakotas. St. Mary's Academy was in Oklahoma. All of her years of stodgy upbringing rescued her. In her heart of hearts, she wanted to stay here, but she was a lady, and a lady didn't stay where she was unwelcome. She refused to demean herself by begging to be kept on—even if Tim and Fuller both agreed, she'd be there on sufferance, and pride demanded she not live under such circumstances.

The very thought of leaving made her want to weep like a

baby. That realization hit her hard. She'd come here planning to return to England. Now the only thing she wanted was to belong here. Even if she couldn't stay at Forsaken, she wouldn't go back to England. The freedom and opportunities here offered her far more latitude than she'd ever enjoy back home. Sydney clamped her lips together, blinked a few times, and continued on. A show of emotion simply wouldn't do.

"Sydney, dinner is on the table," Velma stated from the doorway.

Her head lifted. "Thank you, Velma."

"I fixed bluegill. Pancake caught them in the pond this morning."

"That sounds lovely." Sydney went to the table and took her seat. The fish might have been made of hairpins and moss for all she cared. After picking at a few bites, she rearranged what was left on her plate and rose.

"Something smells great, Velma," Tim hollered as he came tromping in. He stopped at the window and opened it, and a fresh breeze sailed through the room. "Sit back down, Sydney. I didn't mean to interrupt your meal."

"You're not interrupting me. I'm done."

He glanced at her still-full plate and glared at her. "Oh no, you're not! You sit back down there and eat!"

She remained standing. "There's no need to thunder at me. I stated I'm done, and that is all that needs be said. You will not order me about in that manner again."

"Oh yes, I will, Miss Fancy Pants. Fuller left me in charge here and specifically put you in my care. You're under age, and that means you'll obey. Now sit down, or I'll make you sit."

"My uncle put a nonexistent nephew in your care."

"He knows you're a girl now, and he still told me to watch out for you." The chair legs scraped loudly on the floor as Tim yanked it back. "Your seat, Miss Hathwell."

She glowered at him and stiffly sat back down. "*Lady* Hath-well."

"Eat!"

Sydney forced herself to take a few more bites. She knew he watched her and counted every mouthful. His displeasure rolled over her in waves. After struggling to swallow one last bite, she carefully blotted her mouth with the napkin, murmured an unintelligible excuse and slinked away in lady's boots that constricted her feet only a fraction as much as Tim's words constricted her heart.

By suppertime, she'd written to five more possibilities. The task should have taken far less time, but her heart wasn't in it. *If only things could be different. If only I could be Tim's friend again. But that's impossible. He'll never forgive me.* She struggled to compose decent letters and had to rewrite two because of blots. Still, she had the envelopes addressed and ready to go. With a few minutes to spare, she slipped upstairs to comb her hair.

She came back down to find Tim looking at her envelopes. A frown deepened the creases in his forehead. "Mr. Creighton, I would appreciate it if you'd unhand my missives. They are private."

He dropped them. "You discussed the matter with me. I hardly consider it to be a secret. With Fuller gone, I'm bound to watch over you, whether either of us likes it or not." His expression made it clear he didn't like it.

Quelling the desire to weep, she hid behind the emotionless mask she'd been trained to assume. "Sir, you hold no sway over my affairs and the arrangements I make for my future."

"Awww, Sydney! Young women don't strike out like this on their own. I reckoned you'd dabble around in a shop in town— not venture someplace halfway across the country."

I couldn't bear to be close to you and suffer the icy distance you've put between us. "I believe I've been quite clear: Stay out of my affairs."

"Whoa! Wait a minute!"

"No, you wait, Mr. Creighton." Her hands fisted at her sides, and they shook with temper, as did her voice. "More than anything, you made it plain I'm unwelcome. You objected to having to 'nursemaid an English miss.' Don't you dare stand there and suggest that you give a fig about me or my future. I can and will manage."

"You don't have the faintest notion what things cost. I assumed you'd find something local and Fuller could help you out. You can't afford—"

"I specifically searched for positions in which lodging is provided. I'll manage."

Tim shook his head. "That's unnecessary. Sydney, your uncle is rich! You aren't blind . . ." He swept his arm in a wide arc. "Look around you. Fuller will be happy to pay for you to go to the most expensive school."

She directed a cool stare back at him. "I have no need to look about. A man who owns land and cattle as he does is obviously well to do. That doesn't matter a whit. Do you expect me to assume I am to share in my uncle's wealth when I cannot even share his roof? Come, Mr. Creighton, I don't wish to delude myself."

"How can you judge the man? You've never even met him!"

"How can he judge me? He's never met me, either."

He looked thunderstruck for a few seconds. "That's different. You're a woman."

"You, sir, have just relegated me to poverty—a dreadful poverty of spirit simply based on my gender. When you believed me to be a male, I had a future. I could ride and shoot and rope.

I plowed and mucked out stables, I cleared a field and even rescued a child. Now suddenly you limit my horizons because my
form is unlike yours. I may have a narrow waist, but you, Timothy Creighton, have a narrow mind!"

Chapter Eighteen

Sydney's words rang in his ears after she left the room. Tim didn't want to give them credence; they were impertinent and emotional. *But they were also well thought out and true.*

Velma glowered at him from the doorway. "Supper's on."

"Good. I'm hungry."

"Then you're the only one around here who is. You have a way of taking away a body's appetite."

"Just what is that supposed to mean?"

She crammed her hands into the pocket of her apron. "You figure it out. Being as you're the man around here, that makes you the smart one."

"Just what put a crimp in your tail?"

"I took that sweet little gal to town today. She pasted a smile on her face, swallowed her pride, and asked at the emporium about positions as a governess or housekeeper or as a teacher at one of them boardin' schools."

"What?!"

"You heard me just fine."

"She was supposed to be a student at one of those places! What do you mean, she's thinking of being a teacher or housekeeper?"

Velma gave him a chilly glare. "A gal's gotta do what a gal's gotta do. Sydney pretended not to see the townsfolk's surprise or pity, but it was there, plain as day." She gave her head a sorrowful shake. "By now every soul in town knows you're kicking that bitty woman out."

Shame flooded him. "Come on, Velma!"

"Truth's the truth. They got in some of the things she ordered. Lady Sydney insisted on paying for every last thing instead of adding them on Fuller's account."

"She didn't have to do that!"

"Oh yes, she did. She's got too much pride."

"Pride? Pride! She wore britches! No lady with pride would ever be caught dead wearing britches."

"You're a fool to judge a woman's heart by her clothes, Tim Creighton! Don't you tell me otherwise." Velma yanked her hand out of her apron pocket and pointed at the desk. "She sat straight and tall as could be over at that desk all afternoon. Bit her lip, but she didn't shed a single tear. Poor gal has plenty of pluck and even more pride. You're taking it all away, making her feel like she's as worthless as a wad of chewed-up tobacco."

"Tobacco!"

The housekeeper continued on, "She lost her mama and her papa. Did you know the relatives she had left sent her away to New York, hoping to marry her off? Things didn't pan out. Did she moan and groan and whine? No. She hoped maybe she could fit in enough to have a home with her uncle. That's not asking too much. She never asked for money or goods. She doesn't even want us to bow and scrape and serve her."

"I know that, but—"

"Oh, she's been a handful, but she's charming and she tries to help out. She should have married some rich man and lived a life of ease. Now her only goal is to live here somehow. If that doesn't work out, she'll fall back on having her aunt arrange someplace in England for her to watch someone else's brats. Sydney's already said she refuses to let anyone try to arrange another marriage. Poor bitty gal—can't blame her. She's not asking much of life at all. Nuh-unh. Not at all."

Velma wouldn't let him get a word in edgewise. "You didn't like her from the moment she set foot on Forsaken, but she proved herself. You know it's the gospel truth—the very morning, just before you found out she was a girl, you told me you thought Syd, the boy, was a fine youngster and you were proud of him. You *liked* him. Once you discovered he was a she, you suddenly forgot about the pluck and personality and only cared about the package. You act like you were the one who was betrayed by her little deception, but I'm telling you—*she's* the one who's been betrayed. She earned her place here, and you're snatching it away just because she's wearing a petticoat now." Velma gave her head a sorrowful shake and waggled her finger at him as if he were a naughty boy. "Seems to me that with Fuller getting worse each month, he ought to be glad to have his own flesh-and-blood niece to act like a secretary or somethin'."

"I told her she could stay till Fuller gets home!"

Velma gave him a heated look. "Now wasn't it mighty generous of you to offer her bed space in her own uncle's home?"

"Velma! What's gotten into you?"

"Funny. I was wondering the same thing about you!"

Tim gritted his teeth.

"Time's come for you to face up to the truth. You messed up the first part of this. You never bothered to look below the surface. Learn from your mistake. Instead of letting the clothes determine your opinion, look deeper. That gal is steel beneath the dainty lace and ruffles. She doesn't know it yet, though. For all she's gone through, she's going to be fragile as icicles."

Tim shook his head. "Pants or a dress—it makes no difference. She's under my authority while Fuller is gone."

Velma's jaw jutted forward as it did when she went into a snit. "Yep, you're right. Now do a better job with her than you have so far." She walked off.

"I should have known this would happen," Tim muttered. "Get a couple of women together, and they complicate things."

Tim kept waiting for Sydney to come down to eat. She didn't. He ate slowly, and still she didn't appear. Should he go up and talk to her? His palms began to sweat at that thought. The encounter they'd just had didn't go well at all. "Women."

A juicy, rare beefsteak on his plate sat half eaten. It was his favorite dinner, but at the moment, it might just as well have been shoe leather. He hadn't realized how having her sassy comments and saucy grin across the table improved a meal.

As a matter of fact, she'd made several small changes. Velma wasn't one to move at top speed, and things got done when she was of a mind. Truthfully, doing all of the cooking and cleaning for a big house and two bachelors kept her more than busy enough. Sydney saw the details and set them straight. Velma mentioned that Sydney had stitched that sagging curtain ring. He'd seen Sydney sweeping dust from the doorsills and polishing the windows. Velma never bothered with those details.

Linen cloths on the table and bouquets of wildflowers ... years ago, he'd appreciated such things. Louisa saw to those details, and they transformed a house into a home. Since her death, living in a place devoid of those touches suited him. The house had been as barren as his heart. But Sydney set about making changes, and he resented her raking up the pain he'd suppressed.

Tim tried another bite. Half choking on it, he cut another

piece and began to gnaw on it. He glared at the empty place where Fuller usually sat and wished with all of his might that the old guy would get back and put an end to all of this nonsense. In the meantime, he'd foil Sydney's escapade by holding back her letters.

Immediately after supper, Tim went to the desk. Sydney's letters were missing. That fact set his teeth on edge. He found a list of schools. Each bore a tidy checkmark beside it. Next, he found the newspapers, and anger surged. She'd neatly drawn a thin border around five different ads. All were for housekeeper or governess positions. He knew one of the men personally, two of them by reputation, and had no idea who the others were. None of them was good enough to have Lady Sydney Hathwell share a pot of coffee with them, let alone have her brew it on their behalf.

He'd eat dirt before she scrubbed Jake Eddles's floor or mopped his bratty kids' noses. As for her going off to some other man's home . . . Tim passed his hand down his face, as if the gesture might wipe away horrible possibilities flooding his brain. The woman was plain daft if she didn't understand the danger. One look at her, and many a man would haul her straight off to his bed. Tim silently vowed he'd let a mustang drag him five miles before she ever stepped foot off Forsaken to take such a post.

That decision made, he suddenly noticed the downstairs seemed . . . lighter. It took him a minute to realize the drapes now swagged back, permitting the moon to slant in. Odd, how a piddling little change made that kind of difference. Nice, even. Maybe he could mention it when he saw Sydney tomorrow— not that he wanted her to think he was concocting insincere praise to smooth over things. But when she wasn't getting into trouble, the woman did manage to accomplish some decent things.

When he walked upstairs to bed, Tim noted a sliver of light under Sydney's bedchamber door. He had plenty to say, but it would hold until morning.

First thing in the morning, Tim noted Sydney's door was open. When she didn't appear at the breakfast table, he demanded of Velma, "Did Sydney check in with you, or has she gone wandering off after I ordered her not to?"

She gave him a dirty look. "Lady Hathwell got up early in order to take her letters to town. She wanted them to be in this morning's mail pouch."

"How could you let her go do anything so foolish?"

"Lady Hathwell is anxious to leave as soon as possible."

"She's not going anywhere. Leastways, she's not going anywhere without Fuller and me approving of it. Who went with her?"

"No one." Velma's eyes flashed. "The men are all busy. She refused to have me accompany her. She insisted that you still needed me to cook your breakfast."

"For cryin' out loud! She has no business going off all alone."

Velma shook her head. "One minute you're tossing her out on her ear, then next breath, you're shoutin' that the woman can't ride six miles into town without a keeper."

"There are too many men there!"

"There are men everywhere. They'll snap up that baby girl like a buttered hotcake. I bet every last man-jack out there who gets her reply sends for her at once."

Tim gritted his teeth. "She's not going off to some other ranch to work!"

Velma frantically rubbed a nonexistent spot on the table.

"Then that leaves the other option. Big cities have plenty of men. Big cities are where those boarding schools are, too."

Tim's eyes narrowed and he studied the housekeeper carefully. It wasn't like her to be this antsy. "What's really troubling you, Velma?"

"All of this," she mumbled.

"It's something more than that."

"Oh, awright! I can't be sure of those far-away ranches or schools, but my mama ran ads in little city newspapers, acting like her place was a school for gals. Every once in a while, someone responded. By the time they'd spent the last of their money on the train and had a couple of laced drinks to take away their fight, those gals were on their backs and mama got herself a fistful of cash."

Tim let out a roar, grabbed the closest horse, and raced to town.

<hr>

Sydney didn't want to go back to Forsaken. She'd packed the two dresses she wasn't wearing into her valise and seriously considered simply leaving on the train. Once she determined what the boardinghouse in town charged, she decided to stay there overnight. After a sleepless night, she was too tired to ride safely on any public conveyance.

Her financial status was shaky, at best. She counted her money and carefully budgeted. Hopefully any rancher choosing to hire her would send stage fare. When she gave over the envelopes, she'd told the postmistress to hold any replies and she'd send a forwarding address for them. She didn't even mention Abilene because she didn't want Tim to interfere—he didn't want her, so he had no call to stick his nose in her affairs.

Sydney planned to stay at a boardinghouse in Abilene until something appealed to her. She estimated it would take a minimum of a month. During that time, she'd sparingly spend what she must, but one of the reasons she'd go there was so she could work in a restaurant or a dressmaker's shop. A restaurant would be better—she wouldn't have to worry about the cost of her meals. The only problem was, she couldn't cook.

She'd selected Abilene for several reasons, not the least of which was she didn't know the names of any other towns in the area. It must be fairly large, so the opportunities for work would be better. Something inside her longed to know if her uncle looked anything like her mother—if he shared her features or mannerisms. Perhaps she might still be able to make his acquaintance and pay him a visit or two before he went back home to Forsaken.

Of course, it depended on if he'd consent to seeing her at all. She didn't know what Tim wrote in his telegram. Neither did she know precisely what Uncle Fuller's response had been. Back home, ignoring someone was the socially accepted way of giving them the cut. Uncle Fuller hadn't seen fit to write her, so how else was she to interpret his silence?

Burdening a sick man with troubles seemed wrong. Since her uncle didn't want a niece underfoot and Tim would rather dance with every last Richardson girl than face seeing Sydney's face at the supper table again, she'd do the noble thing. She'd relieve Uncle Fuller of the burden by telling him she was ready to pursue adventure elsewhere. Yes, that's what she'd do. She'd visit him and satisfy her heart's desire to at least see Mama's brother, yet not impose on him. In the future, if he found it in his heart to forgive her for her masquerade, maybe they could correspond.

Going to Abilene was a necessity. Velma couldn't be a

sweeter ally, but Tim—Sydney shook her head. During the time Sydney waited for replies to her letters of inquiries, Tim would undoubtedly find ways to swagger into her life for insignificant causes and turn it upside down. And this way, Uncle Fuller wouldn't be caught between allegiance to his partner and an unwanted relative.

Sydney yawned and walked to the window in her room at the boardinghouse. Reaching for the heavy draperies, she stared out in the distance. The fabric bunched in her fisted hand. All she wanted lay within sight, but it couldn't be farther away. She blinked away the tears and closed the draperies.

Indeed, staying here for only one night was the wisest course of action—even if leaving Forsaken nearly tore her heart out. She'd gladly live there for the rest of her life. In their days together, Tim had taught her more than just ranching skills. He'd taught her to love this land. If she couldn't live on Forsaken, at least she'd find a position with another good-hearted western family. She could never go back and live in England after having discovered the freedom and warmth of the wilds of America.

She took off her ankle-high boots and unfastened the uppermost button at the throat of her gown. Too weary to dig her nightdress from the valise, Sydney curled up on the bed and hugged herself. When she stayed busy, she kept the loneliness at bay. But now she was completely on her own. In the days since Tim discovered her identity, he'd also taught her one other painful lesson: Caring about someone did not mean they'd reciprocate.

The train pulled out just as Tim reached town. Sydney's

letters of inquiry were gone along with the puff of the locomotive's gray smoke. Tim looked around and realized he didn't
see Sydney anywhere. He hadn't seen her on the way into town,
either. His heart dropped into his boots. He strode over to the
stationmaster. "Was Lady Sydney on the train?"

The man combed his beard with his fingers. "She had her
valise, but she didn't go today. Said something about tomorrow."

"Her valise?" Tim bellowed in total outrage. "That woman
isn't going anywhere. If she tries to buy a ticket, refuse."

"She doesn't have a ticket yet. I sent her on over to the
boardinghouse."

Tim stormed into the boardinghouse, took off his hat, and
did his level best not to scare the widow who owned the place.
"Mrs. Orion, ma'am, I'm here to fetch Lady Hathwell."

"Mr. Creighton, you know I don't discuss who my boarders
are."

"Ma'am, that's admirable. I detest gossips. That bitty gal's
only seventeen—a minor. Surely you didn't mean to help a run-
away girl."

Mrs. Orion turned and located the spare key for the room.
"I'll fetch her."

Tim paced the parlor and back toward the stairs. *At least this
time it's not the bordello.*

Mrs. Orion started back down the steps. Alone.

Tim's heart skipped a beat. *Don't tell me she sneaked out the back
door.* He rasped, "Where is she?"

"I didn't have the heart to wake her, Big Tim. The poor
thing is crying in her sleep."

Chapter Nineteen

"Sydney," Tim moaned. "Sugar, don't cry." She lay curled on her side, tears wetting the pillow. The blanket was rumpled around her ribs; had she been in a nightdress, matters would have gotten even more sticky. As it was, Mrs. Orion kindly left the door open and stayed out in the hallway—her way of keeping propriety intact while allowing them privacy.

"She's going to be fragile as icicles." Velma's words echoed in his mind.

Tim stroked Sydney's shoulder. "Everything's going to work out." Very briefly, Sydney's crying tapered off. Tim felt a surge of relief until he noted that her face was lax. She languidly shifted a little. He hadn't believed Mrs. Orion about Sydney being asleep. Not with her weeping like she was. Then a whimper shivered out of her, and she began to weep again.

"No, Sydney. No." He groaned as he knelt by the bed and curled over to sort of hug her. How had he ever believed a seventeen-year-old boy could be this petite? The day he discovered her gender and carried her up the stairs, he was too angry to let her size fully register. Now, with nothing to distract him, he visually measured the narrowness of her shoulders and the deep shadows of exhaustion beneath her eyes. Tenderly, he cupped her head with one huge hand and toyed with a stray wisp of her oh-so-soft hair.

He'd forgotten how it felt to protect and comfort a woman. He'd also forgotten how manly he felt when he held a tiny woman in his arms. Somehow, the pain didn't crash over him as it had in the past with those recollections.

The absence of that pain surprised him. For years it nearly tore him apart—days and nights when he almost went crazy missing the precious little family he'd had.

Sydney must be feeling the same terrible emptiness. No wonder she sobbed. He no longer marveled that she'd pretended to be a boy—because by doing so, she'd tried to fill in the terrible void that ached with unspeakable pain. He remembered feeling desperate enough to do anything to make his own grief go away.

Something deep inside shifted. *It's taken me years to heal, but I have. I have to help her through this.* Rocking her, he whispered against her temple, "It hurts. I understand."

Before he knew she was a girl, he'd come to like Sydney. She had a quick wit, a sharp mind, and showed a willingness to work. He'd been wrong about one thing, though. He'd tried to make a man out of Sydney. He should have concentrated on the more important matter. Sydney had a void in her life far greater than the loss of her family: She didn't know the Lord.

Oh, she knew *of* the Lord—but it was an intellectual, philosophical fact to her, not a soul-deep, life-changing decision.

Knowing the Lord had been Tim's only solace in his grief. That, and Fuller's persistence. Fuller pestered him and was patient—but he'd been the only respite from the unbearable loneliness. Sydney wouldn't lean on the Lord because she didn't have faith to sustain her. *That leaves me. She can't bear this all by herself.*

Bowing his head, he softly pressed a kiss on her forehead. "Sydney, sweetheart, wake up."

She shifted a little and drew in a long, choppy breath. Her eyes fluttered open as she lifted her head. After blinking several times, she sucked in a loud gasp. She threw off the covers, scrambled away, and stood on the other side of bed—intentionally out of his reach. "What are you—" She straightened her shoulders. "This is the height of impropriety."

She was embarrassed by her tears, so he'd nettle her into getting angry. "I never did cotton much to silly rules."

"I happen to care about my reputation!"

"If that's the case, explain why you went back to the bordello."

Temper sparked in her eyes. "It was the only way I could be assured of privacy when I bathed!"

He didn't bother to suppress his grin. "To my recollection, that wasn't quite the case."

"Your behavior is despicable!"

"Your vocabulary is impressive. I can see, though, that you got out on the wrong side of the bed."

"Sir, your very presence here is sufficient to give me hives."

Tim laughed. "You're so proper, even your insults sound flattering."

"You're positively barbaric."

He figured he ought to soothe her a little. After all, she wouldn't burst out crying again since he'd piqued her temper. "It's okay, Sydney. Mrs. Orion is just outside the door."

She hastily swiped away her tears.

Looking at her was like peering into his own past. He'd stayed distant and tried to hide his pain from others. "I won't let you gallivant off. Heaven only knows, you'll run headlong into danger."

She glowered at him. "I'm doing quite well without you. I have several fine prospects and—"

"Jake Eddles?" he scoffed. "He worked two wives into early graves while he fiddled with a moonshine still. His ranch boasts all of fifty of the scraggliest cows you've ever seen, and his three sons all have the same habit—they pick their nose. You're going to have to do better than that if you want to survive more than a day on a job."

Even in the dim room, Tim noted how she paled a bit. Good. He needed to scare her into thinking straight. "I saw the other advertisements you sketched around in the *Gazette*. You sure picked a sorry crop of losers. Bill Gravvit's brother lives with him. He spent a stretch in the territorial prison. Don't tell me you're going to feel safe in your bed at night in a ranch house with two bachelors like that."

"I also applied to ladies' academies."

A rusty chuckle erupted from him. "Pardon me, but Fancy Pants Hathwell who chopped off her hair and climbed into men's britches thinks she's going to teach girls how to be proper ladies?"

She smoothed her skirt. "I have two other options if an academy doesn't prove to be satisfactory."

"Yeah?" he drawled in an entertained tone. "Like what?"

Finally, a wobbly smile tilted her lips. A wave of relief washed over him. He wasn't good at handling weepy women. Anything was better than that.

"I still have the britches. I could hire on at another ranch."

Tim jolted to his feet. "Over my dead body!"

"Since I couldn't bear the responsibility for your demise, I'd have to go with my other possibility, then." She paused a moment. When Tim crooked a brow in silent inquiry, she folded her hands in front of herself as if she were going to do a school recitation. "I understand from the advertisements that there is great demand in this part of the world for mail-order bri—"

"That does it!" He grabbed hold of her wrist. "You need to be protected from yourself, woman. I've never known another soul on the face of the earth who concocted half as many hare-brained schemes as you. It's a good thing I came to take you home—elsewise, you'd up and get yourself into more trouble than five reasonable men could untangle." He tugged her toward the door.

Sydney planted her feet and yanked free of his hold. "Just who says men are reasonable to begin with? I'm not going any-where with you, Tim Creighton!"

Tim cupped her shoulders and gently forced her to look up at him. "You'd break Fuller's heart if you skulked away."

She let out an inelegant snort.

"Once he meets you, he's going to lose his heart—just like Velma did. Forsaken is where you belong. I'm sure of it."

"Well, I'm not!"

"What kind of woman would dash off to uncertain dangers when she had folks back home who wanted her?"

"Did you fall off your horse and hit your head?" She slapped her hand over her mouth for all of two seconds before giving up and batting an errant curl off her forehead. "I declare, Mr. Creighton, I'm a perfect lady around anyone else. The min-ute you step in the room, I get in trouble. It's all your fault, though. You say outrageous things, and I cannot help reacting."

"Velma loves you. You know she does. As for Fuller—I've told you I'll speak with him. People mellow with time. After thinking about it, I believe he'll be delighted to have you around."

"That still doesn't change matters."

Tim didn't pretend to misunderstand her. "Life would be

downright boring without you there to stir things up. You keep me on my toes."

She pushed past him and climbed back onto the bed. "You aren't really here. I'm having a nightmare. That's the only explanation for this."

A sampler above the headboard caught his attention. *Let your light so shine before men, that they may see your good works, and glorify your Father.* The verse hit hard. He couldn't make Sydney turn her heart toward the Lord, but he could reflect God's love to her. Talk never got anything done. It was while working alongside "the kid" that Tim taught Syd the essentials. Sydney heard him pray and accompanied him to church—but she'd gotten that much all her life. *She needs an example. Lord, you're going to have to equip me.*

Tim tugged on the blanket and started to tuck her in. "Sleep awhile, sugar."

⁂

Sydney's eyes snapped open. Big Tim was leaning over her. "Did you just call me—"

"Mommy, my shoe broke."

Sydney flung off the coverlet at the sound of a child's voice and gave his shoulder a healthy shove. "Get out of here!"

Mrs. Orion sighed. "Come show me, Heidi."

Sydney yanked Tim back. "No, wait. You can't go out there now." She glanced at the wardrobe, then the bed. Neither would serve as a hiding place for the gigantic man. "Get behind the curtains."

"No."

"Mrs. Orion might well understand your being in here, but her little girl won't." Sydney shook her head. "I don't, either.

You're making a mess of everything!"

Tim leaned so close, his breath washed over her face. "Stop dithering. The best thing to do is act like nothing's wrong."

"Plenty is wrong—you don't belong here!"

"Neither do you."

Compared to Tim Creighton, mules and rocks were cooperative. As soon as Mrs. Orion sent her little girl back downstairs, Sydney decided she'd voice that comparison as she prodded him out of the room.

"Syd, I'll bet the widow can't afford new shoes for her daughter. Help me out here."

Sydney could have resisted just about any ploy of his—but a child in need? "Don't think I'll forget about this. I'll settle it with you later." She stepped back from Tim. "I can't return to Forsaken. Kippy's gait is off. I think a shoe is loose."

"Then we'll see to it before we return to Forsaken."

Sydney sidled past Tim and out into the hallway. Heidi held up a scuffed little shoe for her mother's inspection. "Shoes." Sydney let out a theatrical sigh. "The ones I just purchased simply don't fit right." She dipped her head and confided in a low whisper, "They're rubbing my ankle raw."

"Lady Sydney," Tim appeared in the doorway, holding her ankle boots up for inspection. "Did I overhear you say these don't fit?"

She let out a loud gasp. "You eavesdropped!"

Tim shrugged. "While Kippy's getting shod, I'll take you over to the mercantile and get you shoes, too."

Sydney pressed a hand to her throat. "Sir, are you likening me to a horse?"

"Nope." He grinned as he let the boots drop to the floor. "Horses are biddable. You're not."

Giggles spilled out of Heidi.

Tim tugged on one of her plaits. "I think you'd better come to the mercantile with us. Lady Sydney can't beat me up if I have you along."

Heidi's eyes grew huge. "Would she beat you up?"

"I don't know. She's tiny, but she riles easily." Tim turned to Mrs. Orion. He tilted his head to the side and studied the little shoe she held. "The buckle fell off? We can stop by Matteo's on the way. He's good at leather repairs."

Sydney had to give Tim credit. His off-handed comments sounded so reasonable. *This is an opportunity. He asked me to help him out—and I will. If there's any chance I might stay on at Forsaken, I need to prove to Tim that it's possible for a man and a woman to work together.* She stooped, picked up her boots, and went back into the bedchamber.

Tim's calloused hand kept the door from shutting. "What're you doing?"

"Putting on my shoes."

"But they hurt."

"I can't very well wander out of here and over to the mercantile without shoes on."

"Heidi's going to. Aren't you, Half-pint?"

Heidi wrinkled her nose. "Do I getta take off my stockings, too?"

From the expression on Tim's face, Sydney knew he hadn't anticipated that minor glitch.

Tim hunkered down. "Nah. You're going to get a piggyback ride."

The little girl let out an excited squeal. "Mommy, I getta piggyback ride!"

"You sure do." Tim tugged her over, and she scrambled onto his back.

Heidi scooted higher on his back. "What 'bout Lady Dizzy?"

Tim chortled.

"Lady *Sydney*, Heidi," her mother corrected.

"Okay. Lady Sydney doesn't have her shoes on. Are you gonna give her a piggyback ride, too?"

"No." Sydney wasn't about to let Tim answer the question. "I'll meet you downstairs."

When Sydney joined them, Tim had taken Heidi outside and put her up in Kippy's saddle. "We'll drop Kippy off at the smithy. Right rear shoe's loose. From there, Heidi's going to shift from riding horseback to piggyback."

After dropping off the horse, they stopped by Matteo's. While Tim set Heidi down, Sydney caught Matteo's attention and gave her head a quick shake. Then she smiled. "Heidi's buckle came off her shoe. We'd be ever so appreciative if you could repair it. You can, can't you?"

"Let's see." Matteo accepted the scuffed brown shoe. He gave Sydney an uncertain look, and she again shook her head.

"Hmmmm. I suppose I could try. But the size rivets this needs—they're small. Very small."

"Matteo doesn't make women's shoes." Tim gestured toward the boots along the shelf.

"It's a shame. Truly, it is." Sydney thought of how her shoes pinched. "Would you ever consider . . ."

"No. Never." Matteo scowled. "Men's boots. Some for boys. Saddles."

"There you have it." Tim lifted Heidi and headed to the mercantile. "Sydney, while you find shoes for yourself, do you think you could stir up some for Heidi?"

Heidi sucked in a loud breath. She tugged on Sydney's

hand. When Sydney bent closer, Heidi whispered, "Mommy and me don't have lotsa money."

Tim gave Sydney a take-care-of-this look.

"Yes, well, I need to hire an advisor." Sydney nodded as if to confirm her assertion. "I don't know what young American girls like. What if I hire you as a consultant, and we'll pay you by buying you new shoes?"

Freckled nose wrinkling, Heidi asked, "What am I s'posed to do?"

"I'll explain it after we get our shoes."

Fitting Heidi at the mercantile proved to be quite simple. The first pair Orville Clark brought out fit her perfectly. She did a happy little jig, then hiked up her hem to admire them. "They're brand-new!"

The storekeeper murmured to Sydney, "Mrs. Smith always passes her daughter's things down to Heidi."

Sydney crooked her finger, and Heidi wiggled closer. "While I see about shoes for myself, you can start working with Big Tim. Show him what kind of material little girls like for dresses."

Tim gave her a horrified look and Sydney smiled back sweetly.

Heidi curled her hand around his fingers. "C'mon. It's easy."

"Easy," he echoed in a dubious tone. Heidi started to tow him toward the door. He halted. "Hold on a second. You're going the wrong way."

The little girl gave him a baffled look.

"She's too small to tell where you're going, Tim. Lift her up so she can see over the goods."

"I know where everything is." Heidi's voice carried a hint of exasperation. "Mr. Clark doesn't sell feed. Mr. Vaughn does."

Tim bent forward and rested his hands on his knees. Even so, he towered over the little girl. "I—we aren't leaving Lady Hathwell alone here. We're staying put." He straightened up. "You want bolt goods, don't you, Sydney?"

Heidi's jaw dropped.

She wouldn't mind feed sacks at all, but Sydney didn't want to argue. Besides, the way Mr. Clark kept hovering made her nervous. "Yes, Timothy. That's precisely what we need."

In a child's loud whisper, Heidi asked, "Bolt goods or chicken feed?"

"Bolt goods." Tim nodded once with great emphasis. "You have to understand. Lady Hathwell's family and friends didn't have chickens back home where she came from."

"Oh." Heidi seemed perfectly satisfied with Tim's hasty explanation.

Mr. Clark wanted to help Sydney try on each of the three pair of shoes in her size, but she wasn't about to have him buttoning and unbuttoning anything around her ankles. He kept jabbering, and Sydney wanted to overhear Heidi and Tim. "Mr. Clark, sir, I appreciate your assistance, but I must insist upon being left alone to . . . see to things."

"Yeah." Tim's voice was so close, Sydney jumped. His eyes were steely slits, and his gaze bore through the owner of the mercantile. "While the lady tries on the shoes, you can fetch necessities."

Mr. Clark's jaw thrust forward. "You told me the other morning that Forsaken is fully stocked."

Sydney took the buttonhook from his fingers. "I recall Velma mentioning she was running low on vanilla and paprika. Of course you didn't expect Mr. Creighton to be aware of such minor items. Could you please fetch some?"

Though he looked crestfallen, Orville Clark slouched away.

Tim waited until he was sure Sydney would be left alone, then went back toward the bolt goods. Sydney hastily tried on the boots as she listened to Heidi's clear little voice. Tim's answers were low rumbles. Sydney went over to join them. "How are we doing?"

"Find anything?" Tim countered.

Sydney let out a small sigh. "No."

"Don't be fussy about looks, Sydney. Your hems drag on the floor. Nobody's going to see your shoes."

He had a point. "Then I'll go back to wearing Matteo's—"

Tim's brows shot up. "A proper English lady would wear cowboy boots?"

"In a heartbeat." She turned to Heidi. "You're my consultant. I'm interested in hearing what fabrics you advise."

"I like flowers. And I like pink. And orange. Mama doesn't like them, though. They show the dirt real fast."

"Mr. Creighton is going to help us put the bolts up on the table. Let's choose a few to spread out. They sometimes look different when you unroll a yard or so."

"What is it you have in mind, Sydney?"

"I have a wonderful idea." She tugged Heidi close and motioned to Tim. He leaned toward her. "I want to have a sewing bee. Ladies came and helped me make my dress, and Velma gave me the material. Wouldn't it be fun if we had women come to Forsaken and make dresses for the little girls to wear for church this summer and for school next year?"

Heidi's eyes grew huge. "Girls like me?"

Tim shot Sydney an approving look. "Yeah, Half-pint. Like you. And all the kids on the Smith farm, right, Sydney?"

"Precisely!" A thrill shot through her. Big Tim not only understood her plan; he backed it. For the first time in days, she tasted a hint of the camaraderie they'd once shared. She craved to reestablish their friendship. It would have to be on different grounds—but they both cared about their neighbors. Working together again felt so right. She smiled at him. "What do you think of the plan, Tim?"

"It's good."

Once upon a time, that answer would have crushed her. After having been a "man," Sydney understood that men didn't get all flowery. Curt as it was, his response qualified as a strong endorsement.

Tim tore his gaze from her and hefted Heidi onto the counter. "So what do you like best?"

Sydney's heart warmed at how gentle and kind he was toward Heidi. Some men couldn't be bothered with children— especially if they weren't related. He'd remembered· how she once said they'd concoct a way of helping the Smiths. Teamwork. He'd told her how important it was to work together. He'd been talking about heavy physical labor—but now he showed a willingness to be a partner in her scheme.

"Mandy likes blue." Heidi wiggled. "It's 'portant for me to tell you that. It's my job, right?"

"Indeed."

"Why don't you gals go ahead and get all the foof and poof. I'll go take care of a few things."

Heidi giggled. "Foof and poof!"

Tim colored. "What else do you call all that ribbon and stuff?"

"Ribbon?" Heidi almost fell from the counter. Tim righted her, and she clung to his sleeve. "Really? We get ribbon, too?"

His gaze darted to the ends of her unadorned braids and back. "Yup." He spoke over in the corner to the storekeeper, and Mr. Clark cast a quick look at Sydney. He went red, then blanched and nodded. Tim slapped him on the shoulder and walked out.

For having been so very talkative earlier, Mr. Clark hardly spoke a word while helping her. Sydney wasn't sure what Tim had said, but she suspected he was the reason Mr. Clark suddenly managed to keep to the other side of the cutting counter. By the time Tim returned, Orville Clark finished wrapping up their purchases. Tim eyed the packages. "That doesn't look like very much."

"We got 'terial for me and Mandy and April and Angela and Susannah and 'Lila and . . ." Heidi's brow furrowed.

"Melody," Sydney added.

Mr. Clark reported to Tim, "A frock and an apron apiece."

"And ribbons and buttons. Beee-you-tea-ful buttons!"

Tim cleared his throat.

Sydney's breath froze. *I bought too much. I didn't ask what we could afford to spend!*

"Why don't you, um . . . get a bolt of white?" Tim's gaze slipped away as he mumbled, "For underpinnings."

Heat enveloped her.

Tim paced over to a shelf and grabbed a handful of bandanas. "Put these on the tab for Forsaken, too, Orville."

"I have a full bolt of the best quality white cotton in the back room. Do you want all thirty yards?"

Tim nodded. "I'm sure the ladies will find ways of using it."

"A bolt of white cotton, and . . . how many bandanas do you have there?" Mr. Clark took the pencil from behind his ear and dabbed the lead on his tongue.

"I like to count." Heidi tugged on Tim's jeans. "I'm good at it!"

Tim plunked her up on the counter once again. "Okay, Sunbeam. Count 'em."

A minute later Tim got ready to set her back down. Heidi clung to him. "When I grow up, I wanna marry you."

A flicker crossed his face and his jaw hardened.

"Nonsense." Sydney puffed the shoulder of Heidi's sleeve. "Mr. Creighton is far too old for you. Why, when you marry, he'll be an old man in a rocking chair."

"Mommy says she's too old to marry. Maybe you and Mommy—"

"I'm not a marrying kind of man." Finality rang in his tone.

Chapter Twenty

"I need to marry her at once! What do you mean, you've hit a dead end?" Rex Hume clenched his fists at his side and stared at his investigator, Tyler.

"The Chicago fire destroyed records up to and including 1871. Marriage, birth, death—all of the essential information went up in flames. I've hit an impasse. At this point, you have two choices: Either you abandon your search, or you permit me to speak to the Hathwell family and obtain any facts—however obscure they may seem—in order to locate Lady Sydney."

"There have to be ways of tracing her family."

"I've tried. *Debrett's* provided important information by citing that her father was an attorney. Unfortunately, the name of Robert Johnson is absurdly common. I tracked down Roberts, Robs, Bobs, even R. Johnsons—any and all in the Chicago area."

"Interviewing only attorneys was foolish. He could have retired!"

Tyler flashed a grim smile. "I'm well aware of that, so I tracked down every last one I could locate. Furthermore, there was the possibility that he was appointed into a judiciary position. I spoke with several judges. I've exhausted all leads."

"A woman cannot simply vanish into thin air."

"You're right. At this point, my experience tells me one of two things have happened: Either she was overly trusting and fell in with someone unsavory, or she made contact with a party whom she already knew. In either case, she's lost to you."

"No." Hume slammed his fist down on his desk. Several files slid and fell into a jumble across the carpet, as if to emphasize how his well-ordered existence was precarious and sliding toward a shambles. He refused to stand by and allow that to happen. "Women change their minds. There's the strong possibility that she got cold feet, flitted out, and is too embarrassed to contact me now."

Tyler hitched his shoulder and gave a noncommittal grunt.

"She's my responsibility. I refuse to give up."

"The only other possibility—and it's slim, at best . . ."

Hume leaned forward. "What?"

"Lady Hathwell received a remarkable education. It's possible that she's working under an assumed name as a governess for a wealthy family or teaching at an exclusive finishing school. She wasn't here long enough to send out inquiries. That being the case, she might well be under our noses."

"That makes as much sense as anything else."

The investigator grimaced. "You need to know the chances of that being the case are extremely slim. My advice to you is to go to her family and—"

"Out of the question!" Anger streaked through Hume. Just yesterday *the* local magnate, Blade Rutherford, made a point of stopping by. Rex craved to build a business association with him. Rutherford had just returned from England and heard about Lady Hathwell—and suddenly he'd expressed an interest in exploring the possibilities of doing business together. Of course, he'd invited Rex to bring his bride over for supper.

Only Rex didn't have a bride. He didn't even have a bride-to-be. He'd concocted a story about Sydney doing a little sightseeing and visiting a friend before they settled down and married.

Rutherford's demeanor shifted. Instead of being so congenial, he put up his guard. "I see. Well, then, I can see you're busy. Once the little lady returns, be sure to let us know."

He'd walked out, and Rex knew a fortune blew out the door with him. He couldn't afford for anyone to discover Sydney had gone missing. Especially now.

"There's the matter of my expenses. I've itemized each expenditure to date." Tyler handed him a stack of pages.

Flipping through the pages, Hume quickly ascertained the costs to be within reason. Tyler wasn't listing exorbitant fees for meals, and he traveled by standard train car, not by Pullman sleepers. Even so, this debacle was costly—and Tyler's charges were the mere tip of the iceberg. Thousands and tens of thousands of dollars' worth of business dealings hung in the balance.

The inheritance Lady Hathwell would receive upon their marriage was a mere pittance compared to all he'd gain once she became his wife—but if this went on for much longer, that inheritance would be squandered on this ridiculous, maddening search. The woman didn't know how much she had already cost him; he'd been gentleman enough not to reveal Hume money had covered her cousin's indiscretions and had even bought her trousseau. He'd considered it all an investment—a very safe one. Until now. Well, he couldn't afford for this deal to fall apart. "I'm not giving up. Find her."

Tyler hitched one shoulder. "I'll keep looking, if that's what you want."

"It is. If you'll excuse me a moment, I'll fetch the cash." He

left the study and went upstairs to his bedchamber. A wall safe
located behind the portrait of his parents opened easily. Hume
pulled out what he owed the investigator and added more.
Incentive. Men always worked better with incentive.

Before he shut the safe, he picked up his mother's wedding
ring: a flawless one-carat diamond encircled by a row of sap-
phires. A more beautiful piece of jewelry didn't exist. After he
caught up with Lady Hathwell, it would grace her left hand. She
wasn't worthy of such a piece, but she was worth it financially.

Chapter Twenty-one

"That's a lot of fruit." Sydney cast a surprised look at the back of the buckboard Tim rented from the livery. Since he'd had the blacksmith see to Kippy's shoe, she'd been surprised that Tim rented the buckboard at all ... until she realized they weren't returning to Forsaken with just the fabric and "foof and poof." In his practicality, Tim used the time in town to load up on necessities.

"June's my favorite month. The last of the strawberries and blackberries are still around, and peaches are coming ripe. So are apples. You haven't tasted an apple till you have one grown in Texas."

She looked amused. "Is that so?"

He nodded. "I'm not boasting—it's a fact. The longer an apple stays on a tree, the sweeter it grows. Our sun lends the apples that extra bit, and—well, see for yourself." He leaned back, snagged an apple, and straightened up. After polishing the apple on his sleeve, he handed it to Sydney. "Here you go."

"May I please have your knife?"

"Nope." He crooked a brow. "Remember me telling you not to use tools when they're unnecessary? Just bite."

She took a bitsy nibble.

Tim grabbed her hand, dragged it upward, and took a chomp out of the apple. Pushing it back toward her, he said around his mouthful, "Do the job right, Syd." The nickname slipped out as naturally as could be.

Her eyes grew enormous, and a beautiful smile lifted her lips. *Crunch.* She took a decent bite.

"Good girl."

"Mmmm." She swallowed. "It is wondrously good!"

He yanked the apple from her fingers and munched through it in a few decisive bites. "Nobody's keeping you from taking what you want."

"Is that so?" Her eyes sparkled.

He nodded.

She grabbed the reins.

Tim threw back his head and let out a shout of laughter.

She gave him a saucy grin. "I noticed you bought peaches. They're so far back there, I can't have one until we reach Forsaken, and you're driving too slow."

Throwing the apple core to the side of the road, Tim figured he'd climb back and fetch her a peach.

"Whoa!" The buckboard came to a halt. "Tim Creighton, you can't do that."

"Huh?"

"It's not just manners. If it were, since it's just the two of us, I'd not take offense. But that could become dangerous." Bobbing her head with great certainty, she said, "Go ahead, but remember how much I want a peach. We don't have all day."

He stepped into the back of the buckboard, got a peach for her, and another apple for himself. "Here."

"Why, thank you." She seemed surprised. When he sat back down, she blinked in confusion.

"What's wrong?"

A giggle escaped her. "Oh, Tim, you really do love apples. You're so greedy, you forgot to take care of your road apple. What happens if it takes root? It'll ruin the road."

His hand stopped halfway to his mouth. Incredulity streaked through him. "Who told you that?"

"My father."

How he'd manage to tell her "road apple" happened to be a polite term for . . . Well, he reckoned he might mention mucking and let her draw her own conclusion. But Tim couldn't. Not when her daddy said otherwise. He put his apple on the seat, jumped down, and strode toward the core.

"If you kick it to the side, do you think it really could grow into a tree? Your Texas apples are delicious."

"It's worth a try. We're mighty short on rain this year, though." He jabbed his heel into the dirt, toed the core into the depression, and scuffed a little earth over it. When he sat back down next to her, Tim swiped back the reins. When he grabbed his apple, his fingers dipped into a juicy depression.

"You're right about two things, Big Tim." Sydney's voice rang with merriment. "As I agreed, Texas apples are wondrous. Furthermore, nobody was keeping me from taking what I wanted."

"Speaking about what you want . . ." Tim set the buckboard in motion. "I've thought about it, and I'm standing firm on what I said back at the boardinghouse. You belong at Forsaken."

She nestled the peach in her hands and stared at it, as if fascinated. "America is the land of opportunity. I can make my way—"

"You already made your way straight into Velma's heart. She's delighted to have you there." He pressed on, "Chalk up stuff I said to the heat of the moment. Your uncle has mellowed with age—he'll be tickled to have you here. And me? I think we did pretty good today."

"Teamwork," she said softly.

"Yep. Teamwork." Relieved that she got the drift, he let the subject go.

A yawn overtook her.

Tim's eyes narrowed. He hadn't noticed the dark circles beneath her eyes. As soon as he got her home, he'd send her upstairs to that rose room she thought was so pretty. Order her to take a nice, long nap.

The breeze made the fabric of her sleeve flutter a little, calling his attention to her narrow wrist. How had she managed to clear the garden plot of those rocks? Even more astounding, how did she keep hold of Stauffer's daughter and pull her from the well? That was an absolute miracle.

He watched as Sydney lifted the peach and took a bite. After a week of not doing hard ranch chores, Sydney's hands were already growing soft again. He'd seen her massage rose glycerin lotion into them after she helped Velma with supper dishes. Her nails were clean, but extremely short.

Sydney must have sensed him studying her. She turned to him and raised her brows. "Yes?"

"You're wearing your mama's locket."

Her other hand went up to touch the small golden heart. "I suppose I should do whatever I can to look less boyish."

His hand went up to her hair. He tried to stop himself, but he couldn't. He allowed himself to touch just the tips of her curls. "I wouldn't have cut it if I'd known."

"In England and France, many of the stylish women are wearing their hair in very short curls. I'll have to remember that."

"This isn't England or France."

"And wishing won't make my hair reappear, so I'd do better to make the best of it instead of mourning it until I'm miserable."

"You are a remarkable young woman, Lady Hathwell."

"I was less trouble to you when I was merely Syd." Regret stole the sparkle from her eyes and voice.

Tim almost agreed—but he couldn't. Not honestly. Not when he thought about it. "You weren't less trouble." A slow smile quirked one side of his mouth. "Just a different kind of trouble."

They rounded the corner and he moaned. "Speaking of trouble . . ."

⁕

Mrs. Richardson looked stricken. "Why, Mr. Creighton, can't you spare a bit of time to socialize?"

Tim lifted Sydney down from the buckboard. "Absolutely not, ma'am. I . . ."

Charlotte tugged on his pant leg. "Bethany and me, we've been learning to weave flowers into circles."

"That's nice," he murmured distractedly.

"Because Mama says they make pretty bridal wreaths!"

Sydney took pity on him. "Mr. Creighton, thank you for assisting me with the errands in town today. I know how busy you are." She turned to Mrs. Richardson. "How felicitous that you happened by. I concocted an idea, and you ladies simply must help me work out the details."

Tim took the opportunity and strode away.

"Shall I show you how we conduct tea in England? It's very proper, you understand. There's a whole art to brewing a good cup of tea. Velma is brilliant at it."

Over tea, Mrs. Richardson and her girls heard Sydney's plan for a sewing bee. Mrs. Richardson blinked back tears. "Oh, I can hardly wait! I still remember my very first new dress—pine green with yellow roses."

"Like 'The Yellow Rose of Texas,'" Bethany declared with great assurance.

"That's right. If it weren't for that dress, I don't know where I'd be today."

Sydney set down her teacup. "I'm afraid I don't understand."

"Twenty-five years ago, I was on an orphan train. So was Jeb. That's where we met. The train pulled in late Saturday night. Sunday morning they marched us kids over to the church, and after the service, we all lined up.

"The Richardsons—they lost their boys in the war. Mr. Richardson picked Jeb. Said he needed strapping boys to help on the farm. I grabbed hold of Jeb's hand and pointed at my dress. 'These yellow roses here say I'm supposed to be in Texas.' That's what I told him. Folks all knew some of the orphans wandered off, so I told him and his missus they wouldn't have to worry on that account. So long as Jeb and me were together, we'd work our fingers to the bone for them."

"I never knew that!" Velma wrinkled her nose. "How'd the two of you get hitched if you were both adopted?"

"The Richardsons adopted Jeb. Just in case Jeb and I decided later on we wanted to get married, they took me on and didn't adopt me. And look—it turned out."

"Maybe I should make a dress with yellow roses." Linette sighed. "Then I could grab me a man."

Suddenly the Richardson girls' shenanigans made sense. Sydney patted Linette's hand. "Your mama and papa's story is unique. It broke all the rules."

"What rules?"

"My governess drilled them into me unceasingly. For instance, 'A man hunted is an opportunity blunted.'"

Marcella frowned. "I never heard that before."

"Yes, well, I assure you it is the truth. Men like to pursue."

Linette shook her head. "That's not what worked for Mama. She saw what she wanted and grabbed for it."

"Yes, but she was an orphan. She didn't have the benefits you do of loving parents to advise her. 'A woman's job is to captivate, not capture.'" Sydney let out a trill of laughter. "See? That was another rule. I propose we trade. I'll share all of those little tidbits, and you can teach me something in return."

"Like what?"

Sydney wasn't sure who asked—or, more accurately, who didn't ask. Almost everyone in the parlor had asked the question in unison. She thought a moment. "Baking. Yes, baking. I ate a Texas apple today, and I can only imagine how scrumptious a pie made from them must taste."

"We can start right now!" Marcella hopped to her feet.

"Your enthusiasm is refreshing, but that must wait. I was rather hoping I could depend on you to stop off at some of the neighbors' on your way home, just to extend the invitation to the sewing bee. I know it's a week and a half away, but I'd feel ever so much better if everyone would know in advance to save the day. Back home, we'd be sure to give far more notice than this."

Sydney rose. The Richardson women were a little slow to take the cue that they should leave. Linette groused under her breath.

"That is just the way of things. Chin up, though, my father always said. Pouting gives a woman the most unbecoming wrinkles, you know." With that small jewel of wisdom,

Sydney managed to nudge them out the door.

Once the Richardson women left, Velma shook her head. "I didn't think it was possible, but you've gotten yourself into more trouble yet."

"Not really. In a peculiar way, it all makes sense now. I want a marriage just as my parents had; so do they." *But have I been wrong all along, just as Linette and Marcella have been? Did I expect the wrong things? No . . . no, I didn't. Marriage to Rex Hume would have been dreadful.*

"Syd, are you sure you know what you're doing?"

No. Yes. Well, mostly. At least for them, if not for myself. "I suppose we'll have to work on that situation. I don't want to sound pretentious, but I've been trained all my life in issues of deport-ment and appearance."

"You'd do better learning how to cook than to try to twist one of the Richardson she-cats into something a man'd want."

Sydney gave a dainty shrug. "I daresay I made a case for exchanging our skills."

"Them needing you—that's undeniable. But why would a fancy lady need to cook?"

"Because I'm not a fancy lady any longer—I'm an ordinary woman who may someday need to set a satisfying table for her husband. I want to help those girls, Velma. I feel a pang of sympathy for their plight."

"If you manage to teach those gals a thing, it'll be a miracle."

Sydney helped gather the teacups. "I don't wish to be rude, but I can't for the life of me understand why Uncle Fuller hasn't contacted me. His absence has stretched quite long."

Velma shrugged. "We didn't expect him to be gone this long, but his rheumatiz is getting terrible. There are days he can scarcely bear to sit, and his hips are so stiff, he can't ride at all. I've taken to fixing foods he doesn't have to cut much since his hands are so gnarled, too."

"Dear goodness!"

"He's been so miserable these last few months, I can't hardly blame him for trying to take a cure. Abilene is far enough away that he might stop off at a few towns on his way home to break up the travel."

After supper dishes were done, Sydney sat out on the porch swing and sewed by the waning evening light. Velma shelled peas and hummed. They chatted and worked, much as they usually did. Velma chuckled. "I'll bet my earlobes that the Richardson women flock to our door tomorrow."

"We should plan on it. Do you think I ought to warn Tim?"

The screen door banged behind Tim. "Warn me about what?"

Sydney stabbed her needle into the cloth. "What do you think, Velma?"

"You've pulled some mighty bad stunts. That one might well be unforgivable."

He sat down on the uppermost step, leaned into the post, and gave Sydney a long look. "You're up to no good. That gleam in your eye is enough to make me think about locking you in your room."

Pasting her most innocent look on her face, Sydney pressed a hand to her bosom. "Mr. Creighton, you wound me."

His eyes narrowed. "You're not expecting any of those men you contacted to come fetch you, are you?"

"They couldn't possibly respond so quickly."

He eased back a bit. "I don't want you talking to any of them or writing back, either. Do you hear me?"

"Bellowing as you did, I'm sure most of Texas is well acquainted with your edict."

"Good." He leaned forward again to emphasize his words.

"That'll save me the hassle of kicking them off Forsaken. You're not going anywhere. You're not supposed to have any men sniffing around here, either."

"I simply couldn't receive gentleman callers until Uncle Fuller gives his consent. It just isn't done."

Tim leaned against the post. "Glad you figured that one out."

"Most of the men are pretty decent," Velma judged.

"A bunch of them aren't anywhere near husband material," Tim argued. "They don't earn enough to provide for a gal, or they like going to the saloon too much to keep a wife happy. Nope"—he shook his head—"you shouldn't even think of having any of the men come trying to court you until Fuller gives them a good once-over. Until he does, you'd be wise to keep your company strictly to women."

His adamant little speech amused her. Sydney smoothed the skirt of her dress. "I do believe Velma is correct. I'll probably have some callers, but they'll be women."

"Ahhh. The sewing bee."

"Nope. We decided to have it a week from next Tuesday. That way, we can announce it at church twice," Velma said.

"And it will permit me enough time to write out invitations."

Tim frowned. "Why bother? It's a lot of fuss. Everyone will know about it."

Sydney smiled at him. "It's all part of my grand plan."

Velma gave Tim a warning look. "Sydney promised to start teaching the Richardsons how to act like ladies."

Tim glared at Sydney. "Impossible."

"Timothy—" Sydney clasped her hands. " 'In order to attain the impossible, one must attempt the impossible.'"

"Let me guess: That's another thing Cervantes said."

"It is, and it's right. Just you wait and see."

The next evening, following a fruitful visit from the Richardsons, Sydney carried her picture-perfect pie to the table.

Tim perked up. "Maybe you working with the Richardson gals isn't such a bad idea."

Sydney laughed. "You may have the honors." She set it down in front of him and gave him the server.

Tim cut generous wedges. She sat and waited to take a bite of her own. She wanted to enjoy watching him taste the first bite. He used the side of his fork and cut off an enormous hunk, scooped it up, and grinned as he hefted it to his mouth. As soon as he started to chew, the grin wobbled, faded, and his chewing slowed. His eyes went wide; then his gaze slid from hers. He bravely swallowed but quickly took a big gulp of coffee.

Chapter Twenty-two

Sydney cast a helpless look at Velma, only to see the desperation paint her features as she tried to make her first bite disappear.

"Oh no! What's wrong?"

"Nothing!" Tim blurted out. His answer was too rapid, and the guilty look on his face made it clear he was stretching the truth. "That bite—it just went down the wrong pipe is all." He gamely took another mouthful—but this one was remarkably smaller.

She had to know for herself. Sydney took a dainty bite, and the moment she started to chew, she knew the truth. She choked it down, snatched up her teacup, and tried to politely rinse out the salty taste. "Oh! It's dreadful! How did that happen? Marcella's was delicious!"

"It's a mite salty," Velma admitted.

"It's horrid!" Sydney wailed.

Tim tapped his finger to the glittering crust and dabbed the pad of that finger to his tongue. "Salt."

"That's what Linette and Marcella did," Sydney passionately claimed. "After we crimped the top crust and cut the designs, we sprinkled sal—"

"Supposed to be sugar, child." Velma laughed softly.

Tim peeled back the top crust and continued to eat the filling and bottom crust.

"Oh, do stop! There's no reason to suffer just to assuage my feelings! I'm not a child to be humored!"

"Oh, come on, Syd! The rest of it's just fine. Betcha you don't make that mistake again, so it's no big deal."

"I just wanted to do it right! Linette's and Marcella's were perfect!"

Tim looked over the rim of his coffee cup. "They're country girls."

"I hardly need to be mollified." He'd just as much as told her she didn't belong here. She'd show him. Sydney determined to impress him if it killed her.

⁂

Tim leaned against a fence post and stared at the empty pastureland. They'd moved the cattle again this morning, heading after greener grass . . . as if such a thing existed. He'd mentioned to Sydney that they hadn't had as much rain as usual—but added to the unseasonably dry weather was an early heat wave. Much more of this and the earth would be scorched. Though much of the herd was longhorn crossbred and would carry the heat tolerance and forage better than other breeds when food got scarce, things still looked dicey.

The water level in the pond dropped significantly, and the area where he and Fuller once drilled looked dry as a bone. If Fuller didn't show up in the next few days, Tim determined he'd send a telegram saying they needed to hire someone to come drill elsewhere. Others might sit tight and wait a little longer. Not Tim. Not when so much hung in the balance.

He gazed up at the stars. Stars—those were predictable. Big

Dipper, Little Dipper, Orion, the North Star—God hung them all, and that didn't change. But the weather did. After years of good, it stood to reason that they'd experience some tough times, too. He and Fuller even agreed about setting aside money each year that would see them through a long, dry spell. If he could avert disaster by drilling now, he'd do it. Stauffer had been smart to drill a new well.

Thinking of Stauffer and his well—Tim's gut clenched. Remembering how he'd sent Sydney down that hole made everything within him revolt. Part of him wanted to rattle the teeth out of her head for having participated in that rescue; part of him admired her for the gumption it took. She'd done it, all right—and part of the reason was because he himself had knotted the rope around her and given her a speech about duty. So much could have gone wrong—she could have gotten stuck. The rope might have broken. The air could have run out. The hole could have crumbled and buried her and that little girl alive. She might have gotten little Emmy-Lou, only to have lacked the strength and dropped her. Any of the possibilities left his mouth as dry as the dust at his feet.

Sydney. He didn't know what to do with her.

The pie fiasco after supper was only an indication of a deeper issue. A huge trunk had arrived—and gown after gown now spread across the settee and chairs in the parlor. And they'd only excavated halfway through the trunk before he left. Silks, laces, swags, and such—more foof and poof than he'd ever seen. All suited to a woman of refinement. The dresses she'd been wearing recently were just as much a masquerade costume as the britches had been. The real Sydney Hathwell belonged in drawing rooms, surrounded by men whose polished manners and bottomless bank accounts would pamper her. She no more belonged on Forsaken than a rose belonged in the desert.

Only Sydney wanted to stay here. Or so she thought. Maybe it was a passing whim. Given more time and the lack of excitement and diversions, she'd soon grow bored. So far she hadn't, but what did that mean? He'd brought her back here, telling her she'd stay and even help out her uncle. But they hadn't talked about for how long. He'd intended it to be a permanent arrangement—had she?

Tim cast a glance toward the house. Silhouetted in the window, Sydney tried on a hat. Women were fussy about their hats. Ribbons, netting, feathers, flowers—whatever struck their fancy, women stuck stuff on their hats. Louisa had one she'd prized. Depending on the season, she'd change the decorations around the brim. Though he always thought the whole matter rated as silly, she put great store in it—so he told her it was pretty. Sydney's hatbox alone cost more than any hat a woman around here owned.

Sydney took off her hat and shook her head. *She's not satisfied with it, and it's better than the one she's been using.*

Velma came toward her. Sydney popped the hat on the housekeeper's head. Even in silhouette, Sydney's reaction was unmistakable. She clapped her hands. Velma shook her head and started to remove the bonnet, but Sydney reached up to stop her. She nodded her head, then embraced Velma.

Off in the distance, a rifle shot sounded.

Tim pushed away from the fence post as he listened. A single shot usually indicated a coyote that'd gotten too bold. With water growing scarcer, the coyotes were getting more desperate. Three shots in close succession meant "come running." A second shot sounded.

Tim dashed into the stable, tossed a halter on Hombre, and rode bareback. Velma and Sydney stood at the foot of the porch steps. "Two shots?" Velma called.

"Don't know," he yelled back. The lack of a third shot worried him. Just behind him, men who'd flooded out of the bunkhouse joined up.

Almost two miles later, Tim spotted a rider in the distance. From the wide brim of the sombrero, he knew it was Juan. Juan rode at a modest pace. That meant either there was nothing to worry about, or he was injured and feared falling out of the saddle. Tim kept his pace. When the distance between them narrowed, he cupped his hands to his mouth. "Well?"

"Coyote. Spooked a cow into a prairie dog hole. Broke her leg."

Compared to losing a cowhand, losing a cow rated as good news. The timing could have been better, though. Butchering an animal in daylight was straightforward, even if it made for a bloody mess; doing it by lantern light would turn the task into a huge production. The other hands gathered around Tim. He instructed them to haul the carcass back to the barnyard.

Returning to the house, he halted Hombre at the porch steps. "Lost a cow. I'll go fetch the Smiths to help."

Sydney shook her head. "Don't bother them, Tim. I'll help."

Tim reckoned it would be less hassle to order Lady Sydney to bed than to deal with her reaction once she saw the blood and guts. Having her swoon or puke would make more work for everyone. But she'd shown her mettle several times. He owed her the chance to prove equal to this task, too.

She stared at him. "It's woman's work."

"Sydney——" Velma grabbed her hand and tugged. "We'll need all the help we can get. Go set as much water to boil as you can. Tim, the eldest granddaughter can watch all the children. Bring both women."

As dawn broke, Tim looked down at Sydney. Her hair was a riot of untamed curls, dark circles beneath her eyes tattled on her weariness, and he doubted her apron or dress would ever come clean. Oblivious to his assessment, she waved good-bye to the Smiths. "We'll see you at church!"

"Okay!" Jars and buckets rattled in the bed of the buckboard as it pulled away.

Tim tipped her face up to his. "You sure you'll stay awake through the service?"

"Of course I will. It would be beyond rude to nod off."

"Given the circumstances, I think the preacher would understand."

A surprised laugh bubbled out of her. "I wasn't thinking of him. I was thinking of God. It would be horribly irreverent of me to go pay a visit to His home and ignore Him."

"Attending church is important." He continued to look at her, uncertain if she was awake enough to understand what he felt led to say. "But when we accept Christ, He's with us at all times, wherever we go. Our hearts become His home."

"I recall the vicar saying as much." She flashed him a chipper smile. "He also said that our bodies were the temple of Christ. It was when he tried to convince everyone about the evils of gaming, drinking, and—" Her voice skidded to a halt. She cleared her throat and stammered, "About once a year, he used the pulpit to urge the congregants to be moral pillars."

"It's more than just outward appearance—"

Sydney burst out laughing. She looked down at herself. "I'm glad of that!" A rooster crowed, and she waved one last time as the Smith wagon rounded the corner and went out of sight.

"You were right, Tim. Velma and I did need help."

She'd changed the topic. Tim wasn't sure whether weariness or wariness was behind it. Either way, he felt as if the Holy Spirit was pulling back on the reins for now. Sydney needed time or sleep or space. Maybe all three.

"It was so thoughtful of you to fetch the Smiths," she continued. "You could have selected any of our neighbors, but you chose them, knowing they needed the meat."

"We all help one another out, Sydney. Trying to preserve that much meat would be an impossible task for just you and Velma. As it was, the four of you women worked mighty hard. Those women earned the meat they took home."

"Indeed."

He tucked a wind-tossed curl behind her ear. "You pulled your weight, Sydney."

A lazy smile tilted her mouth and her eyes glittered. "Teamwork, Boss."

She'd taken his praise and turned it back into credit for everyone involved. Tim nodded. "You're a bloody mess, Fancy Pants. You can't very well visit the Lord's house in that shape."

"A coyote robbed me of my Saturday night bath, sir. If you wish to lodge a complaint, I suggest you take up the matter with him." She picked up her skirts and flounced away. Her laughter floated back at him.

"Never woulda thunk it." Pancake shuffled over and shook his head. "Never in a million years. The day Syd dawdled up the road, I reckoned we was all gonna fight for who got to truss up the kid and shove him on the first train outta here. Didn't take much time for the kid to show gumption—and now, look at her. If anyone tried to put her on the train, he'd have to fight me first."

Tim looked at the scrappy cook. By now, everyone knew

Sydney had tried to leave and obtain a position elsewhere. Pancake was issuing a challenge. Earlier, Tim had wondered if she belonged elsewhere—but she'd proven herself yet again. Sydney belonged here. Staring Pancake in the eye, Tim drawled, "Fight him? You could line up after me, old man, but I would have already whupped the fool."

⁂

"Tired?" Tim walked Sydney toward the buckboard after church.

She gave a dainty shrug. "A little."

Velma bustled over. "Tim, you go on ahead and take Sydney home. I'm spending the afternoon with Mrs. Vaughn."

"Shall I come, too?"

Velma gave her a stern look. "You don't belong there." She turned to Tim. "It's her sixth. I ought to be home by supper."

Tim tied Hombre to the buckboard and drove Sydney toward Forsaken. After a few minutes, he cleared his throat. "Sydney, don't get your feelings hurt. Velma's the closest thing we have to a midwife around here."

"Oh, as soon as the need dawned on me, I understood."

"Guess you're more tired than you thought, huh? Don't think you've ever been this quiet."

"I've been thinking about the sermon. Poor Leah. My heart breaks for her. How dreadful must it have been for her, being married to a man who didn't love her."

"I suppose so. But she knew Jacob wanted Rachel, and she pretended to be her sister and fooled Jacob."

"But she was obeying her father. So you think she should have gone against his wishes? And don't you think maybe Jacob got what he deserved, since he practiced trickery to steal Esau's birthright?"

Tim thought for a moment. "I don't count on things being fair or justice to be seen in every situation here on earth. In the end God will judge us all. Even then, none of us will ever measure up. It's only through God's grace that we can be forgiven for our sins."

"The preacher spoke about that, but ..." She sighed.

"But?"

"You know how sorry I am that I masqueraded as a boy. And you've forgiven me. That's the only truly awful thing I've ever done. Nobody got hurt." Sydney smoothed a few wind-ruffled flounces of her lilac taffeta and wished her feelings would fall into order as easily. "I don't understand why I'm not good enough to go to heaven. I always thought I was a Christian—I went to church, and Father was very generous with the vicar. I remember the vicar saying God would forgive our debts as we forgave our debtors. I thought it was a fair deal."

"We can't earn salvation. Isaiah sixty-four, verse six, says, 'But we are all as an unclean thing, and all our righteousnesses are as filthy rags; and we all do fade as a leaf; and our iniquities, like the wind, have taken us away.'" He pulled the reins to the right. Once the buckboard went to the side of the road, he called, "Whoa."

Sydney looked up at him. "So that says we're all sinners." On the heels of that, an appalling thought hit her. "I'm a sinner? Me? I mean, I don't intend to sound proud, but I thought sinners were bad people—like murderers."

Tim wrapped the reins around the brake and said in a slow, quiet tone, "It's a far sight more comfortable to point fingers at others."

He's saying I'm a sinner. Well, not just him. That Bible verse did, too.

He turned to her. "When you put on britches and pretended to be a boy, it didn't make you a boy. You fooled us, but God knew all along who and what you are. People can attend church, pay tithes, and do good works—but those are all props, and they're masquerading. To God, even our best is nothing more than filthy rags."

"That makes it all seem so hopeless." She shook her head, as if to dislodge the troubling thought.

A mild breeze stirred, and a leaf fluttered to earth, then tumbled across the road. "That leaf fell from the branch. Short of a miracle, nothing will ever give it life again. Sin does that to us—separates us from God and carries us away. It doesn't matter whether the sin is large or small—we're deluding ourselves if we say otherwise. The only thing that gives life to our soul again is the miracle of accepting Christ as our Savior."

Her thoughts were muddled. "It used to be so clear to me. Now it's not. I must be more tired than I imagined."

"You can sleep the whole afternoon away." He took up the reins again. "But think about this some more."

She nodded—not because she wanted to agree, but because Sydney knew it would continue to bother her until she figured it out.

When they reached Forsaken, Tim drove the buckboard right up to the porch. Merle and Gulp didn't go to church, so they were pitching horseshoes. Both dashed over to the buckboard. "Lookit you!" Merle gawked at her.

Gulp shoved him aside. "Don't pay him no mind, miss. You look purdy as can be. That's gotta be one of them London gowns of yours." He reached up to help her down.

"Don't." Tim's curt voice made everyone freeze. "Your hands are filthy." Both of the cowboys glanced down to confirm his accusation.

Sydney didn't want the men to pull away. She laughed. "Dirt washes."

"Not out of fancy duds. Not those kind." Merle nodded at her dress. He looked back at his palms. "I wasn't thinking."

"I'd be honored to take both of your hands." Sydney extended an arm toward each of the cowboys. Once their rough palms closed around her hands, she stiffened her arms and made a tiny leap to get free from the buckboard. The minute her boots landed on a step, she turned loose. "Thank you kindly, gentlemen."

Merle grinned. "I heard tell you're the one we ought to thank. Had us a fine breakfast today on account of you."

Sydney raised a hand to hide her grin. Tim must have thought she was yawning, for he swept his hand toward the front door. "Syd, go on up and sleep. I'll eat lunch with the men."

Sydney escaped. She made it into the house and halfway up the stairs before she heard Tim bellow, "She what?!"

Chapter Twenty-three

Sydney walked into the kitchen that evening and stared at the sight before her. Tim looked utterly ridiculous. He'd shoved a dishtowel into his belt to serve as an erstwhile apron. The fire in the stove was far too high——flames sneaked up beneath the burners. "I heard you moving around upstairs and decided to rustle up some chow."

She didn't want to hurt his feelings, but Sydney worried they'd both get sick if he cooked for them. "Velma's not home yet?"

"She got home half an hour ago. Practically cross-eyed from being tired. Ate a ham sandwich and dragged herself off to bed."

"How is Mrs. Vaughn? And the baby?"

"She's fine. Baby boy's fine, too." *Clang.* He plopped a skillet onto the front burner. "We're having eggs for supper."

"Oh."

Tim shot her an accusing look. "Just eggs. No brains. Apparently someone gave half of them to Pancake for the cowboys' breakfast, and the other half went home with the Smiths. Would you know anything about that?"

She didn't bother to smother her smile. "Why, Mr. Creighton, it's a pity Velma isn't here to be a witness."

"Afraid I'm going to strangle you?"

She shook her head. "You'd never hurt me. But it's not often a man confesses he's brainless."

He gave her an outraged look. "For that, Fancy Pants, I'm going to burn your eggs."

"You would have burned them, regardless." She held the coffeepot beneath the pump and started to fill it.

"I happen to be quite adept at making eggs."

"I thought hens laid eggs. You don't look like a hen to me." She paused a moment. "I haven't figured out something, though. How do you know whether the egg is for eating or hatching?"

"You don't." Tim held up an egg. His huge hand dwarfed it. "You take your chances."

"You cannot be serious!" Her voice reflected her horror.

Tim shrugged. Turning toward the pan, he changed his hold on the egg. "Why do you think Velma mixes brains with the eggs?"

"You are perfectly dreadful, Mr. Creighton."

He quickly cracked half a dozen eggs on the side of the skillet and began cooking with practiced ease.

"I'm afraid your talents are being wasted here on a ranch!"

He slid the eggs onto a plate. "Much as I hate to confess it, this is the one and only thing I can make."

"You're welcome to join me while I'm learning." Sydney cut slices of bread from a loaf. "Velma is far more efficient, but the Richardson girls—"

"Don't press your luck." He stuck the plate in the center of the kitchen table.

"They're actually very sweet girls, Timothy. Truly, they are. Did you know that their mother and father were both orphans? Well, they were, and as nice as Mr. and Mrs. Richardson are, they never learned basic social graces. The girls simply need a little guidance."

His mouth twisted wryly. "And I thought I was the one who believed in miracles."

"You're not going to start a debate on what to believe, are you?" Their discussion on the way home from church left her feeling unsettled. Tired as she was, she hadn't slept well.

Tim's eyes met hers. "There's no debate, Sydney; I don't have to convince you. If you seek the truth, it's right there. God is faithful to meet us where we are."

His response stunned her. She'd decided to fall back on the axiom that religion, finances, and politics were subjects best not discussed, and he'd dumped the whole thing back on her shoulders.

Tim seated her and took the chair opposite hers. He folded his hands and bowed his head. How many times had she seen him do that? But something struck her. Until she came here, prayer was merely a rote recitation that blessed food and asked for safety. When the vicar back home prayed, her mind wandered, so she couldn't truly recall what came out of his mouth. She supposed he read the Bible—after all, it was his job, and he quoted from it. But other than the vicar, she'd never known anyone who read his Bible and prayed as Tim did.

Tim said if she sought the truth, God would be faithful to meet her. God was God. He knew where she was. If He wasn't happy with her, why didn't He do something about it? Thoughts whirled through her mind, and Tim's "Amen" took her by surprise.

"Eat." He pressed a fork into her hand. "Why do you look so bewildered?"

She grasped for the first excuse that came to mind. "There's only one plate."

"Yeah, but I don't mind sharing. Eat up, Fancy Pants."

She wagged the tines of her fork at him. "It's the height of impropriety for you to address me in such a manner."

He grinned. "Chalk it up to not knowing any better. I was an orphan, too."

"You were?"

He took a slice of the bread and sopped the corner in egg yolk. "I was teasing, Sydney—but not about losing my folks. I did." He took a bite. "But after you mentioned the Richardsons not knowing any better, I was smarting off." He swallowed and grinned. "You're fun to tease."

"You are a scoundrel, Timothy Creighton."

"If this were a court of law, I'd have to plead guilty to the charge. Do I dare throw myself on your mercy?"

She looked about and poked her nose high into the air. "Mr. Creighton, since Newgate Prison is too far away, I hereby sentence you to one evening of dishwashing."

He glanced down at the plate they shared. "How many times do you expect me to wash this poor plate? If I spend a whole evening doing it, I'll wear a hole in the middle."

"So you're not seeking mercy just for yourself, but for the china as well?"

"And the calf, too."

"What calf?" Her eyes widened as she realized the cow they'd slaughtered left a calf behind. "I didn't realize! Isn't one of the other cows . . ." Her voice died out in embarrassment.

"Not when a calf is this old. I'm bucket-feeding him. It's about time for him to eat, too."

"Can I help?"

"It's slimy."

"You're the man who told me once that a calf would some-day feed a family for a whole winter. I daresay bucket-feeding a calf won't be nearly as slimy as what you asked of me on that occasion." When his eyes narrowed, she asked, "Why are you looking at me like that?"

"How far up can you roll those sleeves?"

Ten minutes later, her sleeve pushed clear up to her elbow, Sydney looked at a burnt orange, speckled calf. He bawled, and she crooned, "Poor baby!"

Pancake sauntered up with a bucket of milk and looked from Tim to her and back. "You sure of this?"

"Positive. Tim's going to teach me what to do."

"Hey, Juan!" Pancake windmilled one arm. "C'mon. Syd's gonna feed the calf."

Tim snatched the bucket from Pancake. "Sydney, give me your hand."

He took her hand, plunged it into the milk bucket, then held it beneath the calf's mouth. Tim's fingers slid downward, and he braced her wrist as the calf slurped her fingers into its mouth. His tongue and lips were warm and—*slimy*. Sydney refused to yank away. She turned her head. Tim's face was right beside hers. She whispered, "Anything on my fingers has to be gone. Do I dip my hand again?"

"Sort of." A lazy grin tilted his mouth.

Warmth stole through her. Then shock. Somehow, he'd lifted the bucket and drew her wrist and hand into the milk. The calf continued to slurp on her fingers. Tim lowered her hand a little at a time until it was completely beneath the milk.

"The trick is to learn to brace the bucket. After he drinks his fill, he's liable to butt it." Tim withdrew their hands slowly and had her help him hang on to the bucket.

"He's so hungry!"

"Yeah." For some reason, having Tim whisper their conversation felt right. Cozy. Sydney didn't want to startle the poor, motherless baby, and apparently Tim shared that sentiment. His warm breath tickled her cheek. "He's pretty big. Give him a couple of days, and he'll stick his head in the bucket without being coaxed. He's already nipping at a little grass, too. Won't be long till he's back out in the pasture full-time."

"I can help until then. Pancake will have to show me how to warm up the milk."

Tim lowered his mouth right by her ear. "He didn't warm it, sugar. It comes that way straight out of the cow."

Heat streaked through her as she gasped.

"No getting goosey on me."

"Boss, Syd's gone red as a pickled beet."

Tim straightened up. "If I don't miss my guess, Sydney's fixing to argue about who feeds this calf."

"Could just forget about it." Pancake rubbed his big belly. "It's been a long time since we had veal."

Sydney jolted, jamming the bucket far up on the poor calf. "You'd better be teasing, Pancake!"

Tim yanked the pail back down as the calf coughed, sneezed, and bawled.

"Look at what you did." Sydney petted the calf. "You scared the poor little creature, Pancake."

"Aww, Boss. Do something. She's getting all sentimental."

"Of course I'm sentimental. I just saved this poor starving little baby. If you had the merest scrap of compassion, you'd come apologize to Moustache so he would stop trembling."

"Moustache?" the men echoed in disbelief.

Pancake moaned loudly. "She named that stupid hunk of beef."

"He's got a milk moustache. And Moustache isn't stupid. He's merely ignorant. It's our duty to be patient and teach him."

Pancake folded his arms across his chest. "Just like we did

with you when you were supposed to be a boy?"

"Exactly so!" Pleased he'd understood, Sydney beamed at him.

Pancake let out a whooping laugh and walked out of the barn. Tim thumped the milk pail onto the floor and kept clearing his throat as he, too, walked away.

"Just what," she wondered aloud, "is so funny? Oh, Tim, come look! Moustache is drinking out of the bucket all on his own. Isn't he brilliant?"

"Sydney, go back inside. Moustache isn't going to need help feeding from now on."

Sydney ran over to Tim. "You're not going to listen to Pancake. You cannot. Moustache is not veal. He's smart!"

"Sydney—"

"Oh, don't you stretch out my name as if I'm testing your patience to the limit. You yourself discussed the matter with Mr. Richardson. It is a scientific fact that the premier animals produce the best offspring."

Tim seemed to find the toes of his boots fascinating. Again, he cleared his throat. "Moustache is not a bull."

"Yes, but he'll grow up and—" Her voice died out as Tim shook his head.

"A steer, Syd. He's a steer."

Thoroughly mortified, she whispered, "I believe I'll go in and wash up."

Sydney scrubbed her hands, then washed the skillet and plate. Though sorely tempted to go hide in her bedchamber, she decided to sit on the parlor settee and read. If Tim came in, she'd look serene—even if it killed her. She lit a lamp and found the *Peterson's Magazine* Mrs. Patterson had left.

Tim's heavy footsteps on the porch warned of his impending arrival. She hastily opened the magazine. A mere moment before Tim found her, she realized she was holding it upside down.

ily flipping the magazine over, she opened it and bowed her head over the page.

"Find something interesting?"

Forcing herself to sound nonchalant, Sydney noted a tiny little insert on the bottom of the right page. "A poem."

Tim's favorite chair groaned as the overstuffed leather yielded to his weight. "What's it about?"

Sydney silently read the title. Disbelief streaked through her. "You'd never believe me."

"Because it's you, I'd believe just about anything. Go ahead and read it aloud."

Only two choices were possible: either she swooned or brazened her way through. Sydney drew in a deep breath. The poem was short enough, she could read the title and race through the eight lines all in one breath. She hoped.

"'True Manhood.'"

Something suspiciously like a snicker erupted from Tim. Sydney ignored him and kept reading.

*"How happy is he born and taught
That serveth not another's will;
Whose armor is his honest thought,
And simple truth his only skill.
This man is freed from servile bands
Of hope to rise or fear to fall;
Lord of himself, thought not of lands;
Yet having nothing, hath all."*

She looked up and flashed a smile at him. *There. That wasn't too dreadful.*

"Sounds like a lot of flowery nonsense to me."

A little debate might help keep their minds engaged so she could get past feeling morbidly self-conscious about her stupidity in the barn. "It's not nonsense. I found it refreshing. Of all people, I'd think you'd appreciate how it upholds honesty and truth."

"Those lines were okay, but the rest—I can't hold with it. I'm not lord of myself; God's the Lord of my life. As for not serving another's will—my aim is to serve His will."

"Does everything have to come back to that?"

Tim studied her for a long moment. "For me, it does."

"I did ask," she admitted grudgingly. Tracing a line on the page, Sydney tried to change the course of the conversation. "I especially like this part: 'freed from servile hands/ Of hope to rise or fear to fall.' You've absolutely no idea how refreshing it's been to not have to mind every tiny nuance and worry about each action. Even the most minor of infractions was cause for gossip back home. I never fully appreciated how stilted my life had become until I came to Texas. I don't mean to say that the ladies here aren't proper; they are. It's just some of the petty rules for decorum aren't adhered to with zeal."

"Like what?" Tim hiked one ankle to the opposite knee and relaxed into his chair.

A flood of answers rushed through her mind. "Calling cards. I've not seen a single one since I arrived."

"Then why all those fancy invitations for the sewing bee? You're not making sense."

"Those were for the greater good." She smiled. "I've noticed the Richardson women are wont to simply traipse in without warning. Doing the invitations permitted me to broach the subject without being unkind. I treasure how neighbors here are so hospitable, but since the girls have made a habit of chasing after men, I hoped it would be a way of—"

"Reining them in. Good idea. So other than giving up on

calling cards, what other rules have you ditched since coming here?"

"Oh," she said with delight. "I no longer have to change clothing multiple times a day."

"Changing clothes? Why?"

"There are morning dresses, walking dresses, tea gowns, dinner gowns, ball gowns, riding skirts, not to mention an Ascot dress, garden party dress ..." She made a dismissive gesture. "Something appropriate for each occasion."

She traced the sketch of a Japanese design for a chair-pillow in the magazine and felt an odd sense of relief that embellished items like this example were out of place at Forsaken. "I never realized how stifling all the rules were until I experienced such freedom here. The notion of ever again trying to be oh-so-very-proper every minute of the day is sufficient to make me do something drastic."

Tim raised a brow. "Like donning britches and ranching?"

"It worked. At least for a while." She gave a dainty shrug. Britches never gave her fits. Velma helped her into her gown this morning, and trying to get out of it alone required acrobatics the likes of which Sydney hadn't ever tried before. Men simply didn't know how lucky they were to yank on jeans and a shirt instead of wearing a plethora of underclothing, yards upon yards of dresses, bustles that made it impossible to sit comfortably ...

"What are you thinking?"

He would ask that now. "Nothing important. So Mrs. Vaughn had a boy. That makes two girls and three boys for them." Sydney frowned. "I thought Velma said it was their sixth."

"They lost a baby two years ago. Something was wrong with her heart, and she only lasted a few days. Velma said this one's loud and pink, so he ought to fare well."

Sydney studied Tim. Something in his tone bothered her. "Were you worried?"

He nodded curtly. "Bill took it hard, losing that little girl."

"Losing my parents has been dreadful. I cannot imagine how horrible it must be to lose a child."

"It's bad."

Tim's quiet tone robbed her of her breath. She couldn't ask, though. Once before, he'd mentioned he'd been married, and on an occasion before that, he told her it was a sore spot. She'd assumed his wife had been unfaithful. Sydney stared at him as a ghastly suspicion swamped her.

Chapter Twenty-four

"Seven years ago," Tim said in a soft, gruff tone, "cholera took my wife and our little baby son."

Tears sprang to her eyes. "I'm so very sorry." The words barely came out in a hushed whisper.

"Running off and starting a new life didn't dull the pain. Time and God's grace do—along with friends."

The print on the magazine blurred. Tim's big, rough hands closed the pages; then he handed her his red bandana. The settee creaked as he sat down beside her. "Coming here isn't going to make you forget your loved ones. After a time, the nice memories linger and you won't ache so bad."

"How long?" she asked in a high, tight voice.

"The way you feel right now, even one minute is an eternity."

The truth of his words hit home. No one had empathized as he just had. Sydney tried to contain her emotions long enough to run upstairs, but Tim didn't let her off the settee. Wrapping his arms about her, he cupped her head to his shoulder and held her as she wept. When she wound down, Tim wiped the tears from her face.

"I'm sorry. I don't know what came over me."

"Grief." He tipped her face up to his. "Even Jesus wept when His friend Lazarus died."

His words erased most of the embarrassment she felt. Still, she'd let her own grief overflow when he'd shared his own loss. "It's ghastly—what you went through."

"It was. Fuller was a stalwart friend to me, even while I shook my fist and railed against God."

Surprise streaked through her sorrow. Sydney didn't know anyone else had felt that way. "At my parents' gravesides, the vicar said God gave and took away and we were supposed to bless His name. I thought that was a vile thing to say."

"It's from the Bible. Job says it. It took me a long time to be thankful for the time God granted me with Louisa and Timmy, instead of resenting Him for taking them away. Longer, still, for memories to bring pleasure instead of pain."

Though sorely tempted to nestle close and draw strength from Tim, Sydney pushed away and smoothed her dress. "It's . . . reassuring to hear it will get easier."

"The most important things take time."

She shook her head. "Not necessarily." A winsome smile lifted her lips. "Mama and Father met and married within a day."

Tim's eyes widened.

She nodded. "Honestly. I suppose that is the proverbial exception that proves the rule."

He chuckled. "I can't blame him if your mother had half your fire and beauty." He rose and started across the parlor. "Since you're enjoying that magazine, we could get you a subscription. Either that, or *Godey's Lady's Book.* Do you have a preference?"

"Why, thank you," she stammered. In her experience, men flattered women because they wanted attention. Tim had paid her the nicest compliment of her life and then had changed the topic just as abruptly. "Either magazine would be lovely."

He cast her a sly smile. "I could recommend a few books on cattle ranching."

Laughter bubbled out of her. He'd held her while she cried, yet now he cheered her up. "You, Timothy Creighton, are a hopeless scoundrel."

"I might well be a scoundrel, but I am far from hopeless."

Tim set aside his Bible and stared out the window. Faint streaks of lavender and gold tinted the predawn sky. *The colors Sydney wears. And she's living in darkness. Lord, she's hurting and so lost.*

The floorboard at the head of the stairs creaked. Tim opened his door. "What are you doing up?"

Sydney turned and whispered, "Shhh. Velma's sleeping."

He picked up his boots and walked down the stairs with Sydney. As they reached the last step, he repeated, "What are you doing up?"

"I thought I'd start coffee, gather eggs, and check on Moustache."

"It's early."

She shrugged. "I had a nap yesterday. Lolling about in bed is useless. Hot as it's getting at midday, I've noticed you're doing a lot of work earlier."

He nodded. While she started coffee, he plopped down and yanked on his boots. "Don't get attached to that calf, Sydney. He's beef on the hoof, not a pet."

"What's wrong with having a pet?"

"A pet shouldn't outweigh its owner."

She smiled. "Moustache doesn't."

"If I were a betting man, I'd wager he already has a good ten to fifteen pounds on you."

"Me?"

"He's five weeks. A solid hundred and five pounds—maybe a shade more." He stomped his foot into his second boot and looked at Sydney's astonished expression. "No offense intended. You're a slight woman is all."

"I have no notion what I might weigh. I've never stepped foot on a scale, but that's not the issue. You and Uncle Fuller own the animals. Compared to a tall, muscular man like you, Moustache—"

"Will pass my weight before Christmas." Her crestfallen look tore at him. "If you're that worried about him, come on out. You can make sure he's bucket-feeding well."

Once they were in the barn, he left Sydney to coo over the calf while he led one of the two milk cows to a stanchion. Sydney approached him. "If you teach me how, I can do that."

Tim snorted. "In that dress?"

"I intend for the milk to go into the pail, not on my clothing."

"You'd break your neck, trying to balance on a milking stool." He pulled out the small log with a board nailed into a T-shape across the top.

"You thought I couldn't ride or shoot, either." She snatched it from him and started to walk behind the cow.

Tim yanked her back. "That's begging for her to kick you. You're right-handed, so you milk from the right. Bessie's used to right-siders. If you went to the left, she'd pitch a fit."

Sydney listened intently. "Thank you for that instruction. Now if you'd be so kind as to turn your head for a moment . . ."

"Why?" He scowled. "The stool doesn't go underneath your skirts!"

"What would you know of it? You've never worn skirts." She stuck her forefinger in the air and twirled it in a silent order for him to turn.

"Oh, brother." Tim turned and prepared to whip back around and catch her as she fell.

"I suppose I should have the pail ready. Might you please hand it to me?"

Tim turned and knelt beside her. The crazy woman had managed to sit on the milking stool properly and even had her skirts artfully arranged to the side, out of the way. Sliding the pail in place, he wondered how he'd manage to tell her what to do without offending her sensibilities.

She tilted her head toward him but didn't look his way. In the barest whisper, she said, "I'm glad you're my friend. That way, I don't have to be embarrassed about this."

Friends. As a "boy," Sydney had become a young protégé— a friend. Ever since he'd discovered the truth, Tim had put distance between them. Only she'd sneaked past his guard all over again. He couldn't deny it. "Yes, Syd. We're friends. Here's what you do."

A while later, she stood back and watched Moustache slurp milk from the bucket. "He's such a bright calf, Tim. See how he's taken to it?"

"Uh-oh." Pancake sauntered over. "Syd's getting moon-eyed over that beast, Tim. Maybe I ought to get some chalk and mark him so she'll see the ribs and roasts and steaks he's gonna become."

"Turn him out to pasture for the day." *If only the calf were female. I could have kept her as a breeder and made Sydney happy.* Tim fought the urge to reassure Sydney that the calf wouldn't go to market. Kids who grew up on a ranch learned early on that the animals represented food, not companionship. Sydney planned to stay; she had to learn it, too.

"I'll go gather eggs." Sydney stopped at the door to the barn. "Pancake? Don't bother with the chalk. Moustache is already marked like he's supposed to become a saddle."

Once she was out of earshot, Pancake kicked a bale of hay. "Blast it. Why'd she go and say that? Bad enough, she named him. Now I'm gonna feel like a snake when we drive him off to market."

It should have been insignificant. Only Tim couldn't get it out of his mind. Sydney had already lost everything. That evening she showed up in the barn, milked the cow, and fed Moustache. Moustache butted the bucket and doused her skirts.

"So that's how you feel about my cooking?" She laughed and picked up the bucket. "I'm sure Tim would agree."

"You're learning." He pointed at her hem. "That's why clothes like that don't belong out here."

"Nonsense. Clothes wash."

"Yeah, but you and Velma finished the laundry this afternoon." His eyes narrowed. "And her washing machine would rip the daylights out of that."

"Her Blackstone machine is a marvel, isn't it?" Sydney plucked a little piece of hay from her sleeve. "Warm as it is, I can hand wash this now, and it'll be dry by bedtime."

When he went to the house, her dress fluttered on the clothesline. Somehow, when she wore her gowns, they seemed ... pretty. Feminine. But on the clothesline, with the skirts all pinned out to keep them from dragging, the creation looked impossibly out of place. Yards upon yards spread out, pinned clear across the line, the delicate ruffles and lace mocking their rugged surroundings.

"Flutter your fan, don't flap it." Sydney stood in the parlor, reached over, and guided Linette's hand.

Marcella laughed. "If you had a fan in the other hand, you'd start flying like a goose!"

Linette's lower lip began to quiver.

Sydney cast a look at Marcella. "'Jests that give pains ...'"

"'... are no jests.'" Marcella completed the quote. "Sorry, Linny."

Linette closed the fan with an awkward slap and wailed, "I can't do this. I'll never catch a man!"

"I hope you never do!" Sydney snatched the fan from her and gave her a playful tap on the wrist with it. "The gentleman is to catch you! If you don't feel comfortable with a fan, you needn't use one."

"But when you use it, you look so ... charming." Linette sniffled.

"Despair is a folly brought on when we compare ourselves." Sydney opened the fan and fluttered it. "Or so my mother told me when I wished with all my might that I'd be a tall, blue-eyed blonde."

"You'll never be tall, blue-eyed, or blond," Katherine said.

"Indeed, I won't. Even though that is all the rage in London. So I learned to use a fan instead. You, Linette, are willowy, blue-eyed, and flaxen-haired. I'm so impressed at how gracefully you're holding yourself. Your posture is positively regal."

"I've been working on it!"

Katherine looked down at her hands. "Mama made up that recipe Velma had with glycerin and rosewater. My hands are so soft now, no one would believe I shucked corn all last week. I was afraid none of the men would want to dance with me when they saw my hands."

"And I, thanks to your wonderful lessons, am able to make applesauce cake. I plan to bake one for the dance." Sydney clasped her hands. "So we're all helping one another. Shall we practice dancing again?"

Marcella moaned. "I'm hopeless. Even Daddy won't dance with me. He said I've broken every one of his toes twice."

"All the more reason to practice." Sydney lifted the vase from the occasional table and placed it on the mantel. "Marcella, would you and Linette please scoot the settee over against that wall there? Yes, below the cross. And, Katherine, you're such a dear to move that table. Look at all this space we've made! Outstanding!"

While they practiced to the tinkling music of a music box, Tim clomped through the house. Linette called out, "Come join us! We need a man!"

Tim shook his head and said in a terse voice, "I've got work to do. Velma? Pancake needs your tweezers. He's got a splinter."

After Tim strode back outside with the tweezers, Linette sighed. "He's never going to fall in love with me. It breaks my heart. I wish I were beautiful."

"You are beautiful." Sydney held Linette's hands and squeezed. "You know how I adore Cervantes."

"You quote his writings the way the parson quotes the Bible."

Sydney smiled. "Well, he wrote many wise things, and one of them comes to mind right this very minute: 'All kinds of beauty don't inspire love; there is a kind that pleases on the sight, but does not captivate the affections.' You wouldn't want a man who merely wanted you to be a decoration on his arm. How very empty a marriage would be if all that mattered to your husband was your appearance! You want a husband who will love your zest for life and appreciate the gentleness you show children."

Tim didn't venture near the house again until long after the Richardsons left. He didn't say much at supper, so Sydney waited to speak until Velma left the supper table to get the applesauce cake. She cleared her throat to gain his attention. "Tim, if it bothers you so much for the Richardson girls to come here, I could go to their farm."

"No." The word lashed out of him. He pointed his fork at her. "You're staying put. If anyone caught wind of you being there, men would storm the place."

"That would be wonderful!"

He scowled. "No man is getting within ten feet of you unless Fuller approves of him."

"But think how lovely it would be for Linette and—"

"Sydney, you're doing a right fine job with 'em from what little I've seen, but any man in the world would ignore them with you around. Those girls are dull as dishwater compared to you." He stabbed his fork in his meat and muttered, "Then again, water is getting so scarce ..." His head shot back up. "But you're staying on Forsaken. I'll put up with those girls being here as long as I don't get trapped into anything."

<hr/>

"Sydney, I told you that gown's too fancy for you to wear while milking and feeding—see there?" Tim shook his head.

"Everything rinsed out last time. Is it my imagination, or is Moustache growing bigger?" She merely laughed when the calf licked at her hand and skirt.

Tim pushed the calf away. "I'm putting him out to pasture.

He's plenty big enough now. Has been for days."

She compressed her lips and nodded.

Feeling like a brute, Tim knew he couldn't let her continue to dote on the beast. "You knew this would happen. This is the way things have to be. Don't be disappointed."

Sydney reached over and petted the calf's red face and traced the edge of the white moustache. "It's not your fault, Tim. I understand."

"Good. If you think on it, I'm sure you can come up with one of Cervantes' axioms that will apply." There. That would give her something to occupy her mind.

"'Man appoints, and God disappoints.'"

"Sydney!" Horror streaked through him. Was that her image of God?

"I'd better go rinse out my dress." Her expression was guarded. "You told me not to be disappointed, and that's what popped into my mind. I know you believe the reverse—that God appoints and man disappoints. Maybe both are true. Please don't say anything. I don't want to discuss religion just now."

Tim fought the urge to chase after her after she turned and walked away. Instead, he stared up at the heavens. "Lord, Sydney's got so much roiling inside. Ever since she figured she's a sinner, too, she's been struggling. I don't know what to do or how to help. That girl needs you. She needs you bad."

The next morning, Sydney hastened outside after breakfast to hang out her dress so it could finish drying again. Tim shook his head.

Velma poked his arm. "Don't you go back to judging her by her duds, Big Tim. She's got a plan, and if you say anything, you'll spoil it. By the way, Sydney made a couple of big, fat sandwiches for you and put them in a bucket with an apple. That way, you don't have to wade past the Richardson gals while we're having our sewing bee today."

He grunted and walked off.

It wasn't long before just about every woman and child for miles around arrived. Mrs. Orion and Heidi rode in a buckboard with the pastor's wife and some of the other town women. Heidi waved to him. "Mr. Creighton! Come look!"

He strode over and helped the ladies alight. The Widow O'Toole paraded into the house carrying a cake. Heidi wiggled by his side until he helped the last woman. "Look!" The little girl stuck out her foot. "Mr. Matteo—he fixed my old shoes extra special!"

Tim grinned. Matteo had replaced the rivet for the buckle—but he'd also cut out the toes to turn the almost-too-small shoes into sandals. He'd stained them red, too. "Aren't those a sight!"

"Jesus wore sandals. Mama says it's a reminder to me to be good like Jesus wants me to."

"Come, Heidi. Mr. Creighton's a busy man." Mrs. Orion took hold of the wooden handle of her sewing box and grabbed Heidi's hand.

Tim winked at the little girl. "Your mama's right about those sandals. Show them to Lady Sydney."

"Big Tim," the parson's wife said, "could you please carry this crate into the house?"

"Sure thing, Mrs. Bradle."

As he walked up the porch steps, Heidi was showing Sydney her sandals. On his way back out, Sydney said, "Isn't that true, Big Tim?"

"What?"

"Mrs. Orion was admiring that dress I hung up to finish drying. I told her it's unsuitable for ranch life. You said so yourself, didn't you?"

"I did."

"See?" Sydney grabbed Mrs. Orion's hands in hers. "My second cousin's wife understood my wishes to wear proper mourning for Father. I fear she went a bit overboard, though. It's been over a year now—" Sydney closed her eyes, then took a steadying breath. "Gray, mauve, purple, lavender, lilac, white and burgundy—they're permitted after the first year. It's been more than a year for you, hasn't it?"

"Why, yes, but—"

"I nearly ruined that dress yesterday, spilling milk all down the skirts. And that shade of lilac would be so pretty on you. I might sound dreadfully vain, but that gown always makes me look sickly. Sallow. It's the red in my hair, you see."

"Your hair is a beautiful shade of chestnut."

Tim slipped away before he got drawn further into the conversation. Velma warned him Sydney had a plan. He hoped it was simply to give Mrs. Orion the dress and not to corner him into paying the widow any compliments. At the earliest opportunity, he'd drag Sydney off and make sure she knew not to try matchmaking.

"Boss." Gulp's indignant tone sent Tim in his direction. As he drew closer, Gulp motioned toward the barnyard. School had still been in session the day the women came to sew the dress for Sydney. Free for the summer, children now filled Forsaken's yard. "Boss, you've gotta do something!"

Tim crooked a brow.

"A bunch of boys turned my lariat into a swing—a *swing!*"

Tim laughed in sheer disbelief.

"Go ahead and laugh. That ain't no skippin' rope over yonder. Them girls stole your lariat."

"We're sorry. We didn't mean to break your clothesline." The Smith boys stared at their feet.

Sydney patted Harvey's shoulder. "We're just glad you didn't get hurt, aren't we, Big Tim?"

Tim stared at the jumble of rope, wood, and blankets on the ground.

Since he hadn't responded, Sydney felt obliged to explain. "The boys were building a tent."

"We use Ma's line at home. Hers must be stronger."

Harvey wrinkled his freckled nose. "We always drag the blankets across Ma's. We never tried tightrope walking the blankets across before today."

Sydney gasped. "You could have broken your necks!"

"No, ma'am, we were careful. We walked on two lines apiece and had hold of each other's shoulder with one hand."

Tim folded his arms across his chest. "You boys are lucky the fancy dress Lady Sydney gave to Mrs. Orion wasn't hanging there anymore. Now shake out the blankets and go spread them out for lunch."

The boys scurried to do his bidding.

"I'm sorry, Tim." Sydney stooped and inspected the cracked wooden supports.

"Velma's been after me to put up a bigger one made of pipe."

"That's very forgiving of you. I know how busy you are."

He took her hand and helped her back up. "I've been forgiven far worse."

She grinned. "I can imagine you were quite a handful as a boy. Even so, nobody's perfect."

"I was a rascal, but you're right: Nobody's perfect."

"So then why doesn't God appreciate it when we do our best?" She pressed her fingers to her mouth. She couldn't believe she'd blurted out that question. "My apologies. Ever since I discovered I'm a sinner, this has all ..." She made a helpless gesture.

"It was a reasonable question, Syd. God gave us His best—His Son. It's by His grace we are forgiven, not because of our actions."

Sydney didn't want to think about what he'd said. Then again, she'd been thinking of little else for days. She gestured toward the broken clothesline. "Well, our clothes are certainly bound to be as filthy rags right now!"

"The outside doesn't matter; the inside does." He tapped his shirt pocket over his heart.

You and Velma have a peace in your hearts that I envy. Everything inside me feels so topsy-turvy.

"So it's not God who disappoints. We're the ones who disappoint Him because we mess up."

"Exactly."

"Rasselfrass!" Merle's shout caused them both to wheel around. "Boogers and brains! Stinkin'—"

Sydney hiked up her skirts and chased after Tim toward the source of the noise.

"Merle!" Tim's booming voice silenced the hand's odd tirade. "What is going on here?"

"This is what's going on." Merle jabbed his finger through a hole in his hat. It came out through the brim and wiggled like a worm. "Nobody messes with my hat. Nobody!"

From her time as a man, Sydney knew nobody touched another cowboy's hat or saddle.

"It was by the rubbish. I thought you were going to burn it." Melody's lower lip began to quiver. "The boys said I couldn't hit it, and I wanted to prove they were wrong." As she spoke, she squished herself up against Sydney's side.

330

Tim stuck out his hand, and one of Melody's brothers sheepishly laid his pocketknife across Tim's palm. "Really didn't think Sis could hit the broadside of a barn."

Melody gripped Sydney's hand. "You tell 'em. You tell 'em girls can do stuff just as good as boys can!"

"Just because you *can* do something doesn't mean you ought to." Sydney nodded toward the hat. "Sometimes things are ruined when you don't think matters through." *Or even when you do think them through. Because nobody's perfect.*

"Like my hat. My hat is ruint." Merle continued to wiggle his finger in the hole and mourn his hat.

Melody's eyes filled with tears.

Tim shot Sydney the same helpless, *get-me-out-of-this-fix* look he'd had when he'd been cornered in the Richardsons' hen-house.

"But Merle's birthday is coming up." Sydney smiled. "And that hat, though it is a fine one, has seen a lot of use. It's why he likes it so much. But for his birthday, Tim, Velma, and I want to get him a new hat. Don't we, Tim?"

"Yep."

"It's almost lunchtime. You children go wash up and help the younger ones, too." Sydney shooed them away. She looked from Tim to Merle. "I'm sorry. Truly, I am. The children all seem to be in high spirits today. If you would rather not join us for the picnic, I'll understand if you men grab a plate and go off somewhere else to eat."

"I thought I taught you better than that." A slow smile crept across Tim's rugged features. "Never turn your back on the enemy."

Merle squinted at her. "How'd you know my birthday's almost here?"

"A little birdie told me." She turned and walked off. She

couldn't recall precisely where she'd heard it, but the important thing was that she'd restored peace. She turned back. "Oh, and one other thing, Merle. I'm very proud of you."

"You are?"

She nodded. "You've finally broken that terrible habit you had of cursing."

By the time everyone sat down for the picnic, all of the garments were cut out and sewing had begun. A few of the babies and toddlers slept on pallets in the parlor, and Sydney decided things had turned a corner and the day would turn out well in spite of the rough start.

Then Widow O'Toole picked up her cake and carried it over to the blankets where the men sat. "You can bet that's not a rum cake," Velma whispered to Sydney.

Sydney's smothered giggle turned into a gasp as the widow knelt down in front of Merle. "It's your birthday. I baked you a cake."

"Oh." If he'd looked horrified earlier about his hat, he now looked sick enough to be on death's door.

"That was mighty nice of you." Tim reached out to take it from her.

She jerked it back, looked into Merle's eyes, and began to warble, "Beautiful dreamer, wake unto me...."

<hr />

"Wasn't it a wonderful day?" Sydney opened her napkin and slid it onto her lap. "We made six dresses and five pinafores."

Velma reached over and patted Sydney's hand. "Aprons. We call 'em aprons."

"Aprons. Five aprons." Sydney beamed.

Tim asked the blessing.

"Some of the older girls used scraps and stitched a blanket for the Vaughns' new baby." Sydney took a sip of coffee. "Wasn't that thoughtful of them?"

"Is that why they stopped using my lariat as a skip rope?"

"It was so generous of you to loan it to them. Velma, might I please have a little butter? Several of the children took turns with the butter churn, Tim."

"I suppose that explains why they were all eating popcorn."

"When Christmas draws nigh, we'll have to invite them all over to make popcorn balls. Oh! And a taffy pull. Wouldn't that be jolly?"

Tim arched a brow. "By then, Merle might forget about his hat—but you'll have to take care that Widow O'Toole doesn't come. It'll take a long time before he recovers from this afternoon."

Beneath the table, Velma kicked Tim and said, "All in all, we got a lot done today."

"Yup. Considering that the men didn't have ropes, they did a fair job of rounding up the horses."

"You do have them well trained." Sydney buttered a biscuit. "I meant the horses, but the same could be said of Forsaken's hands."

Tim drummed his fingers on the tabletop. "Sydney . . ."

She heaved a remarkably unladylike sigh. "Oh, very well. I confess. This was the first time I've entertained in America. Cervantes says, 'To be prepared is half the victory.' I thought I'd planned adequately and wanted everything to go perfectly, but I failed abysmally."

Velma shot Tim a look-what-you-did scowl.

"You got the dresses and aprons made." Tim nodded to emphasize his assertion. "That's what counts. Roast tastes good, Velma."

Sydney sliced off a miniscule bite of meat.

"Your plan worked, Sydney." Velma poked at her potato. "Bet Mrs. Orion wears that fancy gown to church next week."

"She'll look lovely in it."

Tim cleared his throat. "Syd—you're not playing match-maker, are you?"

"Merciful heavens, no! I'm no good at romance—my own or anyone else's." Hectic red tinted her cheeks. "Timothy, did you know that Americans misquote the Bible?"

Her change of subject astonished him—not only the change, but the topic she chose. Then again, over by the broken clothesline, she'd said matters were weighing heavily on her soul. Tim speared several green beans. "How's that?"

"Fearing what else might go awry or what Widow O'Toole might do, I blurted out that perhaps someone might want to read aloud to us as we sewed. Before I could suggest a story from *Peterson's Magazine,* Mrs. Bradle pulled a Bible from her sewing box."

"She has a Bible with her wherever she goes," Velma commented.

Tim wondered, "What did she read?"

"Nothing." Sydney continued to play with the food on her plate. "She passed her Bible to Etta and stole the baby from her. Etta said she'd been reading from Matthew. You'll never believe it, but she read that verse we talked about on the way home from church. Where Jesus prays. He said, 'Forgive us our debts, as we forgive our debtors.' A verse or two later, it talks about transgressions."

Tim nodded slowly. It never ceased to amaze him how God worked. Even so, he didn't want to pressure Sydney. He'd told her he wouldn't debate her on spiritual matters.

"But at lunch, Mrs. Bradle prayed for the food and started

that prayer. Everyone joined in. But you all said it differently. You don't say debts. You say trespasses."

Lord, guide me and give me the words you would have her hear. Tim put his elbows on the table. "What do the words mean to you?"

"My aunt Serena said men care about money, property, and title. Debt is about money. Trespassing is property." She frowned. "I can't match up transgressions and title, though."

"Title is about family." He looked at her.

A small *V* formed between her brows as she nodded.

"Transgressions separate us from God. We've trespassed out of His will and into the land of sin and darkness. There's no way we can buy our way back into His grace. The debt was canceled when Christ shed His blood on the cross. Because of His sacrifice, God is willing to adopt us as full heirs in His family."

"So debts, trespasses, and transgressions are all synonyms."

Tim nodded. "You could say that."

"And disappointments," Sydney added softly.

Tim understood her reference and nodded.

"I'll never forget Fuller explaining salvation to me." Velma's voice had a catch in it. "God was willing to overlook my past all because of Jesus. One minute, I was a whore's daughter, and the next minute I was a daughter of the King. All I had to do was confess that I'd sinned and ask for forgiveness through the grace of Christ Jesus."

"That's all?" Sydney looked flummoxed.

"Yes," Tim and Velma said in unison.

Sydney shook her head. "No, it can't be that simple. It's not a little thing, like me confessing that I was a miserable host-ess today. A soul is different. Momentous." She couldn't fathom that anything so life-changing would be that casual.

"There's always a proper way to do things. Rules."

"In the Old Testament times, that was true." Tim nodded. "Sacrifices had to be made in strict accordance with detailed laws. Only the High Priest could enter the Holy of Holies in the temple to commune with God. But because of Christ, the curtain to the Holy of Holies was torn apart. He fulfilled all the laws. We call upon His name, and we are saved."

Sydney placed her fork on the edge of her plate with exacting care. Her hands were shaking, and her heart thundered in her chest. "You mean to tell me, I spent countless months learning all of the etiquette—months of learning precisely how to walk and how far to bow and the proper way to hold my skirts and dip my head—all so I could make my bow to the queen of England, yet I don't have to do anything whatsoever to approach the Lord? I could ask Him to adopt me, and I don't have to wear something special or go somewhere important?"

Tim smiled. "God is with us everywhere. We don't have to go to Him."

"I was sitting in a railroad car when Fuller explained it to me." Velma reached up and poked in an errant hairpin. "Noisy and drafty, with raindrops comin' in the window we couldn't shut all the way. But that didn't matter. In fact, I sorta think it was fitting. I was leaving behind everything I used to be, and God was moving me on to a new life, washing and blowing away all the past."

Velma's words seemed almost poetic. "I guess it doesn't matter if someone has one small sin or a million big ones—they're still not Christian."

Tim looked at her, his eyes patient and steady. Slowly, he nodded. Sydney wasn't sure whether he was merely agreeing with her, or urging her to continue to think aloud. "You said the outside doesn't matter; the inside does."

"Men judge by outward appearance, but God looks at our hearts."

Even so, she glanced down at her bodice. She wouldn't receive callers or pay a visitation on someone if her gown were soiled. God deserved at least that much consideration. It wasn't vanity; it was respect. Satisfied that she wasn't smudged, she looked at Tim, slid her hands into her lap, and clasped them tightly together.

"What's bothering you, Sydney?" Velma asked.

"Even if I accept that clothing doesn't matter, surely conduct does. One doesn't barge in on royalty and say whatever one pleases. Especially when seeking an extraordinary favor. Jesus gave us the proper words—that prayer. So which word is right? Debts or trespasses?"

Tim's eyes turned a somber gray. "Are you asking out of simple curiosity?"

"You said if I searched, the answers would be there for me. There's a verse about asking and seeking and tapping."

Tim nodded. "It's in the seventh chapter of Matthew. 'Ask, and it shall be given you; seek, and ye shall find; knock, and it shall be opened unto you: For every one that asketh receiveth; and he that seeketh findeth; and to him that knocketh it shall be opened.'"

"Knocking. That implies I'm supposed to find a door." She pushed away from the table. "I always thought rules complicated things. Now I wish I knew the rules." Suddenly everything she wanted seemed so very close, yet she didn't know how to reach out for it. Her knees shook and the tightness in her chest grew unbearably. She chewed on her lower lip, then blurted out, "Something this important must be done properly."

"The important thing," Tim said as he rose, "is to ask

the Lord's forgiveness and pledge to live for Him from now on. It's not just a fleeting thing, Sydney. As His child, you live to please Him."

"Pleasing my father brought me joy. If God adopts me, I'll want to do whatever pleases Him."

"The Lord's invitation is open to anyone who sincerely wishes to be His, Sydney. There's no question as to whether He'll adopt you. He'd love to make you His daughter. All you have to do is ask."

"Would you mind terribly if I borrowed your Bible? I'm likely to mess up and say transgressing and tapping instead of trespasses and knocking."

Tim stood before her and took her hands in his. Until that moment, she hadn't realized she'd been wringing them. "Would you like Velma or me to help you?"

"Would you? You wouldn't mind?"

"I'd be honored."

While he went upstairs to get his Bible, Velma gave her a hug. "The parlor would be nice. We have that cross up on the wall. You can sit on the settee or kneel there if you'd like."

Sydney had bowed to the queen. She figured she ought to kneel before God.

Tim came back downstairs. "Sydney, as you read the prayer, would you like to personalize it? Instead of saying 'forgive us,' you can say 'forgive me.'"

She nodded and accepted his arm. He escorted her toward the parlor, but she stopped in the entry. "There's not a door."

"You could knock on the wall," Velma suggested.

Tim shook his head. "Sydney, did your father ever hear your footsteps and call out to welcome you?"

Her breath caught. "Oh yes."

"The heavenly Father hears you coming. It's no mistake

that there's no door here. Jesus opened the door for you, and God is waiting to welcome you."

She fought the urge to run into the parlor. Sydney stepped into the room, approached the far wall, and bowed as deeply as she'd been taught to for royalty. As she rose, she whispered, "Tim, I'd like to kneel here at the cross, too."

Tim nodded. "That's appropriate. The cross is empty, though, because Christ gives victory over death." He went down on one knee beside her and opened his Bible. His hands were steady as he braced the pages for her.

Sydney took a deep breath. "I'm a sinner." Ever since their discussion on Sunday, that realization had weighed heavily on her heart. Confessing it aloud now made her want to sob. Guilty tears spilled down her cheeks.

"You've come to the right place. The foot of the cross is where we lay our burdens."

In the past days, the weight of her sins had become an unbearable burden. The knowledge that she'd be free of them because of Christ's sacrifice overwhelmed her. She didn't know how long she knelt and wept. She only knew that what Tim said was true: God was meeting her where she was.

Sydney wiped away her tears. She'd bowed before the queen, and it hadn't made much difference in her life—but this moment when she knelt before God would change everything. He'd be her Lord and Father and King. Awe and gratitude filled her.

Tim leaned a little closer, and the lamp shone on the pages of the book of Matthew.

"My Father who is in heaven, hallowed be thy name. Thy kingdom come. Thy will be done in earth, as it is in heaven. Give me this day my daily bread. And forgive me my debts, as I forgive my debtors. And lead me not into temptation, but deliver me from evil; For thine is the kingdom, and the power, and the glory, for ever. Amen."

She turned to Tim, her heart strangely warm and light.

His eyes glowed like buffed pewter. "Welcome to the family of God, Sydney."

Chapter Twenty-five

"Rex!" Todd Pinter tilted his head toward the door.

Hume nodded and finished explaining, "The shipments are as regular as clockwork. I'm sure you'd find it a satisfactory investment. Think about it, Rutherford. There's no hurry. Now if you'll excuse me . . ." He schooled himself to saunter away as if he didn't have a care in the world. The truth was, he'd worked hard to manipulate matters so Todd Pinter would invite Blade Rutherford to this event. If Rutherford invested, others would rush to follow.

So what was so important that Todd was pulling him away?

Todd stood outside the doorway. "There's a . . . person who says it's an urgent matter. He's on the portico."

Hume's shoes beat out an impatient rhythm as he crossed the well-polished marble floor and out into the night air. The minute he spied Tyler, his pace escalated.

"I found her."

"Where?"

"Texas. The Ashton servant wrote. She was cleaning Serena Hathwell's room and found a shipping form for a large steamer trunk. Lady Hathwell's aunt arranged for it to be sent via New Orleans to an address in Texas. I've taken the liberty of buying seats on the train. It leaves at quarter to eleven."

Snatching his pocket watch from his vest pocket, Hume said, "Give me . . . ten minutes. I have to sew up a deal here."

"The train stops in that town only twice a week. We'll have to get off ten miles before."

"I'll rent or buy mounts when we get there." He calculated the time remaining and knew he was cutting it too close. The documents he'd secreted in the false-bottomed desk drawer were essential for when he confronted Sydney. Either he gave up his deal with Blade Rutherford or . . .

"There's a false bottom to the upper right desk drawer in my study. It's imperative I have the contents with me. Take this." He handed Tyler his watch. "Show it to the butler, and he'll allow you in."

Tyler slid off into the dark.

Hume rubbed his hands together and strode back inside. It was about time. He'd have Rutherford in his pocket and Lady Hathwell on his arm in no time at all.

Chapter Twenty-six

The acrid smells of sweat, singed hair, and leather filled the area. Tim pressed the branding iron to the calf, waited a quick count, then removed it. Boaz and Juan turned loose of the bawling calf and let it run back to its mama. Merle and Gulp already had the next one ready.

Ropes sang through the air and dogs yipped and nipped at the heels of recalcitrant Herefords. The dogs were smart enough to stay clear from the longhorns.

Pancake and two other men had their hands full, dehorning some of the yearling steers. At a year, those that took after the longhorn genes had already reached half of their horn length. The railroad didn't take kindly to fitting steers with six-foot horn spans into the cars. Fuller and Tim considered the issue and determined they'd leave any longhorned cows alone—they'd protect their calves from coyotes. Since bulls wouldn't go to the meat market, their horns were left alone, too. But if the steers were dehorned at a year, any regrowth before going to market wouldn't cause shipping problems.

Looking cool as a spring breeze, Sydney carried a big aluminum washtub over to the fence. She set it down, lifted a glass from it, and smiled at him.

Tim let out a loud whistle. The men finished whatever they were doing and followed him over to the fence.

"Here you go!" Sydney balanced a smaller pail on the fence post.

Tim stripped off his gloves and grabbed one of the wet dish towels. Soaked in cold well water, it cut through the brutal heat, bringing relief and pleasure. "Ahhhh," he moaned.

The men eagerly followed suit. They all pushed off their hats, squeezed the water onto their heads, then swabbed their gritty faces, necks, and hands. Glass after glass of lemonade came across the fence, only to be drained and returned. Velma arrived with two more pitchers that the men emptied in a matter of minutes.

Velma looked at him. "About an hour till lunch?"

Tim glanced around. "Yeah. That's good."

The men went back to work. As Tim dragged on his gloves and Velma walked off, he looked at Sydney. "Thanks. That was a real treat."

"*That,*" she pointed her chin toward the cattle, "is hot, hard work."

"You'd know." The moment color washed her cheeks, Tim reached over to touch her, but drew back before making contact. His gloves were filthy. "Don't take that the wrong way, Sydney. Women know their men work hard, and plenty pitch in as best they can. You—you actually understand the demands, and look what you did—came up with a way to help."

A saucy smile lit her face. "Teamwork, Boss."

A cloud of dust appeared on the horizon. "Sydney, I know there's a barn raising and square dance next week, and you've been working with the Richardson girls."

"They're coming along quite nicely, Tim. Truly, I think all they need is a little direction and tutoring."

The dust cloud came closer, and he fought to keep his voice level. "You're not having the Richardson girls over today, are you?"

"No." She shook her head. "They have dropped by un-invited, but we've covered that *faux pas,* so I don't think it'll be a problem anymore. Why are you asking?" She turned and followed his gaze. "That can't be the Richardsons. They always use a buckboard. Who'd use a buggy?"

"Doc does, but he knows better than to come here. Velma almost clobbered him with her rolling pin years ago." That left only two possibilities: Either Widow O'Toole was coming back, and Merle vowed that very morning if she stepped foot on Forsaken, he'd quit; or one of the men had decided to impress Sydney by renting a rig and taking her for a ride. Tim wouldn't stand for that.

The buggy rounded the turn, and he spotted one of the Bradle boys. Tim's temper flared hotter than the branding iron. He leapt over the fence and ripped off his gloves.

"What is it?"

"Trouble."

"Who is it?" Sydney shaded her eyes and stood on tiptoe.

Tim started to shove her behind his back, then reconsidered. "Go on in the house."

"To get Velma? Do you think someone's sick or hurt?"

No, but I'm sorely tempted to knock some sense into that kid. No one's courting her. Not even after Fuller gets back. No one but me. She's mine.

"Tim?"

Just as quickly as he made that decision, Tim belted out a laugh. Wasn't it just like God to time things this way? Tim grabbed Sydney's hand. "C'mon."

She picked up her skirts and ran alongside him. "What is it?"

"Fuller."

Sydney stopped dead in her tracks. "My uncle?"

"Yeah." He tugged on her arm, but she didn't budge. "Sydney . . ."

She pulled away and started fussing with her skirts.

"Stop being a girl and get over here."

Eyes huge, she whispered in a voice that crackled with emotion, "I am a girl. That's the problem. He doesn't like girls and didn't want a niece."

"He knows you're a girl. Now c'mon."

She stopped wringing her hands only long enough to make a shooing motion. "You go on ahead. He'll be glad to see you."

"He'll be glad to see you, too."

"I'm not ready to meet him yet. I need time to prepare myself."

"Sugar, you look fine." *Cervantes. She quoted him about how being prepared was half the victory. Well, she's already won the war and doesn't know it.* "I promise: You're not going anywhere. I'll see to it that you stay on Forsaken." She looked less than convinced, so he wrapped an arm about her and propelled her along. "Fuller!"

"Tim!"

He reached the buggy, stuck his right hand up, and carefully closed his fingers around his partner's gnarled hand. "Glad to have you home."

Fuller shook hands as best he was able. "Glad to be home."

"Let's get you down from there. I've got someone here for you to meet." Tim carefully grasped Fuller's arm. "She's nervous, so let's not keep her waiting."

Once Tim got Fuller out of the buggy and set him on his feet, he said, "Sydney, this is your uncle, Fuller Johnson. Fuller, your niece, Sydney Hathwell."

Sydney made a curtsy. "It's lovely to make your acquaintance. Mama spoke lovingly of you."

Fuller let out a rusty chuckle. "Oh, you're every bit as pretty as your mama."

"Thank you, sir."

"Call me Uncle."

"And you must call me Sydney."

"'Course I will. What else would I call you?"

Sydney shot Tim a glance.

Tim chortled. "I've been known to call her 'Fancy Pants.'"

"Pay that scoundrel no mind." Embarrassment colored her cheeks and tone. Sydney bowed her head. "I'm sorry. That wasn't right. Timothy isn't a scoundrel. He's a good man. I've been the troublemaker. I won't hold it against you for being angry about my ruse."

"'Urgent necessity prompts many to do things.'"

Sydney startled. "Cervantes! You quoted Cervantes! Mama loved Cervantes so."

Fuller chuckled. "I remember. She used that quote on more than one occasion to explain a rash act."

Color rushed to Sydney's cheeks. "My actions—"

"Hold it right there." Fuller swayed his hand from side to side, as if to wipe away any of her words. "Child, we'll make a deal. I won't be angry about it if you'll forgive me for making you feel unwanted just for being a girl."

Sydney took her uncle's hand in her own—gently, yet without any fuss. "You're too kind. I shouldn't have stood here dithering. Travel is wearisome. I'm sure you'd relish resting in the shade. Are you hungry? You can sit in the kitchen and tell me all about yourself. Velma and I are making sandwiches for everyone, and you shall have the first."

Tim reached out to take Fuller's valise from the parson's son. "Thanks for driving him home."

"It's no trouble for me to carry this in, Tim." The kid hopped down.

Tim didn't like how that Bradle boy gawked at Sydney. He opened his mouth to shoo off the pest.

"Yeah, go on ahead and tote that on inside." Fuller patted Sydney. "I'll meet you in the kitchen."

Tim's mouth snapped shut.

Sydney excused herself. Her skirts whispered as she turned and went up the steps. Bradle marched alongside her—far too close, too.

Fuller knocked his knobby hand on Tim's arm. "I'd have to be blind not to know the look on your face. Wondered if I'd ever see the day that you'd let a woman into your heart."

Tim grinned and shrugged. "She didn't play fair."

"Neither did I." Fuller let out a raspy chuckle. "Over the years, the correspondence between my sister and me dwindled away. I assumed she'd had kids I didn't know. When you sent that telegram, I realized my mistake. For me—I'd gladly have come home that day. I reckoned if she was anything like her mama, she'd give you fits and you'd bolt before you saw what a prize she is."

Tim folded his arms across his chest. "You old goat!"

"Velma wrote that you'd told Sydney she couldn't accept gentleman callers until I came home. I gave you a head start. You can thank me later." Fuller hobbled away a few steps and turned back. "Don't you have anything more to say?"

It took one large stride to close the distance between them. "Until last night, Sydney wasn't a believer. I couldn't be un-equally yoked."

Fuller grabbed Tim's sleeve. "Until last night?"

"Yeah, Fuller. She found salvation."

"Glory be!"

"Hey, Creighton!" Gulp hollered.

"Coming!" Tim gave his partner a mock scowl. "Velma wrote to you? Don't think I won't blister your ears later."

"Ha!" Fuller waggled his brows. "You won't. You have to ask my permission to marry Sydney."

<hr/>

Sydney couldn't wait for her uncle to come into the kitchen. She met him in the entryway. "Uncle Fuller, I would have recognized you right away. You have my mama's eyes."

He patted her cheek. "You're the spittin' image of Crystal."

"I carried your satchel to the top of the stairs." Leo Bradle descended the stairs.

Manners demanded she invite the parson's eldest son to stay for lunch, but Sydney didn't want to.

Uncle Fuller winked at her. "Bradle, lots of work goin' on outside. Ask Tim if he can use your help."

"Oh. Okay. Yeah, I'll do that!"

As she and Fuller walked toward the kitchen, he murmured, "He's a nice boy."

"Yes, he is." *You just got here, and you're trying to match me up?*

"Yep, a real nice boy. Fine family, too."

Pasting on a smile she was far from feeling, Sydney said, "Had I any brothers, I imagine they'd be like him and the other Bradle boys."

Velma shouted from the kitchen, "Sydney, drag that old rascal in here. I've got a sandwich ready for him."

"Who're you calling old?" Fuller stopped and stared at the dining table. "Velma? What's your special tablecloth doing out?"

Velma stood in the doorway. "Now that I have Sydney to

help me, I'm going to civilize you."

"It'll take a lot more than Irish linen to do that." He chuckled and shuffled to the kitchen.

Sydney stood across the kitchen table and made sandwiches as he ate. Velma chattered about everything that he'd missed while gone. Fuller latched on to any man mentioned and pointed out his strengths. "Jakob Stauffer's a good man. Dependable. Sad, him being a widower. I'll bet he's mighty grateful to you for saving his daughter."

"It was teamwork. I just happened to be at the end of the rope."

Orville Clark, the owner of the mercantile, was pronounced "a man who'd be a steady provider," Jim Whitsley's "family's been here forever—he's well-respected," and even Jake Eddles got painted with a generous, "another widower who's trying to do well for his kids, and all three are boys."

Sydney slapped the last sandwich onto a tray and bit her tongue so she wouldn't say something she'd regret. Just because Uncle Fuller had Mama's eyes didn't mean he had her loving heart. He'd been honest from the start—he didn't want a girl underfoot. And he'd just crowed about Jake Eddles having sons. Sydney felt certain if a snake oil salesman came knocking on the door, Uncle Fuller would gladly push her into the stranger's arms just to get her off Forsaken.

Velma lifted the lid on a pot on the stove. "I'll stir those." Sydney grabbed a spoon and swirled the baked beans.

"Might want to add a pinch of salt." Velma picked up a crate that held plates, silverware, and mugs. "Now that they're almost done, it won't toughen them. A hint of salt brings out the sweet of the molasses."

As Velma left, Fuller mused, "So a high-society English gal's learned her way around a kitchen?"

"Velma's been a wonderful teacher." Sydney couldn't help herself. "So have the Richardson girls."

He choked and took a gulp of coffee. "You brought them here?"

"You may as well hear it from me. Since I've been here, we've had two sewing bees for the ladies of the town, and the Richardson girls have come calling at least twice a week. Tim allowed it, but now that you're back I understand things are bound to change."

He pursed his lips and nodded. "Plenty's about to change around here."

"Okay, Sydney," Velma called. "Let's get the food out there."

After the hands had been served, Uncle Fuller stayed at the kitchen table and talked as Velma and Sydney washed the lunch plates and made supper. He wanted to know everything that had happened in his absence—only since Tim would fill him in on the matters pertaining to the ranch, he asked about everything else. *Everybody* else—who was male and unmarried.

Pan after pan of cornbread went into and came out of the oven. Sydney helped Velma strip the stems and seeds from several pods of chili. Then, as Velma simmered, mashed, and strained those chilies, Sydney chopped up onions and garlic to add to the pot of meat on the stove. She'd never seen a pot half as vast as the one that covered multiple burners.

Fuller extolled Checkered Past's Henry, who could eat a whole plate of the hottest chili peppers God ever made. Then he went on to talk about Milton Baumgartner. According to Fuller, the blacksmith's strength would never leave a woman worrying about protection. Sydney started to measure in the cumin, oregano, paprika, and chili powder.

Uncle Fuller continued to talk faster than a gypsy horse

trader. Apparently Ephraim Somebody-or-other could dowse for water with a branch from any of Jakob Stauffer's fine peach trees. "It's gotten hot while I was gone, Velma. How many wells did Ephraim start? Two? Five?"

Sydney paused for a second. All that talk made her almost lose count of how many spoons of chili powder she'd added. Three. She'd only done three so far. She added more.

"Three. No, wait. He went south seven or eight miles to dowse for a rancher there. I heard he found another there, too. That makes four. Tim's decided we need to drill another well."

Fuller nodded. "Yep. Hottest part of the year isn't even close yet. Reminds me of the summer of eighty-five."

Velma said they were tripling the recipe. That meant she needed fifteen tablespoons.

Fuller chuckled. "Ephraim's going to boast that he's up to seventeen now, but I reckon it's closer to fifteen. Still, that's nothing to sneeze at. He can make ours his sixteenth."

Fifteen. She'd measured in fifteen. Or was it fourteen? At that point, what difference would one more spoonful make? Sydney added one last tablespoon of chili and grabbed the oregano.

The men finished branding and dehorning. After they washed up, they filed past the kitchen door and got dinner. Sydney didn't want to be rude, but the last thing she wanted to do was sit across from her uncle. By now, he had to have run out of eligible men in the state of Texas, but given the opportunity, he'd likely start listing friends of his all across America.

The cowboys sat along the back porch. She took a bowl after everyone else had been served and slipped off to the front porch swing.

"Sydney?" Tim called to her. "Hey, Syd? Where are you?"

She took a bite. For an instant, she thought the temperature of the chili was too hot. Then, the full impact hit. She slapped her hand over her mouth, and her eyes started to tear. Her tongue and the roof of her mouth began to burn unbearably. Desperate, she swallowed.

It got worse. She hadn't thought it possible, but it had. Fire streaked from her stomach clear to the roots of her hair.

"Sydney!" Tim shouted.

She suspected he was going to bellow at her for how she'd managed to ruin the meal. Not that she cared—at least not much, not now. Spying the pump out in the barnyard, she picked up her skirts and ran for the relief it promised. Abandoning every last shred of decorum, she grabbed the handle and stuck her mouth by the spigot.

Chapter Twenty-seven

"No!" Tim grabbed her by the waist and jerked her from the stream of cool water.

"Aaaarghhh!" She struggled against his hold.

"No. No water."

Wiggling with all her might, she couldn't break free. He swept her into his arms. She grabbed his shoulders and shook him. "Bur. Ha! Wa-ur!"

Ignoring her plea, he headed up the porch steps.

Even her lips felt scorched. It was impossible to tell what was worse—the heat that built up if her mouth was closed, or the searing flames that streaked across her tongue if she breathed with her mouth open.

"Velma, get some milk!" How Tim managed to open the screen door didn't register. The minute he set foot in the house, Sydney twisted to snatch the pitcher from the washstand. If Tim tried to take it away, she decided she'd be fully justified in smacking him in the head with it—after she drank the contents.

Velma swiped the pitcher from her and pressed a glass into Sydney's hands. "Drink that. Quick."

Anything. Sydney would drink anything if it would lessen the burning. The first gulp didn't help whatsoever. Desperation had her taking a second, then a third. Tears rolled down her cheeks.

"Keep drinking it. Milk stops the burning."

"Ire."

"Did she just call you a liar?" Fuller hobbled over.

"Fire. She's saying her mouth's on fire." Tim sat on a chair in the dining room and kept her on his lap. "We're going to need more milk. Or sour cream."

"Cheese works pretty good," Fuller said. "Don't know why she's having trouble. I've eaten hotter."

Sydney was sure her hair was singed. It had to be. She glugged the rest of the first glass with a complete lack of restraint. Maybe after she had the ninth or tenth glass, her hair might stop smoking. It would take at least a month or more before she could breathe or talk. She figured it was God's way of keeping her quiet, because she wanted to tell Uncle Fuller the only chili that could possibly be hotter had to be in Lucifer's kitchen.

Fuller took another bite. "Whoo-eee! I take that back. This has a delayed kick."

Pancake knocked and let himself in. "The men are wild about the chili. They want me to get your recipe."

Sydney grabbed the next glass of milk and gulped it. She was afraid they'd misconstrue her answer. As a Christian, it wasn't proper to tell someone to go to hell—even if that had to be where the recipe originated from.

❦

Two hours later, Sydney looked out at the moonlit barnyard. After the weeks of working as a ranch hand, then working as a western woman alongside Velma, she'd come to love the land

and this way of life. She knew each acre of fencing, each twist and rut in the road. At night, she knew which floorboards to avoid because they squeaked. Her heart told her she belonged here.

What would it be like to live on Forsaken, to be Tim's wife, to rear a houseful of children who knew how to rope and ride and romp without worrying what others would think? A daughter who could go barefoot in wet grass and whistle with birds? And a son who would ride at his father's side. . . . Best of all, they'd grow up knowing about Jesus.

She wilted onto the porch swing, wondering how to pray. At mealtimes, Tim and Velma talked to God as if He were sitting right there at the table with them. *Tim said God is with me wherever I go. Lord, that means you are here right now. You're supposed to know what's in my heart. Well, I'm scared and hurt. I have feelings for Tim. He's never done anything to make me think he's interested in me. And now Uncle Fuller is trying to fob me off on whoever will take me. I don't know what to do, God. Could you help me, please? Thank you. Amen.*

Sydney straightened her sleeve cuffs. As prayers went, that hadn't been eloquent, but she felt okay, anyway. God was her Father. He wouldn't care if she wasn't perfect. That's the way fathers were.

"Thought you might like this." Tim came out with a glass of milk for her and a cup of coffee for himself. He eased himself down on the porch swing and started to move it with a bit more effort. It no longer merely swayed a few inches each direction, but rocked a good two feet forward and back. The creaking of the chains made Tim grin. "I'm going to have to oil those."

"They do make a racket."

"It's going to be a pain in the neck if I don't." He winked. "Want me to take it down and move it back a foot or so?"

"Why?" She accepted her milk and sipped.

Tim emptied his mug with a few healthy swigs, then leaned a bit closer. "It wouldn't be as easy to see from the barnyard."

Her brows knit. "Don't you want me to watch what's going on?"

Tucking a stray curl behind her shoulder, he asked, "Don't they have courting swings in England?"

"A courting swing?" She tried her best to modulate her voice. Disappointment swamped her. Tim must have changed his mind and decided to agree with Fuller.

"When a man wants to be with his sweetheart, he asks her out onto the porch. They sit and visit while they swing. Most a man can do is hold his sweetheart's hand on one of these things, because if he wants to crank up enough courage to kiss her, the rhythm of the swing changes, or it stops altogether. Believe you me, if the chains stop making noise, her parents find an excuse to walk on out to check on them!"

"Oh."

He gave her an odd look. "You don't seem very happy about the idea."

Staring at the contents of her glass, Sydney confessed, "I'm not. I don't want to go anywhere else. Uncle Fuller must have spoken to you by now. It's obvious he wants me gone."

"What in the world gave you that notion?"

"He spent the entire afternoon bringing up every last one of your neighbors and telling me about their strong points and fortes. To hear him talk, you'd think all of the unmarried men for miles around are paragons. I daresay if the Hunchback of Notre Dame were a neighbor, my uncle would declare I'd be hearing beautiful music for my entire marriage."

Tim let out a bark of a laugh.

She didn't bother to say anything more. Tim hadn't been there and heard Fuller. Worse, he didn't seem in the least bit sorry she'd be leaving. It wouldn't surprise her if Velma was upstairs at this very moment, packing for her. *I thought we were all friends, but their loyalty still belongs to Fuller. Friends. That's how Tim thinks of me. I love him, and he thinks of me as a comrade. I did this to myself. I masqueraded as a man, and this is the consequence.* Heart burning worse than her mouth, she lifted the glass and took a sip.

"That was Fuller being Fuller. In all the time I've known him, I've never once heard him say a bad thing about anyone else. He sees the best in others. It's one of his finest qualities."

She swallowed and forced herself to admit, "Admirable."

"He wasn't trying to pair you up with anyone, Sugar."

If she squeezed the glass any tighter, it would shatter. "Are you sure?"

Tim trailed his fingernail back and forth over the shoulder seam of her dress. "Positive. I thought maybe you'd like the swing set back. I sure would. I don't cotton to having the men in the bunkhouse watching us sit together."

"Us?" She could hardly believe her ears. A moment ago, she'd convinced herself that he didn't have feelings for her. Was he declaring himself?

"Yes, us." He took the glass from her. As the swing arced backward, he set the glass on the porch planks, then turned toward her. "I have you just where I want you."

She could barely whisper, "And where is that?"

He slid his hand back to cup her neck. His mouth came closer as he murmured, "At home with me, where you belong."

A loud whistle and hoot from the yard made them pull apart at once. Tim growled, "I'm moving the swing!"

"Yes, I think," Sydney agreed in a shaky tone, "that is a brilliant idea."

"I heard the swing stop creaking," Velma observed from the

door. As Tim chuckled, Velma winked. "Figured I'd best check up on the two of you."

"No need, Velma." Tim gave her a sharkish grin. "Fuller's given me permission to chase after her."

By midmorning the next day, Tim wanted to stomp up to the porch and kiss Sydney. Then he'd knock a few heads together for good measure. He wasn't a man given to violence, but this situation was unique. Once the men knew Fuller had returned, they reckoned she was fair game. Tim wanted to be sure to show them they'd reckoned wrong.

To his disgust, four lovesick swains tripped all over themselves and each other to be with her. Two others had already been here and left. The blacksmith had even brought her flowers. Like a fool, Tim hadn't ever given her flowers. He should have thought to do that by now. Women liked flowers. Sydney had gathered them and filled her boots, and still, he hadn't gotten the hint. He growled under his breath.

Sydney sat on the porch swing, holding court—the porch swing *he'd* moved. Not only moved, but oiled. He determined that until he scared some sense into this flock of idiots, he'd put her swing up front during the day and set it back at night.

Tim started toward the porch. He saw red when Alex Denton rested his hand on Sydney's knee. Just before Tim bellowed, though, Sydney smartly rapped Denton directly across the knuckles with her fan and chided, "Behave yourself or leave, sir!"

While Denton tried to frame a suitable apology, Milton Baumgartner gave him a punch in the arm. "Try that again, and I'll pinch that pimple you call a head clean off of your neck!"

"Oh my." Sydney opened her fan and fluttered it.

Tim thundered up the steps. "That's no way to—"

"Talk in the presence of a lady," Fuller interrupted as he came out of the house.

Baumgartner groused, "I didn't mean any offense."

"Of course you didn't." Fuller gave the blacksmith a nod of acknowledgment. "I'm sure we all want what is best for my niece. It's plain to me already that she's just like her mama— smart, pretty, and softhearted. There's not a man alive who doesn't want to snap up a gal like her and hold her safe and tight."

A chorus of agreement left Tim ready to knock heads together again.

"I do hope you will all understand." Sydney rose. "I only met my uncle yesterday and need to become better acquainted with him today."

The second Sydney got up, the men came to their feet.

"We've all missed him, too," Mr. Clark said. "Fuller, I brought some boots for Miss Hathwell to try on. Special ordered from Boston. If you'll write down whatever tonic the doctor in Abilene used to treat you, I'll be sure to stock it at the mercantile."

"I'll bring Sydney to town later in the week to take care of those matters."

His patience exhausted, Tim jerked his thumb to the side. "Out of here, all of you."

"Of course they're leaving." Fuller nodded sagely. "They're busy men with plenty of hard work to do. I'm honored you all took the time to come welcome me home."

As the men rode off, Sydney slid her hand into Tim's. "They're our neighbors. Just like the Richardsons."

He gave her a surly look. "They can pester those girls. You're taken."

⟶⟵

Checking his pocket watch, Hume fought a persistent sense of impatience. The first leg of their journey had tested him sorely. When Tyler said he'd gotten tickets for the train, Rex didn't for a moment imagine the investigator had purchased standard seats.

Rexall Hume the Third did not travel with commoners and riffraff. Since they'd barely jumped aboard the train before it departed, Rex attempted to talk the purser into moving him to a Pullman car—but none was available. At a brief stop, Rex dashed to the telegraph station and ordered a private Pullman be prepared so it could be added onto the train in Chicago.

Indeed, his maxim proved true yet again: Anything could be obtained for the right price. *Snap.* The cover closed on his watch. In a matter of days, he'd also have the wife he'd paid so dearly for.

It couldn't be soon enough.

"The train ought to be pulling into the station in about an hour." Tyler gazed out the window. "The purser mentioned we have a thirty-minute stop."

Hume nodded. The investigator possessed the singular ability to sit still and silent for hours on end, yet remain fully attentive the whole while. It stood to reason—his line of work would require such a temperament. Nonetheless, as antsy as Hume felt, it irritated him that his hireling seemed to be in far better control.

A moment at the washstand. Yes, that would be wise. The cool water refreshed him and helped him regain some sense of order. He noted the starch in his shirt was long gone. When he caught up with Lady Hathwell, he couldn't possibly look this rumpled.

"What are the chances that the backwater town we stop at will have a tailor?"

Tyler shrugged. "I couldn't say."

"I'll settle for a ready-made shirt if I must." Hume dragged his comb through his hair. A ready-made shirt would be quite a comedown, and every bit as bad, the too-long sleeves would require him to wear sleeve garters. Back home he had a closet full of fine cotton shirts tailored to his exact specifications. That being the case, the very thought of sleeve garters galled him. He ought to have thought to instruct Tyler to order the maid to pack a few necessities for him whilst Tyler picked up the papers.

Ah, the papers. The packet rested in the inside pocket of his suit coat. That coat presently swayed to and fro on a highly polished brass hook with the train's motion. A fresh brushing by the purser would restore the suit coat sufficiently . . . and the sleeve garters wouldn't be visible beneath the coat. Cheered by that thought, Hume grinned at his reflection.

"Have you decided whether to purchase mounts when we reach our destination," Tyler asked, "or will we rent?"

"It depends on how much time we have in Abilene. We haven't been on time for a single leg of this trip."

"Most men have a preference when it comes to breed. Anything particular you like? Tennessee Walker? Arabian?"

"Dappled gray." Hume walked the length of the Pullman, took a cigar from the box, and sniffed it appreciatively. "Whatever you ride doesn't matter, but I'm firm about my mount."

"Dappled grays are fine. Rare in this region. Cowboys go for mustangs, pintos, workhorses. We could wire ahead, but I discourage that. If your name gets out, Lady Hathwell might overhear it and bolt."

A knock sounded, and the purser entered. "Sir, will you be dining here or in the dining car this evening?"

"Here. I trust the fare will have improved over the other meals?"

"The menu is pre-arranged, sir. If I might be so bold, Mildred's is a mere stone's throw from the train station. The offerings there are superior. I particularly recommend the roast rabbit."

"Tyler, see to that."

As soon as the train ground to a halt, Tyler went to fetch the meal. Hume headed toward the tailor. To his disgust, the shop was closed. He banged on the door, hoping the proprietor was in the back room. No such luck. Vexed, Hume hastened on to the general store.

He never darkened the door of such an establishment, for his servants saw to the marketing. The smell of pickle brine and moldy cheese assailed him as he entered the store. Without the luxury of time or choice, Rex knew he had to make do. "Show me your shirts."

The owner gestured to a shelf. "Got a bunch in last week. Take your pick."

Rex stared in revulsion at the display. The shirts were all folded. The creases in them would proclaim them to be precisely what they were: a working man's ready-made, cheap garment. Well, if a meal could be cooked on the train, there had to be a stove. That meant the purser could slap an iron on it. Rex gritted his teeth and snatched up a white shirt. Two. No, three. He'd need changes for the next few days.

"They're on special. Buy four, get one free."

"Fine." He added a couple more. Tyler could use a change.

Aware time was short, Hume slapped them down on the counter. "Sleeve garters."

"How many pair?"

"Two." A case caught Hume's attention. He strode over and looked inside. He'd not been able to bring along his mother's wedding ring. Then again, as much trouble as his fiancée had caused, it was justice that she begin the marriage with a plain gold band. *After she gives me a son, she'll get Mother's ring. I'm not giving her any reason to quibble or demure. I have her guardian's written consent for her to wed as well as a license. A ring is all I need.* He jabbed his finger against the jewelry case. "Give me that band."

Friday afternoon, Tim returned from the Smiths' to find Jake Eddles yammering at Sydney as she helped Velma weed the garden. All three of his boys squabbled under a nearby tree.

"Ben! Bob! Buck! Knock it off!" Jake hollered, then turned back to her. "They're good boys, Miss Hathwell. They need a woman's touch is all."

Velma sat back on her heels. "Jake, the gal's told you no twice now."

"If you don't wanna marry up, I'll understand." Jake shuffled. "But I'm willing to hire you as a housekeeper. The boys can move into my bedroom and you can have theirs."

Sydney tugged at a dandelion. "I'm afraid—"

"You don't gotta be afraid of anything. It'll all be on the up-and-up."

"Eddles, forget it." Tim put down the sack he carried and stepped in front of him. "She writ a letter!"

Something about Jake's desperation evoked sympathy. Tim

said in a low tone, "Things change."

"Yeah. So if she changes her mind—" His voice died out as Tim shook his head.

"Sydney is where she belongs." Tim looked him in the eye. "With me."

Velma stood and dusted off her hands. "Jake, come on round to the kitchen. We did some baking; I'll send you home with a pie."

Jake traipsed after Velma. "Heard tell 'bout Miss Hathwell's chili. Brimstone in a bowl. Women like her are rare as hens' teeth."

Kneeling, Tim muttered, "I feel bad for him."

"Remember that when you see him walk by with an apple pie." Sydney looked up at him. A smile faltered on her face, then she turned away.

"Hey, what's wrong?"

Uncaring of her frilly skirts, she sat in the dirt. "I know you were trying to be kind . . ."

"But?"

"I saw you take Moustache away. You were right. I grew quite attached to him. I've never had a pet, you see."

"I took him to the Smiths. They can raise him, and I traded so you could have a real pet." Tim reached over and grabbed the sack. "Here, Sugar."

Sydney's eyes widened as the sack wiggled. "What's in there?"

"Take a look." He felt downright smug.

The knot came loose, and a damp black nose poked out. "Oh!" Delight rang in that single sound. The pup wriggled from the burlap bag and gamboled into her lap. "You're darling! Tim, really? Is he for me?"

He grinned as the puppy lapped at Sydney's fingers. "Yes,

she's for you. Looks like she's as taken with you as I am."

Sydney lifted the puppy and rubbed noses with it. "You're darling, too."

Stunned, Tim looked at her, then chuckled. "Did you call me darling a second ago?"

A self-conscious smile tilted her mouth. "Yes. I suppose it doesn't sound very masculine, though. Was I too forward in speaking such a sentiment?"

"Are you kidding? I've waited for half of forever."

"Truly?"

"When you came down those stairs at the saloon with your head held proud and those pretty shoulders tilted back in an I-dare-you pose, I couldn't imagine ever feeling such fire in my veins."

She giggled. "That's because you were mad!"

"Yep. But that should have told me plenty. I thought I'd lost a good friend. Only I didn't, did I?"

"That was the worst part of it for me, too. I was so certain you'd never forgive me." A beautiful smile lit her face. "You did forgive me, and God has, too. I've never been happier."

"I'm glad, Sugar."

Her eyes sparkled. "You used to call me something else." She looked at the puppy and played with her ears. "What are we going to call you?"

"The Smith kids already named most of the litter. They were calling this one 'Boots.' Boots for my Fancy Pants."

She laughed as she tapped the puppy's brown paws. "Yes, look at her markings. She's a lucky little rascal. Nothing's more comfortable than cowboy boots. Let's keep that name."

Tim slid his hand atop Sydney's. "I'd like to change your name, though. I love you. With all my heart, I love you. Nothing would sound better to me than calling you mine. Will you marry me?"

Her eyes shone brightly. "Tim, I've never known a better man. My heart overflows with love for you. Yes, I'd adore being your wife."

He leaned close, took Boots from her lap, and pulled Sydney into his arms. "Seal it with a kiss."

Just before their lips met, Fuller hollered, "Hey! That's my niece!"

Tim groaned and pulled back. "She's your niece, but she's going to be my wife!"

"No kissing until you're at the altar."

Sydney had turned a fetching shade of pink and giggled in embarrassment. It was all Tim could do to keep from kissing her silly. He heaved a sigh. "Syd, Sugar, desperate times call for desperate measures."

"What does that mean?"

"It means we're going to follow a family tradition. I'm hauling you to the pastor right now."

"We can't! You've seen me today. It's bad luck. Father waited to marry Mama until the next day."

"Tomorrow, then. That's it."

<hr />

"You look like a princess!" Heidi hopped up and down as Velma and Mrs. Orion helped Sydney with her veil.

"Thank you."

"There." Velma stepped back. "I'm going to dash over to the church now and remind him what to say. If I don't, instead of giving you away, he'll stand there and tell everyone what a good man Tim is."

"God never made a better man." Sydney smiled.

"Yes, well, it's too hot today for everyone to spend extra time sitting there waiting to see a wedding."

As Velma, Mrs. Orion, and Heidi crossed the street, Forsaken's cowboys all crowded around the boardinghouse parlor. Hair slicked down with pomade, crisp white shirts and string ties on them all. "Handsome. Every one of you," Sydney pronounced.

Pancake stepped up. "We've got it all figured out. Juan and Gulp are gonna carry you. The rest of the men're gonna hang on to all them skirts and train so's they don't drag in the dirt. I've got your posies here."

The church was across the street and down about twenty yards. Sydney wanted to run the whole distance herself—but she couldn't very well behave like a hoyden when she'd started making inroads with the Richardson girls.

To her relief, the men decided to cut across the street diagonally to expedite the trip. Suddenly, Pancake held up his hand. "Someone's coming. Let me stop 'em so's Syd's dress don't get all dusty." He trotted ahead about ten feet and motioned the two men to stop.

They didn't. One kneed his dappled gray past Pancake and came right up to her. Sydney gasped.

Chapter Twenty-eight

"Well, well." Hume's gaze passed over her gown. "This is convenient. I've waited long enough to marry you."

"Mister, you've got the wrong gal," Merle growled. "Back off."

"Lady Hathwell," he said her name in a clipped tone, "is to marry me."

The men couldn't decide exactly what to do. Juan and Gulp both pulled in opposite directions, almost dropping her. Pancake stood in the street and gave her an odd look. "Syd, so you know this feller?"

Whoever was playing the piano in the church started playing louder.

Uncle Fuller stepped out of the church. "What's taking so long?"

"Fuller, we got us a problem. Get Big Tim out here."

A moment later, Tim barreled out of the church. He came straight up to Sydney, pulled her into his arms, and looked at her. "What's wrong?"

His strength poured into her. "Nothing."

"Only because she didn't make it to the altar with you." Hume dismounted. "I'm Rexall Hume the Third and that woman is my bride. It's all arranged."

"No, it isn't." Sydney shook her head. "I told you we didn't suit."

"Nonsense." Hume brushed dust from his jacket, and another man joined him. It didn't escape her notice that the other man wore a double holster.

"Just because I came to America didn't mean I had to marry you."

Hume's eyes narrowed. "There was far more involved."

Tim's hold tightened imperceptibly. "Sydney is entitled to marry whomever she wants. I'm that man."

She nodded.

"Tim?" Parson Bradle drew close. At that moment, Sydney realized everyone had exited the church and was watching the scene.

"I see from your collar that you're a man of the cloth." A stingy smile flickered across Hume's face. "You, of all people, understand matters of honor. I suggest we retire to a private setting and resolve this."

"There's nothing to resolve." Tim's rock-steady voice carried the assurance Sydney needed.

Parson Bradle's chin came up. "The Good Book says, 'Come now, let us reason together.' We'll follow that admonition. The parlor in the parsonage will serve nicely."

It took a minute of haggling, but the pastor allowed Hume's man to come along—provided he left his weapons with the sheriff. Fuller insisted that as Sydney's uncle, he was entitled to be there.

As Tim carried Sydney to the parsonage, Velma bustled alongside them, fussing about how her skirts and train were getting filthy.

Hume stopped her at the door.

Velma stuck out her forefinger and prodded him in the center of his chest, poking with each syllable as she said, "I'm not about to leave that gal in there without a woman present. You've already caused enough trouble. Now get out of my way."

Velma came over, got up on tiptoe, and whispered, "Big Tim, put Sydney down. It'll save time when you have to punch that man in the nose."

A grim smile crossed Tim's face, but he gave Sydney a reassuringly tight squeeze before setting her down.

"Let's all take a seat," the parson urged.

No one seemed to think that was a good idea.

Hume folded his arms across his chest. "Lady Hathwell is to be my wife."

"Lady Hathwell," Tim said, "is to be *my* wife."

"I'm certain we can clear up this matter." The preacher clasped his hands together. "Surely, there's a misunderstanding."

"There's no misunderstanding." Sydney tucked her hand into Tim's. "I want to marry Tim."

Hume's face went ruddy. "Enough of this, Sydney."

"Oh, so at least you got her name right this time." Velma planted herself on Sydney's other side. "She told me about you. You called her Cindy the last time you ordered her to marry you."

"Well!" Mrs. Richardson huffed from outside the parsonage window.

The man accompanying Hume strode over and slammed the window shut.

Sydney held tight to Tim. "I knew I could never love him. I told him so twice. You're the man I love."

"There was an agreement." Hume's face was hard as stone. His expression told Sydney that it didn't matter to him that she didn't love him. Worse still, he didn't even care that she loved Tim. "You're honor bound to marry me."

"She doesn't have to do anything she doesn't want to." Tim stepped in front of her.

"I had a gentleman's agreement. I even waited for a whole year so she could mourn her father."

She fought her skirts and sidled up beside Tim. "I promised Father I'd come meet him. I didn't agree to become his bride."

"Your cousin made the commitment." Hume pulled a packet of papers from the inside of his coat. "I have all of the documents here."

Tim squeezed Sydney close. "I'll take care of this, Syd. We'll be at the altar in just a few minutes."

"She'll be there with me. I have the marriage license. Harold Hathwell is Lady Hathwell's guardian. She has not yet reached her majority, so his consent is necessary for her to wed. He gave that consent to me."

"Cousin Harold?" she gasped.

Hume gave her a frigid smile. "I might add, Lady Hathwell, I paid dearly for his consent. I can see the money was well spent, too. I approve of that gown."

She shuddered. "You didn't—"

"Oh, but I did. Harold seems to have a predilection for card games, and his luck is abysmal. He was more than happy to accept my money. Appearances are important, and I stipulated that you were to be well-outfitted when he sent you to me."

"Slavery was abolished twenty-five years ago, Hume. You can't buy anyone"—Tim's voice dropped to a rumble—"and Sydney is not a woman who can be bought or paid for."

"She is a woman accustomed to cobblestones and carriages, not dirt and drudgery. I'll continue to provide for her in accordance to her station." Hume's gaze swept out the window, then across the parsonage's humble parlor and finally settled on Sydney. "This does not suit you."

"It's perfectly suited to me, and I'll be happy here." Sydney looked up at Tim. "My father wasn't like Laban. He wouldn't force me to marry a man who didn't love me and be miserable all of my life as Leah was."

"You have no justification for thinking you'd be miserable as my wife."

Sydney pressed closer to Tim. "I overheard you, Mr. Hume. All you wanted were legitimate heirs and access to the peerage to further your business."

"You planned to use Sydney as a pawn so you could make more money?" Outrage vibrated in Tim's words. "What kind of man are you?"

"I won't apologize for being successful. I'll provide for Lady Hathwell far better than any cowboy ever could."

"Gentlemen, let's keep this civil." The parson cleared his throat. "Mr. Hume, I'm sure you didn't mean to imply Miss Hathwell's happiness hinges solely upon material wealth."

"My happiness wasn't his concern." Sydney stared at Hume. "You ignored me while I was a guest in your home. And . . ." Her voice trailed off.

"She's trying to find a nice way of saying something downright ugly." Velma shook her finger at Hume. "You have a mistress and plan to keep her even after you marry."

Pushing Sydney behind himself, Tim roared, "I'm giving you a chance to deny that."

Hume snapped, "It's none of your affair."

"I disagree." The parson asserted, "At the outset, Mr. Hume, you stated this was a matter of honor. Was it your intention to take the vows of holy matrimony only to break them?"

"Decent women don't relish their marital duty. I assumed the lady would be relieved that I'd spare her. Since that's not the case, I give my word as a gentleman that I'd be faithful."

"You just implied Sydney is not a decent—"

"No!" Hume interrupted Tim. "That wasn't my intent. I searched for over six months to find a bride. Days after her father gave his approval, he passed on—yet I adhered to my word and waited a full year for Lady Sydney to mourn. I've spent the last months searching for her yet again. Clearly, I'm committed to this marriage."

Fuller finally spoke. "It appears to me you're committed to *a* marriage, not to my niece. As her uncle, I'm closer kin than a second cousin somewhere off in England."

"And he's given me his consent to marry Sydney." Tim grabbed her wrist. "Come on, Sugar. This has gone far enough."

"Wait." She pretended not to see Tim's fury. "Tim, when I marry or reach my majority—whichever comes first, I receive an inheritance. Can we give that to Mr. Hume?"

Hume heaved a mighty sigh. "The money isn't as important to me as having a bride."

"Were you telling the truth?" Sydney stared at him. "On your word of honor, would you be faithful to your bride?"

"Yes."

Tim tugged on her. "Sydney . . ."

The parson gawked at her. "Lady Hathwell, are you reconsidering?"

"Goodness, no! But if Mr. Hume is serious, I know any number of eligible young ladies in England. Girls with impeccable pedigrees."

"You're playing matchmaker?" Tim shook his head.

"Why not? I'm going to marry the man of my dreams. Who better to—"

Tim scowled. "Now is not the time. He can have the money. I couldn't care less. All I want is you."

"That's sweet, and I love you with all my heart. It's just that I can't. Not today."

"Why not?" he shouted.

She gestured toward herself.

"Her pretty gown got filthy on the way over here," Fuller said.

"I'll help her dust it off," Tim proclaimed.

"That ain't it." Velma shook her head. "Syd can't get married in a dress Hume paid for."

"I'll pay the man for it!"

"I could overlook those things, Tim," she started.

"Good." Tim swept her into his arms.

"But it's ruined. Even if you think it's superstitious nonsense, it's a family tradition. The groom can't see the bride on their wedding day until she's walking down the aisle to him."

Tim groaned, "You're serious about this, aren't you?"

She nodded.

Hume chuckled. "You're a better man than I."

"That's why I love him."

Tim stood at the front of the church, praying God would have mercy and let everything go well. He'd run out of patience. All he wanted was to put a ring on Sydney's finger, kiss her, and start in on their "happily ever after."

Parson Bradle had already planned to preach about Christ's first miracle at the wedding in Cana. He'd offered to marry Tim and Sydney, then conduct the worship service. Once that was arranged yesterday, the women all flocked to the boardinghouse to help sew Sydney a wedding dress.

The pianist started to play the "Wedding March" and everyone rose. Tim stood straighter and craned his neck to catch his first glimpse of Sydney.

He'd thought she looked perfect yesterday. He'd been mistaken. Fuller slipped her hand into Tim's, and Sydney glanced downward. He followed her gaze. She was wearing the cowboy boots he'd bought her. He knew in an instant it was her way of showing him beneath all the foof and poof, his bride had grit. She wasn't just accepting this new life; she was embracing it with zeal. He looked up at her saucy smile and grinned.

Tim led her to the altar. They exchanged vows; then he pulled her into his arms and gave her a kiss. Afterward, Parson Bradle stepped forward. "I'd like to present Mr. and Mrs. Timothy Creighton to you. They've asked for the privilege of leading the congregation in prayer."

Tim cradled Sydney close to his side and laced his left hand with hers. They bowed their heads and began together, "Our Father, which art in heaven ..."

His thumb brushed over her wedding band as they said, "Give *us* this day ..." Her fingers squeezed his back.

Tim escorted her to the front pew and sat beside her. She positively glowed. Never before had a bride boasted such a gown. It framed her beautifully, and she wore it like a princess. He promised himself he'd go to his grave without ever mentioning that he recognized the fabric. It was Velma's treasured Irish linen tablecloth.

More Laugh-Out-Loud Historical Fiction From
Cathy Marie Hake

Ruth Caldwell has always tried to live up to her mother's expectations of what a lady should be, often with less than impressive results. When she's forced to journey west to meet the father she's never seen, Ruth hopes this might be the place she'll finally fit in. But her arrival brings more mayhem than even Ruth is used to.

Letter Perfect by Cathy Marie Hake

When Galen O'Sullivan is forced to the altar in a true shotgun wedding—to another woman—Laney McCain is devastated. Though Laney believes in his innocence, honor binds Galen to Ivy. As Galen and Laney struggle to surrender their hopes for the future, they come to learn a truly bittersweet lesson on learning to live in God's will and trusting Him.

Bittersweet by Cathy Marie Hake

Looking for More Good Books to Read?